THE TIDES OF BARNEGAT

A REPRINT OF THE ORIGINAL NOVEL
By
F. HOPKINSON SMITH

WITH A NEW INTRODUCTION
By
JOHN BAILEY LLOYD

HARVEY CEDARS, NEW JERSEY

THE TIDES OF
BARNEGAT

LUCY HUNG BACK UNTIL THE LAST.

THE TIDES OF BARNEGAT

BY

F. HOPKINSON SMITH

ILLUSTRATED BY

GEORGE WRIGHT

NEW YORK

CHARLES SCRIBNER'S SONS

1906

Introduction copyright ©2001 John Bailey Lloyd.
New material and design ©2001 Down The Shore
Publishing Corp.

For information, address:
Down The Shore Publishing Corp.
Box 3100, Harvey Cedars, NJ 08008
www.down-the-shore.com

*The words "Down The Shore" and logos
are registered U.S. Trademarks.*

A complete facsimile reprint of the original book.

Printed in the United States of America.
10 9 8 7 6 5 4 3 2 1

*Cover painting © Marilyn Ganss
Cover design by Leslee Ganss*

Library of Congress Cataloging-in-Publication Data

Smith, Francis Hopkinson, 1838-1915.
    The tides of Barnegat / by F. Hopkinson Smith ; with a new introduction
    by John Bailey Lloyd.
        p. cm.
    "A reprint of the original novel."
    ISBN 0-945582-83-8 (cloth) -- ISBN 0-945582-82-X (pbk.)
        1. Barnegat Bay Region (N.J.)--Fiction. 2. Illegitimate children--Fiction.
    3. Adopted children--Fiction. 4. Lifesaving--Fiction. 5. Sisters--Fiction.
    6. Storms--Fiction.   I. Title.
PS2864 .T53 2001
813'.4--dc21

                                                    2001042334

CONTENTS

CONTENTS

INTRODUCTION

There has always been a general feeling that *The Tides of Barnegat* has something important to say about the history of the Shore and ought to be kept. A lot of this has to do with the original book's handsome cloth cover, with its rolling waves in gold and the magic name of "Barnegat". However, *The Tides Of Barnegat* is also the only full length, adult novel ever written that uses Long Beach Island and southern Ocean County, New Jersey as its setting. Published in 1906, it has long been out of print — until now.

The Tides Of Barnegat is a sentimental romance spanning a twenty year period from 1854 until 1874, with a highly melodramatic final chapter involving the newly organized U.S. Life Saving Service in a tragic ship wreck. If the dialogue is a little stilted by today's standards, and some of the characters impossibly virtuous and high minded as they spend the best years of their lives trying to cover up for a character who lacks all virtue, the novel is still very much worth reading for its vivid portrait of a time and place. People familiar with the region, however, should be alerted to one special problem with the book. That problem is geography.

The author has taken real mainland villages like Barnegat, and another he calls "Warehold", and put them within less than a half hour's walking distance of the ocean and the light house, and, in so doing, completely ignores the existence of sizeable bodies of water like Barnegat and Little Egg Harbor bays. The characters never need to sail a boat or row one; they just walk from town out across the marshes, climb the big dunes and they're on the beach. Fiction writer's license of this sort might be overlooked by many readers, but those who live along the Shore in the region purportedly used by the author will be confused. Toms River, Forked River, and the town of Barnegat on the mainland, as well as the Barnegat Inlet — all actual places — are mentioned in this story and some of the action takes place in Beach Haven where, in another geographical stretch, one can sit on the piazza of a brand new hotel there and count boats going through the Barnegat Inlet. In reality, these two points are nearly sixteen miles apart. In the book, the life saving station has been placed midway in this foreshortened distance between the hotel at Beach Haven and Barnegat Light. This imaginary shoreline is called "Barnegat Beach" which is, historically, one of the old names for Long Beach Island.

In the 1850's, when the novel opens, most of the action takes place in "Warehold", a name created from real place names like Freehold and Waretown. Described by the author as being two miles south of

Barnegat, "Warehold" would have to be Manahawkin. Warehold has one tavern, one church and a minister, one judge and one lawyer, a doctor, and a retired ship captain. The towns people stand around like extras in the elm lined main street commenting on the activities of the two Cobden sisters who live in a stately ancestral manor house called Yardley. Kind, gentle Jane Cobden is loved and respected by everyone. Her younger sister, Lucy, is beautiful but also very vain and selfish. At seventeen, she has just returned from two years at a boarding school in Philadelphia, and her first act is to take up with Bart Holt, the handsome, shiftless son of the much respected Captain Nat Holt. As the summer progresses, Lucy and Bart spend a lot of time alone together in an old life saving hut — too much, in fact, for their own good, for Lucy soon discovers she is with child. She confides only in her sister Jane, whereupon the two of them abruptly pack up and leave for a voyage to Europe so that she may hide her sin. Bart's father, Captain Nat Holt, who has been told the truth, has a violent confrontation with his son and banishes him from Warehold and the region. Bart runs off to South America. When, after two years, news comes that Bart has died of the yellow fever, Captain Nat is filled with remorse.

At about the same time "Plain Jane" Cobden, now twenty-eight years old, returns from Europe with a handsome two year old boy named Archie, whom she convinces everyone she has adopted. No one but Captain Holt and the good village doctor, John Cavendish, know the real parents. Captain Holt is sworn to secrecy, and Doctor Cavendish would do anything to protect his beloved Jane.

Lucy stays in Paris where she eventually marries a very wealthy older man. Jane, living alone with little Archie in the old mansion in Warehold, really ought to marry Doctor John Cavendish who loves her as much as she loves him, but she is preoccupied with raising Lucy's child. Jane and the doctor often get together, but both are so noble and reserved that they do little more than sit for hours on end holding hands and talking.

Twenty years pass, and the now widowed Lucy at last returns to Warehold. At thirty-seven, she is beautiful, sophisticated, immensely wealthy and as vain and insensitive as ever. She pays no attention to Archie, who has never been told that she is his real mother. Lucy has a socially prominent lover from Philadelphia in tow, and the two of them go off to spend two months in the new summer resort at Beach Haven, staying in a brand new hotel — in separate suites.

Captain Holt is as scrupulously noble as Jane is about protecting the unworthy Lucy, thus he has never been able to reveal to Archie, now grown into a fine young man, that he is his grandfather. The two are very close, however, and Archie works at the newly commissioned U.S. Life Saving station where the Captain is the keeper. Meanwhile, Lucy, who plans to remarry, is terrified lest her fiance discover her secret past. Suddenly, word comes to Captain Holt that his son Bart did not die of yellow fever and is coming home to Warehold. Now a wealthy mine operator in Brazil, Bart wants to marry Lucy and acknowledge the son he has never seen. He has written to his father from Perth Amboy and will be sailing down the coast in two days. Lucy rejects Bart's plan in horror. Jane, to protect her sister, once more urges the Captain not to reveal the truth to Archie just yet. It is mid September and a great storm is brewing. As the storm gathers force, it brings all the characters together in an almost Shakespearean finale. This scene of high drama comes as the resolution of a tightly constructed novel by a remarkable man.

Francis Hopkinson Smith was born in Baltimore in 1838 to a distinguished family. He was a great grandson of Francis Hopkinson, poet and signer of the Declaration of Independence for New Jersey. Raised in an artistic and intellectual household, Smith planned to go to college until family financial reverses made this impossible. He worked at a number of jobs eventually becoming an engineer specializing in marine projects. The greatest achievement of his long career was the design and building of Race Rock Light House at the entrance to Long Island Sound, eight miles out at sea where the tide rips in at seven miles an hour. It took thirteen years to build and was completed in 1879. It is there to this day. His firm also built the foundation for the Statue of Liberty and fulfilled numerous other marine contracts.

It is a matter of regret that Smith the novelist, with his knowledge of engineering, did not have a single thing to say about the construction and design of Barnegat Light in *The Tides Of Barnegat*. While the action of the story covers more than twenty years during which the old 1835 Barnegat Light fell into the sea and was replaced, in 1859, by the present tower, he may have seen it as a distraction from the story itself. One of his novels, however, *Caleb West, Master Diver*, was drawn from his experiences building the Race Rock Light.

Writing was, in fact, Smith's third career and one he did not begin until he was over fifty. By then, he was not only a very successful engineer but also an acclaimed and popular artist. Smith painted as a hobby and was mainly self taught. His paintings, often of scenes from his European travels, convey place and atmosphere in much the way his writing does. He worked mostly in water color and liked to paint *en plein air.* He worked with great speed; one summer in Venice he painted a picture a day for fifty-three days to the amazement of fellow artists. Smith believed that anyone who loved art for its own sake should have another career to provide a living and then "in his evenings and on his Sundays...take down his Aladdin's lamp and give it a rub." His writing career began when he decided to capitalize on his skill as a raconteur and put some of his after dinner stories into print, illustrating them with sketches. When his first novel, *Colonel Carter Of Cartersville*, proved successful, Smith gave up his engineering career and retired to a life of travel, painting and writing in Spain, Italy and Constantinople. He produced a long line of travel books, short story collections and longer works of fiction. He died in New York in 1915.

John Bailey Lloyd
Beach Haven, New Jersey

ILLUSTRATIONS

THE TIDES OF BARNEGAT

CHAPTER I

THE DOCTOR'S GIG

One lovely spring morning—and this story begins
on a spring morning some fifty years or more ago—
a joy of a morning that made one glad to be alive,
when the radiant sunshine had turned the ribbon
of a road that ran from Warehold village to Barnegat
Light and the sea to satin, the wide marshes to
velvet, and the belts of stunted pines to bands of pur-
ple—on this spring morning, then, Martha Sands,
the Cobdens' nurse, was out with her dog Meg. She
had taken the little beast to the inner beach for a
bath—a custom of hers when the weather was fine
and the water not too cold—and was returning to
Warehold by way of the road, when, calling the dog
to her side, she stopped to feast her eyes on the picture unrolled at her feet.

To the left of where she stood curved the coast,
glistening like a scimitar, and the strip of yellow
beach which divided the narrow bay from the open

1

sea; to the right, thrust out into the sheen of silver, lay the spit of sand narrowing the inlet, its edges scalloped with lace foam, its extreme point dominated by the grim tower of Barnegat Light; aloft, high into the blue, soared the gulls, flashing like jewels as they lifted their breasts to the sun, while away and beyond the sails of the fishing-boats, gray or silver in their shifting tacks, crawled over the wrinkled sea.

The glory of the landscape fixed in her mind, Martha gathered her shawl about her shoulders, tightened the strings of her white cap, smoothed out her apron, and with the remark to Meg that he'd "never see nothin' so beautiful nor so restful," resumed her walk.

They were inseparable, these two, and had been ever since the day she had picked him up outside the tavern, half starved and with a sore patch on his back where some kitchen-maid had scalded him. Somehow the poor outcast brought home to her a sad page in her own history, when she herself was homeless and miserable, and no hand was stretched out to her. So she had coddled and fondled him, gaining his confidence day by day and talking to him by the hour of whatever was uppermost in her mind.

Few friendships presented stronger contrasts: She stout and motherly-looking—too stout for any waistline—with kindly blue eyes, smooth gray hair—

gray, not white—her round, rosy face, framed in a cotton cap, aglow with the freshness of the morning —a comforting, coddling-up kind of woman of fifty, with a low, crooning voice, gentle fingers, and soft, restful hollows about her shoulders and bosom for the heads of tired babies; Meg thin, rickety, and sneak-eyed, with a broken tail that hung at an angle, and but one ear (a black-and-tan had ruined the other)— a sandy-colored, rough-haired, good-for-nothing cur of multifarious lineage, who was either crouching at her feet or in full cry for some hole in a fence or rift in a wood-pile where he could flatten out and sulk in safety.

Martha continued her talk to Meg. While she had been studying the landscape he had taken the opportunity to wallow in whatever came first, and his wet hair was bristling with sand and matted with burrs.

" Come here, Meg—you measly rascal ! " she cried, stamping her foot. " Come here, I tell ye ! "

The dog crouched close to the ground, waited until Martha was near enough to lay her hand upon him, and then, with a backward spring, darted under a bush in full blossom.

" Look at ye now ! " she shouted in a commanding tone. " ' Tain't no use o' my washin' ye. Ye're full o' thistles and jest as dirty as when I throwed ye in the water. Come out o' that, I tell ye ! Now,

Meg, darlin' "—this came in a coaxing tone—" come out like a good dog—sure I'm not goin' in them brambles to hunt ye! "

A clatter of hoofs rang out on the morning air. A two-wheeled gig drawn by a well-groomed sorrel horse and followed by a brown-haired Irish setter was approaching. In it sat a man of thirty, dressed in a long, mouse-colored surtout with a wide cape falling to the shoulders. On his head was a soft gray hat and about his neck a white scarf showing above the lapels of his coat. He had thin, shapely legs, a flat waist, and square shoulders, above which rose a clean-shaven face of singular sweetness and refinement.

At the sound of the wheels the tattered cur poked his head from between the blossoms, twisted his one ear to catch the sound, and with a side-spring bounded up the road toward the setter.

"Well, I declare, if it ain't Dr. John Cavendish and Rex!" Martha exclaimed, raising both hands in welcome as the horse stopped beside her. "Good-mornin' to ye, Doctor John. I thought it was you, but the sun blinded me, and I couldn't see. And ye never saw a better nor a brighter mornin'. These spring days is all blossoms, and they ought to be. Where ye goin', anyway, that ye're in such a hurry? Ain't nobody sick up to Cap'n Holt's, be there?" she added, a shade of anxiety crossing her face.

4

"No, Martha; it's the dressmaker," answered the doctor, tightening the reins on the restless sorrel as he spoke. The voice was low and kindly and had a ring of sincerity through it.

"What dressmaker?"

"Why, Miss Gossaway!" His hand was extended now—that fine, delicately wrought, sympathetic hand that had soothed so many aching heads.

"You've said it," laughed Martha, leaning over the wheel so as to press his fingers in her warm palm. "There ain't no doubt 'bout that skinny fright being 'Miss,' and there ain't no doubt 'bout her stayin' so. Ann Gossaway she is, and Ann Gossaway she'll die. Is she took bad?" she continued, a merry, questioning look lighting up her kindly face, her lips pursed knowingly.

"No, only a sore throat," the doctor replied, loosening his coat.

"Throat!" she rejoined, with a wry look on her face. "Too bad 'twarn't her tongue. If ye could snip off a bit o' that some day it would help folks considerable 'round here."

The doctor laughed in answer, dropped the lines over the dashboard and leaned forward in his seat, the sun lighting up his clean-cut face. Busy as he was—and there were few busier men in town, as every hitching-post along the main street of Warehold village from Billy Tatham's, the driver of the country stage, to Captain Holt's, could prove—he always had time for a word with the old nurse.

"And where have *you* been, Mistress Martha?" he asked, with a smile, dropping his whip into the socket, a sure sign that he had a few more minutes to give her.

"Oh, down to the beach to git some o' the dirt off Meg. Look at him—did ye ever see such a rapscallion! Every time I throw him in he's into the sand ag'in wallowin' before I kin git to him."

The doctor bent his head, and for an instant watched the two dogs: Meg circling about Rex, all four legs taut, his head jerking from side to side in his eagerness to be agreeable to his roadside acquaintance; the agate-eyed setter returning Meg's attentions with the stony gaze of a club swell ignoring a shabby relative. The doctor smiled thoughtfully. There was nothing he loved to study so much as dogs —they had a peculiar humor of their own, he often said, more enjoyable sometimes than that of men— then he turned to Martha again.

"And why are you away from home this morning of all others?" he asked. "I thought Miss Lucy was expected from school to-day?"

"And so she is, God bless her! And that's why I'm here. I was that restless I couldn't keep still, and so I says to Miss Jane, 'I'm goin' to the beach with Meg and watch the ships go by; that's the only thing that'll quiet my nerves. They're never in a hurry with everybody punchin' and haulin' them.' Not that there's anybody doin' that to me, 'cept like it is to-day when I'm waitin' for my blessed baby to come back to me. Two years, doctor—two whole years since I had my arms round her. Wouldn't ye think I'd be nigh crazy?"

"She's too big for your arms now, Martha," laughed the doctor, gathering up his reins. "She's a woman—seventeen, isn't she?"

"Seventeen and three months, come the fourteenth of next July. But she's not a woman to me, and she never will be. She's my wee bairn that I took from her mother's dyin' arms and nursed at my own breast, and she'll be that wee bairn to me as long as I live. Ye'll be up to see her, won't ye, doctor?"

"Yes, to-night. How's Miss Jane?" As he made the inquiry his eyes kindled and a slight color suffused his cheeks.

"She'll be better for seein' ye," the nurse answered with a knowing look. Then in a louder and more positive tone, "Oh, ye needn't stare so with them big brown eyes o' yourn. Ye can't fool old Martha, none o' you young people kin. Ye think I go round with my eyelids sewed up. Miss Jane knows what she wants—she's proud, and so are you; I never knew a Cobden nor a Cavendish that warn't. I haven't a word to say—it'll be a good match when

7

it comes off. Where's that Meg? Good-by, doctor. I won't keep ye a minute longer from *Miss* Gossaway. I'm sorry it ain't her tongue, but if it's only her throat she may get over it. Go 'long, Meg!"

Dr. Cavendish laughed one of his quiet laughs— a laugh that wrinkled the lines about his eyes, with only a low gurgle in his throat for accompaniment, picked up his whip, lifted his hat in mock courtesy to the old nurse, and calling to Rex, who, bored by Meg's attentions, had at last retreated under the gig, chirruped to his horse, and drove on.

Martha watched the doctor and Rex until they were out of sight, walked on to the top of the low hill, and finding a seat by the roadside—her breath came short these warm spring days—sat down to rest, the dog stretched out in her lap. The little outcast had come to her the day Lucy left Warehold for school, and the old nurse had always regarded him with a certain superstitious feeling, persuading herself that nothing would happen to her bairn as long as this miserable dog was well cared for.

" Ye heard what Doctor John said about her bein' a woman, Meg?" she crooned, when she had caught her breath. " And she with her petticoats up to her knees! That's all he knows about her. Ye'd know better than that, Meg, wouldn't ye—if ye'd seen her grow up like he's done? But grown up or not, Meg" —here she lifted the dog's nose to get a clearer view

8

of his sleepy eyes—" she's my blessed baby and she's comin' home this very day, Meg, darlin'; d'ye hear that, ye little ruffian? And she's not goin' away ag'in, never, never. There'll be nobody drivin' round in a gig lookin' after her—nor nobody else as long as I kin help it. Now git up and come along; I'm that restless I can't sit still," and sliding the dog from her lap, she again resumed her walk toward Warehold.

Soon the village loomed in sight, and later on the open gateway of " Yardley," the old Cobden Manor, with its two high brick posts topped with white balls and shaded by two tall hemlocks, through which could be seen a level path leading to an old colonial house with portico, white pillars supporting a balcony, and a sloping roof with huge chimneys and dormer windows.

Martha quickened her steps, and halting at the gate-posts, paused for a moment with her eyes up the road. It was yet an hour of the time of her bairn's arrival by the country stage, but her impatience was such that she could not enter the path without this backward glance. Meg, who had followed behind his mistress at a snail's pace, also came to a halt and, as was his custom, picked out a soft spot in the road and sat down on his haunches.

Suddenly the dog sprang up with a quick yelp and darted inside the gate. The next instant a young girl in white, with a wide hat shading her joyous face, jumped from behind one of the big hemlocks and with a cry pinioned Martha's arms to her side.

" Oh, you dear old thing, you! where have you been? Didn't you know I was coming by the early stage?" she exclaimed in a half-querulous tone.

The old nurse disengaged one of her arms from the tight clasp of the girl, reached up her hand until she found the soft cheek, patted it gently for an instant as a blind person might have done, and then reassured, hid her face on Lucy's shoulder and burst into tears. The joy of the surprise had almost stopped her breath.

" No, baby, no," she murmured. " No, darlin', I didn't. I was on the beach with Meg. No, no— Oh, let me cry, darlin'. To think I've got you at last. I wouldn't have gone away, darlin', but they told me you wouldn't be here till dinner-time. Oh, darlin', is it you? And it's all true, isn't it? and ye've come back to me for good? Hug me close. Oh, my baby bairn, my little one! Oh, you precious!" and she nestled the girl's head on her bosom, smoothing her cheek as she crooned on, the tears running down her cheeks.

Before the girl could reply there came a voice calling from the house: " Isn't she fine, Martha?" A woman above the middle height, young and of slender figure, dressed in a simple gray gown and without her hat, was stepping from the front porch to meet them.

"Too fine, Miss Jane, for her old Martha," the nurse called back. "I've got to love her all over again. Oh, but I'm that happy I could burst meself with joy! Give me hold of your hand, darlin'—I'm afraid I'll lose ye ag'in if ye get out of reach of me."

The two strolled slowly up the path to meet Jane, Martha patting the girl's arm and laying her cheek against it as she walked. Meg had ceased barking and was now sniffing at Lucy's skirts, his bent tail wagging slowly, his sneaky eyes looking up into Lucy's face.

"Will he bite, Martha?" she asked, shrinking to one side. She had an aversion to anything physically imperfect, no matter how lovable it might be to others. This tattered example struck her as particularly objectionable.

"No, darlin'—nothin' 'cept his food," and Martha laughed.

"What a horrid little beast!" Lucy said half aloud to herself, clinging all the closer to the nurse. "This isn't the dog sister Jane wrote me about, is it? She said you loved him dearly—you don't, do you?"

"Yes, that's the same dog. You don't like him, do you, darlin'?"

11

" No, I think he's awful," retorted Lucy in a positive tone.

" It's all I had to pet since you went away,"
Martha answered apologetically.

" Well, now I'm home, give him away, please.
Go away, you dreadful dog! " she cried, stamping
her foot as Meg, now reassured, tried to jump upon
her.

The dog fell back, and crouching close to Martha's
side raised his eyes appealingly, his ear and tail
dragging.

Jane now joined them. She had stopped to pick
some blossoms for the house.

" Why, Lucy, what's poor Meg done? " she asked,
as she stooped over and stroked the crestfallen beast's
head. " Poor old doggie—we all love you, don't
we? "

" Well, just please love him all to yourselves,
then," retorted Lucy with a toss of her head. " I
wouldn't touch him with a pair of tongs. I never
saw anything so ugly. Get away, you little brute! "

" Oh, Lucy, dear, don't talk so," replied the older
sister in a pitying tone. " He was half starved when
Martha found him and brought him home—and look
at his poor back——"

" No, thank you; I don't want to look at his poor
back, nor his poor tail, nor anything else poor about
him. And you will send him away, won't you, like

a dear good old Martha?" she added, patting
Martha's shoulder in a coaxing way. Then encir-
cling Jane's waist with her arm, the two sisters sauntered slowly back to the house.

Martha followed behind with Meg.

Somehow, and for the first time where Lucy was
concerned, she felt a tightening of her heart-strings,
all the more painful because it had followed so
closely upon the joy of their meeting. What had
come over her bairn, she said to herself with a sigh,
that she should talk so to Meg—to anything that
her old nurse loved, for that matter? Jane interrupted her reveries.

" Did you give Meg a bath, Martha?" she asked
over her shoulder. She had seen the look of disappointment in the old nurse's face and, knowing
the cause, tried to lighten the effect.

" Yes—half water and half sand. Doctor John
came along with Rex shinin' like a new muff, and
I was ashamed to let him see Meg. He's comin' up
to see you to-night, Lucy, darlin'," and she bent forward and tapped the girl's shoulder to accentuate
the importance of the information.

Lucy cut her eye in a roguish way and twisted
her pretty head around until she could look into
Jane's eyes.

" Who do you think he's coming to see, sister?"

" Why, you, you little goose. They're all coming

13

—Uncle Ephraim has sent over every day to find out when you would be home, and Bart Holt was here early this morning, and will be back to-night."

"What does Bart Holt look like?"—she had stopped in her walk to pluck a spray of lilac blossoms. "I haven't seen him for years; I hear he's another one of your beaux," she added, tucking the flowers into Jane's belt. "There, sister, that's just your color; that's what that gray dress needs. Tell me, what's Bart like?"

"A little like Captain Nat, his father," answered Jane, ignoring Lucy's last inference, "not so stout and——"

"What's he doing?"

"Nothin', darlin', that's any good," broke in Martha from behind the two. "He's sailin' a boat when he ain't playin' cards or scarin' everybody down to the beach with his gun, or shyin' things at Meg."

"Don't you mind anything Martha says, Lucy," interrupted Jane in a defensive tone. "He's got a great many very good qualities; he has no mother and the captain has never looked after him. It's a great wonder that he is not worse than he is."

She knew Martha had spoken the truth, but she still hoped that her influence might help him, and then again, she never liked to hear even her acquaintances criticised.

14

"Playing cards! That all?" exclaimed Lucy, arching her eyebrows; her sister's excuses for the delinquent evidently made no impression on her. "I don't think playing cards is very bad; and I don't blame him for throwing anything he could lay his hands on at this little wretch of Martha's. We all played cards up in our rooms at school. Miss Sarah never knew anything about it—she thought we were in bed, and it was just lovely to fool her. And what does the immaculate Dr. John Cavendish look like? Has he changed any?" she added with a laugh.

"No," answered Jane simply.

"Does he come often?" She had turned her head now and was looking from under her lids at Martha. "Just as he used to and sit around, or has he—" Here she lifted her eyebrows in inquiry, and a laugh bubbled out from between her lips.

"Yes, that's just what he does do," cried Martha in a triumphant tone; "every minute he kin git. And he can't come too often to suit me. I jest love him, and I'm not the only one, neither, darlin'," she added with a nod of her head toward Jane.

"And Barton Holt as well?" persisted Lucy. "Why, sister, I didn't suppose there would be a man for me to look at when I came home, and you've got two already! Which one are you going to take?" Here her rosy face was drawn into solemn lines.

Jane colored. "You've got to be a great tease,

15

Lucy," she answered as she leaned over and kissed her on the cheek. " I'm not in the back of the doctor's head, nor he in mine—he's too busy nursing the sick—and Bart's a boy ! "

" Why, he's twenty-five years old, isn't he ? " exclaimed Lucy in some surprise.

" Twenty-five years young, dearie—there's a difference, you know. That's why I do what I can to help him. If he'd had the right influences in his life and could be thrown a little more with nice women it would help make him a better man. Be very good to him, please, even if you do find him a little rough."

They had mounted the steps of the porch and were now entering the wide colonial hall—a bare white hall, with a staircase protected by spindling mahogany banisters and a handrail. Jane passed into the library and seated herself at her desk. Lucy ran on upstairs, followed by Martha to help unpack her boxes and trunks.

When they reached the room in which Martha had nursed her for so many years—the little crib still occupied one corner—the old woman took the wide hat from the girl's head and looked long and searchingly into her eyes.

" Let me look at ye, my baby," she said, as she pushed Lucy's hair back from her forehead; " same blue eyes, darlin', same pretty mouth I kissed so

16

often, same little dimples ye had when ye lay in my arms, but ye've changed—how I can't tell. Somehow, the face is different."

Her hands now swept over the full rounded shoulders and plump arms of the beautiful girl, and over the full hips.

" The doctor's right, child," she said with a sigh, stepping back a pace and looking her over critically; " my baby's gone—you've filled out to be a woman."

CHAPTER II

For days the neighbors in and about the village of Warehold had been looking forward to Lucy's home-coming as one of the important epochs in the history of the Manor House, quite as they would have done had Lucy been a boy and the expected function one given in honor of the youthful heir's majority. Most of them had known the father and mother of these girls, and all of them loved Jane, the gentle mistress of the home—a type of woman eminently qualified to maintain its prestige.

It had been a great house in its day. Built in early Revolutionary times by Archibald Cobden, who had thrown up his office under the Crown and openly espoused the cause of the colonists, it had often been the scene of many of the festivities and social events following the conclusion of peace and for many years thereafter: the rooms were still pointed out in which Washington and Lafayette had slept, as well as the small alcove where the dashing Bart de Klyn passed the night whenever he drove over in his coach with outriders from Bow Hill to Barnegat and the sea.

With the death of Colonel Creighton Cobden, who held a commission in the War of 1812, all this magnificence of living had changed, and when Morton Cobden, the father of Jane and Lucy, inherited the estate, but little was left except the Manor House, greatly out of repair, and some invested property which brought in but a modest income. On his death-bed Morton Cobden's last words were a prayer to Jane, then eighteen, that she would watch over and protect her younger sister, a fair-haired child of eight, taking his own and her dead mother's place, a trust which had so dominated Jane's life that it had become the greater part of her religion.

Since then she had been the one strong hand in the home, looking after its affairs, managing their income, and watching over every step of her sister's girlhood and womanhood. Two years before she had placed Lucy in one of the fashionable boarding-schools of Philadelphia, there to study " music and French," and to perfect herself in that " grace of manner and charm of conversation," which the two maiden ladies who presided over its fortunes claimed in their modest advertisements they were so competent to teach. Part of the curriculum was an enforced absence from home of two years, during which time none of her own people were to visit her except in case of emergency.

To-night, the once famous house shone with something of its old-time color. The candles were lighted in the big bronze candelabra—the ones which came from Paris; the best glass and china and all the old plate were brought out and placed on the sideboard and serving-tables; a wood fire was started (the nights were yet cold), its cheery blaze lighting up the brass fender and andirons before which many of Colonel Cobden's cronies had toasted their shins as they sipped their toddies in the old days; easy-chairs and hair-cloth sofas were drawn from the walls; the big lamps lighted, and many minor details perfected for the comfort of the expected guests.

Jane entered the drawing-room in advance of Lucy and was busying herself putting the final touches to the apartment,—arranging the sprays of blossoms over the clock and under the portrait of Morton Cobden, which looked calmly down on the room from its place on the walls, when the door opened softly and Martha—the old nurse had for years been treated as a member of the family—stepped in, bowing and curtsying as would an old woman in a play, the skirt of her new black silk gown that Ann Gossaway had made for her held out between her plump fingers, her mob-cap with its long lace strings bobbing with every gesture. With her rosy cheeks, silver-rimmed spectacles, self-satisfied smile, and big puffy sleeves, she looked as if she might have stepped out of one of the old frames lining the walls.

" What do ye think of me, Miss Jane? I'm proud as a peacock—that I am!" she cried, twisting herself about. " Do ye know, I never thought that skinny dressmaker could do half as well. Is it long enough?" and she craned her head in the attempt to see the edge of the skirt.

" Fits you beautifully, Martha. You look fine," answered Jane in all sincerity, as she made a survey of the costume. " How does Lucy like it?"

" The darlin' don't like it at all; she says I look like a pall-bearer, and ye ought to hear her laughin' at the cap. Is there anything the matter with it? The pastor's wife's got one, anyhow, and she's a year younger'n me."

" Don't mind her, Martha—she laughs at everything; and how good it is to hear her! She never saw you look so well," replied Jane, as she moved a jar from a table and placed it on the mantel to hold the blossoms she had picked in the garden. " What's she doing upstairs so long?"

" Prinkin'—and lookin' that beautiful ye wouldn't know her. But the width and the thickness of her "—here the wrinkled fingers measured the increase with a half circle in the air—" and the way she's plumped out—not in one place, but all over— well, I tell ye, ye'd be astonished! She knows it, too, bless her heart! I don't blame her. Let her git all the comfort she kin when she's young—that's

the time for laughin'—the cryin' always comes
later."

No part of Martha's rhapsody over Lucy described
Jane. Not in her best moments could she have been
called beautiful—not even to-night when Lucy's
home-coming had given a glow to her cheeks and a
lustre to her eyes that nothing else had done for
months. Her slender figure, almost angular in its
contour with its closely drawn lines about the hips
and back; her spare throat and neck, straight arms,
thin wrists and hands—transparent hands, though
exquisitely wrought, as were those of all her race
—all so expressive of high breeding and refinement, carried with them none of the illusions of
beauty. The mould of the head, moreover, even
when softened by her smooth chestnut hair, worn
close to her ears and caught up in a coil behind, was
too severe for accepted standards, while her features
wonderfully sympathetic as they were, lacked the
finer modeling demanded in perfect types of female
loveliness, the eyebrows being almost straight, the
cheeks sunken, with little shadows under the cheek-
bones, and the lips narrow and often drawn.

And yet with all these discrepancies and, to some
minds, blemishes there was a light in her deep gray
eyes, a melody in her voice, a charm in her manner,
a sureness of her being exactly the sort of woman
one hoped she would be, a quick responsiveness to

any confidence, all so captivating and so satisfying that those who knew her forgot her slight physical shortcomings and carried away only the remembrance of one so much out of the common and of so distinguished a personality that she became ever after the standard by which they judged all good women.

There were times, too—especially whenever Lucy entered the room or her name was mentioned—that there shone through Jane's eyes a certain instantaneous kindling of the spirit which would irradiate her whole being as a candle does a lantern—a light betokening not only uncontrollable tenderness but unspeakable pride, dimmed now and then when some word or act of her charge brought her face to face with the weight of the responsibility resting upon her—a responsibility far outweighing that which most mothers would have felt. This so dominated Jane's every motion that it often robbed her of the full enjoyment of the companionship of a sister so young and so beautiful.

If Jane, to quote Doctor John, looked like a lily swaying on a slender stem, Lucy, when she bounded into the room to-night, was a full-blown rose tossed by a summer breeze. She came in with throat and neck bare; a woman all curves and dimples, her skin as pink as a shell; plump as a baby, and as fair, and yet with the form of a wood-nymph; dressed in a clinging, soft gown, the sleeves caught up at the shoulders revealing her beautiful arms, a spray of blossoms on her bosom, her blue eyes dancing with health, looking twenty rather than seventeen; glad of her freedom, glad of her home and Jane and Martha, and of the lights and blossoms and the glint on silver and glass, and of all that made life breathable and livable.

" Oh, but isn't it just too lovely to be at home! " she cried as she skipped about. " No lights out at nine, no prayers, no getting up at six o'clock and turning your mattress and washing in a sloppy little washroom. Oh, I'm so happy! I can't realize it's all true." As she spoke she raised herself on her toes so that she could see her face in the mirror over the mantel. " Why, do you know, sister," she rattled on, her eyes studying her own face, " that Miss Sarah used to make us learn a page of dictionary if we talked after the silence bell! "

" You must know the whole book by heart, then, dearie," replied Jane with a smile, as she bent over a table and pushed back some books to make room for a bowl of arbutus she held in her hand.

" Ah, but she didn't catch us very often. We used to stuff up the cracks in the doors so she couldn't hear us talk and smother our heads in the pillows. Jonesy, the English teacher, was the worst." She was still looking in the glass, her fingers busy with the spray of blossoms on her bosom. " She always wore felt slippers and crept around like a cat. She'd tell on anybody. We had a play one night in my room after lights were out, and Maria Collins was Claude Melnotte and I was Pauline. Maria had a mustache blackened on her lips with a piece of burnt cork and I was all fixed up in a dressing-gown and sash. We never heard Jonesy till she put her hand on the knob; then we blew out the candle and popped into bed. She smelled the candle-wick and leaned over and kissed Maria good-night, and the black all came off on her lips, and next day we got three pages apiece—the mean old thing! How do I look, Martha? Is my hair all right?" Here she turned her head for the old woman's inspection.

"Beautiful, darlin'. There won't one o' them know ye; they'll think ye're a real livin' princess stepped out of a picture-book." Martha had not taken her eyes from Lucy since she entered the room.

"See my little beau-catchers," she laughed, twisting her head so that Martha could see the tiny Spanish curls she had flattened against her temples. "They are for Bart Holt, and I'm going to cut sister out. Do you think he'll remember me?" she prattled on, arching her neck.

"It won't make any difference if he don't," Martha retorted in a positive tone. "But Cap'n

Nat will, and so will the doctor and Uncle Ephraim and—who's that comin' this early?" and the old nurse paused and listened to a heavy step on the porch. "It must be the cap'n himself; there ain't nobody but him's got a tread like that; ye'd think he was trampin' the deck o' one of his ships."

The door of the drawing-room opened and a bluff, hearty, round-faced man of fifty, his iron-gray hair standing straight up on his head like a shoe-brush, dressed in a short pea-jacket surmounted by a low sailor collar and loose necktie, stepped cheerily into the room.

"Ah, Miss Jane!" Somehow all the neighbors, even the most intimate, remembered to prefix "Miss" when speaking to Jane. "So you've got this fly-away back again? Where are ye? By jingo! let me look at you. Why! why! why! Did you ever! What have you been doing to yourself, lassie, that you should shed your shell like a bug and come out with wings like a butterfly? Why you're the prettiest thing I've seen since I got home from my last voyage."

He had Lucy by both hands now, and was turning her about as if she had been one of Ann Gossaway's models.

"Have I changed, Captain Holt?"

"No—not a mite. You've got a new suit of flesh and blood on your bones, that's all. And it's the best in the locker. Well! *Well!* WELL!" He was still twisting her around. "She does ye proud, Martha," he called to the old nurse, who was just leaving the room to take charge of the pantry, now that the guests had begun to arrive. "And so ye're home for good and all, lassie?"

"Yes—isn't it lovely?"

"Lovely? That's no name for it. You'll be settin' the young fellers crazy 'bout here before they're a week older. Here come two of 'em now."

Lucy turned her head quickly, just as the doctor and Barton Holt reached the door of the drawing-room. The elder of the two, Doctor John, greeted Jane as if she had been a duchess, bowing low as he approached her, his eyes drinking in her every movement; then, after a few words, remembering the occasion as being one in honor of Lucy, he walked slowly toward the young girl.

"Why, Lucy, it's so delightful to get you back!" he cried, shaking her hand warmly. "And you are looking so well. Poor Martha has been on pins and needles waiting for you. I told her just how it would be—that she'd lose her little girl—and she has," and he glanced at her admiringly. "What did she say when she saw you?"

"Oh, the silly old thing began to cry, just as they all do. Have you seen her dog?"

The answer jarred on the doctor, although he excused her in his heart on the ground of her youth and her desire to appear at ease in talking to him.

"Do you mean Meg?" he asked, scanning her face the closer.

"I don't know what she calls him—but he's the ugliest little beast I ever saw."

"Yes—but so amusing. I never get tired of watching him. What is left of him is the funniest thing alive. He's better than he looks, though. He and Rex have great times together."

"I wish you would take him, then. I told Martha this morning that he mustn't poke his nose into my room, and he won't. He's a perfect fright."

"But the dear old woman loves him," he protested with a tender tone in his voice, his eyes fixed on Lucy.

He had looked into the faces of too many young girls in his professional career not to know something of what lay at the bottom of their natures. What he saw now came as a distinct surprise.

"I don't care if she does," she retorted; "no, I don't," and she knit her brow and shook her pretty head as she laughed.

While they stood talking Bart Holt, who had lingered at the threshold, his eyes searching for the fair arrival, was advancing toward the centre of the room. Suddenly he stood still, his gaze fixed on the vision of the girl in the clinging dress, with the blossoms resting on her breast. The curve of her back, the round of the hip; the way her moulded shoulders rose above the lace of her bodice; the bare, full arms tapering to the wrists;—the color, the movement, the grace of it all had taken away his breath. With only a side nod of recognition toward Jane, he walked straight to Lucy and with an " Excuse me," elbowed the doctor out of the way in his eagerness to reach the girl's side. The doctor smiled at the young man's impetuosity, bent his head to Lucy, and turned to where Jane was standing awaiting the arrival of her other guests.

The young man extended his hand. " I'm Bart Holt," he exclaimed; " you haven't forgotten me, Miss Lucy, have you? We used to play together. Mighty glad to see you—been expecting you for a week."

Lucy colored slightly and arched her head in a coquettish way. His frankness pleased her; so did the look of unfeigned admiration in his eyes.

" Why, of course I haven't forgotten you, Mr. Holt. It was so nice of you to come," and she gave him the tips of her fingers—her own eyes meanwhile, in one comprehensive glance, taking in his round head with its closely cropped curls, searching brown eyes, wavering mouth, broad shoulders, and shapely body, down to his small, well-turned feet. The young fellow lacked the polish and well-bred

29

grace of the doctor, just as he lacked his well-cut clothes and distinguished manners, but there was a sort of easy effrontery and familiar air about him that some of his women admirers encouraged and others shrank from. Strange to say, this had appealed to Lucy before he had spoken a word.

"And you've come home for good now, haven't you?" His eyes were still drinking in the beauty of the girl, his mind neither on his questions nor her answers.

"Yes, forever and ever," she replied, with a laugh that showed her white teeth.

"Did you like it at school?" It was her lips now that held his attention and the little curves under her dimpled chin. He thought he had never seen so pretty a mouth and chin.

"Not always; but we used to have lots of fun," answered the girl, studying him in return—the way his cravat was tied and the part of his hair. She thought he had well-shaped ears and that his nose and eyebrows looked like a picture she had in her room upstairs.

"Come and tell me about it. Let's sit down here," he continued as he drew her to a sofa and stood waiting until she took her seat.

"Well, I will for a moment, until they begin to come in," she answered, her face all smiles. She liked the way he behaved towards her—not asking her permission, but taking the responsibility and by his manner compelling a sort of obedience. " But I can't stay," she added. " Sister won't like it if I'm not with her to shake hands with everybody."

" Oh, she won't mind me; I'm a great friend of Miss Jane's. Please go on; what kind of fun did you have? I like to hear about girls' scrapes. We had plenty of them at college, but I couldn't tell you half of them." He had settled himself beside her now, his appropriating eyes still taking in her beauty.

" Oh, all kinds," she replied as she bent her head and glanced at the blossoms on her breast to be assured of their protective covering.

" But I shouldn't think you could have much fun with the teachers watching you every minute," said Bart, moving nearer to her and turning his body so he could look squarely into her eyes.

" Yes, but they didn't find out half that was going on." Then she added coyly, " I don't know whether you can keep a secret—do you tell everything you hear? "

" Never tell anything."

" How do I know? "

" I'll swear it." In proof he held up one hand and closed both eyes in mock reverence as if he were taking an oath. He was getting more interested now in her talk; up to this time her beauty had dazzled

31

him. " Never! So help me—" he mumbled impressively.

" Well, one day we were walking out to the park— Now you're sure you won't tell sister, she's so easily shocked ? " The tone was the same, but the inflection was shaded to closer intimacy.

Again Bart cast up his eyes.

" And all the girls were in a string with Miss Griggs, the Latin teacher, in front, and we all went in a cake shop and got a big piece of gingerbread apiece. We were all eating away hard as we could when we saw Miss Sarah coming. Every girl let her cake go, and when Miss Sarah got to us the whole ten pieces were scattered along the sidewalk."

Bart looked disappointed over the mild character of the scrape. From what he had seen of her he had supposed her adventures would be seasoned with a certain spice of deviltry.

" I wouldn't have done that, I'd have hidden it in my pocket," he replied, sliding down on the sofa until his head rested on the cushion next her own.

" We tried, but she was too close. Poor old Griggsey got a dreadful scolding. She wasn't like Miss Jones—she wouldn't tell on the girls."

" And did they let any of the fellows come to see you ? " Bart asked.

" No; only brothers and cousins once in a long while. Maria Collins tried to pass one of her beaux,

Max Feilding, off as a cousin, but Miss Sarah went down to see him and poor Maria had to stay up-stairs."

" I'd have got in," said Bart with some emphasis, rousing himself from his position and twisting his body so he could again look squarely in her face. This escapade was more to his liking.

" How ? " asked Lucy in a tone that showed she not only quite believed it, but rather liked him the better for saying so.

" Oh I don't know. I'd have cooked up some story." He was leaning over now, toying with the lace that clung to Lucy's arms. " Did you ever have any one of your own friends treated in that way ? "

Jane's voice cut short her answer. She had seen the two completely absorbed in each other, to the exclusion of the other guests who were now coming in, and wanted Lucy beside her.

The young girl waved her fan gayly in answer, rose to her feet, turned her head close to Bart's, pointed to the incoming guests, whispered something in his ear that made him laugh, listened while he whispered to her in return, and in obedience to the summons crossed the room to meet a group of the neighbors, among them old Judge Woolworthy, in a snuff-colored coat, high black stock, and bald head, and his bustling little wife. Bart's last whisper to Lucy was in explanation of the little wife's manner

—who now, all bows and smiles, was shaking hands with everybody about her.

Then came Uncle Ephraim Tipple, and close beside him walked his spouse, Ann, in a camel's-hair shawl and poke-bonnet, the two preceded by Uncle Ephraim's stentorian laugh, which had been heard before their feet had touched the porch outside. Mrs. Cromartin now bustled in, accompanied by her two daughters—slim, awkward girls, both dressed alike in high waists and short frocks; and after them the Bunsbys, father, mother, and son—all smiles, the last a painfully thin young lawyer, in a low collar and a shock of whitey-brown hair, "looking like a patent window-mop resting against a wall," so Lucy described him afterward to Martha when she was putting her to bed; and finally the Colfords and Bronsons, young and old, together with Pastor Dellenbaugh, the white-haired clergyman who preached in the only church in Warehold.

When Lucy had performed her duty and the several greetings were over, and Uncle Ephraim had shaken the hand of the young hostess in true pump-handle fashion, the old man roaring with laughter all the time, as if it were the funniest thing in the world to find her alive; and the good clergyman in his mildest and most impressive manner had said she grew more and more like her mother every day— which was a flight of imagination on the part of

Bart's last whisper to Lucy was in explanation of the little wife's manner.

the dear man, for she didn't resemble her in the least; and the two thin girls had remarked that it must be so " perfectly blissful " to get home; and the young lawyer had complimented her on her wonderful, almost life-like resemblance to her grandfather, whose portrait hung in the court-house—and which was nearer the truth—to all of which the young girl replied in her most gracious tones, thanking them for their kindness in coming to see her and for welcoming her so cordially—the whole of Lucy's mind once more reverted to Bart.

Indeed, the several lobes of her brain had been working in opposition for the past hour. While one-half of her mind was concocting polite speeches for her guests the other was absorbed in the fear that Bart would either get tired of waiting for her return and leave the sofa, or that some other girl friend of his would claim him and her delightful talk be at an end.

To the young girl fresh from school Bart represented the only thing in the room that was entirely alive. The others talked platitudes and themselves. He had encouraged her to talk of *herself* and of the things she liked. He had, too, about him an assurance and dominating personality which, although it made her a little afraid of him, only added to his attractiveness.

While she stood wondering how many times the

35

white-haired young lawyer would tell her it was so nice to have her back, she felt a slight pressure on her arm and turned to face Bart.

"You are wanted, please, Miss Lucy; may I offer you my arm? Excuse me, Bunsby—I'll give her to you again in a minute."

Lucy slipped her arm into Bart's, and asked simply, "What for?"

"To finish our talk, of course. Do you suppose I'm going to let that tow-head monopolize you?" he answered, pressing her arm closer to his side with his own.

Lucy laughed and tapped Bart with her fan in rebuke, and then there followed a bit of coquetry in which the young girl declared that he was "too mean for anything, and that she'd never seen anybody so conceited, and if he only knew, she might really prefer the 'tow head' to his own;" to which Bart answered that his only excuse was that he was so lonely he was nearly dead, and that he had only come to save his life—the whole affair culminating in his conducting her back to the sofa with a great flourish and again seating himself beside her.

"I've been watching you," he began when he had made her comfortable with a small cushion behind her shoulders and another for her pretty feet. "You don't act a bit like Miss Jane." As he spoke he leaned forward and flicked an imaginary something from her bare wrist with that air which always characterized his early approaches to most women.

"Why?" Lucy asked, pleased at his attentions and thanking him with a more direct look.

"Oh, I don't know. You're more jolly, I think. I don't like girls who turn out to be solemn after you know them a while; I was afraid you might. You know it's a long time since I saw you."

"Why, then, sister can't be solemn, for everybody says you and she are great friends," she replied with a light laugh, readjusting the lace of her bodice.

"So we are; nobody about here I think as much of as I do of your sister. She's been mighty good to me. But you know what I mean: I mean those don't-touch-me kind of girls who are always thinking you mean a lot of things when you're only trying to be nice and friendly to them. I like to be a brother to a girl and to go sailing with her, and fishing, and not have her bother me about her feet getting a little bit wet, and not scream bloody murder when the boat gives a lurch. That's the kind of girl that's worth having."

"And you don't find them?" laughed Lucy, looking at him out of the corners of her eyes.

"Well, not many. Do you mind little things like that?"

As he spoke his eyes wandered over her bare shoulders until they rested on the blossoms, the sort of roaming, critical eyes that often cause a woman to wonder whether some part of her toilet has not been carelessly put together. Then he added, with a sudden lowering of his voice: " That's a nice posy you've got. Who sent it?" and he bent his head as if to smell the cluster on her bosom.

Lucy drew back and a slight flush suffused her cheek; his audacity frightened her. She was fond of admiration, but this way of expressing it was new to her. The young man caught the movement and recovered himself. He had ventured on a thin spot, as was his custom, and the sound of the cracking ice had warned him in time.

" Oh, I see, they're apple blossoms," he added carelessly as he straightened up. " We've got a lot in our orchard. You like flowers, I see." The even tone and perfect self-possession of the young man reassured her.

" Oh, I adore them; don't you?" Lucy answered in a relieved, almost apologetic voice. She was sorry she had misjudged him. She liked him rather the better now for her mistake.

" Well, that depends. Apple blossoms never looked pretty to me before; but then it makes a good deal of difference where they are," answered Bart with a low chuckle.

Jane had been watching the two and had noticed Bart's position and manner. His easy familiarity

of pose offended her. Instinctively she glanced about
the room, wondering if any of her guests had seen it.
That Lucy did not resent it surprised her. She
supposed her sister's recent training would have
made her a little more fastidious.

" Come, Lucy," she called gently, moving toward
her, " bring Bart over here and join the other
girls."

" All right, Miss Jane, we'll be there in a minute,"
Bart answered in Lucy's stead. Then he bent his
head and said in a low voice:

" Won't you give me half those blossoms ? "

" No; it would spoil the bunch."

" Please——"

" No, not a single one. You wouldn't care for
them, anyway."

" Yes, I would." Here he stretched out his hand
and touched the blossoms on her neck.

Lucy ducked her head in merry glee, sprang up,
and with a triumphant curtsy and a " No, you don't,
sir—not this time," joined her sister, followed by
Bart.

The guests were now separated into big and little
groups. Uncle Ephraim and the judge were hob-
nobbing around the fireplace, listening to Uncle
Ephraim's stories and joining in the laughter which
every now and then filled the room. Captain Nat
was deep in a discussion with Doctor John over some

seafaring matter, and Jane and Mrs. Benson were discussing a local charity with Pastor Dellenbaugh.

The younger people being left to themselves soon began to pair off, the white-haired young lawyer disappearing with the older Miss Cromartin and Bart soon following with Lucy:—the outer porch and the long walk down the garden path among the trees, despite the chilliness of the night, seemed to be the only place in which they could be comfortable.

During a lull in the discussion of Captain Nat's maritime news and while Mrs. Benson was talking to the pastor, Doctor John seized the opportunity to seat himself again by Jane.

" Don't you think Lucy improved ? " she asked, motioning the doctor to a place beside her.

" She's much more beautiful than I thought she would be," he answered in a hesitating way, looking toward Lucy, and seating himself in his favorite attitude, hands in his lap, one leg crossed over the other and hanging straight beside its fellow; only a man like the doctor, of more than usual repose and of a certain elegance of form, Jane always said, could sit this way any length of time and be comfortable and unconscious of his posture. Then he added slowly, and as if he had given the subject some consideration, " You won't keep her long, I'm afraid."

" Oh, don't say that," Jane cried with a nervous

start. " I don't know what I would do if she should marry."

" That don't sound like you, Miss Jane. You would be the first to deny yourself. You are too good to do otherwise." He spoke with a slight quiver in his voice, and yet with an emphasis that showed he believed it.

" No; it is you who are good to think so," she replied in a softer tone, bending her head as she spoke, her eyes intent on her fan. " And now tell me," she added quickly, raising her eyes to his as if to bar any further tribute he might be on the point of paying to her—" I hear your mother takes greatly to heart your having refused the hospital appointment."

" Yes, I'm afraid she does. Mother has a good many new-fashioned notions nowadays." He laughed —a mellow, genial laugh; more in the spirit of apology than of criticism.

" And you don't want to go ? " she asked, her eyes fixed on his.

" Want to go ? No, why should I ? There would be nobody to look after the people here if I went away. You don't want me to leave, do you ? " he added suddenly in an anxious tone.

" Nobody does, doctor," she replied, parrying the question, her face flushing with pleasure.

Here Martha entered the room hurriedly and

bending over Jane's shoulder, whispered something in her ear. The doctor straightened himself and leaned back out of hearing.

" Well, but I don't think she will take cold," Jane whispered in return, looking up into Martha's face. " Has she anything around her ? "

" Yes, your big red cloak; but the child's head is bare and there's mighty little on her neck, and she ought to come in. The wind's begun to blow and it's gettin' cold."

" Where is she ? " Jane continued, her face showing her surprise at Martha's statement.

" Out by the gate with that dare-devil. He don't care who he gives cold. I told her she'd get her death, but she won't mind me."

" Why, Martha, how can you talk so ! " Jane retorted, with a disapproving frown. Then raising her voice so that the doctor could be brought into the conversation, she added in her natural tone, " Whom did you say she was with ? "

" Bart Holt," cried Martha aloud, nodding to the doctor as if to get his assistance in saving her bairn from possible danger.

Jane colored slightly and turned to Doctor John.

" You go please, doctor, and bring them all in, or you may have some new patients on your hands."

The doctor looked from one to the other in doubt

42

as to the cause of his selection, but Jane's face showed none of the anxiety in Martha's.

"Yes, certainly," he answered simply; "but I'll get myself into a hornet's nest. These young people don't like to be told what's good for them," he added with a laugh, rising from his seat. "And after that you'll permit me to slip away without telling anybody, won't you? My last minute has come," and he glanced at his watch.

"Going so soon? Why, I wanted you to stay for supper. It will be ready in a few minutes." Her voice had lost its buoyancy now. She never wanted him to go. She never let him know it, but it pained her all the same.

"I would like to, but I cannot." All his heart was in his eyes as he spoke.

"Someone ill?" she asked.

"Yes, Fogarty's child. The little fellow may develop croup before morning. I saw him to-day, and his pulse was not right. He's a sturdy little chap with a thick neck, and that kind always suffers most. If he's worse Fogarty is to send word to my office," he added, holding out his hand in parting.

"Can I help?" Jane asked, retaining the doctor's hand in hers as if to get the answer.

"No, I'll watch him closely. Good-night," and with a smile he bent his head and withdrew.

Martha followed the doctor to the outer door,

and then grumbling her satisfaction went back to the pantry to direct the servants in arranging upon the small table in the supper-room the simple refreshments which always characterized the Cobdens' entertainments.

Soon the girls and their beaux came trooping in to join their elders on the way to the supper-room. Lucy hung back until the last (she had not liked the doctor's interference), Jane's long red cloak draped from her shoulders, the hood hanging down her back, her cheeks radiant, her beautiful blond hair ruffled with the night wind, an aureole of gold framing her face. Bart followed close behind, a pleased, almost triumphant smile playing about his lips.

He had carried his point. The cluster of blossoms which had rested upon Lucy's bosom was pinned to the lapel of his coat.

CHAPTER III

LITTLE TOD FOGARTY

With the warmth of Jane's parting grasp lingering in his own Doctor John untied the mare, sprang into his gig, and was soon clear of the village and speeding along the causeway that stretched across the salt marshes leading past his own home to the inner beach beyond. As he drove slowly through his own gate, so as to make as little noise as possible, the cottage, blanketed under its clinging vines, seemed in the soft light of the low-lying moon to be fast asleep. Only one eye was open; this was the window of his office, through which streamed the glow of a lamp, its light falling on the gravel path and lilac bushes beyond.

Rex gave a bark of welcome and raced beside the wheels.

"Keep still, old dog! Down, Rex! Been lonely, old fellow?"

The dog in answer leaped in the air as his master drew rein, and with eager springs tried to reach his hands, barking all the while in short and joyful yelps.

Doctor John threw the lines across the dash-board, jumped from the gig, and pushing open the hall door—it was never locked—stepped quickly into his office, and turning up the lamp, threw himself into a chair at his desk. The sorrel made no attempt to go to the stable—both horse and man were accustomed to delays—sometimes of long hours and sometimes of whole nights.

The appointments and fittings of the office—old-fashioned and practical as they were—reflected in a marked degree the aims and tastes of the occupant. While low bookcases stood against the walls surmounted by rows of test-tubes, mortars and pestles, cases of instruments, and a line of bottles labelled with names of various mixtures (in those days doctors were chemists as well as physicians), there could also be found a bust of the young Augustus; one or two lithographs of Heidelberg, where he had studied; and some line engravings in black frames—one a view of Oxford with the Thames wandering by, another a portrait of the Duke of Wellington, and still another of Nell Gwynn. Scattered about the room were easy-chairs and small tables piled high with books, a copy of Tacitus and an early edition of Milton being among them, while under the wide, low window stood a narrow bench crowded with flowering plants in earthen pots, the remnants of the winter's bloom. There were also souvenirs of his

46

earlier student life—a life which few of his friends in Warehold, except Jane Cobden, knew or cared anything about—including a pair of crossed foils and two boxing-gloves; these last hung over a portrait of Macaulay.

What the place lacked was the touch of a woman's hand in vase, flower, or ornament—a touch that his mother, for reasons of her own, never gave and which no other woman had yet dared suggest.

For an instant the doctor sat with his elbows on the desk in deep thought, the light illuminating his calm, finely chiselled features and hands—those thin, sure hands which could guide a knife within a hair's breadth of instant death—and leaning forward, with an indrawn sigh examined some letters lying under his eye. Then, as if suddenly remembering, he glanced at the office slate, his face lighting up as he found it bare of any entry except the date.

Rex had been watching his master with ears cocked, and was now on his haunches, cuddling close, his nose resting on the doctor's knee. Doctor John laid his hand on the dog's head and smoothing the long, silky ears, said with a sigh of relief, as he settled himself in his chair:

" Little Tod must be better, Rex, and we are going to have a quiet night."

The anxiety over his patients relieved, his thoughts reverted to Jane and their talk. He remembered the

47

tone of her voice and the quick way in which she
had warded off his tribute to her goodness; he recalled
her anxiety over Lucy; he looked again into the deep,
trusting eyes that gazed into his as she appealed to
him for assistance; he caught once more the poise
of the head as she listened to his account of little
Tod Fogarty's illness and heard her quick offer to
help, and felt for the second time her instant tenderness and sympathy, never withheld from the sick
and suffering, and always so generous and sponta-
neous.

A certain feeling of thankfulness welled up in
his heart. Perhaps she had at last begun to depend
upon him—a dependence which, with a woman such
as Jane, must, he felt sure, eventually end in love.

With these thoughts filling his mind, he settled
deeper in his chair. These were the times in which
he loved to think of her—when, with pipe in mouth,
he could sit alone by his fire and build castles in the
coals, every rosy mountain-top aglow with the love
he bore her; with no watchful mother's face trying
to fathom his thoughts; only his faithful dog
stretched at his feet.

Picking up his brierwood, lying on a pile of books
on his desk, and within reach of his hand, he started
to fill the bowl, when a scrap of paper covered with
a scrawl written in pencil came into view. He
turned it to the light and sprang to his feet.

"Tod worse," he said to himself. "I wonder how long this has been here."

The dog was now beside him looking up into the doctor's eyes. It was not the first time that he had seen his master's face grow suddenly serious as he had read the tell-tale slate or had opened some note awaiting his arrival.

Doctor John lowered the lamp, stepped noiselessly to the foot of the winding stairs that led to the sleeping rooms above—the dog close at his heels, watching his every movement—and called gently:

"Mother! mother, dear!" He never left his office when she was at home and awake without telling her where he was going.

No one answered.

"She is asleep. I will slip out without waking her. Stay where you are, Rex—I will be back some time before daylight," and throwing his night-cloak about his shoulders, he started for his gig.

The dog stopped with his paws resting on the outer edge of the top step of the porch, the line he was not to pass, and looked wistfully after the doctor. His loneliness was to continue, and his poor master to go out into the night alone. His tail ceased to wag, only his eyes moved.

Once outside Doctor John patted the mare's neck as if in apology and loosened the reins. "Come, old girl," he said; "I'm sorry, but it can't be helped,"

49

and springing into the gig, he walked the mare clear of the gravel beyond the gate, so as not to rouse his mother, touched her lightly with the whip, and sent her spinning along the road on the way to Fogarty's.

The route led toward the sea, branching off within the sight of the cottage porch, past the low, conical ice-houses used by the fishermen in which to cool their fish during the hot weather, along the sand-dunes, and down a steep grade to the shore. The tide was making flood, and the crawling surf spent itself in long shelving reaches of foam. These so packed the sand that the wheels of the gig hardly made an impression upon it. Along this smooth surface the mare trotted briskly, her nimble feet wet with the farthest reaches of the incoming wash.

As he approached the old House of Refuge, black in the moonlight and looking twice its size in the stretch of the endless beach, he noticed for the hundredth time how like a crouching woman it appeared, with its hipped roof hunched up like a shoulder close propped against the dune and its overhanging eaves but a draped hood shading its thoughtful brow; an illusion which vanished when its square form, with its wide door and long platform pointing to the sea, came into view.

More than once in its brief history the doctor had seen the volunteer crew, aroused from their cabins along the shore by the boom of a gun from some stranded vessel, throw wide its door and with a wild cheer whirl the life-boat housed beneath its roof into the boiling surf, and many a time had he helped to bring back to life the benumbed bodies drawn from the merciless sea by their strong arms.

There were other houses like it up and down the coast. Some had remained unused for years, desolate and forlorn, no unhappy ship having foundered or struck the breakers within their reach; others had been in constant use. The crews were gathered from the immediate neighborhood by the custodian, who was the only man to receive pay from the Government. If he lived near by he kept the key; if not, the nearest fisherman held it. Fogarty, the father of the sick child, and whose cabin was within gunshot of this house, kept the key this year. No other protection was given these isolated houses and none was needed. These black-hooded Sisters of the Coast, keeping their lonely vigils, were as safe from beach-combers and sea-prowlers as their white-capped namesakes would have been threading the lonely suburbs of some city.

The sound of the mare's feet on the oyster-shell path outside his cabin brought Fogarty, a tall, thin, weather-beaten fisherman, to the door. He was still wearing his hip-boots and sou'wester—he was just in from the surf—and stood outside the low doorway with a lantern. Its light streamed over the sand and made wavering patterns about the mare's feet.

"Thought ye'd never come, Doc," he whispered, as he threw the blanket over the mare. "Wife's nigh crazy. Tod's fightin' for all he's worth, but there ain't much breath left in him. I was off the inlet when it come on."

The wife, a thick-set woman in a close-fitting cap, her arms bared to the elbow, her petticoats above the tops of her shoes, met him inside the door. She had been crying and her eyelids were still wet and her cheeks swollen. The light of the ship's lantern fastened to the wall fell upon a crib in the corner, on which lay the child, his short curls, tangled with much tossing, smoothed back from his face. The doctor's ears had caught the sound of the child's breathing before he entered the room.

"When did this come on?" Doctor John asked, settling down beside the crib upon a stool that the wife had brushed off with her apron.

"'Bout sundown, sir," she answered, her tear-soaked eyes fixed on little Tod's face. Her teeth chattered as she spoke and her arms were tight pressed against her sides, her fingers opening and shutting in her agony. Now and then in her nervousness she would wipe her forehead with the back of her wrist as if it were wet, or press her two fingers deep into her swollen cheek.

LITTLE TOD FOGARTY

Fogarty had followed close behind the doctor and now stood looking down at the crib with fixed eyes, his thin lips close shut, his square jaw sunk in the collar of his shirt. There were no dangers that the sea could unfold which this silent surfman had not met and conquered, and would again. Every fisherman on the coast knew Fogarty's pluck and skill, and many of them owed their lives to him. To-night, before this invisible power slowly closing about his child he was as powerless as a skiff without oars caught in the swirl of a Barnegat tide.

" Why didn't you let me know sooner, Fogarty ? You understood my directions ? " Doctor John asked in a surprised tone. " You shouldn't have left him without letting me know." It was only when his orders were disobeyed and life endangered that he spoke thus.

The fisherman turned his head and was about to reply when the wife stepped in front of him.

" My husband got ketched in the inlet, sir," she said in an apologetic tone, as if to excuse his absence. " The tide set ag'in him and he had hard pullin' makin' the p'int. It cuts in turrible there, you know, doctor. Tod seemed to be all right when he left him this mornin'. I had husband's mate take the note I wrote ye. Mate said nobody was at home and he laid it under your pipe. He thought ye'd sure find it there when ye come in."

Doctor John was not listening to her explanations; he was leaning over the rude crib, his ear to the child's breast. Regaining his position, he smoothed the curls tenderly from the forehead of the little fellow, who still lay with eyes closed, one stout brown hand and arm clear of the coverlet, and stood watching his breathing. Every now and then a spasm of pain would cross the child's face; the chubby hand would open convulsively and a muffled cry escape him. Doctor John watched his breathing for some minutes, laid his hand again on the child's forehead, and rose from the stool.

" Start up that fire, Fogarty," he said in a crisp tone, turning up his shirt-cuffs, slipping off his evening coat, and handing the garment to the wife, who hung it mechanically over a chair, her eyes all the time searching Doctor John's face for some gleam of hope.

" Now get a pan," he continued, " fill it with water and some corn-meal, and get me some cotton cloth— half an apron, piece of an old petticoat, anything, but be quick about it."

The woman, glad of something to do, hastened to obey. Somehow, the tones of his voice had put new courage into her heart. Fogarty threw a heap of driftwood on the smouldering fire and filled the kettle; the dry splinters crackled into a blaze.

The noise aroused the child.

The doctor held up his finger for silence and again caressed the boy's forehead. Fogarty, with a fresh look of alarm in his face, tiptoed back of the crib and stood behind the restless sufferer. Under the doctor's touch the child once more became quiet.

" Is he bad off ? " the wife murmured when the doctor moved to the fire and began stirring the mush she was preparing. " The other one went this way; we can't lose him. You won't lose him, will ye, doctor, dear ? I don't want to live if this one goes. Please, doctor——"

The doctor looked into the wife's eyes, blurred with tears, and laid his hand tenderly on her shoulder.

" Keep a good heart, wife," he said; " we'll pull him through. Tod is a tough little chap with plenty of fight in him yet. I've seen them much worse. It will soon be over; don't worry."

Mrs. Fogarty's eyes brightened and even the fisherman's grim face relaxed. Silent men in grave crises suffer most; the habit of their lives precludes the giving out of words that soothe and heal; when others speak them, they sink into their thirsty souls like drops of rain after a long drought. It was just such timely expressions as these that helped Doctor John's patients most—often their only hope hung on some word uttered with a buoyancy of spirit that for a moment stifled all their anxieties.

The effect of the treatment began to tell upon the little sufferer—his breathing became less difficult, the spasms less frequent. The doctor whispered the change to the wife, sitting close at his elbow, his impassive face brightening as he spoke; there was an even chance now for the boy's life.

The vigil continued.

No one moved except Fogarty, who would now and then tiptoe quickly to the hearth, add a fresh log to the embers, and as quickly move back to his position behind the child's crib. The rising and falling of the blaze, keeping rhythm, as it were, to the hopes and fears of the group, lighted up in turn each figure in the room. First the doctor sitting with hands resting on his knees, his aquiline nose and brow clearly outlined against the shadowy background in the gold chalk of the dancing flames, his black evening clothes in strong contrast to the high white of the coverlet, framing the child's face like a nimbus. Next the bent body of the wife, her face in half-tones, her stout shoulders in high relief, and behind, swallowed up in the gloom, out of reach of the fire-gleam, the straight, motionless form of the fisherman, standing with folded arms, grim and silent, his unseen eyes fixed on his child.

Far into the night, and until the gray dawn streaked the sky, this vigil continued; the doctor, assisted by Fogarty and the wife, changing the poul-

The vigil continued far into the night and until the gray dawn streaked the sky.

tices, filling the child's lungs with hot steam by means of a paper funnel, and encouraging the mother by his talk. At one time he would tell her in half-whispered tones of a child who had recovered and who had been much weaker than this one. Again he would turn to Fogarty and talk of the sea, of the fishing outside the inlet, of the big three-masted schooner which had been built by the men at Tom's River, of the new light they thought of building at Barnegat to take the place of the old one—anything to divert their minds and lessen their anxieties, stopping only to note the sound of every cough the boy gave or to change the treatment as the little sufferer struggled on fighting for his life.

When the child dozed no one moved, no word was spoken. Then in the silence there would come to their ears above the labored breathing of the boy the long swinging tick of the clock, dull and ominous, as if tolling the minutes of a passing life; the ceaseless crunch of the sea, chewing its cud on the beach outside or the low moan of the outer bar turning restlessly on its bed of sand.

Suddenly, and without warning, and out of an apparent sleep, the child started up from his pillow with staring eyes and began beating the air for breath.

The doctor leaned quickly forward, listened for a moment, his ear to the boy's chest, and said in a quiet, restrained voice:

"Go into the other room, Mrs. Fogarty, and stay there till I call you." The woman raised her eyes to his and obeyed mechanically. She was worn out, mind and body, and had lost her power of resistance.

As the door shut upon her Doctor John sprang from the stool, caught the lamp from the wall, handed it to Fogarty, and picking the child up from the crib, laid it flat upon his knees.

He now slipped his hand into his pocket and took from it a leather case filled with instruments.

"Hold the light, Fogarty," he said in a firm, decided tone, "and keep your nerve. I thought he'd pull through without it, but he'll strangle if I don't."

"What ye goin' to do—not cut him?" whispered the fisherman in a trembling voice.

"Yes. It's his only chance. I've seen it coming on for the last hour—no nonsense now. Steady, old fellow. It'll be over in a minute. . . . There, my boy, that'll help you. Now, Fogarty, hand me that cloth. . . . All right, little man; don't cry; it's all over. Now open the door and let your wife in," and he laid the child back on the pillow.

When the doctor took the blanket from the sorrel tethered outside Fogarty's cabin and turned his horse's head homeward the sails of the fishing-boats lying in a string on the far horizon flashed silver in the morning sun. His groom met him at the stable door, and without a word led the mare into the barn.

The lamp in his study was still burning in yellow mockery of the rosy dawn. He laid his case of instruments on the desk, hung his cloak and hat to a peg in the closet, and ascended the staircase on the way to his bedroom. As he passed his mother's open door she heard his step.

" Why, it's broad daylight, son," she called in a voice ending in a yawn.

" Yes, mother."

" Where have you been ? "

" To see little Tod Fogarty," he answered simply.

" What's the matter with him ? "

" Croup."

" Is he going to die ? "

" No, not this time."

" Well, what did you stay out all night for ? " The voice had now grown stronger, with a petulant tone through it.

" Well, I could hardly help it. They are very simple people, and were so badly frightened that they were helpless. It's the only child they have left to them—the last one died of croup."

" Well, are you going to turn nurse for half the paupers in the county ? All children have croup, and they don't all die ! " The petulant voice had now developed into one of indignation.

" No, mother, but I couldn't take any risks. This little chap is worth saving."

There came a pause, during which the tired man waited patiently.

" You were at the Cobdens'? "

" Yes; or I should have reached Fogarty's sooner."

" And Miss Jane detained you, of course."

" No, mother."

" Good-night, John."

" Say rather ' Good-day,' mother," he answered with a smile and continued on to his room.

CHAPTER IV

ANN GOSSAWAY'S RED CLOAK

The merrymakings at Yardley continued for weeks, a new impetus and flavor being lent them by the arrival of two of Lucy's friends—her schoolmate and bosom companion, Maria Collins, of Trenton, and Maria's devoted admirer, Max Feilding, of Walnut Hill, Philadelphia.

Jane, in her joy over Lucy's home-coming, and in her desire to meet her sister's every wish, gladly welcomed the new arrivals, although Miss Collins, strange to say, had not made a very good impression upon her. Max she thought better of. He was a quiet, well-bred young fellow; older than either Lucy or Maria, and having lived abroad a year, knew something of the outside world. Moreover, their families had always been intimate in the old days, his ancestral home being always open to Jane's mother when a girl.

The arrival of these two strangers only added to the general gayety. Picnics were planned to the woods back of Warehold to which the young people of the town were invited, and in which Billy Tatham with his team took a prominent part. Sailing and fishing parties outside of Barnegat were gotten up; dances were held in the old parlor, and even tableaux were arranged under Max's artistic guidance. In one of these Maria wore a Spanish costume fashioned out of a white lace shawl belonging to Jane's grandmother draped over her head and shoulders, and made the more bewitching by a red japonica fixed in her hair, and Lucy appeared as a dairy-maid decked out in one of Martha's caps, altered to fit her shapely head.

The village itself was greatly stirred.

"Have you seen them two fly-up-the-creeks?" Billy Tatham, the stage-driver, asked of Uncle Ephraim Tipple as he was driving him down to the boat-landing.

"No, what do they look like?"

"The He-one had on a two-inch hat with a green ribbon and wore a white bob-tail coat that 'bout reached to the top o' his pants. Looks like he lived on water-crackers and milk, his skin's that white. The She-one had a set o' hoops on her big as a circus tent. Much as I could do to git her in the 'bus —as it was, she come in sideways. And her trunk! Well, it oughter been on wheels—one o' them travellin' houses. I thought one spell I'd take the old plug out the shafts and hook on to it and git it up that-a-way."

"Some of Lucy's chums, I guess," chuckled Uncle Ephraim. "Miss Jane told me they were coming. How long are they going to stay?"

"Dunno. Till they git fed up and fattened, maybe. If they was mine I'd have killin' time to-day."

Ann Gossaway and some of her cronies also gave free rein to their tongues.

"Learned them tricks at a finishin' school, did they?" broke out the dressmaker. (Lucy had been the only young woman in Warehold who had ever enjoyed that privilege.) "Wearin' each other's hats, rollin' round in the sand, and hollerin' so you could hear 'em clear to the lighthouse. If I had my way I'd finish 'em. And that's where they'll git if they don't mind, and quick, too!"

The Dellenbaughs, Cromartins, and Bunsbys, being of another class, viewed the young couple's visit in a different light. "Mr. Feilding has such nice hands and wears such lovely cravats," the younger Miss Cromartin said, and "Miss Collins is too sweet for anything." Prim Mr. Bunsby, having superior notions of life and deportment, only shook his head. He looked for more dignity, he said; but then this Byronic young man had not been invited to any of the outings.

In all these merrymakings and outings Lucy was the central figure. Her beauty, her joyous nature,

63

her freedom from affectation and conventionality, her love of the out-of-doors, her pretty clothes and the way she wore them, all added to her popularity. In the swing and toss of her freedom, her true temperament developed. She was like a summer rose, making everything and everybody glad about her, loving the air she breathed as much for the color it put into her cheeks as for the new bound it gave to her blood. Just as she loved the sunlight for its warmth and the dip and swell of the sea for its thrill. So, too, when the roses were a glory of bloom, not only would she revel in the beauty of the blossoms, but intoxicated by their color and fragrance, would bury her face in the wealth of their abundance, taking in great draughts of their perfume, caressing them with her cheeks, drinking in the honey of their petals.

This was also true of her voice—a rich, full, vibrating voice, that dominated the room and thrilled the hearts of all who heard her. When she sang she sang as a bird sings, as much to relieve its own overcharged little body, full to bursting with the music in its soul, as to gladden the surrounding woods with its melody—because, too, she could not help it and because the notes lay nearest her bubbling heart and could find their only outlet through the lips.

Bart was her constant companion. Under his instructions she had learned to hold the tiller in sail-

ing in and out of the inlet; to swim over hand; to
dive from a plank, no matter how high the jump; and
to join in all his outdoor sports. Lucy had been his
constant inspiration in all of this. She had surveyed the field that first night of their meeting and
had discovered that the young man's personality
offered the only material in Warehold available for
her purpose. With him, or someone like him—one
who had leisure and freedom, one who was quick
and strong and skilful (and Bart was all of these)—
the success of her summer would be assured. Without him many of her plans could not be carried
out.

And her victory over him had been an easy one.
Held first by the spell of her beauty and controlled
later by her tact and stronger will, the young man's
effrontery—almost impudence at times—had changed
to a certain respectful subservience, which showed
itself in his constant effort to please and amuse her.
When they were not sailing they were back in the
orchard out of sight of the house, or were walking
together nobody knew where. Often Bart would call
for her immediately after breakfast, and the two
would pack a lunch-basket and be gone all day, Lucy
arranging the details of the outing, and Bart entering into them with a dash and an eagerness which,
to a man of his temperament, cemented the bond
between them all the closer. Had they been two

fabled denizens of the wood—she a nymph and he a dryad—they could not have been more closely linked with sky and earth.

As for Jane, she watched the increasing intimacy with alarm. She had suddenly become aroused to the fact that Lucy's love affair with Bart was going far beyond the limits of prudence. The son of Captain Nathaniel Holt, late of the Black Ball Line of packets, would always be welcome as a visitor at the home, the captain being an old and tried friend of her father's; but neither Bart's education nor prospects, nor, for that matter, his social position—a point which usually had very little weight with Jane —could possibly entitle him to ask the hand of the granddaughter of Archibald Cobden in marriage. She began to regret that she had thrown them together. Her own ideas of reforming him had never contemplated any such intimacy as now existed between the young man and her sister. The side of his nature which he had always shown her had been one of respectful attention to her wishes; so much so that she had been greatly encouraged in her efforts to make something more of him than even his best friends predicted could be done; but she had never for one instant intended that her friendly interest should go any further, nor could she have conceived of such an issue.

And yet Jane did nothing to prevent the meetings

and outings of the young couple, even after Maria's and Max's departure.

When Martha, in her own ever-increasing anxiety, spoke of the growing intimacy she looked grave, but she gave no indication of her own thoughts. Her pride prevented her discussing the situation with the old nurse and her love for Lucy from intervening in her pleasures.

" She has been cooped up at school so long, Martha, dear," she answered in extenuation, " that I hate to interfere in anything she wants to do. She is very happy; let her alone. I wish, though, she would return some of the calls of these good people who have been so kind to her. Perhaps she will if you speak to her. But don't worry about Bart; that will wear itself out. All young girls must have their love-affairs."

Jane's voice had lacked the ring of true sincerity when she spoke about " wearing itself out," and Martha had gone to her room more dissatisfied than before. This feeling became all the more intense when, the next day, from her window she watched Bart tying on Lucy's hat, puffing out the big bow under her chin, smoothing her hair from the flying strings. Lucy's eyes were dancing, her face turned toward Bart's, her pretty lips near his own. There was a knot or a twist, or a collection of knots and twists, or perhaps Bart's fingers bungled, for minutes passed before the hat could be fastened to suit either of them. Martha's head had all this time been thrust out of the casement, her gaze apparently fixed on a bird-cage hung from a hook near the shutter.

Bart caught her eye and whispered to Lucy that that " old spy-cat " was watching them; whereupon Lucy faced about, waved her hand to the old nurse, and turning quickly, raced up the orchard and out of sight, followed by Bart carrying a shawl for them to sit upon.

After that Martha, unconsciously, perhaps, to her-self, kept watch, so far as she could, upon their movements, without, as she thought, betraying her-self: making excuses to go to the village when they two went off together in that direction; traversing the orchard, ostensibly looking for Meg when she knew all the time that the dog was sound asleep in the woodshed; or yielding to a sudden desire to give the rascal a bath whenever Lucy announced that she and Bart were going to spend the morning down by the water.

As the weeks flew by and Lucy had shown no will-ingness to assume her share of any of the responsibil-ities of the house,—any that interfered with her per-sonal enjoyment,—Jane became more and more rest-less and unhappy. The older village people had shown her sister every attention, she said to herself,— more than was her due, considering her youth,—and yet Lucy had never crossed any one of their thresholds. She again pleaded with the girl to remember her social duties and to pay some regard to the neighbors who had called upon her and who had shown her so much kindness; to which the happy-hearted sister had laughed back in reply:

"What for, you dear sister? These old fossils don't want to see me, and I'm sure I don't want to see them. Some of them give me the shivers, they are so prim."

It was with glad surprise, therefore, that Jane heard Lucy say in Martha's eharing one bright afternoon:

"Now, I'm going to begin, sister, and you won't have to scold me any more. Everyone of these old tabbies I will take in a row: Mrs. Cavendish first, and then the Cromartins, and the balance of the bunch when I can reach them. I am going to Rose Cottage to see Mrs. Cavendish this very afternoon."

The selection of Mrs. Cavendish as first on her list only increased Jane's wonder. Rose Cottage lay some two miles from Warehold, near the upper end of the beach, and few of their other friends lived near it. Then again, Jane knew that Lucy had not liked the doctor's calling her into the house the night of her arrival, and had heretofore made one excuse after another when urged to call on his mother.

Her delight, therefore, over Lucy's sudden sense of duty was all the more keen.

" I'll go with you, darling," she answered, slipping her arm about Lucy's waist, " and we'll take Meg for a walk."

So they started, Lucy in her prettiest frock and hat and Jane with her big red cloak over her arm to protect the young girl from the breeze from the sea, which in the early autumn was often cool, especially if they should sit out on Mrs. Cavendish's piazza.

The doctor's mother met them on the porch. She had seen them enter the garden gate, and had left her seat by the window, and was standing on the top step to welcome them. Rex, as usual, in the doctor's absence, did the honors of the office. He loved Jane, and always sprang straight at her, his big paws resting on her shoulders. These courtesies, however, he did not extend to Meg. The high-bred setter had no other salutation for the clay-colored remnant than a lifting of his nose, a tightening of his legs, and a smothered growl when Meg ventured too near his lordship.

" Come up, my dear, and let me look at you," were Mrs. Cavendish's first words of salutation to Lucy. " I hear you have quite turned the heads of all the gallants in Warehold. John says you are very beautiful, and you know the doctor is a good judge, is he not, Miss Jane?" she added, holding out her hands to them both. "And he's quite right; you are just like your dear mother, who was known as the Rose of Barnegat long before you were born. Shall we sit here, or will you come into my little *salon* for a cup of tea?" It was always a *" salon "* to Mrs. Cavendish, never a "sitting-room."

"Oh, please let me sit here," Lucy answered, checking a rising smile at the word, "the view is so lovely," and without further comment or any reference to the compliments showered upon her, she took her seat upon the top step and began to play with Rex, who had already offered to make friends with her, his invariable habit with well-dressed people.

Jane meanwhile improved the occasion to ask the doctor's mother about the hospital they were building near Barnegat, and whether she and one or two of the other ladies at Warehold would not be useful as visitors, and, perhaps, in case of emergency, as nurses.

While the talk was in progress Lucy sat smoothing Rex's silky ears, listening to every word her hostess spoke, watching her gestures and the expressions that crossed her face, and settling in her mind for all time, after the manner of young girls, what sort of woman the doctor's mother might be; any opinions she might have had two years before being now outlawed by this advanced young woman in her present mature judgment.

In that comprehensive glance, with the profound wisdom of her seventeen summers to help her, she had come to the conclusion that Mrs. Cavendish was a high-strung, nervous, fussy little woman of fifty, with an outward show of good-will and an inward intention to rip everybody up the back who opposed her; proud of her home, of her blood, and of her son, and determined, if she could manage it, to break off his attachment for Jane, no matter at what cost. This last Lucy caught from a peculiar look in the little old woman's eyes and a slightly scornful curve of the lower lip as she listened to Jane's talk about the hospital, all of which was lost on " plain Jane Cobden," as the doctor's mother invariably called her sister behind her back.

Then the young mind-reader turned her attention to the house and grounds and the buildings lying above and before her, especially to the way the matted vines hung to the porches and clambered over the roof and dormers. Later on she listened to Mrs. Cavendish's description of its age and ancestry: How it had come down to her from her grandfather, whose large estate was near Trenton, where as a girl she had spent her life; how in those days it was but a small villa to which old Nicholas Erskine, her great-uncle, would bring his guests when the August days made Trenton unbearable; and how in later years under the big trees back of the house and over the lawn—" you can see them from where you sit, my dear "—tea had been served to twenty or more of " the first gentlemen and ladies of the land."

Jane had heard it all a dozen times before, and so had every other visitor at Rose Cottage, but to Lucy it was only confirmation of her latter-day opinion of her hostess. Nothing, however, could be more gracious than the close attention which the young girl gave Mrs. Cavendish's every word when the talk was again directed to her, bending her pretty head and laughing at the right time—a courtesy which so charmed the dear lady that she insisted on giving first Lucy, and then Jane, a bunch of roses from her " own favorite bush " before the two girls took their leave.

With these evidences of her delight made clear, Lucy pushed Rex from her side—he had become presuming and had left the imprint of his dusty paw upon her spotless frock—and with the remark that she had other visits to pay, her only regret being that this one was so short, she got up from her seat on the step, called Meg, and stood waiting for Jane with some slight impatience in her manner.

Jane immediately rose from her chair. She had been greatly pleased at the impression Lucy had made. Her manner, her courtesy, her respect for the older woman, her humoring her whims, showed her to be the daughter of a Cobden. As to her own place during the visit, she had never given it a thought. She would always be willing to act as foil to her accomplished, brilliant sister if by so doing she could make other people love Lucy the more.

As they walked through the doctor's study, Mrs. Cavendish preceding them, Jane lingered for a moment and gave a hurried glance about her. There stood his chair and his lounge where he had thrown himself so often when tired out. There, too, was the closet where he hung his coat and hat, and the desk covered with books and papers. A certain feeling of reverence not unmixed with curiosity took possession of her, as when one enters a sanctuary in the absence of the priest. For an instant she passed her hand gently over the leather back of the chair where his head rested, smoothing it with her fingers. Then her eyes wandered over the room, noting each appointment in detail. Suddenly a sense of injustice rose in her mind as she thought that nothing of beauty had ever been added to these plain surroundings; even the plants in the boxes by the windows looked half faded. With a quick glance at the open door she slipped a rose from the bunch in her hand, leaned over, and with the feeling of a devotee laying an offering on the altar, placed the flower hurriedly

74

on the doctor's slate. Then she joined Mrs. Cavendish.

Lucy walked slowly from the gate, her eyes every now and then turned to the sea. When she and Jane had reached the cross-road that branched off toward the beach—it ran within sight of Mrs. Cavendish's windows—Lucy said:

" The afternoon is so lovely I'm not going to pay any more visits, sister. Suppose I go to the beach and give Meg a bath. You won't mind, will you? Come, Meg! "

" Oh, how happy you will make him! " cried Jane. " But you are not dressed warm enough, dearie. You know how cool it gets toward evening. Here, take my cloak. Perhaps I'd better go with you——"

" No, do you keep on home. I want to see if the little wretch will be contented with me alone. Goodby," and without giving her sister time to protest, she called to Meg, and with a wave of her hand, the red cloak flying from her shoulders, ran toward the beach, Meg bounding after her.

Jane waved back in answer, and kept her eyes on the graceful figure skipping along the road, her head and shoulders in silhouette against the blue sea, her white skirts brushing the yellow grass of the sand-dune. All the mother-love in her heart welled up in her breast. She was so proud of her, so much in love with her, so thankful for her! All these foolish love affairs and girl fancies would soon be over and Bart and the others like him out of Lucy's mind and heart. Why worry about it? Some great strong soul would come by and by and take this child in his arms and make a woman of her. Some strong soul——

She stopped short in her walk and her thoughts went back to the red rose lying on the doctor's desk.

"Will he know?" she said to herself; "he loves flowers so, and I don't believe anybody ever puts one on his desk. Poor fellow! how hard he works and how good he is to everybody! Little Tod would have died but for his tenderness." Then, with a prayer in her heart and a new light in her eyes, she kept on her way.

Lucy, as she bounded along the edge of the bluff, Meg scurrying after her, had never once lost sight of her sister's slender figure. When a turn in the road shut her from view, she crouched down behind a sand-dune, waited until she was sure Jane would not change her mind and join her, and then folding the cloak over her arm, gathered up her skirts and ran with all her speed along the wet sand to the House of Refuge. As she reached its side, Bart Holt stepped out into the afternoon light.

"I thought you'd never come, darling," he said, catching her in his arms and kissing her.

" I couldn't help it, sweetheart. I told sister I was going to see Mrs. Cavendish, and she was so delighted she said she would go, too."

" Where is she ? " he interrupted, turning his head and looking anxiously up the beach.

" Gone home. Oh, I fixed that. I was scared to death for a minute, but you trust me when I want to get off."

" Why didn't you let her take that beast of a dog with her ? We don't want him," he rejoined, pointing to Meg, who had come to a sudden standstill at the sight of Bart.

" Why, you silly! That's how I got away. She thought I was going to give him a bath. How long have you been waiting, my precious ? " Her hand was on his shoulder now, her eyes raised to his.

" Oh, 'bout a year. It really seems like a year, Luce " (his pet name for her), " when I'm waiting for you. I was sure something was up. Wait till I open the door." The two turned toward the house.

" Why! can we get in ? I thought Fogarty, the fisherman, had the key," she asked, with a tone of pleasant surprise in her voice.

" So he has," he laughed. " Got it now hanging up behind his clock. I borrowed it yesterday and had one made just like it. I'm of age." This came with a sly wink, followed by a low laugh of triumph.

Lucy smiled. She liked his daring; she liked, too, his resources. When a thing was to be done, Bart always found the way to do it. She waited until he had fitted the new bright key into the rusty lock, her hand in his.

" Now, come inside," he cried, swinging wide the big doors. " Isn't it a jolly place?" He slipped his arm about her and drew her to him. " See, there's the stove with the kindling-wood all ready to light when anything comes ashore, and up on that shelf are life-preservers; and here's a table and some stools and a lantern—two of 'em; and there's the big life-boat, all ready to push out. Good place to come Sundays with some of the fellows, isn't it? Play all night here, and not a soul would find you out," he chuckled as he pointed to the different things. " You didn't think, now, I was going to have a cubby-hole like this to hide you in where that old spot-cat Martha can't be watching us, did you?" he added, drawing her toward him and again kissing her with a sudden intensity.

Lucy slipped from his arms and began examining everything with the greatest interest. She had never seen anything but the outside of the house before and she always wondered what it contained, and as a child had stood up on her toes and tried to peep in through the crack of the big door. When she had looked the boat all over and felt the oars, and wondered whether the fire could be lighted quick enough, and pictured in her mind the half-drowned people huddled around it in their sea-drenched clothes, she moved to the door. Bart wanted her to sit down inside, but she refused.

"No, come outside and lie on the sand. Nobody comes along here," she insisted. "Oh, see how beautiful the sea is! I love that green," and drawing Jane's red cloak around her, she settled herself on the sand, Bart throwing himself at her feet.

The sun was now nearing the horizon, and its golden rays fell across their faces. Away off on the sky-line trailed the smoke of an incoming steamer; nearer in idled a schooner bound in to Barnegat Inlet with every sail set. At their feet the surf rose sleepily under the gentle pressure of the incoming tide, its wavelets spreading themselves in widening circles as if bent on kissing the feet of the radiant girl.

As they sat and talked, filled with the happiness of being alone, their eyes now on the sea and now looking into each other's, Meg, who had amused himself by barking at the swooping gulls, chasing the sand-snipe and digging holes in the sand for imaginary muskrats, lifted his head and gave a short yelp. Bart, annoyed by the sound, picked up a bit of driftwood and hurled it at him, missing him by a few inches. The narrowness of the escape silenced the dog and sent him to the rear with drooping tail and ears.

Bart should have minded Meg's warning. A broad beach in the full glare of the setting sun, even when protected by a House of Refuge, is a poor place to be alone in.

A woman was passing along the edge of the bluffs, carrying a basket in one hand and a green umbrella in the other; a tall, thin, angular woman, with the eye of a ferret. It was Ann Gossaway's day for visiting the sick, and she had just left Fogarty's cabin, where little Tod, with his throat tied up in red flannel, had tried on her mitts and played with her spectacles. Miss Gossaway had heard Meg's bark and had been accorded a full view of Lucy's back covered by Jane's red cloak, with Bart sitting beside her, their shoulders touching.

Lovers with their heads together interested the gossip no longer, except as a topic to talk about. Such trifles had these many years passed out of the dressmaker's life.

So Miss Gossaway, busy with her own thoughts, kept on her way unnoticed by either Lucy or Bart.

When she reached the cross-road she met Doctor John driving in. He tightened the reins on the sorrel and stopped.

"Lovely afternoon, Miss Gossaway. Where are you from—looking at the sunset?"

" No, I ain't got no time for spoonin'. I might be if I was Miss Jane and Bart Holt. Just see 'em a spell ago squattin' down behind the House o' Refuge. She wouldn't look at me. I been to Fogarty's; she's on my list this week, and it's my day for visitin', fust in two weeks. That two-year-old of hers is all right ag'in after your sewing him up; they'll never get over tellin' how you set up all night with him. You ought to hear Mrs. Fogarty go on— ' Oh, the goodness of him ! ' " and she mimicked the good woman's dialect. " ' If Tod 'd been his own child he couldn't a-done more for him.' That's the way she talks. I heard, doctor, ye never left him till daylight. You're a wonder."

The doctor touched his hat and drove on.

Miss Gossaway's sharp, rasping voice and incisive manner of speaking grated upon him. He liked neither her tone nor the way in which she spoke of the mistress of Yardley. No one else dared as much. If Jane was really on the beach and with Bart, she had some good purpose in her mind. It may have been her day for visiting, and Bart, perhaps, had accompanied her. But why had Miss Gossaway not met Miss Cobden at Fogarty's, his being the only cabin that far down the beach ? Then his face brightened. Perhaps, after all, it was Lucy whom she had seen. He had placed that same red cloak around her shoulders the night of the reception at Yardley—and when she was with Bart, too.

Mrs. Cavendish was sitting by her window when the doctor entered his own house. She rose, and putting down her book, advanced to meet him.

"You should have come earlier, John," she said with a laugh; "such a charming girl and so pretty and gracious. Why, I was quite overcome. She is very different from her sister. What do you think Miss Jane wants to do now? Nurse in the new hospital when it is built! Pretty position for a lady, isn't it?"

"Any position she would fill would gain by her presence," said the doctor gravely. "Have they been gone long?" he asked, changing the subject. He never discussed Jane Cobden with his mother if he could help it.

"Oh, yes, some time. Lucy must have kept on home, for I saw Miss Jane going toward the beach alone."

"Are you sure, mother?" There was a note of anxiety in his voice.

"Yes, certainly. She had that red cloak of hers with her and that miserable little dog; that's how I know. She must be going to stay late. You look tired, my son; have you had a hard day?" added she, kissing him on the cheek.

"Yes, perhaps I am a little tired, but I'll be all

right. Have you looked at the slate lately? I'll go myself," and he turned and entered his office.

On the slate lay the rose. He picked it up and held it to his nose in a preoccupied way.

"One of mother's," he said listlessly, laying it back among his papers. "She so seldom does that sort of thing. Funny that she should have given it to me to-day; and after Miss Jane's visit, too." Then he shut the office door, threw himself into his chair, and buried his face in his hands. He was still there when his mother called him to supper.

When Lucy reached home it was nearly dark. She came alone, leaving Bart at the entrance to the village. At her suggestion they had avoided the main road and had crossed the marsh by the foot-path, the dog bounding on ahead and springing at the nurse, who stood in the gate awaiting Lucy's return.

"Why, he's as dry as a bone!" Martha cried, stroking Meg's rough hair with her plump hand. "He didn't get much of a bath, did he?"

"No, I couldn't get him into the water. Every time I got my hand on him he'd dart away again."

"Anybody on the beach, darlin'?"

"Not a soul except Meg and the sandsnipe."

CHAPTER V

When Martha, with Meg at her heels, passed Ann Gossaway's cottage the next morning on her way to the post-office—her daily custom—the dressmaker, who was sitting in the window, one eye on her needle and the other on the street, craned her head clear of the calico curtain framing the sash and beckoned to her.

This perch of Ann Gossaway's was the eyrie from which she swept the village street, bordered with a double row of wide-spreading elms and fringed with sloping grassy banks spaced at short intervals by hitching-posts and horse-blocks. Her own cottage stood somewhat nearer the flagged street path than the others, and as the garden fences were low and her lookout flanked by two windows, one on each end of her corner, she could not only note what went on about the fronts of her neighbors' houses, but much of what took place in their back yards. From this angle, too, she could see quite easily, and without more than twisting her attenuated neck, the whole village street from the Cromartins' gate to the spire

84

of the village church, as well as everything that passed up and down the shadow-flecked road: which child, for instance, was late for school, and how often, and what it wore and whether its clothes were new or inherited from an elder sister; who came to the Bronsons' next door, and how long they stayed, and whether they brought anything with them or carried anything away; the peddler with his pack; the gunner on his way to the marshes, his two dogs following at his heels in a leash; Dr. John Cavendish's gig, and whether it was about to stop at Uncle Ephraim Tipple's or keep on, as usual, and whirl into the open gate of Cobden Manor; Billy Tatham's passenger list, as the ricketty stage passed with the side curtains up, and the number of trunks and bags, and the size of them, all indicative of where they were bound and for how long; details of village life—no one of which concerned her in the least—being matters of profound interest to Miss Gossaway.

These several discoveries she shared daily with a faded old mother who sat huddled up in a rocking-chair by the stove, winter and summer, whether it had any fire in it or not.

Uncle Ephraim Tipple, in his outspoken way, always referred to these two gossips as the " spiders." " When the thin one has sucked the life out of you," he would say with a laugh, " she passes you on to her old mother, who sits doubled up inside the web, and when she gets done munching there isn't anything left but your hide and bones."

It was but one of Uncle Ephraim's jokes. The mother was only a forlorn, half-alive old woman who dozed in her chair by the hour—the relict of a fisherman who had gone to sea in his yawl some twenty years before and who had never come back. The daughter, with the courage of youth, had then stepped into the gap and had alone made the fight for bread. Gradually, as the years went by the roses in her cheeks—never too fresh at any time—had begun to fade, her face and figure to shrink, and her brow to tighten. At last, embittered by her responsibilities and disappointments, she had lost faith in human kind and had become a shrew. Since then her tongue had swept on as relentlessly as a scythe, sparing neither flower nor noxious weed, a movement which it was wise, sometimes, to check.

When, therefore, Martha, with Meg now bounding before her, caught sight of Ann Gossaway's beckoning hand thrust out of the low window of her cottage —the spider-web referred to by Uncle Ephraim—she halted in her walk, lingered a moment as if undecided, expressed her opinion of the dressmaker to Meg in an undertone, and swinging open the gate with its ball and chain, made her way over the grass-plot and stood outside the window, level with the sill.

" Well, it ain't none of my business, of course, Martha Sands," Miss Gossaway began, " and that's just what I said to mother when I come home, but if I was some folks I'd see my company in my parlor, long as I had one, 'stead of hidin' down behind the House o' Refuge. I said to mother soon's I got in, ' I'm goin' to tell Martha Sands fust minute I see her. She ain't got no idee how them girls of hers is carryin' on or she'd stop it.' That's what I said, didn't I, mother ? "

Martha caught an inarticulate sound escaping from a figure muffled in a blanket shawl, but nothing else followed.

" I thought fust it was you when I heard that draggle-tail dog of yours barkin', but it was only Miss Jane and Bart Holt."

" Down on the beach ! When ? " asked Martha. She had not understood a word of Miss Gossaway's outburst.

" Why, yesterday afternoon, of course—didn't I tell ye so ? I'd been down to Fogarty's; it's my week. Miss Jane and Bart didn't see me—didn't want to. Might a' been a pair of scissors, they was that close together."

" Miss Jane warn't on the beach yesterday afternoon," said Martha in a positive tone, still in the dark.

" She warn't, warn't she ? Well, I guess I know

Miss Jane Cobden. She and Bart was hunched up that close you couldn't get a bodkin 'tween 'em. She had that red cloak around her and the hood up over her head. Not know her, and she within ten feet o' me? Well, I guess I got my eyes left, ain't I?"

Martha stood stunned. She knew now who it was. She had taken the red cloak from Lucy's shoulders the evening before. Then a cold chill crept over her as she remembered the lie Lucy had told—"not a soul on the beach but Meg and the sandsnipe." For an instant she stood without answering. But for the window-sill on which her hand rested she would have betrayed her emotion in the swaying of her body. She tried to collect her thoughts. To deny Jane's identity too positively would only make the situation worse. If either one of the sisters were to be criticised Jane could stand it best.

" You got sharp eyes and ears, Ann Gossaway, nobody will deny you them, but still I don't think Miss Jane was on the beach yesterday."

" Don't think, don't you? Maybe you think I can't tell a cloak from a bed blanket, never havin' made one, and maybe ye think I don't know my own clo'es when I see 'em on folks. I made that red cloak for Miss Jane two years ago, and I know every stitch in it. Don't you try and teach Ann Gossaway how to cut and baste or you'll git worsted," and the gossip looked over her spectacles at Martha and shook her side-curls in a threatening way.

Miss Gossaway had no love for the old nurse. There had been a time when Martha " weren't no better'n she oughter be, so everybody said," when she came to the village, and the dressmaker never let a chance slip to humiliate the old woman. Martha's open denunciation of the dressmaker's vinegar tongue had only increased the outspoken dislike each had for the other. She saw now, to her delight, that the incident which had seemed to be only a bit of flotsam that had drifted to her shore and which but from Martha's manner would have been forgotten by her the next day, might be a fragment detached from some floating family wreck. Before she could press the matter to an explanation Martha turned abruptly on her heel, called Meg, and with the single remark, " Well, I guess Miss Jane's of age," walked quickly across the grass-plot and out of the gate, the ball and chain closing it behind her with a clang.

Once on the street Martha paused with her brain on fire. The lie which Lucy had told frightened her. She knew why she had told it, and she knew, too, what harm would come to her bairn if that kind of gossip got abroad in the village. She was no longer the gentle, loving nurse with the soft caressing hand, but a woman of purpose. The sudden terror aroused in her heart had the effect of tightening her grip and bracing her shoulders as if the better to withstand some expected shock.

She forgot Meg; forgot her errand to the post-office; forgot everything, in fact, except the safety of the child she loved. That Lucy had neglected and even avoided her of late, keeping out of her way even when she was in the house, and that she had received only cool indifference in place of loyal love, had greatly grieved her, but it had not lessened the idolatry with which she worshipped her bairn. Hours at a time she had spent puzzling her brain trying to account for the change which had come over the girl during two short years of school. She had until now laid this change to her youth, her love of admiration, and had forgiven it. Now she understood it; it was that boy Bart. He had a way with him. He had even ingratiated himself into Miss Jane's confidence. And now this young girl had fallen a victim to his wiles. That Lucy should lie to her, of all persons, and in so calm and self-possessed a manner; and about Bart, of all men— sent a shudder through her heart, that paled her cheek and tightened her lips. Once before she had consulted Jane and had been rebuffed. Now she would depend upon herself.

Retracing her steps and turning sharply to the right, she ordered Meg home in a firm voice, watched the dog slink off and then walked straight down a side road to Captain Nat Holt's house. That the captain occupied a different station in life from herself did not deter her. She felt at the moment that the honor of the Cobden name lay in her keeping. The family had stood by her in her trouble; now she would stand by them.

The captain sat on his front porch reading a newspaper. He was in his shirt-sleeves and bareheaded, his straight hair standing straight out like the bristles of a shoe-brush. Since the death of his wife a few years before he had left the service, and now spent most of his days at home, tending his garden and enjoying his savings. He was a man of positive character and generally had his own way in everything. It was therefore with some astonishment that he heard Martha say when she had mounted the porch steps and pushed open the front door, her breath almost gone in her hurried walk, " Come inside."

Captain Holt threw down his paper and rising hurriedly from his chair, followed her into the sitting-room. The manner of the nurse surprised him. He had known her for years, ever since his old friend, Lucy's father, had died, and the tones of her voice, so different from her usual deferential air, filled him with apprehension.

" Ain't nobody sick, is there, Martha ? "

" No, but there will be. Are ye alone ? "

" Yes."

" Then shut that door behind ye and sit down. I've got something to say."

The grizzled, weather-beaten man who had made twenty voyages around Cape Horn, and who was known as a man of few words, and those always of command, closed the door upon them, drew down the shade on the sunny side of the room and faced her. He saw now that something of more than usual importance absorbed her.

" Now, what is it ? " he asked. His manner had by this time regained something of the dictatorial tone he always showed those beneath him in authority.

" It's about Bart. You've got to send him away." She had not moved from her position in the middle of the room.

The captain changed color and his voice lost its sharpness.

" Bart! What's he done now ? "

" He sneaks off with our Lucy every chance he gets. They were on the beach yesterday hidin' behind the House o' Refuge with their heads together. She had on Miss Jane's red cloak, and Ann Gossaway thought it was Miss Jane, and I let it go at that."

The captain looked at Martha incredulously for a moment, and then broke into a loud laugh as the absurdity of the whole thing burst upon him. Then dropping back a step, he stood leaning against the old-fashioned sideboard, his elbows behind him, his large frame thrust toward her.

"Well, what if they were—ain't she pretty enough?" he burst out. "I told her she'd have 'em all crazy, and I hear Bart ain't done nothin' but follow in her wake since he seen her launched."

Martha stepped closer to the captain and held her fist in his face.

"He's got to stop it. Do ye hear me?" she shouted. "If he don't there'll be trouble, for you and him and everybody. It's me that's crazy, not him."

"Stop it!" roared the captain, straightening up, the glasses on the sideboard ringing with his sudden lurch. "My boy keep away from the daughter of Morton Cobden, who was the best friend I ever had and to whom I owe more than any man who ever lived! And this is what you traipsed up here to tell me, is it, you mollycoddle?"

Again Martha edged nearer; her body bent forward, her eyes searching his—so close that she could have touched his face with her knuckles.

"Hold your tongue and stop talkin' foolishness," she blazed out, the courage of a tigress fighting for her young in her eyes, the same bold ring in her voice. "I tell ye, Captain Holt, it's got to stop short

off, and NOW! I know men; have known 'em to my
misery. I know when they're honest and I know
when they ain't, and so do you, if you would open
your eyes. Bart don't mean no good to my bairn.
I see it in his face. I see it in the way he touches
her hand and ties on her bonnet. I've watched him
ever since the first night he laid eyes on her. He
ain't a man with a heart in him; he's a sneak with a
lie in his mouth. Why don't he come round like any
of the others and say where he's goin' and what he
wants to do instead of peepin' round the gate-posts
watchin' for her and sendin' her notes on the sly,
and makin' her lie to me, her old nurse, who's done
nothin' but love her? Doctor John don't treat Miss
Jane so—he loves her like a man ought to love a
woman and he ain't got nothin' to hide—and you
didn't treat your wife so. There's something here
that tells me "—and she laid her hand on her bosom
—" tells me more'n I dare tell ye. I warn ye now
ag'in. Send him to sea—anywhere, before it is too
late. She ain't got no mother; she won't mind a word
I say; Miss Jane is blind as a bat; out with him and
now!"

The captain straightened himself up, and with his
clenched fist raised above his head like a hammer
about to strike, cried:

"If he harmed the daughter of Morton Cobden
I'd kill him!" The words jumped hot from his

throat with a slight hissing sound, his eyes still aflame.

" Well, then, stop it before it gets too late. I walk the floor nights and I'm scared to death every hour I live." Then her voice broke. " Please, captain, please," she added in a piteous tone. " Don't mind me if I talk wild, my heart is breakin', and I can't hold in no longer," and she burst into a paroxysm of tears.

The captain leaned against the sideboard again and looked down upon the floor as if in deep thought. Martha's tears did not move him. The tears of few women did. He was only concerned in getting hold of some positive facts upon which he could base his judgment.

" Come, now," he said in an authoritative voice, " let me get that chair and set down and then I'll see what all this amounts to. Sounds like a yarn of a horse-marine." As he spoke he crossed the room and, dragging a rocking-chair from its place beside the wall, settled himself in it. Martha found a seat upon the sofa and turned her tear-stained face toward him.

" Now, what's these young people been doin' that makes ye so almighty narvous ? " he continued, lying back in his chair and looking at her from under his bushy eyebrows, his fingers supporting his forehead.

" Everything. Goes out sailin' with her and goes driftin' past with his head in her lap. Fogarty's man who brings fish to the house told me." She had regained something of her old composure now.

" Anything else ? " The captain's voice had a relieved, almost condescending tone in it. He had taken his thumb and forefinger from his eyebrow now and sat drumming with his stiffened knuckles on the arm of the rocker.

" Yes, a heap more—ain't that enough along with the other things I've told ye ? " Martha's eyes were beginning to blaze again.

" No, that's just as it ought to be. Boys and girls will be boys and girls the world over." The tone of the captain's voice indicated the condition of his mind. He had at last arrived at a conclusion. Martha's head was muddled because of her inordinate and unnatural love for the child she had nursed. She had found a spookship in a fog bank, that was all. Jealousy might be at the bottom of it or a certain nervous fussiness. Whatever it was it was too trivial for him to waste his time over.

The captain rose from his chair, crossed the sitting-room, and opened the door leading to the porch, letting in the sunshine. Martha followed close at his heels.

" You're runnin' on a wrong tack, old woman, and first thing ye know ye'll be in the breakers," he said, with his hand on the knob. " Ease off a little and don't be too hard on 'em. They'll make harbor all right. You're makin' more fuss than a hen over one chicken. Miss Jane knows what she's about. She's got a level head, and when she tells me that my Bart ain't good enough to ship alongside the daughter of Morton Cobden, I'll sign papers for him somewhere else, and not before. I'll have to get you to excuse me now; I'm busy. Good-day," and picking up his paper, he re-entered the house and closed the door upon her.

CHAPTER VI

A GAME OF CARDS

Should Miss Gossaway have been sitting at her lookout some weeks after Martha's interview with Captain Nat Holt, and should she have watched the movements of Doctor John's gig as it rounded into the open gate of Cobden Manor, she must have decided that something out of the common was either happening or about to happen inside Yardley's hospitable doors. Not only was the sorrel trotting at her best, the doctor flapping the lines along her brown back, his body swaying from side to side with the motion of the light vehicle, but as he passed her house he was also consulting the contents of a small envelope which he had taken from his pocket.

" Please come early," it read. " I have something important to talk over with you."

A note of this character signed with so adorable a name as " Jane Cobden " was so rare in the doctor's experience that he had at once given up his round of morning visits and, springing into his waiting gig, had started to answer it in person.

He was alive with expectancy. What could she want with him except to talk over some subject that they had left unfinished? As he hurried on there came into his mind half a dozen matters, any one of which it would have been a delight to revive. He knew from the way she worded the note that nothing had occurred since he had seen her—within the week, in fact—to cause her either annoyance or suffering. No; it was only to continue one of their confidential talks, which were the joy of his life.

Jane was waiting for him in the morning-room. Her face lighted up as he entered and took her hand, and immediately relaxed again into an expression of anxiety.

All his eagerness vanished. He saw with a sinking of the heart, even before she had time to speak, that something outside of his own affairs, or hers, had caused her to write the note.

" I came at once," he said, keeping her hand in his. " You look troubled; what has happened? "

" Nothing yet," she answered, leading him to the sofa. " It is about Lucy. She wants to go away for the winter."

" Where to? " he asked. He had placed a cushion at her back and had settled himself beside her.

" To Trenton, to visit her friend Miss Collins and study music. She says Warehold bores her."

" And you don't want her to go? "

" No; I don't fancy Miss Collins, and I am afraid she has too strong an influence over Lucy. Her personality grates on me; she is so boisterous, and she laughs so loud; and the views she holds are unaccountable to me in so young a girl. She seems to have had no home training whatever. Why Lucy likes her, and why she should have selected her as an intimate friend, has always puzzled me." She spoke with her usual frankness and with that directness which always characterized her in matters of this kind. " I had no one else to talk to and am very miserable about it all. You don't mind my sending for you, do you? "

" Mind! Why do you ask such a question? I am never so happy as when I am serving you."

That she should send for him at all was happiness. Not sickness this time, nor some question of investment, nor the repair of the barn or gate or outbuildings—but Lucy, who lay nearest her heart! That was even better than he had expected.

" Tell me all about it, so I can get it right," he continued in a straightforward tone—the tone of the physician, not the lover. She had relied on him, and he intended to give her the best counsel of which he was capable. The lover could wait.

" Well, she received a letter a week ago from Miss Collins, saying she had come to Trenton for the winter and had taken some rooms in a house belonging to her aunt, who would live with her. She wants to be within reach of the same music-teacher who taught the girls at Miss Parkham's school. She says if Lucy will come it will reduce the expenses and they can both have the benefit of the tuition. At first Lucy did not want to go at all, now she insists, and, strange to say, Martha encourages her."

" Martha wants her to leave ? " he asked in surprise.

" She says so."

The doctor's face assumed a puzzled expression. He could account for Lucy's wanting the freedom and novelty of the change, but that Martha should be willing to part with her bairn for the winter mystified him. He knew nothing of the flirtation, of course, and its effect on the old nurse, and could not, therefore, understand Martha's delight in Lucy's and Bart's separation.

" You will be very lonely," he said, and a certain tender tone developed in his voice.

" Yes, dreadfully so, but I would not mind if I thought it was for her good. But I don't think so. I may be wrong, and in the uncertainty I wanted to talk it over with you. I get so desolate sometimes. I never seemed to miss my father so much as now. Perhaps it is because Lucy's babyhood and childhood are over and she is entering upon womanhood with all the dangers it brings. And she frightens me so sometimes," she continued after a slight pause. " She is different; more self-willed, more self-centred. Besides, her touch has altered. She doesn't seem to love me as she did—not in the same way."

" But she could never do anything else but love you," he interrupted quickly, speaking for himself as well as Lucy, his voice vibrating under his emotions. It was all he could do to keep his hands from her own; her sending for him alone restrained him.

" I know that, but it is not in the old way. It used to be ' Sister, darling, don't tire yourself,' or ' Sister, dear, let me go upstairs for you,' or ' Cuddle close here, and let us talk it all out together.' There is no more of that. She goes her own way, and when I chide her laughs and leaves me alone until I make some new advance. Help me, please, and with all the wisdom you can give me; I have no one else in whom I can trust, no one who is big enough to know what should be done. I might have talked to Mr. Dellenbaugh about it, but he is away."

" No; talk it all out to me," he said simply. " I so want to help you "—his whole heart was going out to her in her distress.

" I know you feel sorry for me." She withdrew her hand gently so as not to hurt him; she too did not want to be misunderstood—having sent for him. " I know how sincere your friendship is for me, but put all that aside. Don't let your sympathy for me cloud your judgment. What shall I do with Lucy? Answer me as if you were her father and mine," and she looked straight into his eyes.

The doctor tightened the muscles of his throat, closed his teeth, and summoned all his resolution. If he could only tell her what was in his heart how much easier it would all be! For some moments he sat perfectly still, then he answered slowly—as her man of business would have done:

" I should let her go."

" Why do you say so ? "

" Because she will find out in that way sooner than in any other how to appreciate you and her home. Living in two rooms and studying music will not suit Lucy. When the novelty wears off she will long for her home, and when she comes back it will be with a better appreciation of its comforts. Let her go, and make her going as happy as you can."

And so Jane gave her consent—it is doubtful whether Lucy would have waited for it once her mind was made up—and in a week she was off, Doctor John taking her himself as far as the Junction, and seeing her safe on the road to Trenton. Martha was evidently delighted at the change, for the old nurse's face was wreathed in smiles that last morning as they all stood out by the gate while Billy

Tatham loaded Lucy's trunks and boxes. Only once did a frown cross her face, and that was when Lucy leaned over and whispering something in Bart's ear, slipped a small scrap of paper between his fingers. Bart crunched it tight and slid his hand carelessly into his pocket, but the gesture did not deceive the nurse: it haunted her for days thereafter.

As the weeks flew by and the letters from Trenton told of the happenings in Maria's home, it became more and more evident to Jane that the doctor's advice had been the wisest and best. Lucy would often devote a page or more of her letters to recalling the comforts of her own room at Yardley, so different from what she was enduring at Trenton, and longing for them to come again. Parts of these letters Jane read to the doctor, and all of them to Martha, who received them with varying comment. It became evident, too, that neither the excitement of Bart's letters, nor the visits of the occasional school friends who called upon them both, nor the pursuit of her new accomplishment, had satisfied the girl.

Jane was not surprised, therefore, remembering the doctor's almost prophetic words, to learn of the arrival of a letter from Lucy begging Martha to come to her at once for a day or two. The letter was enclosed in one to Bart and was handed to the nurse by that young man in person. As he did so he remarked meaningly that Miss Lucy wanted Martha's visit to be kept a secret from everybody but Miss Jane, "just as a surprise," but Martha answered in a positive tone that she had no secrets from those who had a right to know them, and that he could write Lucy she was coming next day, and that Jane and everybody else who might inquire would know of it before she started.

She rather liked Bart's receiving the letter. As long as that young man kept away from Trenton and confined himself to Warehold, where she could keep her eyes on him, she was content.

To Jane Martha said: "Oh, bless the darlin'! She can't do a day longer without her Martha. I'll go in the mornin'. It's a little pettin' she wants— that's all."

So the old nurse bade Meg good-by, pinned her big gray shawl about her, tied on her bonnet, took a little basket with some delicacies and a pot of jelly, and like a true Mother Hubbard, started off, while Jane, having persuaded herself that perhaps "the surprise" was meant for her, and that she might be welcoming two exiles instead of one the following night, began to put Lucy's room in order and to lay out the many pretty things she loved, especially the new dressing-gown she had made for her, lined with blue silk—her favorite color.

All that day and evening, and far into the next afternoon, Jane went about the house with the refrain of an old song welling up into her heart—one that had been stifled for months. The thought of the round-about way in which Lucy had sent for Martha did not dull its melody. That ruse, she knew, came from the foolish pride of youth, the pride that could not meet defeat. Underneath it she detected, with a thrill, the love of home; this, after all, was what her sister could not do without. It was not Bart this time. That affair, as she had predicted and had repeatedly told Martha, had worn itself out and had been replaced by her love of music. She had simply come to herself once more and would again be her old-time sister and her child. Then, too—and this sent another wave of delight tingling through her—it had all been the doctor's doing! But for his advice she would never have let Lucy go.

Half a dozen times, although the November afternoon was raw and chilly, with the wind fresh from the sea and the sky dull, she was out on the front porch without shawl or hat, looking down the path, covered now with dead leaves, and scanning closely every team that passed the gate, only to return again to her place by the fire, more impatient than ever.

Meg's quick ear first caught the grating of the wheels. Jane followed him with a cry of joyous expectation, and flew to the door to meet the stage, which for some reason—why, she could not tell—had stopped for a moment outside the gate, dropping only one passenger, and that one the nurse.

"And Lucy did not come, Martha!" Jane exclaimed, with almost a sob in her voice. She had reached her side now, followed by Meg, who was springing straight at the nurse in the joy of his welcome.

The old woman glanced back at the stage, as if afraid of being overheard, and muttered under her breath:

"No, she couldn't come."

"Oh, I am so disappointed! Why not?"

Martha did not answer. She seemed to have lost her breath. Jane put her arm about her and led her up the path. Once she stumbled, her step was so unsteady, and she would have fallen but for Jane's assistance.

The two had now reached the hand-railing of the porch. Here Martha's trembling foot began to feel about for the step. Jane caught her in her arms.

"You're ill, Martha!" she cried in alarm. "Give me the bag. What's the matter?"

Again Martha did not answer.

"Tell me what it is."

"Upstairs! Upstairs!" Martha gasped in reply. "Quick!"

"What has happened?"

" Not here; upstairs."

They climbed the staircase together, Jane half carrying the fainting woman, her mind in a whirl.

" Where were you taken ill? Why did you try to come home? Why didn't Lucy come with you? "

They had reached the door of Jane's bedroom now, Martha clinging to her arm.

Once inside, the nurse leaned panting against the door, put her hands to her face as if she would shut out some dreadful spectre, and sank slowly to the floor.

" It is not me," she moaned, wringing her hands, " not me—not——"

" Who? "

" Oh, I can't say it! "

" Lucy? "

" Yes."

" Not ill? "

" No; worse! "

" Oh, Martha! Not dead? "

" O God, I wish she were! "

An hour passed—an hour of agony, of humiliation and despair.

Again the door opened and Jane stepped out— slowly, as if in pain, her lips tight drawn, her face ghastly white, the thin cheeks sunken into deeper

"It is not me," she moaned, "not me."

hollows, the eyes burning. Only the mouth preserved its lines, but firmer, more rigid, more severe, as if tightened by the strength of some great resolve. In her hand she held a letter.

Martha lay on the bed, her face to the wall, her head still in her palms. She had ceased sobbing and was quite still, as if exhausted.

Jane leaned over the banisters, called to one of the servants, and dropping the letter to the floor below, said:

"Take that to Captain Holt's. When he comes bring him upstairs here into my sitting-room."

Before the servant could reply there came a knock at the front door. Jane knew its sound—it was Doctor John's. Leaning far over, grasping the top rail of the banisters to steady herself, she said to the servant in a low, restrained voice:

"If that is Dr. Cavendish, please say to him that Martha is just home from Trenton, greatly fatigued, and I beg him to excuse me. When the doctor has driven away, you can take the letter."

She kept her grasp on the hand-rail until she heard the tones of his voice through the open hall door and caught the note of sorrow that tinged them.

"Oh, I'm so sorry! Poor Martha!" she heard him say. "She is getting too old to go about alone. Please tell Miss Jane she must not hesitate to send for me if I can be of the slightest service." Then she re-entered the room where Martha lay and closed the door.

Another and louder knock now broke the stillness of the chamber and checked the sobs of the nurse; Captain Holt had met Jane's servant as he was passing the gate. He stopped for an instant in the hall, slipped off his coat, and walked straight upstairs, humming a tune as he came. Jane heard his firm tread, opened the door of their room, and she and Martha crossed the hall to a smaller apartment where Jane always attended to the business affairs of the house. The captain's face was wreathed in a broad smile as he extended his hand to Jane in welcome.

"It's lucky ye caught me, Miss Jane. I was just goin' out, and in a minute I'd been gone for the night. Hello, Mother Martha! I thought you'd gone to Trenton."

The two women made no reply to his cheery salutation, except to motion him to a seat. Then Jane closed the door and turned the key in the lock.

When the captain emerged from the chamber he stepped out alone. His color was gone, his eyes flashing, his jaw tight set. About his mouth there hovered a savage, almost brutal look, the look of a bull-dog who bares his teeth before he tears and strangles

—a look his men knew when someone of them purposely disobeyed his orders. For a moment he stood as if dazed. All he remembered clearly was the white, drawn face of a woman gazing at him with staring, tear-drenched eyes, the slow dropping of words that blistered as they fell, and the figure of the nurse wringing her hands and moaning: " Oh, I told ye so! I told ye so! Why didn't ye listen?" With it came the pain of some sudden blow that deadened his brain and stilled his heart.

With a strong effort, like one throwing off a stupor, he raised his head, braced his shoulders, and strode firmly along the corridor and down the stairs on his way to the front door. Catching up his coat, he threw it about him, pulled his hat on, with a jerk, slamming the front door, plunged along through the dry leaves that covered the path, and so on out to the main road. Once beyond the gate he hesitated, looked up and down, turned to the right and then to the left, as if in doubt, and lunged forward in the direction of the tavern.

It was Sunday night, and the lounging room was full. One of the inmates rose and offered him a chair—he was much respected in the village, especially among the rougher class, some of whom had sailed with him—but he only waved his hand in thanks.

" I don't want to sit down; I'm looking for Bart.

Has he been here?" The sound came as if from between closed teeth.

"Not as I know of, cap'n," answered the landlord; "not since sundown, nohow."

"Do any of you know where he is?" The look in the captain's eyes and the sharp, cutting tones of his voice began to be noticed.

"Do ye want him bad?" asked a man tilted back in a chair against the wall.

"Yes."

"Well, I kin tell ye where to find him."

"Where?"

"Down on the beach in the Refuge shanty. He and the boys have a deck there Sunday nights. Been at it all fall—thought ye knowed it."

Out into the night again, and without a word of thanks, down the road and across the causeway to the hard beach, drenched with the ceaseless thrash of the rising sea. He followed no path, picked out no road. Stumbling along in the half-gloom of the twilight, he could make out the heads of the sand-dunes, bearded with yellow grass blown flat against their cheeks. Soon he reached the prow of the old wreck with its shattered timbers and the water-holes left by the tide. These he avoided, but the smaller objects he trampled upon and over as he strode on, without caring where he stepped or how often he stumbled. Outlined against the sand-hills, bleached

112

white under the dull light, he looked like some evil presence bent on mischief, so direct and forceful was his unceasing, persistent stride.

When the House of Refuge loomed up against the gray froth of the surf he stopped and drew breath. Bending forward, he scanned the beach ahead, shading his eyes with his hand as he would have done on his own ship in a fog. He could make out now some streaks of yellow light showing through the cracks one above the other along the side of the house and a dull patch of red. He knew what it meant. Bart and his fellows were inside, and were using one of the ship lanterns to see by.

This settled in his mind, the captain strode on, but at a slower pace. He had found his bearings, and would steer with caution.

Hugging the dunes closer, he approached the house from the rear. The big door was shut and a bit of matting had been tacked over the one window to deaden the light. This was why the patch of red was dull. He stood now so near the outside planking that he could hear the laughter and talk of those within. By this time the wind had risen to half a gale and the moan on the outer bar could be heard in the intervals of the pounding surf. The captain crept under the eaves of the roof and listened. He wanted to be sure of Bart's voice before he acted.

At this instant a sudden gust of wind burst in the

113

big door, extinguishing the light of the lantern, and Bart's voice rang out:

"Stay where you are, boys! Don't touch the cards. I know the door, and can fix it; it's only the bolt that's slipped."

As Bart passed out into the gloom the captain darted forward, seized him with a grip of steel, dragged him clear of the door, and up the sand-dunes out of hearing. Then he flung him loose and stood facing the cowering boy.

"Now stand back and keep away from me, for I'm afraid I'll kill you!"

"What have I done?" cringed Bart, shielding his face with his elbow as if to ward off a blow. The suddenness of the attack had stunned him.

"Don't ask me, you whelp, or I'll strangle you. Look at me! That's what you been up to, is it?"

Bart straightened himself, and made some show of resistance. His breath was coming back to him.

"I haven't done anything—and if I did——"

"You lie! Martha's back from Trenton and Lucy told her. You never thought of me. You never thought of that sister of hers whose heart you've broke, nor of the old woman who nursed her like a mother. You thought of nobody but your stinkin' self. You're not a man! You're a cur! a dog! Don't move! Keep away from me, I tell ye, or I may lose hold of myself."

Bart was stretching out his hands now, as if in supplication. He had never seen his father like this—the sight frightened him.

"Father, will you listen——" he pleaded.

"I'll listen to nothin'——"

"Will you, please? It's not all my fault. She ought to have kept out of my way——"

"Stop! Take that back! You'd blame *her,* would ye—a child just out of school, and as innocent as a baby? By God, you'll do right by her or you'll never set foot inside my house again!"

Bart faced his father again.

"I want to tell you the whole story before you judge me. I want to——"

"You'll tell me nothin'! Will you act square with her?"

"I must tell you first. You wouldn't understand unless——"

"You won't? That's what you mean—you mean you *won't!* Damn ye!" The captain raised his clenched fist, quivered for an instant as if struggling against something beyond his control, dropped it slowly to his side and whirling suddenly, strode back up the beach.

Bart staggered back against the planking, threw out his hand to keep from falling, and watched his father's uncertain, stumbling figure until he was swallowed up in the gloom. The words rang in his

115

ears like a knell. The realization of his position and what it meant, and might mean, rushed over him. For an instant he leaned heavily against the planking until he had caught his breath. Then, with quivering lips and shaking legs, he walked slowly back into the house, shutting the big door behind him.

"Boys," he said with a forced smile, "who do you think's been outside? My father! Somebody told him, and he's just been giving me hell for playing cards on Sunday."

CHAPTER VII

THE EYES OF AN OLD PORTRAIT

Before another Sunday night had arrived Warehold village was alive with two important pieces of news.

The first was the disappearance of Bart Holt.

Captain Nat, so the story ran, had caught him carousing in the House of Refuge on Sunday night with some of his boon companions, and after a stormy interview in which the boy pleaded for forgiveness, had driven him out into the night. Bart had left town the next morning at daylight and had shipped as a common sailor on board a British bark bound for Brazil. No one had seen him go—not even his companions of the night before.

The second announcement was more startling.

The Cobden girls were going to Paris. Lucy Cobden had developed an extraordinary talent for music during her short stay in Trenton with her friend Maria Collins, and Miss Jane, with her customary unselfishness and devotion to her younger sister, had decided to go with her. They might be gone two

117

years or five—it depended on Lucy's success. Martha would remain at Yardley and take care of the old home.

Bart's banishment coming first served as a target for the fire of the gossip some days before Jane's decision had reached the ears of the villagers.

"I always knew he would come to no good end," Miss Gossaway called out to a passer-by from her eyrie; "and there's more like him if their fathers would look after 'em. Guess sea's the best place for him."

Billy Tatham, the stage-driver, did not altogether agree with the extremist.

"You hearn tell, I s'pose, of how Captain Nat handled his boy t'other night, didn't ye?" he remarked to the passenger next to him on the front seat. "It might be the way they did things 'board the Black Ball Line, but 'tain't human and decent, an' I told Cap'n Nat so to-day. Shut his door in his face an' told him he'd kill him if he tried to come in, and all because he ketched him playin' cards on Sunday down on the beach. Bart warn't no worse than the others he run with, but ye can't tell what these old sea-dogs will do when they git riled. I guess it was the rum more'n the cards. Them fellers used to drink a power o' rum in that shanty. I've seen 'em staggerin' home many a Monday mornin' when I got down early to open up for my team. It's the rum that riled the cap'n, I guess. He wouldn't stand it aboard ship and used to put his men in irons, I've hearn tell, when they come aboard drunk. What gits me is that the cap'n didn't know them fellers met there every night they could git away, week-days as well as Sundays. Everybody 'round here knew it 'cept him and the light-keeper, and he's so durned lazy he never once dropped on to 'em. He'd git bounced if the Gov'ment found out he was lettin' a gang run the House o' Refuge whenever they felt like it. Fogarty, the fisherman's, got the key, or oughter have it, but the light-keeper's responsible, so I hearn tell. Git-up, Billy," and the talk drifted into other channels.

The incident was soon forgotten. One young man more or less did not make much difference in Warehold. As to Captain Nat, he was known to be a scrupulously honest, exact man who knew no law outside of his duty. He probably did it for the boy's good, although everybody agreed that he could have accomplished his purpose in some more merciful way.

The other sensation—the departure of the two Cobden girls, and their possible prolonged stay abroad—did not subside so easily. Not only did the neighbors look upon the Manor House as the show-place of the village, but the girls themselves were greatly beloved, Jane being especially idolized from Warehold to Barnegat and the sea. To lose Jane's presence among them was a positive calamity entailing a sorrow that most of her neighbors could not bring themselves to face. No one could take her place.

Pastor Dellenbaugh, when he heard the news, sank into his study chair and threw up his hands as if to ward off some blow.

"Miss Jane going abroad!" he cried; "and you say nobody knows when she will come back! I can't realize it! We might as well close the school; no one else in the village can keep it together."

The Cromartins and the others all expressed similar opinions, the younger ladies' sorrow being aggravated when they realized that with Lucy away there would be no one to lead in their merrymakings.

Martha held her peace; she would stay at home, she told Mrs. Dellenbaugh, and wait for their return and look after the place. Her heart was broken with the loneliness that would come, she moaned, but what was best for her bairn she was willing to bear. It didn't make much difference either way; she wasn't long for this world.

The doctor's mother heard the news with ill-concealed satisfaction.

"A most extraordinary thing has occurred here, my dear," she said to one of her Philadelphia friends who was visiting her—she was too politic to talk openly to the neighbors. "You have, of course, met

120

that Miss Cobden who lives at Yardley—not the pretty one—the plain one. Well, she is the most quixotic creature in the world. Only a few weeks ago she wanted to become a nurse in the public hospital here, and now she proposes to close her house and go abroad for nobody knows how long, simply because her younger sister wants to study music, as if a school-girl couldn't get all the instruction of that kind here that is necessary. Really, I never heard of such a thing."

To Mrs. Benson, a neighbor, she said, behind her hand and in strict confidence: " Miss Cobden is morbidly conscientious over trifles. A fine woman, one of the very finest we have, but a little too strait-laced, and, if I must say it, somewhat commonplace, especially for a woman of her birth and education."

To herself she said: " Never while I live shall Jane Cobden marry my John! She can never help any man's career. She has neither the worldly knowledge, nor the personal presence, nor the money."

Jane gave but one answer to all inquiries—and there were many.

" Yes, I know the move is a sudden one," she would say, " but it is for Lucy's good, and there is no one to go with her but me." No one saw beneath the mask that hid her breaking heart. To them the drawn face and the weary look in her eyes only showed her grief at leaving home and those who loved her: to Mrs. Cavendish it seemed part of Jane's peculiar temperament.

Nor could they watch her in the silence of the night tossing on her bed, or closeted with Martha in her search for the initial steps that had led to this horror. Had the Philadelphia school undermined her own sisterly teachings or had her companions been at fault? Perhaps it was due to the blood of some long-forgotten ancestor, which in the cycle of years had cropped out in this generation, poisoning the fountain of her youth. Bart, she realized, had played the villain and the ingrate, but yet it was also true that Bart, and all his class, would have been powerless before a woman of a different temperament. Who, then, had undermined this citadel and given it over to plunder and disgrace? Then with merciless exactness she searched her own heart. Had it been her fault? What safeguard had she herself neglected? Wherein had she been false to her trust and her promise to her dying father? What could she have done to avert it? These ever-haunting, ever-recurring doubts maddened her.

One thing she was determined upon, cost what it might—to protect her sister's name. No daughter of Morton Cobden's should be pointed at in scorn. For generations no stain of dishonor had tarnished the family name. This must be preserved, no matter who suffered. In this she was sustained by Martha, her only confidante.

Doctor John heard the news from Jane's lips before it was known to the villagers. He had come to inquire after Martha.

She met him at the porch entrance, and led him into the drawing-room, without a word of welcome. Then shutting the door, she motioned him to a seat opposite her own on the sofa. The calm, determined way with which this was done—so unusual in one so cordial—startled him. He felt that something of momentous interest, and, judging from Jane's face, of serious import, had happened. He invariably took his cue from her face, and his own spirits always rose or fell as the light in her eyes flashed or dimmed.

" Is there anything the matter ? " he asked nervously. " Martha worse ? "

" No, not that; Martha is around again—it is about Lucy and me." The voice did not sound like Jane's.

The doctor looked at her intently, but he did not speak. Jane continued, her face now deathly pale, her words coming slowly.

" You advised me some time ago about Lucy's going to Trenton, and I am glad I followed it. You thought it would strengthen her love for us all and teach her to love me the better. It has—so much so that hereafter we will never be separated. I hope now you will also approve of what I have just decided upon. Lucy is going abroad to live, and I am going with her."

As the words fell from her lips her eyes crept up to his face, watching the effect of her statement. It was a cold, almost brutal way of putting it, she knew, but she dared not trust herself with anything less formal.

For a moment he sat perfectly still, the color gone from his cheeks, his eyes fixed on hers, a cold chill benumbing the roots of his hair. The suddenness of the announcement seemed to have stunned him.

" For how long ? " he asked in a halting voice.

" I don't know. Not less than two years; perhaps longer."

" *Two years?* Is Lucy ill ? "

" No; she wants to study music, and she couldn't go alone."

" Have you made up your mind to this ? " he asked, in a more positive tone. His self-control was returning now.

" Yes."

Doctor John rose from his chair, paced the room slowly for a moment, and crossing to the fireplace with his back to Jane, stood under her father's portrait, his elbows on the mantel, his head in his hand. Interwoven with the pain which the announcement

124

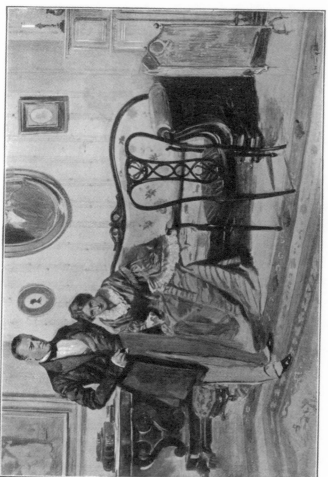

Doctor John rose from his chair and slowly paced the room.

had given him was the sharper sorrow of her neglect of him. In forming her plans she had never once thought of her lifelong friend.

"Why did you not tell me something of this before?" The inquiry was not addressed to Jane, but to the smouldering coals. "How have I ever failed you? What has my daily life been but an open book for you to read, and here you leave me for years, and never give me a thought."

Jane started in her seat.

"Forgive me, my dear friend!" she answered quickly in a voice full of tenderness. "I did not mean to hurt you. It is not that I love all my friends here the less—and you know how truly I appreciate your own friendship—but only that I love my sister more; and my duty is with her. I only decided last night. Don't turn your back on me. Come and sit by me, and talk to me," she pleaded, holding out her hand. "I need all your strength." As she spoke the tears started to her eyes and her voice sank almost to a whisper.

The doctor lifted his head from his palm and walked quickly toward her. The suffering in her voice had robbed him of all resentment.

"Forgive me, I did not mean it. Tell me," he said, in a sudden burst of tenderness—all feeling about himself had dropped away—"why must you go so soon? Why not wait until spring?" He had taken his seat beside her now and sat looking into her eyes.

"Lucy wants to go at once," she replied, in a tone as if the matter did not admit of any discussion.

"Yes, I know. That's just like her. What she wants she can never wait a minute for, but she certainly would sacrifice some pleasure of her own to please you. If she was determined to be a musician it would be different, but it is only for her pleasure, and as an accomplishment." He spoke earnestly and impersonally, as he always did when she consulted him on any of her affairs. He was trying, too, to wipe from her mind all remembrance of his impatience.

Jane kept her eyes on the carpet for a moment, and then said quietly, and he thought in rather a hopeless tone:

"It is best we go at once."

The doctor looked at her searchingly—with the eye of a scientist, this time, probing for a hidden meaning.

"Then there is something else you have not told me; someone is annoying her, or there is someone with whom you are afraid she will fall in love. Who is it? You know how I could help in a matter of that kind."

"No; there is no one."

Doctor John leaned back thoughtfully and tapped

the arm of the sofa with his fingers. He felt as if a door had been shut in his face.

" I don't understand it," he said slowly, and in a baffled tone. " I have never known you to do a thing like this before. It is entirely unlike you. There is some mystery you are keeping from me. Tell me, and let me help."

" I can tell you nothing more. Can't you trust me to do my duty in my own way?" She stole a look at him as she spoke and again lowered her eyelids."

" And you are determined to go?" he asked in his former cross-examining tone.

" Yes."

Again the doctor kept silence. Despite her assumed courage and determined air, his experienced eye caught beneath it all the shrinking helplessness of the woman.

" Then I, too, have reached a sudden resolve," he said in a manner almost professional in its precision. " You cannot and shall not go alone."

" Oh, but Lucy and I can get along together," she exclaimed with nervous haste. " There is no one we could take but Martha, and she is too old. Besides she must look after the house while we are away."

" No; Martha will not do. No woman will do. I know Paris and its life; it is not the place for two women to live in alone, especially so pretty and light-hearted a woman as Lucy."

" I am not afraid."

" No, but I am," he answered in a softened voice, " very much afraid." It was no longer the physician who spoke, but the friend.

" Of what ? "

" Of a dozen things you do not understand, and cannot until you encounter them," he replied, smoothing her hand tenderly.

" Yes, but it cannot be helped. There is no one to go with us." This came with some positiveness, yet with a note of impatience in her voice.

" Yes, there is," he answered gently.

" Who ? " she asked slowly, withdrawing her hand from his caress, an undefined fear rising in her mind.

" Me. I will go with you."

Jane looked at him with widening eyes. She knew now. She had caught his meaning in the tones of his voice before he had expressed it, and had tried to think of some way to ward off what she saw was coming, but she was swept helplessly on.

" Let us go together, Jane," he burst out, drawing closer to her. All reserve was gone. The words which had pressed so long for utterance could no longer be held back. " I cannot live here alone without you. You know it, and have always known it.

128

I love you so—don't let us live apart any more. If you must go, go as my wife."

A thrill of joy ran through her. Her lips quivered. She wanted to cry out, to put her arms around his neck, to tell him everything in her heart. Then came a quick, sharp pain that stifled every other thought. For the first time the real bitterness of the situation confronted her. This phase of it she had not counted upon.

She shrank back a little. "Don't ask me that!" she moaned in a tone almost of pain. "I can stand anything now but that. Not now—not now!"

Her hand was still under his, her fingers lying limp, all the pathos of her suffering in her face: determination to do her duty, horror over the situation, and above them all her overwhelming love for him.

He put his arm about her shoulders and drew her to him.

"You love me, Jane, don't you?"

"Yes, more than all else in the world," she answered simply. "Too well"—and her voice broke —"to have you give up your career for me or mine."

"Then why should we live apart? I am willing to do as much for Lucy as you would. Let me share the care and responsibility. You needn't, perhaps, be gone more than a year, and then we will all come back together, and I take up my work again. I need you, my beloved. Nothing that I do seems of any use without you. You are my great, strong light, and have always been since the first day I loved you. Let me help bear these burdens. You have carried them so long alone."

His face lay against hers now, her hand still clasped tight in his. For an instant she did not answer or move; then she straightened a little and lifted her cheek from his.

" John," she said—it was the first time in all her life she had called him thus—" you wouldn't love me if I should consent. You have work to do here and I now have work to do on the other side. We cannot work together; we must work apart. Your heart is speaking, and I love you for it, but we must not think of it now. It may come right some time— God only knows! My duty is plain—I must go with Lucy. Neither you nor my dead father would love me if I did differently."

" I only know that I love you and that you love me and nothing else should count," he pleaded impatiently. " Nothing else shall count. There is nothing you could do would make me love you less. You are practical and wise about all your plans. Why has this whim of Lucy's taken hold of you as it has? And it is only a whim; Lucy will want something else in six months. Oh, I cannot—cannot let you go. I'm so desolate without you—my whole life is yours—everything I do is for you. O Jane, my beloved, don't shut me out of your life! I will not let you go without me!" His voice vibrated with a certain indignation, as if he had been unjustly treated. She raised one hand and laid it on his forehead, smoothing his brow as a mother would that of a child. The other still lay in his.

"Don't, John," she moaned, in a half-piteous tone. "Don't! Don't talk so! I can only bear comforting words to-day. I am too wretched—too utterly broken and miserable. Please! please, John!"

He dropped her hand and leaning forward put both of his own to his head. He knew how strong was her will and how futile would be his efforts to change her mind unless her conscience agreed.

"I won't," he answered, as a strong man answers who is baffled. "I did not mean to be impatient or exacting." Then he raised his head and looked steadily into her eyes. "What would you have me do, then?"

"Wait."

"But you give me no promise."

"No, I cannot—not now. I am like one staggering along, following a dim light that leads hither and thither, and which may any moment go out and leave me in utter darkness."

"Then there is something you have not told me?"

"O John! Can't you trust me?"

" And yet you love me ? "

" As my life, John."

When he had gone and she had closed the door upon him, she went back to the sofa where the two had sat together, and with her hands clasped tight above her head, sank down upon its cushions. The tears came like rain now, bitter, blinding tears that she could not check.

" I have hurt him," she moaned. " He is so good, and strong, and helpful. He never thinks of himself; it is always of me—me, who can do nothing. The tears were in his eyes—I saw them. Oh, I've hurt him—hurt him! And yet, dear God, thou knowest I could not help it."

Maddened with the pain of it all she sprang up, determined to go to him and tell him everything. To throw herself into his arms and beg forgiveness for her cruelty and crave the protection of his strength. Then her gaze fell upon her father's portrait! The cold, steadfast eyes were looking down upon her as if they could read her very soul. " No! No! " she sobbed, putting her hands over her eyes as if to shut out some spectre she had not the courage to face. " It must not be—it *cannot* be," and she sank back exhausted.

When the paroxysm was over she rose to her feet, dried her eyes, smoothed her hair with both hands, and then, with lips tight pressed and faltering steps, walked upstairs to where Martha was getting Lucy's things ready for the coming journey. Crossing the room, she stood with her elbows on the mantel, her cheeks tight pressed between her palms, her eyes on the embers. Martha moved from the open trunk and stood behind her.

"It was Doctor John, wasn't it?" she asked in a broken voice that told of her suffering.

"Yes," moaned Jane from between her hands.

"And ye told him about your goin'?"

"Yes, Martha." Her frame was shaking with her sobs.

"And about Lucy?"

"No, I could not."

Martha leaned forward and laid her hand on Jane's shoulder.

"Poor lassie!" she said, patting it softly. "Poor lassie! That was the hardest part. He's big and strong and could 'a' comforted ye. My heart aches for ye both!"

CHAPTER VIII

With the departure of Jane and Lucy the old homestead took on that desolate, abandoned look which comes to most homes when all the life and joyousness have gone from them. Weeds grew in the roadway between the lilacs, dandelions flaunted themselves over the grass-plots; the shutters of the porch side of the house were closed, and the main gate, always thrown wide day and night in ungoverned welcome, was seldom opened except to a few intimate friends of the old nurse.

At first Pastor Dellenbaugh had been considerate enough to mount the long path to inquire for news of the travelers and to see how Martha was getting along, but after the receipt of the earlier letters from Jane telling of their safe arrival and their sojourn in a little village but a short distance out of Paris, convenient to the great city, even his visits ceased. Captain Holt never darkened the door; nor did he ever willingly stop to talk to Martha when he met her on the road. She felt the slight, and avoided

134

him when she could. This resulted in their seldom speaking to each other, and then only in the most casual way. She fancied he might think she wanted news of Bart, and so gave him no opportunity to discuss him or his whereabouts; but she was mistaken. The captain never mentioned his name to friend or stranger. To him the boy was dead for all time. Nor had anyone of his companions heard from him since that stormy night on the beach.

Doctor John's struggle had lasted for months, but he had come through it chastened and determined. For the first few days he went about his work as one in a dream, his mind on the woman he loved, his hand mechanically doing its duty. Jane had so woven herself into his life that her sudden departure had been like the upwrenching of a plant, tearing out the fibres twisted about his heart, cutting off all his sustenance and strength. The inconsistencies of her conduct especially troubled him. If she loved him—and she had told him that she did, and with their cheeks touching—how could she leave him in order to indulge a mere whim of her sister's? And if she loved him well enough to tell him so, why had she refused to plight him her troth? Such a course was unnatural, and out of his own and everyone else's experience. Women who loved men with a great, strong, healthy love, the love he could give her, and the love he knew she could give him, never permitted such trifles to come between them and their life's happiness. What, he asked himself a thousand times, had brought this change?

As the months went by these doubts and speculations one by one passed out of his mind, and only the image of the woman he adored, with all her qualities—loyalty to her trust, tenderness over Lucy, and unquestioned love for himself—rose clear. No, he would believe in her to the end! She was still all he had in life. If she would not be his wife she should be his friend. That happiness was worth all else to him in the world. His was not to criticise, but to help. Help as *she* wanted it; preserving her standard of personal honor, her devotion to her ideals, her loyalty, her blind obedience to her trust.

Mrs. Cavendish had seen the change in her son's demeanor and had watched him closely through his varying moods, but though she divined their cause she had not sought to probe his secret.

His greatest comfort was in his visits to Martha. He always dropped in to see her when he made his rounds in the neighborhood; sometimes every day, sometimes once a week, depending on his patients and their condition—visits which were always prolonged when a letter came from either of the girls, for at first Lucy wrote to the old nurse as often as did Jane. Apart from this the doctor loved the patient caretaker, both for her loyalty and for her gentleness. And she loved him in return; clinging to him as an older woman clings to a strong man, following his advice (he never gave orders) to the minutest detail when something in the management or care of house or grounds exceeded her grasp. Consulting him, too, and this at Jane's special request—regarding any financial complications which needed prompt attention, and which, but for his services, might have required Jane's immediate return to disentangle. She loved, too, to talk of Lucy and of Miss Jane's goodness to her bairn, saying she had been both a sister and a mother to her, to which the doctor would invariably add some tribute of his own which only bound the friendship the closer.

His main relief, however, lay in his work, and in this he became each day more engrossed. He seemed never to be out of his gig unless at the bedside of some patient. So long and wearing had the routes become—often beyond Barnegat and as far as Westfield—that the sorrel gave out, and he was obliged to add another horse to his stable. His patients saw the weary look in his eyes—as of one who had often looked on sorrow—and thought it was the hard work and anxiety over them that had caused it. But the old nurse knew better.

" His heart's breakin' for love of her," she would say to Meg, looking down into his sleepy eyes—she cuddled him more than ever these days—" and I don't wonder. God knows how it 'll all end."

Jane wrote to him but seldom; only half a dozen letters in all during the first year of her absence; among them one to tell him of their safe arrival, another to thank him for his kindness to Martha, and a third to acknowledge the receipt of a letter of introduction to a student friend of his who was now a prominent physician in Paris, and who might be useful in case either of them fell ill. He had written to his friend at the same time, giving the address of the two girls, but the physician had answered that he had called at the street and number, but no one knew of them. The doctor reported this to Jane in his next letter, asking her to write to his friend so that he might know of their whereabouts should they need his services, for which Jane, in a subsequent letter, thanked him, but made no mention of sending to his friend should occasion require. These subsequent letters said very little about their plans and carefully avoided all reference to their daily life or to Lucy's advancement in her studies, and never once set any time for their coming home. He wondered at her neglect of him, and when no answer came to his continued letters, except at long intervals, he could contain himself no longer, and laid the whole matter before Martha.

" She means nothing, doctor, dear," she had answered, taking his hand and looking up into his troubled face. " Her heart is all right; she's goin' through deep waters, bein' away from everybody she loves—you most of all. Don't worry; keep on lovin' her, ye'll never have cause to repent it."

That same night Martha wrote to Jane, giving her every detail of the interview, and in due course of time handed the doctor a letter in which Jane wrote: " He *must not* stop writing to me; his letters are all the comfort I have "—a line not intended for the doctor's eyes, but which the good soul could not keep from him, so eager was she to relieve his pain.

Jane's letter to him in answer to his own expressing his unhappiness over her neglect was less direct, but none the less comforting to him. " I am constantly moving about," the letter ran, " and have much to do and cannot always answer your letters, so please do not expect them too often. But I am always thinking of you and your kindness to dear Martha. You do for me when you do for her."

After this it became a settled habit between them, he writing by the weekly steamer, telling her every thought of his life, and she replying at long intervals. In these no word of love was spoken on her side; nor was any reference made to their last interview. But this fact did not cool the warmth of his affection nor weaken his faith. She had told him she loved him, and with her own lips. That was enough—

enough from a woman like Jane. He would lose
faith when she denied it in the same way. In the
meantime she was his very breath and being.

One morning two years after Jane's departure,
while the doctor and his mother sat at breakfast,
Mrs. Cavendish filling the tea-cups, the spring sunshine lighting up the snow-white cloth and polished
silver, the mail arrived and two letters were laid
at their respective plates, one for the doctor and the
other for his mother.

As Doctor John glanced at the handwriting his
face flushed, and his eyes danced with pleasure.
With eager, trembling fingers he broke the seal and
ran his eyes hungrily over the contents. It had
been his habit to turn to the bottom of the last page
before he read the preceding ones, so that he might
see the signature and note the final words of affection or friendship, such as " Ever your friend,"
or " Affectionately yours," or simply " Your friend,"
written above Jane's name. These were to him
the thermometric readings of the warmth of her
heart.

Half way down the first page—before he had time
to turn the leaf—he caught his breath in an effort
to smother a sudden outburst of joy. Then with a
supreme effort he regained his self-control and read
the letter to the end. (He rarely mentioned Jane's
name to his mother, and he did not want his delight

over the contents of the letter to be made the basis of comment.)

Mrs. Cavendish's outburst over the contents of her own envelope broke the silence and relieved his tension.

" Oh, how fortunate!" she exclaimed. " Listen, John; now I really have good news for you. You remember I told you that I met old Dr. Pencoyd the last time I was in Philadelphia, and had a long talk with him. I told him how you were buried here and how hard you worked and how anxious I was that you should leave Barnegat, and he promised to write to me, and he has. Here's his letter. He says he is getting too old to continue his practice alone, that his assistant has fallen ill, and that if you will come to him at once he will take you into partnership and give you half his practice. I always knew something good would come out of my last visit to Philadelphia. Aren't you delighted, my son?"

" Yes, perfectly overjoyed," answered the doctor, laughing. He was more than delighted—brimming over with happiness, in fact—but not over his mother's news; it was the letter held tight in his grasp that was sending electric thrills through him. " A fine old fellow is Dr. Pencoyd—known him for years," he continued; " I attended his lectures before I went abroad. Lives in a musty old house on Chestnut Street, stuffed full of family portraits and old mahogany furniture, and not a comfortable chair or sofa in the place; wears yellow Nankeen waist-coats, takes snuff, and carries a fob. Oh, yes, same old fellow. Very kind of him, mother, but wouldn't you rather have the sunlight dance in upon you as it does here and catch a glimpse of the sea through the window than to look across at your neighbors' back walls and white marble steps?" It was across that same sea that Jane was coming, and the sunshine would come with her!

"Yes; but, John, surely you are not going to refuse this without looking into it?" she argued, eyeing him through her gold-rimmed glasses. "Go and see him, and then you can judge. It's his practice you want, not his house."

"No; that's just what I don't want. I've got too much practice now. Somehow I can't keep my people well. No, mother, dear, don't bother your dear head over the old doctor and his wants. Write him that I am most grateful, but that the fact is I need an assistant myself, and if he will be good enough to send someone down here, I'll keep him busy every hour of the day and night. Then, again," he continued, a more serious tone in his voice, "I couldn't possibly leave here now, even if I wished to, which I do not."

Mrs. Cavendish eyed him intently. She had expected just such a refusal. Nothing that she ever planned for his advancement did he agree to.

" Why not ? " she asked, with some impatience.

" The new hospital is about finished, and I am going to take charge of it."

" Do they pay you for it ? " she continued, in an incisive tone.

" No, I don't think they will, nor can. It's not that kind of a hospital," answered the doctor gravely.

" And you will look after these people just as you do after Fogarty and the Branscombs, and everybody else up and down the shore, and never take a penny in pay ! " she retorted with some indignation.

" I am afraid I will, mother. A disappointing son, am I not ? But there's no one to blame but yourself, old lady," and with a laugh he rose from his seat, Jane's letter in his hand, and kissed his mother on the cheek.

" But, John, dear," she exclaimed in a pleading petulance as she looked into his face, still holding on to the sleeve of his coat to detain him the longer, " just think of this letter of Pencoyd's ; nothing has ever been offered you better than this. He has the very best people in Philadelphia on his list, and you would get——"

The doctor slipped his hand under his mother's chin, as he would have done to a child, and said with a twinkle in his eye—he was very happy this morning :

" That's precisely my case—I've got the very best

people in three counties on my list. That's much
better than the old doctor."

" Who are they, pray ? " She was softening under
her son's caress.

" Well, let me think. There's the distinguished
Mr. Tatham, who attends to the transportation of
the cities of Warehold and Barnegat; and the Right
Honorable Mr. Tipple, and Mrs. and Miss Gossaway,
renowned for their toilets——"

Mrs. Cavendish bit her lip. When her son was
in one of these moods it was all she could do to keep
her temper.

" And the wonderful Mrs. Malmsley, and——"

Mrs. Cavendish looked up. The name had an aris-
tocratic sound, but it was unknown to her.

" Who is she ? "

" Why, don't you know the wonderful Mrs. Malmsley ? " inquired the doctor, with a quizzical smile.

" No, I never heard of her."

" Well, she's just moved into Warehold. Poor
woman, she hasn't been out of bed for years ! She's
the wife of the new butcher, and——"

" The butcher's wife ? "

" The butcher's wife, my dear mother, a most
delightful old person, who has brought up three
sons, and each one a credit to her."

Mrs. Cavendish let go her hold on the doctor's
sleeve and settled back in her chair.

"And you won't even write to Dr. Pencoyd?" she asked in a disheartened way, as if she knew he would refuse.

"Oh, with pleasure, and thank him most kindly, but I couldn't leave Barnegat; not now. Not at any time, so far as I can see."

"And I suppose when Jane Cobden comes home in a year or so she will work with you in the hospital. She wanted to turn nurse the last time I talked to her." This special arrow in her maternal quiver, poisoned with her jealousy, was always ready.

"I hope so," he replied, with a smile that lighted up his whole face; "only it will not be a year. Miss Jane will be here on the next steamer."

Mrs. Cavendish put down her tea-cup and looked at her son in astonishment. The doctor still kept his eyes on her face.

"Be here by the next steamer! How do you know?"

The doctor held up the letter.

"Lucy will remain," he added. "She is going to Germany to continue her studies."

"And Jane is coming home alone?"

"No, she brings a little child with her, the son of a friend, she writes. She asks that I arrange to have Martha meet them at the dock."

"Somebody, I suppose, she has picked up out of

the streets. She is always doing these wild, unpractical things. Whose child is it?"

"She doesn't say, but I quite agree with you that it was helpless, or she wouldn't have protected it."

"Why don't Lucy come with her?"

The doctor shrugged his shoulders.

"And I suppose you will go to the ship to meet her?"

The doctor drew himself up, clicked his heels together with the air of an officer saluting his superior—really to hide his joy—and said with mock gravity, his hand on his heart:

"I shall, most honorable mother, be the first to take her ladyship's hand as she walks down the gangplank." Then he added, with a tone of mild reproof in his voice: "What a funny, queer old mother you are! Always worrying yourself over the unimportant and the impossible," and stooping down, he kissed her again on the cheek and passed out of the room on the way to his office.

"That woman always comes up at the wrong moment," Mrs. Cavendish said to herself in a bitter tone. "I knew he had received some word from her, I saw it in his face. He would have gone to Philadelphia but for Jane Cobden."

CHAPTER IX

The doctor kept his word. His hand was the first that touched Jane's when she came down the gangplank, Martha beside him, holding out her arms for the child, cuddling it to her bosom, wrapping her shawl about it as if to protect it from the gaze of the inquisitive.

" O doctor! it was so good of you! " were Jane's first words. It hurt her to call him thus, but she wanted to establish the new relation clearly. She had shouldered her cross and must bear its weight alone and in her own way. " You don't know what it is to see a face from home! I am so glad to get here. But you should not have left your people; I wrote Martha and told her so. All I wanted you to do was to have her meet me here. Thank you, dear friend, for coming."

She had not let go his hand, clinging to him as a timid woman in crossing a narrow bridge spanning an abyss clings to the strong arm of a man.

He helped her to the dock as tenderly as if she had been a child; asking her if the voyage had been

147

a rough one, whether she had been ill in her berth, and whether she had taken care of the baby herself, and why she had brought no nurse with her. She saw his meaning, but she did not explain her weakness or offer any explanation of the cause of her appearance or of the absence of a nurse. In a moment she changed the subject, asking after his mother and his own work, and seemed interested in what he told her about the neighbors.

When the joy of hearing her voice and of looking into her dear face once more had passed, his skilled eyes probed the deeper. He noted with a sinking at the heart the dark circles under the drooping lids, the drawn, pallid skin and telltale furrows that had cut their way deep into her cheeks. Her eyes, too, had lost their lustre, and her step lacked the spring and vigor of her old self. The diagnosis alarmed him. Even the mould of her face, so distinguished, and to him so beautiful, had undergone a change; whether through illness, or because of some mental anguish, he could not decide.

When he pressed his inquiries about Lucy she answered with a half-stifled sigh that Lucy had decided to remain abroad for a year longer; adding that it had been a great relief to her, and that at first she had thought of remaining with her, but that their affairs, as he knew, had become so involved at home that she feared their means of living might be jeopardized if she did not return at once. The child, however, would be a comfort to both Martha and herself until Lucy came. Then she added in a constrained voice:

"Its mother would not, or could not care for it, and so I brought it with me."

Once at home and the little waif safely tucked away in the crib that had sheltered Lucy in the old days, the neighbors began to flock in; Uncle Ephraim among the first.

"My, but I'm glad you're back!" he burst out. "Martha's been lonelier than a cat in a garret, and down at our house we ain't much better. And so that Bunch of Roses is going to stay over there, is she, and set those Frenchies crazy?"

Pastor Dellenbaugh took both of Jane's hands into his own and looking into her face, said:

"Ah, but we've missed you! There has been no standard, my dear Miss Jane, since you've been gone. I have felt it, and so has everyone in the church. It is good to have you once more with us."

Mrs. Cavendish could hardly conceal her satisfaction, although she was careful what she said to her son. Her hope was that the care of the child would so absorb Jane that John would regain his freedom and be no longer subservient to Miss Cobden's whims.

149

" And so Lucy is to stay in Paris ? " she said, with one of her sweetest smiles. " She is so charming and innocent, that sweet sister of yours, my dear Miss Jane, and so sympathetic. I quite lost my heart to her. And to study music, too ? A most noble accomplishment, my dear. My grandmother, who was an Erskine, you know, played divinely on the harp, and many of my ancestors, especially the Dagworthys, were accomplished musicians. Your sister will look lovely bending over a harp. My grandmother had her portrait painted that way by Peale, and it still hangs in the old house in Trenton. And they tell me you have brought a little angel with you to bring up and share your loneliness ? How pathetic, and how good of you ! "

The village women—they came in groups—asked dozens of questions before Jane had had even time to shake each one by the hand. Was Lucy so in love with the life abroad that she would never come back ? was she just as pretty as ever ? what kind of bonnets were being worn ? etc., etc.

The child in Martha's arms was, of course, the object of special attention. They all agreed that it was a healthy, hearty, and most beautiful baby; just the kind of a child one would want to adopt if one had any such extraordinary desires.

This talk continued until they had gained the highway, when they also agreed—and this without a single dissenting voice—that in all the village Jane Cobden was the only woman conscientious enough to want to bring up somebody else's child, and a foreigner at that, when there were any quantity of babies up and down the shore that could be had for the asking. The little creature was, no doubt, helpless, and appealed to Miss Jane's sympathies, but why bring it home at all? Were there not places enough in France where it could be brought up? etc., etc. This sort of gossip went on for days after Jane's return, each dropper-in at tea-table or village gathering having some view of her own to express, the women doing most of the talking.

The discussion thus begun by friends was soon taken up by the sewing societies and church gatherings, one member in good standing remarking loud enough to be heard by everybody:

"As for me, I ain't never surprised at nothin' Jane Cobden does. She's queerer than Dick's hatband, and allus was, and I've knowed her ever since she used to toddle up to my house and I baked cookies for her. I've seen her many a time feed the dog with what I give her, just because she said he looked hungry, which there warn't a mite o' truth in, for there ain't nothin' goes hungry round my place, and never was. She's queer, I tell ye."

"Quite true, dear Mrs. Pokeberry," remarked Pastor Dellenbaugh in his gentlest tone—he had heard the discussion as he was passing through the room and had stopped to listen—" especially when mercy and kindness is to be shown. Some poor little outcast, no doubt, with no one to take care of it, and so this grand woman brings it home to nurse and educate. I wish there were more Jane Cobdens in my parish. Many of you talk good deeds, and justice, and Christian spirit; here is a woman who puts them into practice."

This statement having been made during the dispersal of a Wednesday night meeting, and in the hearing of half the congregation, furnished the key to the mystery, and so for a time the child and its new-found mother ceased to be an active subject of discussion.

Ann Gossaway, however, was not satisfied. The more she thought of the pastor's explanation the more she resented it as an affront to her intelligence.

" If folks wants to pick up stray babies," she shouted to her old mother on her return home one night, " and bring 'em home to nuss, they oughter label 'em with some sort o' pedigree, and not keep the village a-guessin' as to who they is and where they come from. I don't believe a word of this outcast yarn. Guess Miss Lucy is all right, and she knows enough to stay away when all this tomfoolery's goin' on. She doesn't want to come back to a child's nussery." To all of which her mother nodded her head, keeping it going like a toy mandarin long after the subject of discussion had been changed.

Little by little the scandal spread: by innuendoes; by the wise shakings of empty heads; by nods and winks; by the piecing out of incomplete tattle. For the spread of gossip is like the spread of fire: First a smouldering heat—some friction of ill-feeling, perhaps, over a secret sin that cannot be smothered, try as we may; next a hot, blistering tongue of flame creeping stealthily; then a burst of scorching candor and the roar that ends in ruin. Sometimes the victim is saved by a dash of honest water—the outspoken word of some brave friend. More often those who should stamp out the burning brand stand idly by until the final collapse and then warm themselves at the blaze.

Here in Warehold it began with some whispered talk: Bart Holt had disappeared; there was a woman in the case somewhere; Bart's exile had not been entirely caused by his love of cards and drink. Reference was also made to the fact that Jane had gone abroad but a short time *after* Bart's disappearance, and that knowing how fond she was of him, and how she had tried to reform him, the probability was that she had met him in Paris. Doubts having been expressed that no woman of Jane Cobden's position would go to any such lengths to oblige so young a fellow as Bart Holt, the details of their intimacy were passed from mouth to mouth, and when this was again scouted, reference was made to Miss Gossaway, who was supposed to know more than she was willing to tell. The dressmaker denied all responsibility for the story, but admitted that she had once seen them on the beach " settin' as close together as they could git, with the red cloak she had made for Miss Jane wound about 'em.

" 'Twarn't none o' my business, and I told Martha so, and 'tain't none o' my business now, but I'd rather die than tell a lie or scandalize anybody, and so if ye ask me if I saw 'em I'll have to tell ye I did. I don't believe, howsomever, that Miss Jane went away to oblige that good-for-nothin' or that she's ever laid eyes on him since. Lucy is what took her. She's one o' them flyaways. I see that when she was home, and there warn't no peace up to the Cobdens' house till they'd taken her somewheres where she could git all the runnin' round she wanted. As for the baby, there in't nobody knows where Miss Jane picked that up, but there ain't no doubt but what she loves it same's if it was her own child. She's named it Archie, after her grandfather, anyhow. That's what Martha and she calls it. So they're not ashamed of it."

When the fire had spent itself, only one spot remained unscorched: this was the parentage of little Archie. That mystery still remained unsolved.

154

Those of her own class who knew Jane intimately admired her kindness of heart and respected her silence; those who did not soon forgot the boy's existence.

The tavern loungers, however, some of whom only knew the Cobden girls by reputation, had theories of their own; theories which were communicated to other loungers around other tavern stoves, most of whom would not have known either of the ladies on the street. The fact that both women belonged to a social stratum far above them gave additional license to their tongues; they could never be called in question by anybody who overheard, and were therefore safe to discuss the situation at their will. Condensed into illogical shape, the story was that Jane had met a foreigner who had deserted her, leaving her to care for the child alone; that Lucy had refused to come back to Warehold, had taken what money was coming to her, and, like a sensible woman, had stayed away. That there was not the slightest foundation for this slander did not lessen its acceptance by a certain class; many claimed that it offered the only plausible solution to the mystery, and must, therefore, be true.

It was not long before the echoes of these scandals reached Martha's ears. The gossips dare not affront Miss Jane with their suspicions, but Martha was different. If they could irritate her by speaking lightly of her mistress, she might give out some information which would solve the mystery.

One night a servant of one of the neighbors stopped Martha on the road and sent her flying home; not angry, but terrified.

"They're beginnin' to talk," she broke out savagely, as she entered Jane's room, her breath almost gone from her run to the house. "I laughed at it and said they dare not one of 'em say it to your face or mine, but they're beginnin' to talk."

"Is it about Barton Holt? have they heard anything from him?" asked Jane. The fear of his return had always haunted her.

"No, and they won't. He'll never come back here ag'in. The captain would kill him."

"It isn't about Lucy, then, is it?" cried Jane, her color going.

Martha shook her head in answer to save her breath.

"Who, then?" cried Jane, nervously. "Not Archie?"

"Yes, Archie and you."

"What do they say?" asked Jane, her voice fallen to a whisper.

"They say it's your child, and that ye're afraid to tell who the father is."

Jane caught at the chair for support and then sank slowly into her seat.

" Who says so ? " she gasped.

" Nobody that you or I know; some of the beach-combers and hide-by-nights, I think, started it. Pokeberry's girl told me; her brother works in the shipyard."

Jane sat looking at Martha with staring eyes.

" How dare they——"

" They dare do anything, and we can't answer back. That's what's goin' to make it hard. It's nobody's business, but that don't satisfy 'em. I've been through it meself; I know how mean they can be."

" They shall never know—not while I have life left in me," Jane exclaimed firmly.

" Yes, but that won't keep 'em from lyin'."

The two sat still for some minutes, Martha gazing into vacancy, Jane lying back in her chair, her eyes closed. One emotion after another coursed through her with lightning rapidity—indignation at the charge, horror at the thought that any of her friends might believe it, followed by a shivering fear that her father's good name, for all her care and suffering, might be smirched at last.

Suddenly there arose the tall image of Doctor John, with his frank, tender face. What would he think of it, and how, if he questioned her, could she answer him ? Then there came to her that day of parting in Paris. She remembered Lucy's willingness to give up the child forever, and so cover up all traces of her sin, and her own immediate determination to risk everything for her sister's sake. As this last thought welled up in her mind and she recalled her father's dying command, her brow relaxed. Come what might, she was doing her duty. This was her solace and her strength.

"Cruel, cruel people!" she said to Martha, relaxing her hands. "How can they be so wicked? But I am glad it is I who must take the brunt of it all. If they would treat me so, who am innocent, what would they do to my poor Lucy?"

CHAPTER X

These rumors never reached the doctor. No scandalmonger ever dared talk gossip to him. When he first began to practise among the people of Warehold, and some garrulous old dame would seek to enrich his visit by tittle-tattle about her neighbors, she had never tried it a second time. Doctor John of Barnegat either received the news in silence or answered it with some pleasantry; even Ann Gossaway held her peace whenever the doctor had to be called in to prescribe for her oversensitive throat.

He was aware that Jane had laid herself open to criticism in bringing home a child about which she had made no explanation, but he never spoke of it nor allowed anyone to say so to him. He would have been much happier, of course, if she had given him her confidence in this as she had in many other matters affecting her life; but he accepted her silence as part of her whole attitude toward him. Knowing her as he did, he was convinced that her sole incentive was one of loving kindness, both for the child and for the poor mother whose sin or whose poverty she was concealing. In this connection, he remembered how in one of her letters to Martha she had told of the numberless waifs she had seen and how her heart ached for them; especially in the hospitals which she had visited and among the students. He recalled that he himself had had many similar experiences in his Paris days, in which a woman like Jane Cobden would have been a veritable angel of mercy.

Mrs. Cavendish's ears were more easily approached by the gossips of Warehold and vicinity; then, again she was always curious over the inmates of the Cobden house, and any little scraps of news, reliable or not, about either Jane or her absent sister were eagerly listened to. Finding it impossible to restrain herself any longer, she had seized the opportunity one evening when she and her son were sitting together in the *salon,* a rare occurrence for the doctor, and only possible when his patients were on the mend.

" I'm sorry Jane Cobden was so foolish as to bring home that baby," she began.

" Why ? " said the doctor, without lifting his eyes from the book he was reading.

" Oh, she lays herself open to criticism. It is, of course, but one of her eccentricities, but she owes something to her position and birth and should not invite unnecessary comment."

"Who criticises her?" asked the doctor, his eyes still on the pages.

"Oh, you can't tell; everybody is talking about it. Some of the gossip is outrageous, some I could not even repeat."

"I have no doubt of it," answered the doctor quietly. "All small places like Warehold and Barnegat need topics of conversation, and Miss Jane for the moment is furnishing one of them. They utilize you, dear mother, and me, and everybody else in the same way. But that is no reason why we should lend our ears or our tongues to spread and encourage it."

"I quite agree with you, my son, and I told the person who told me how foolish and silly it was, but they will talk, no matter what you say to them."

"What do they say?" asked the doctor, laying down his book and rising from his chair.

"Oh, all sorts of things. One rumor is that Captain Holt's son, Barton, the one that quarrelled with his father and who went to sea, could tell something of the child, if he could be found."

The doctor laughed. "He can be found," he answered. "I saw his father only last week, and he told me Bart was in Brazil. That is some thousand of miles from Paris, but a little thing like that in geography doesn't seem to make much difference to some of our good people. Why do you listen to such nonsense?" he added as he kissed her tenderly and, with a pat on her cheek, left the room for his study. His mother's talk had made but little impression upon him. Gossip of this kind was always current when waifs like Archie formed the topic; but it hurt nobody, he said to himself—nobody like Jane.

Sitting under his study lamp looking up some complicated case, his books about him, Jane's sad face came before him. "Has she not had trouble enough," he said to himself, "parted from Lucy and with her unsettled money affairs, without having to face these gnats whose sting she cannot ward off?" With this came the thought of his own helplessness to comfort her. He had taken her at her word that night before she left for Paris, when she had refused to give him her promi c and had told him to wait, and he was still ready to come at her call; loving her, watching over her, absorbed in every detail of her daily life, and eager to grant her slightest wish, and yet he could not but see that she had, since her return, surrounded herself with a barrier which he could neither understand nor break down whenever he touched on their personal relations.

Had he loved her less he would, in justice to himself, have faced all her opposition and demanded an answer—Yes or No—as to whether she would yield to his wishes. But his generous nature forbade any such stand and his reverence for her precluded any such mental attitude.

Lifting his eyes from his books and gazing dreamily into the space before him, he recalled, with a certain sinking of the heart, a conversation which had taken place between Jane and himself a few days after her arrival—an interview which had made a deep impression upon him. The two, in the absence of Martha—she had left the room for a moment— were standing beside the crib watching the child's breathing. Seizing the opportunity, one he had watched for, he had told her how much he had missed her during the two years, and how much happier his life was now that he could touch her hand and listen to her voice. She had evaded his meaning, making answer that his pleasure was nothing compared to her own when she thought how safe the baby would be in his hands; adding quickly that she could never thank him enough for remaining in Barnegat and not leaving her helpless and without a " physician." The tone with which she pronounced the word had hurt him. He thought he detected a slight inflection, as if she were making a distinction between his skill as an expert and his love as a man, but he was not sure.

Still gazing into the shadows before him, his unread book in his hand, he recalled a later occasion when she appeared rather to shrink from him than to wish to be near him, speaking to him with down-cast eyes and without the frank look in her face which was always his welcome. On this day she was more unstrung and more desolate than he had ever seen her. At length, emboldened by his intense desire to help, and putting aside every obstacle, he had taken her hand and had said with all his heart in his voice:

"Jane, you once told me you loved me. Is it still true?"

He remembered how at first she had not answered, and how after a moment she had slowly withdrawn her hand and had replied in a voice almost inarticulate, so great was her emotion.

"Yes, John, and always will be, but it can never go beyond that—never, never. Don't ask me any more questions. Don't talk to me about it. Not now, John—not now! Don't hate me! Let us be as we have always been—please, John! You would not refuse me if you knew."

He had started forward to take her in his arms; to insist that now every obstacle was removed she should give him at once the lawful right to protect her, but she had shrunk back, the palms of her hands held out as barriers, and before he could reason with her Martha had entered with something for little Archie, and so the interview had come to an end.

Then, still absorbed in his thoughts, his eyes suddenly brightened and a certain joy trembled in his heart as he remembered that with all these misgivings and doubts there were other times—and their sum was in the ascendency—when she showed the same confidence in his judgment and the same readiness to take his advice; when the old light would once more flash in her eyes as she grasped his hand and the old sadness again shadow her face when his visits came to an end. With this he must be for a time content.

These and a hundred other thoughts raced through Doctor John's mind as he sat to-night in his study chair, the lamplight falling on his open books and thin, delicately modelled hands.

Once he rose from his seat and began pacing his study floor, his hands behind his back, his mind on Jane, on her curious and incomprehensible moods, trying to solve them as he walked, trusting and leaning upon him one day and shrinking from him the next. Baffled for the hundredth time in this mental search, he dropped again into his chair, and adjusting the lamp, pulled his books toward him to devote his mind to their contents. As the light flared up he caught the sound of a step upon the gravel outside, and then a heavy tread upon the porch. An instant later his knocker sounded. Doctor Cavendish gave a sigh—he had hoped to have one night at home— and rose to open the door.

Captain Nat Holt stood outside.

His pea-jacket was buttoned close up under his chin, his hat drawn tight down over his forehead. His weather-beaten face, as the light fell upon it, looked cracked and drawn, with dark hollows under the eyes, which the shadows from the lamplight deepened.

" It's late, I know, doctor," he said in a hoarse, strained voice; " ten o'clock, maybe, but I got somethin' to talk to ye about," and he strode into the room. " Alone, are ye ? " he continued, as he loosened his coat and laid his hat on the desk. " Where's the good mother ? Home, is she ? "

" Yes, she's inside," answered the doctor, pointing to the open door leading to the *salon* and grasping the captain's brawny hand in welcome. " Why ? Do you want to see her ? "

" No, I don't want to see her; don't want to see nobody but you. She can't hear, can she ? 'Scuse me—I'll close this door."

The doctor looked at him curiously. The captain seemed to be laboring under a nervous strain, unusual in one so stolid and self-possessed.

The door closed, the captain moved back a cushion, dropped into a corner of the sofa, and sat looking at the doctor, with legs apart, his open palms resting on his knees.

" I got bad news, doctor—awful bad news for

everybody," as he spoke he reached into his pocket and produced a letter with a foreign postmark.

" You remember my son Bart, of course, don't ye, who left home some two years ago ? " he went on.

The doctor nodded.

" Well, he's dead."

" Your son Bart dead ! " cried the doctor, repeating his name in the surprise of the announcement. " How do you know ? "

" This letter came by to-day's mail. It's from the consul at Rio. Bart come in to see him dead broke and he helped him out. He'd run away from the ship and was goin' up into the mines to work, so the consul wrote me. He was in once after that and got a little money, and then he got down with yellow fever and they took him to the hospital, and he died in three days. There ain't no doubt about it. Here's a list of the dead in the paper; you kin read his name plain as print."

Doctor John reached for the letter and newspaper clipping and turned them toward the lamp. The envelope was stamped " Rio Janeiro " and the letter bore the official heading of the consulate.

" That's dreadful, dreadful news, captain," said the doctor in sympathetic tones. " Poor boy! it's too bad. Perhaps, however, there may be some mistake, after all. Foreign hospital registers are not always reliable," added the doctor in a hopeful tone.

"No, it's all true, or Benham wouldn't write me what he has. I've known him for years. He knows me, too, and he don't go off half-cocked. I wrote him to look after Bart and sent him some money and give him the name of the ship, and he watched for her and sent for him all right. I was pretty nigh crazy that night he left, and handled him, maybe, rougher'n I ou'ter, but I couldn't help it. There's some things I can't stand, and what he done was one of 'em. It all comes back to me now, but I'd do it ag'in." As he spoke the rough, hard sailor leaned forward and rested his chin on his hand. The news had evidently been a great shock to him.

The doctor reached over and laid his hand on the captain's knee. "I'm very, very sorry, captain, for you and for Bart; and the only son you have, is it not?"

"Yes, and the only child we ever had. That makes it worse. Thank God, his mother's dead! All this would have broken her heart." For a moment the two men were silent, then the captain continued in a tone as if he were talking to himself, his eyes on the lamp:

"But I couldn't have lived with him after that, and I told him so—not till he acted fair and square, like a man. I hoped he would some day, but that's over now."

A LATE VISITOR

"We're none of us bad all the way through, captain," reasoned the doctor, "and don't you think of him in that way. He would have come to himself some day and been a comfort to you. I didn't know him as well as I might, and only as I met him at Yardley, but he must have had a great many fine qualities or the Cobdens wouldn't have liked him. Miss Jane used often to talk to me about him. She always believed in him. She will be greatly distressed over this news."

"That's what brings me here. I want you to tell her, and not me. I'm afraid it 'll git out and she'll hear it, and then she'll be worse off than she is now. Maybe it's best to say nothin' 'bout it to nobody and let it go. There ain't no one but me to grieve for him, and they don't send no bodies home, not from Rio, nor nowheres along that coast. Maybe, too, it ain't the time to say it to her. I was up there last week to see the baby, and she looked thinner and paler than I ever see her. I didn't know what to do, so I says to myself, ' There's Doctor John, he's at her house reg'lar and knows the ins and outs of her, and I'll go and tell him 'bout it and ask his advice.' I'd rather cut my hand off than hurt her, for if there's an angel on earth she's one. She shakes so when I mention Bart's name and gits so flustered, that's why I dar'n't tell her. Now he's dead there won't be nobody to do right by Archie. I can't;

I'm all muzzled up tight. She made me take an oath, same as she has you, and I ain't goin' to break it any more'n you would. The little feller 'll have to git 'long best way he kin now."

Doctor John bent forward in his chair and looked at the captain curiously. His words conveyed no meaning to him. For an instant he thought that the shock of his son's death had unsettled the man's mind.

" Take an oath! What for? "

" 'Bout Archie and herself."

" But I've taken no oath! "

" Well, perhaps it isn't your habit; it ain't some men's. I did."

" What about? "

It was the captain's turn now to look searchingly into his companion's face. The doctor's back was toward the lamp, throwing his face into shadow, but the captain could read its expression plainly.

" You mean to tell me, doctor, you don't know what's goin' on up at Yardley? You do, of course, but you won't say—that's like you doctors! "

" Yes, everything. But what has your son Bart got to do with it? "

" Got to do with it! Ain't Jane Cobden motherin' his child? "

The doctor lunged forward in his seat, his eyes staring straight at the captain. Had the old sailor struck him in the face he could not have been more astounded.

"His child!" he cried savagely.

"Certainly! Whose else is it? You knew, didn't ye?"

The doctor settled back in his chair with the movement of an ox felled by a sudden blow. With the appalling news there rang in his ears the tones of his mother's voice retailing the gossip of the village. This, then, was what she could not repeat.

After a moment he raised his head and asked in a low, firm voice:

"Did Bart go to Paris after he left here?"

"No, of course not! Went 'board the *Corsair* bound for Rio, and has been there ever since. I told you that before. There weren't no necessity for her to meet him in Paris."

The doctor sprang from his chair and with eyes blazing and fists tightly clenched, stood over the captain.

"And you dare to sit there and tell me that Miss Jane Cobden is that child's mother?"

The captain struggled to his feet, his open hands held up to the doctor as if to ward off a blow.

"Miss Jane! No, by God! *No!* Are you crazy? Sit down, sit down, I tell ye!"

"Who, then? Speak!"

"Lucy! That's what I drove Bart out for. Mort

Cobden's daughter—Mort, mind ye, that was a brother to me since I was a boy! Jane that child's mother! Yes, all the mother poor Archie's got! Ask Miss Jane, she'll tell ye. Tell ye how she sits and eats her heart out to save her sister that's too scared to come home. I want to cut my tongue out for tellin' ye, but I thought ye knew. Martha told me you loved her and that she loved you, and I thought she'd told ye. Jane Cobden crooked! No more'n the angels are. Now, will you tell her Bart's dead, or shall I?"

"I will tell her," answered the doctor firmly, "and to-night."

The doctor stood over the captain with eyes blazing and fists tightly clenched.

CHAPTER XI

The cold wind from the sea freighted with the raw mist churned by the breakers cut sharply against Doctor John's cheeks as he sprang into his gig and dashed out of his gate toward Yardley. Under the shadow of the sombre pines, along the ribbon of a road, dull gray in the light of the stars, and out on the broader highway leading to Warehold, the sharp click of the mare's hoofs striking the hard road echoed through the night. The neighbors recognized the tread and the speed, and Uncle Ephraim threw up a window to know whether it was a case of life or death, an accident, or both; but the doctor only nodded and sped on. It *was* life and death—life for the woman he loved, death for all who traduced her. The strange news that had dropped from the captain's lips did not affect him except as would the ending of any young life; neither was there any bitterness in his heart against the dead boy who had wrecked Lucy's career and brought Jane humiliation and despair. All he thought of was the injustice of Jane's sufferings. Added to this was an over-

173

powering desire to reach her side before her misery should continue another moment; to fold her in his arms, stand between her and the world; help her to grapple with the horror which was slowly crushing out her life. That it was past her hour for retiring, and that there might be no one to answer his summons, made no difference to him. He must see her at all hazards before he closed his eyes.

As he whirled into the open gates of Yardley and peered from under the hood of the gig at the outlines of the old house, looming dimly through the avenue of bushes, he saw that the occupants were asleep; no lights shone from the upper windows and none burned in the hall below. This discovery checked to some extent the impetus with which he had flung himself into the night, his whole being absorbed and dominated by one idea. The cool wind, too, had begun to tell upon his nerves. He drew rein on the mare and stopped. For the first time since the captain's story had reached his ears his reason began to work. He was never an impetuous man; always a thoughtful and methodical one, and always overparticular in respecting the courtesies of life. He began suddenly to realize that this midnight visit was at variance with every act of his life. Then his better judgment became aroused. Was it right for him to wake Jane and disturb the house at this hour, causing her, perhaps, a sleepless night, or should he wait until the morning, when he could break the news to her in a more gentle and less sen-sensational way?

While he sat thus wondering, undetermined whether to drive lightly out of the gate again or to push forward in the hope that someone would be awake, his mind unconsciously reverted to the figure of Jane making her way with weary steps down the gangplank of the steamer, the two years of her suffer-ing deep cut into every line of her face. He recalled the shock her appearance had given him, and his per-plexity over the cause. He remembered her refusal to give him her promise, her begging him to wait, her unaccountable moods since her return.

Then Lucy's face came before him, her whole career, in fact (in a flash, as a drowning man's life is pictured), from the first night after her return from school until he had bade her good-by to take the train for Trenton. Little scraps of talk sounded in his ears, and certain expressions about the corners of her eyes revealed themselves to his memory. He thought of her selfishness, of her love of pleasure, of her disregard of Jane's wishes, of her recklessness.

Everything was clear now.

" What a fool I have been! " he said to himself. " What a fool—*fool!* I ought to have known! "

Next the magnitude of the atonement, and the cruelty and cowardice of the woman who had put her sister into so false a position swept over him. Then there arose, like the dawning of a light, the grand figure of the woman he loved, standing clear of all entanglements, a Madonna among the saints, more precious than ever in the radiance of her own sacrifice.

With this last vision his mind was made up. No, he would not wait a moment. Once this terrible secret out of the way, Jane would regain her old self and they two fight the world together.

As he loosened the reins over the sorrel a light suddenly flashed from one of the upper windows, disappeared for a moment, and reappeared again at one of the smaller openings near the front steps. He drew rein again. Someone was moving about—who he did not know; perhaps Jane, perhaps one of the servants. Tying the lines to the dashboard, he sprang from the gig, tethered the mare to one of the lilac bushes, and walked briskly toward the house. As he neared the steps the door was opened and Martha's voice rang clear:

"Meg, you rascal, come in, or shall I let ye stay out and freeze?"

Doctor John stepped upon the porch, the light of Martha's candle falling on his face and figure.

"It's I, Martha, don't be frightened; it's late, I know, but I hoped Miss Jane would be up. Has she gone to bed?"

The old nurse started back. "Lord, how ye skeered me! I don't know whether she's asleep or not. She's upstairs with Archie, anyhow. I come out after this rapscallion that makes me look him up every night. I've talked to him till I'm sore, and he's promised me a dozen times, and here he is out ag'in. Here! Where are ye? In with ye, ye little beast!" The dog shrank past her and darted into the hall. "Now, then, doctor, come in out of the cold."

Doctor John stepped softly inside and stood in the flare of the candle-light. He felt that he must give some reason for his appearance at this late hour, even if he did not see Jane. It would be just as well, therefore, to tell Martha of Bart's death at once, and not let her hear it, as she was sure to do, from some-one on the street. Then again, he had kept few secrets from her where Jane was concerned; she had helped him many times before, and her advice was always good. He knew that she was familiar with every detail of the captain's story, but he did not propose to discuss Lucy's share in it with the old nurse. That he would reserve for Jane's ears alone.

"Bring your candle into the sitting-room, Martha; I have something to tell you," he said gravely, loosening the cape of his overcoat and laying his hat on the hall table.

The nurse followed. The measured tones of the doctor's voice, so unlike his cheery greetings, especially to her, unnerved her. This, in connection with the suppressed excitement under which he seemed to labor and the late hour of his visit, at once convinced her that something serious had happened.

"Is there anything the matter?" she asked in a trembling voice.

"Yes."

"Is it about Lucy? There ain't nothin' gone wrong with her, doctor dear, is there?"

"No, it is not about Lucy. It's about Barton Holt."

"Ye don't tell me! Is he come back?"

"No, nor never will. He's dead!"

"That villain dead! How do you know?" Her face paled and her lips quivered, but she gave no other sign of the shock the news had been to her.

"Captain Nat, his father, has just left my office. I promised I would tell Miss Jane to-night. He was too much broken up and too fearful of its effect upon her to do it himself. I drove fast, but perhaps I'm too late to see her."

"Well, ye could see her no doubt,—she could throw somethin' around her—but ye mustn't tell her *that* news. She's been downhearted all day and is tired out. Bart's dead, is he?" she repeated with an effort at indifference. "Well, that's too bad. I

178

s'pose the captain's feelin' purty bad over it. Where did he die?"

"He died in Rio Janeiro of yellow fever," said the doctor slowly, wondering at the self-control of the woman. Wondering, too, whether she was glad or sorry over the event, her face and manner showing no index to her feelings.

"And will he be brought home to be buried?" she asked with a quick glance at the doctor's face.

"No; they never bring them home with yellow fever."

"And is that all ye come to tell her?" She was scrutinizing Doctor John's face, her quick, nervous glances revealing both suspicion and fear.

"I had some other matters to talk about, but if she has retired, perhaps I had better come tomorrow," answered the doctor in undecided tones, as he gazed abstractedly at the flickering candle.

The old woman hesitated. She saw that the doctor knew more than he intended to tell her. Her curiosity and her fear that some other complication had arisen—one which he was holding back—got the better of her judgment. If it was anything about her bairn, she could not wait until the morning. She had forgotten Meg now.

"Well, maybe if ye break it to her easy-like she can stand it. I don't suppose she's gone to bed yet. Her door was open on a crack when I come down, and she always shuts it 'fore she goes to sleep. I'll light a couple o' lamps so ye can see, and then I'll send her down to ye if she'll come. Wait here, doctor, dear."

The lamps lighted and Martha gone, Doctor John looked about the room, his glance resting on the sofa where he had so often sat with her; on the portrait of Morton Cobden, the captain's friend; on the work-basket filled with needlework that Jane had left on a small table beside her chair, and upon the books her hands had touched. He thought he had never loved her so much as now. No one he had ever known or heard of had made so great a sacrifice. Not for herself this immolation, but for a sister who had betrayed her confidence and who had repaid a life's devotion with unforgivable humiliation and disgrace. This was the woman whose heart he held. This was the woman he loved with every fibre of his being. But her sufferings were over now. He was ready to face the world and its malignity beside her. Whatever sins her sister had committed, and however soiled were Lucy's garments, Jane's robes were as white as snow. He was glad he had yielded to the impulse and had come at once. The barrier between them once broken down and the terrible secret shared, her troubles would end.

The whispering of her skirts on the stairs announced her coming before she entered the room. She had been sitting by Archie's crib and had not waited to change her loose white gown, whose clinging folds accentuated her frail, delicate form. Her hair had been caught up hastily and hung in a dark mass, concealing her small, pale ears and making her face all the whiter by contrast.

"Something alarming has brought you at this hour," she said, with a note of anxiety in her voice, walking rapidly toward him. "What can I do? Who is ill?"

Doctor John sprang forward, held out both hands, and holding tight to her own, drew her close to him.

"Has Martha told you?" he said tenderly.

"No; only that you wanted me. I came as soon as I could."

"It's about Barton Holt. His father has just left my office. I have very sad news for you. The poor boy——"

Jane loosened her hands from his and drew back. The doctor paused in his recital.

"Is he ill?" she inquired, a slight shiver running through her.

"Worse than ill! I'm afraid you'll never see him again."

"You mean that he is dead? Where?"

"Yes, dead, in Rio. The letter arrived this morning."

"And you came all the way up here to tell me this?" she asked, with an effort to hide her astonishment. Her eyes dropped for a moment and her voice trembled. Then she went on. "What does his father say?"

"I have just left him. He is greatly shaken. He would not tell you himself, he said; he was afraid it might shock you too much, and asked me to come up. But it is not altogether that, Jane. I have heard something to-night that has driven me half out of my mind. That you should suffer this way alone is torture to me. You cannot, you shall not live another day as you have! Let me help!"

Instantly there flashed into her mind the story Martha had brought in from the street. "He has heard it," she said to herself, "but he does not believe it, and he comes to comfort me. I cannot tell the truth without betraying Lucy."

She drew a step farther from him.

"You refer to what the people about us call a mystery—that poor little child upstairs?" she said slowly, all her self-control in her voice. "You think it is a torture for me to care for this helpless baby? It is not a torture; it is a joy—all the joy I have now." She stood looking at him as she spoke with searching eyes, wondering with the ever-questioning doubt of those denied love's full expression.

"But I know——"

"You know nothing—nothing but what I have told you; and what I have told you is the truth. What I have not told you is mine to keep. You love me too well to probe it any further. I am sorry for the captain. He has an iron will and a rough exterior, but he has a warm heart underneath. If you see him before I do give him my deepest sympathy. Now, my dear friend, I must go back to Archie; he is restless and needs me. Good-night," and she held out her hand and passed out of the room.

She was gone before he could stop her. He started forward as her hand touched the door, but she closed it quickly behind her, as if to leave no doubt of her meaning. He saw that she had misunderstood him. He had intended to talk to her of Archie's father, and of Lucy, and she had supposed he had only come to comfort her about the village gossip.

For some minutes he stood like one dazed. Then a feeling of unspeakable reverence stole over him. Not only was she determined to suffer alone and in silence, but she would guard her sister's secret at the cost of her own happiness. Inside that sacred precinct he knew he could never enter; that wine-press she intended to tread alone.

Then a sudden indignation, followed by a contempt of his own weakness took possession of him. Being the older and stronger nature, he should have compelled her to listen. The physician as well as the friend should have asserted himself. No woman could be well balanced who would push away the hand of a man held out to save her from ruin and misery. He would send Martha for her again and insist upon her listening to him.

He started for the door and stopped irresolute. A new light broke in upon his heart. It was not against himself and her own happiness that she had taken this stand, but to save her father's and her sister's name. He knew how strong was her devotion to her duty, how blind her love for Lucy, how sacred she held the trust given to her by her dead father. No; she was neither obstinate nor quixotic. Hers was the work of a martyr, not a fanatic. No one he had ever known or heard of had borne so great a cross or made so noble a sacrifice. It was like the deed of some grand old saint, the light of whose glory had shone down the ages. He was wrong, cruelly wrong. The only thing left for him to do was to wait. For what he could not tell. Perhaps God in his mercy would one day find the way.

Martha's kindly voice as she opened the door awoke him from his revery.

" Did she take it bad ? " she asked.

" No," he replied aimlessly, without thinking of what he said. " She sent a message to the captain. I'll go now. No, please don't bring a light to the door. The mare's only a short way down the road."

When the old nurse had shut the front door after him she put out the lamps and ascended the stairs. The other servants were in bed. Jane's door was partly open. Martha pushed it gently with her hand and stepped in. Jane had thrown herself at full length on the bed and lay with her face buried in her hands. She was talking to herself and had not noticed Martha's footsteps.

" O God! what have I done that this should be sent to me?" Martha heard her say between her sobs. "You would be big enough, my beloved, to bear it all for my sake; to take the stain and wear it; but I cannot hurt you—not you, not you, my great, strong, sweet soul. Your heart aches for me and you would give me all you have, but I could not bear your name without telling you. You would forgive me, but I could never forgive myself. No, no, you shall stand unstained if God will give me strength!"

Martha walked softly to the bed and bent over Jane's prostrate body.

"It's me, dear. What did he say to break your heart?"

Jane slipped her arm about the old nurse's neck, drawing her closer, and without lifting her own head from the pillow talked on.

"Nothing, nothing. He came to comfort me, not to hurt me."

"Do ye think it's all true 'bout Bart?" Martha whispered.

Jane raised her body from the bed and rested her head on Martha's shoulder.

"Yes, it's all true about Bart," she answered in a stronger and more composed tone. "I have been expecting it. Poor boy, he had nothing to live for, and his conscience must have given him no rest."

"Did the captain tell him about——" and Martha pointed toward the bed of the sleeping child. She could never bring herself to mention Lucy's name when speaking either of Bart or Archie.

Jane sat erect, brushed the tears from her eyes, smoothed her hair back from her temples, and said with something of her customary poise:

"No, I don't think so. The captain gave me his word, and he will not break it. Then, again, he will never discredit his own son. The doctor doesn't know, and there will be nobody to tell him. That's not what he came to tell me. It was about the stories you heard last week and which have only just reached his ears. That's all. He wanted to protect me from their annoyance, but I would not listen to him. There is trouble enough without bringing him into it. Now go to bed, Martha."

As she spoke Jane regained her feet, and crossing the room, settled into a chair by the boy's crib. Long after Martha had closed her own door for the night

Jane sat watching the sleeping child. One plump pink hand lay outside the cover; the other little crumpled rose-leaf was tucked under the cheek, the face half-hidden in a tangle of glossy curls, now spun-gold in the light of the shaded lamp.

" Poor little waif," she sighed, " poor little motherless, fatherless waif! Why didn't you stay in heaven ? This world has no place for you."

Then she rose wearily, picked up the light, carried it across the room to her desk, propped a book in front of it so that its rays would not fall upon the sleeping child, opened her portfolio, and sat down to write.

When she had finished and had sealed her letter it was long past midnight. It was addressed to Lucy in Dresden, and contained a full account of all the doctor had told her of Bart's death.

CHAPTER XII

For the first year Jane watched Archie's growth
and development with the care of a self-appointed
nurse temporarily doing her duty by her charge.
Later on, as the fact became burned into her mind
that Lucy would never willingly return to Warehold,
she clung to him with that absorbing love and devotion which an unmarried woman often lavishes upon
a child not her own. In his innocent eyes she saw the
fulfilment of her promise to her father. He would
grow to be a man of courage and strength, the stain
upon his birth forgotten, doing honor to himself, to
her, and to the name he bore. In him, too, she sought
refuge from that other sorrow which was often
greater than she could bear—the loss of the closer
companionship of Doctor John—a companionship
which only a wife's place could gain for her. The
true mother-love—the love which she had denied herself, a love which had been poured out upon Lucy
since her father's death—found its outlet, therefore,
in little Archie.

Under Martha's watchful care the helpless infant

grew to be a big, roly-poly boy, never out of her arms when she could avoid it. At five he had lost his golden curls and short skirts and strutted about in knee-trousers. At seven he had begun to roam the streets, picking up his acquaintances wherever he found them.

Chief among them was Tod Fogarty, the son of the fisherman, now a boy of ten, big for his age and bubbling over with health and merriment, and whose life Doctor John had saved when he was a baby. Tod had brought a basket of fish to Yardley, and sneaking Meg, who was then alive—he died the year after—had helped himself to part of the contents, and the skirmish over its recovery had resulted in a friendship which was to last the boys all their lives. The doctor believed in Tod, and always spoke of his pluck and of his love for his mother, qualities which Jane admired—but then technical class distinctions never troubled Jane—every honest body was Jane's friend, just as every honest body was Doctor John's.

The doctor loved Archie with the love of an older brother; not altogether because he was Jane's ward, but for the boy's own qualities—for his courage, for his laugh—particularly for his buoyancy. Often, as he looked into the lad's eyes brimming with fun, he would wish that he himself had been born with the same kind of temperament. Then again the boy satisfied to a certain extent the longing in his heart

for home, wife, and child—a void which he knew
now would never be filled. Fate had decreed that
he and the woman he loved should live apart—with
this he must be content. Not that his disappointments had soured him; only that this ever-present
sorrow had added to the cares of his life, and in later
years had taken much of the spring and joyousness
out of him. This drew him all the closer to Archie,
and the lad soon became his constant companion;
sitting beside him in his gig, waiting for him at the
doors of the fishermen's huts, or in the cabins of the
poor on the outskirts of Barnegat and Warehold.

"There goes Doctor John of Barnegat and his
curly-head," the neighbors would say; "when ye
see one ye see t'other."

Newcomers in Barnegat and Warehold thought
Archie was his son, and would talk to the doctor about
him:

"Fine lad you got, doctor—don't look a bit like
you, but maybe he will when he gets his growth."
At which the doctor would laugh and pat the boy's
head.

During all these years Lucy's letters came but
seldom. When they did arrive, most of them were
filled with elaborate excuses for her prolonged stay.
The money, she wrote, which Jane had sent her from
time to time was ample for her needs; she was making many valuable friends, and she could not see

how she could return until the following spring—a spring which never came. In no one of them had she ever answered Jane's letter about Bart's death, except to acknowledge its receipt. Nor, strange to say, had she ever expressed any love for Archie. Jane's letters were always filled with the child's doings; his illnesses and recoveries; but whenever Lucy mentioned his name, which was seldom, she invariably referred to him as " your little ward " or " your baby," evidently intending to wipe that part of her life completely out. Neither did she make any comment on the child's christening—a ceremony which took place in the church, Pastor Dellenbaugh officiating—except to write that perhaps one name was as good as another, and that she hoped he would not disgrace it when he grew up.

These things, however, made but little impression on Jane. She never lost faith in her sister, and never gave up hope that one day they would all three be reunited; how or where she could not tell or foresee, but in some way by which Lucy would know and love her son for himself alone, and the two live together ever after—his parentage always a secret. When Lucy once looked into her boy's face she was convinced she would love and cling to him. This was her constant prayer.

All these hopes were dashed to the ground by the receipt of a letter from Lucy with a Geneva postmark. She had not written for months, and Jane broke the seal with a murmur of delight, Martha leaning forward, eager to hear the first word from her bairn. As she read Jane's face grew suddenly pale.

"What is it?" Martha asked in a trembling voice.

For some minutes Jane sat staring into space, her hand pressed to her side. She looked like one who had received a death message. Then, without a word, she handed the letter to Martha.

The old woman adjusted her glasses, read the missive to the end without comment, and laid it back on Jane's lap. The writing covered but part of the page, and announced Lucy's coming marriage with a Frenchman: "A man of distinction; some years older than myself, and of ample means. He fell in love with me at Aix."

There are certain crises in life with conclusions so evident that no spoken word can add to their clearness. There is no need of comment; neither is there room for doubt. The bare facts stand naked. No sophistry can dull their outlines nor soften the insistence of their high lights; nor can any reasoning explain away the results that will follow. Both women, without the exchange of a word, knew instantly that the consummation of this marriage meant the loss of Lucy forever. Now she would never come back, and Archie would be motherless for life. They foresaw, too, that all their yearning to clasp Lucy once more in their arms would go unsatisfied. In this marriage she had found a way to slip as easily from out the ties that bound her to Yardley as she would from an old dress.

Martha rose from her chair, read the letter again to the end, and without opening her lips left the room. Jane kept her seat, her head resting on her hand, the letter once more in her lap. The revulsion of feeling had paralyzed her judgment, and for a time had benumbed her emotions. All she saw was Archie's eyes looking into hers as he waited for an answer to that question he would one day ask and which now she knew she could never give.

Then there rose before her, like some disembodied spirit from a long-covered grave, the spectre of the past. An icy chill crept over her. Would Lucy begin this new life with the same deceit with which she had begun the old? And if she did, would this Frenchman forgive her when he learned the facts? If he never learned them—and this was most to be dreaded—what would Lucy's misery be all her life if she still kept the secret close? Then with a pathos all the more intense because of her ignorance of the true situation—she fighting on alone, unconscious that the man she loved not only knew every pulsation of her aching heart, but would be as willing as herself to guard its secret, she cried:

"Yes, at any cost she must be saved from this living death! I know what it is to sit beside the man I love, the man whose arm is ready to sustain me, whose heart is bursting for love of me, and yet be always held apart by a spectre which I dare not face."

With this came the resolve to prevent the marriage at all hazards, even to leaving Yardley and taking the first steamer to Europe, that she might plead with Lucy in person.

While she sat searching her brain for some way out of the threatened calamity, the rapid rumbling of the doctor's gig was heard on the gravel road outside her open window. She knew from the speed with which he drove that something out of the common had happened. The gig stopped and the doctor's voice rang out:

"Come as quick as you can, Jane, please. I've got a bad case some miles out of Warehold, and I need you; it's a compound fracture, and I want you to help with the chloroform."

All her indecision vanished and all her doubts were swept away as she caught the tones of his voice. Who else in the wide world understood her as he did, and who but he should guide her now? Had he ever failed her? When was his hand withheld or his lips silent? How long would her pride shut out his sympathy? If he could help in the smaller things of life why not trust him in this larger sorrow?—one that threatened to overwhelm her, she whose heart ached for tenderness and wise counsel. Perhaps she could lean upon him without betraying her trust. After all, the question of Archie's birth— the one secret between them—need not come up. It was Lucy's future happiness which was at stake. This must be made safe at any cost short of exposure.

"Better put a few things in a bag," Doctor John continued. "It may be a case of hours or days—I can't tell till I see him. The boy fell from the roof of the stable and is pretty badly hurt; both legs are broken, I hear; the right one in two places."

She was upstairs in a moment, into her nursing dress, always hanging ready in case the doctor called for her, and down again, standing beside the gig, her bag in her hand, before he had time to turn his horse and arrange the seat and robes for her comfort.

"Who is it?" she asked hurriedly, resting her hand in his as he helped her into the seat and took the one beside her, Martha and Archie assisting with her bag and big driving cloak.

"Burton's boy. His father was coming for me and met me on the road. I have everything with me, so we will not lose any time. Good-by, my boy," he called to Archie. "One day I'll make a doctor of you, and then I won't have to take your dear mother from you so often. Good-by, Martha. You want to take care of that cough, old lady, or I shall have to send up some of those plasters you love so."

They were off and rattling down the path between the lilacs before either Archie or the old woman could answer. To hearts like Jane's and the doctor's, a suffering body, no matter how far away, was a sinking ship in the clutch of the breakers. Until the lifeboat reached her side everything was forgotten.

The doctor adjusted the robe over Jane's lap and settled himself in his seat. They had often driven thus together, and Jane's happiest hours had been spent close to his side, both intent on the same errand of mercy, and *both working together*. That was the joy of it!

They talked of the wounded boy and of the needed treatment and what part each should take in the operation; of some new cases in the hospital and the remedies suggested for their comfort; of Archie's life on the beach and how ruddy and handsome he was growing, and of his tender, loving nature; and of the thousand and one other things that two people who know every pulsation of each other's hearts are apt to discuss—of everything, in fact, but the letter in her pocket. " It is a serious case," she said to herself—" this to which we are hurrying—and nothing must disturb the sureness of his sensitive hand."

A LETTER FROM PARIS

Now and then, as he spoke, the two would turn their heads and look into each other's eyes.

When a man's face lacks the lines and modellings that stand for beauty the woman who loves him is apt to omit in her eager glance every feature but his eyes. His eyes are the open doors to his soul; in these she finds her ideals, and in these she revels. But with Jane every feature was a joy—the way the smoothly cut hair was trimmed about his white temples; the small, well-turned ears lying flat to his head; the lines of his eyebrows; the wide, sensitive nostrils and the gleam of the even teeth flashing from between well-drawn, mobile lips; the white, smooth, polished skin. Not all faces could boast this beauty; but then not all souls shone as clearly as did Doctor John's through the thin veil of his face.

And she was equally young and beautiful to him. Her figure was still that of her youth; her face had not changed—he still caught the smile of the girl he loved. Often, when they had been driving along the coast, the salt wind in their faces, and he had looked at her suddenly, a thrill of delight had swept through him as he noted how rosy were her cheeks and how ruddy the wrists above the gloves, hiding the dear hands he loved so well, the tapering fingers tipped with delicate pink nails. He could, if he sought them, find many telltale wrinkles about the corners of the mouth and under the eyelids (he knew and loved them all), showing where the acid of anxiety had bitten deep into the plate on which the record of her life was being daily etched, but her beautiful gray eyes still shone with the same true, kindly light, and always flashed the brighter when they looked into his own. No, she was ever young and ever beautiful to him!

To-day, however, there was a strange tremor in her voice and an anxious, troubled expression in her face—one that he had not seen for years. Nor had she once looked into his eyes in the old way.

"Something worries you, Jane," he said, his voice echoing his thoughts. "Tell me about it."

"No—not now—it is nothing," she answered quickly.

"Yes, tell me. Don't keep any troubles from me. I have nothing else to do in life but smooth them out. Come, what is it?"

"Wait until we get through with Burton's boy. He may be hurt worse than you think."

The doctor slackened the reins until they rested on the dashboard, and with a quick movement turned half around and looked searchingly into Jane's eyes.

"It is serious, then. What has happened?"

"Only a letter from Lucy."

"Is she coming home?"

"No, she is going to be married."

A LETTER FROM PARIS

The doctor gave a low whistle. Instantly Archie's laughing eyes looked into his; then came the thought of the nameless grave of his father.

"Well, upon my soul! You don't say so! Who to, pray?"

"To a Frenchman." Jane's eyes were upon his, reading the effect of her news. His tone of surprise left an uncomfortable feeling behind it.

"How long has she known him?" he continued, tightening the reins again and chirruping to the mare.

"She does not say—not long, I should think."

"What sort of a Frenchman is he? I've known several kinds in my life—so have you, no doubt," and a quiet smile overspread his face. "Come, Bess! Hurry up, old girl."

"A gentleman, I should think, from what she writes. He is much older than Lucy, and she says very well off."

"Then you didn't meet him on the other side?"

"No."

"And never heard of him before?"

"Not until I received this letter."

The doctor reached for his whip and flecked off a fly that had settled on the mare's neck.

"Lucy is about twenty-seven, is she not?"

"Yes, some eight years younger than I am. Why do you ask, John?"

"Because it is always a restless age for a woman.

She has lost the protecting ignorance of youth and she has not yet gained enough of the experience of age to steady her. Marriage often comes as a balance-weight. She is coming home to be married, isn't she ? "

" No; they are to be married in Geneva at his mother's."

" I think that part of it is a mistake," he said in a decided tone. " There is no reason why she should not be married here; she owes that to you and to herself." Then he added in a gentler tone, " And this worries you ? "

" More than I can tell you, John." There was a note in her voice that vibrated through him. He knew now how seriously the situation affected her.

" But why, Jane ? If Lucy is happier in it we should do what we can to help her."

" Yes, but not in this way. This will make her all the more miserable. I don't want this marriage; I want her to come home and live with me and Archie. She makes me promises every year to come, and now it is over six years since I left her and she has always put me off. This marriage means that she will never come. I want her here, John. It is not right for her to live as she does. Please think as I do ! "

The doctor patted Jane's hand—it was the only mark of affection he ever allowed himself—not in a caressing way, but more as a father would pat the hand of a nervous child.

" Well, let us go over it from the beginning. Maybe I don't know all the facts. Have you the letter with you ? "

She handed it to him. He passed the reins to her and read it carefully to the end.

" Have you answered it yet ? "

" No, I wanted to talk to you about it. What do you think now ? "

" I can't see that it will make any difference. She is not a woman to live alone. I have always been surprised that she waited so long. You are wrong, Jane, about this. It is best for everybody and everything that Lucy should be married."

" John, dear," she said in a half-pleading tone— there were some times when this last word slipped out—" I don't want this marriage at all. I am so wretched about it that I feel like taking the first steamer and bringing her home with me. She will forget all about him when she is here; and it is only her loneliness that makes her want to marry. I don't want her married ; I want her to love me and Martha and—Archie—and she will if she sees him."

" Is that better than loving a man who loves her ? " The words dropped from his lips before he could recall them—forced out, as it were, by the pressure of his heart.

Jane caught her breath and the color rose in her cheeks. She knew he did not mean her, and yet she saw he spoke from his heart. Doctor John's face, however, gave no sign of his thoughts.

"But, John, I don't know that she does love him. She doesn't say so—she says *he* loves her. And if she did, we cannot all follow our own hearts."

"Why not?" he replied calmly, looking straight ahead of him: at the bend in the road, at the crows flying in the air, at the leaden sky between the rows of pines. If she wanted to give him her confidence he was ready now with heart and arms wide open. Perhaps his hour had come at last.

"Because—because," she faltered, "our duty comes in. That is holier than love." Then her voice rose and steadied itself—"Lucy's duty is to come home."

He understood. The gate was still shut; the wall still confronted him. He could not and would not scale it. She had risked her own happiness—even her reputation—to keep this skeleton hidden, the secret inviolate. Only in the late years had she begun to recover from the strain. She had stood the brunt and borne the sufferings of another's sin without complaint, without reward, giving up everything in life in consecration to her trust. He, of all men, could not tear the mask away, nor could he stoop by the more subtle paths of of friendship, love, or duty to seek to look behind it—not without her own free and willing hand to guide him. There was nothing else in all her life that she had not told him. Every thought was his, every resolve, every joy. She would entrust him with this if it was hers to give. Until she did his lips would be sealed. As to Lucy, it could make no difference. Bart lying in a foreign grave would never trouble her again, and Archie would only be a stumbling-block in her career. She would never love the boy, come what might. If this Frenchman filled her ideal, it was best for her to end her days across the water—best certainly for Jane, to whom she had only brought unhappiness.

For some moments he busied himself with the reins, loosening them from where they were caught in the harness; then he bent his head and said slowly, and with the tone of the physician in consultation:

"Your protest will do no good, Jane, and your trip abroad will only be a waste of time and money. If Lucy has not changed, and this letter shows that she has not, she will laugh at your objections and end by doing as she pleases. She has always been a law unto herself, and this new move of hers is part of her life-plan. Take my advice: stay where you are; write her a loving, sweet letter and tell her how happy you hope she will be, and send her your congratulations. She will not listen to your objections, and your opposition might lose you her love."

Before dark they were both on their way back to Yardley. Burton's boy had not been hurt as badly as his father thought; but one leg was broken, and this was soon in splints, and without Jane's assistance.

Before they had reached her door her mind was made up.

The doctor's words, as they always did, had gone down deep into her mind, and all thoughts of going abroad, or of even protesting against Lucy's marriage, were given up. Only the spectre remained. That the doctor knew nothing of, and that she must meet alone.

Martha took Jane's answer to the post-office herself. She had talked its contents over with the old nurse, and the two had put their hearts into every line.

"Tell him everything," Jane wrote. "Don't begin a new life with an old lie. With me it is different. I saved you, my sister, because I loved you, and because I could not bear that your sweet girlhood should be marred. I shall live my life out in this duty. It came to me, and I could not put it from me, and would not now if I could, but I know the tyranny of a secret you cannot share with the man who loves you. I know, too, the cruelty of it all. For years I have answered kindly meant inquiry with discourteous silence, bearing insinuations, calumny, insults—and all because I cannot speak. Don't, I beseech you, begin your new life in this slavery. But whatever the outcome, take him into your confidence. Better have him leave you now than after you are married. Remember, too, that if by this declaration you should lose his love you will at least gain his respect. Perhaps, if his heart is tender and he feels for the suffering and wronged, you may keep both. Forgive me, dear, but I have only your happiness at heart, and I love you too dearly not to warn you against any danger which would threaten you. Martha agrees with me in the above, and knows you will do right by him."

When Lucy's answer arrived weeks afterward—after her marriage, in fact—Jane read it with a clutching at her throat she had not known since that fatal afternoon when Martha returned from Trenton.

"You dear, foolish sister," Lucy's letter began, "what should I tell him for? He loves me devotedly and we are very happy together, and I am not going to cause him any pain by bringing any disagreeable thing into his life. People don't do those wild, old-fashioned things over here. And then, again, there is no possibility of his finding out. Maria agrees with me thoroughly, and says in her funny way that men nowadays know too much already." Then followed an account of her wedding.

This letter Jane did not read to the doctor—no part of it, in fact. She did not even mention its receipt, except to say that the wedding had taken place in Geneva, where the Frenchman's mother lived, it being impossible, Lucy said, for her to come home, and that Maria Collins, who was staying with her, had been the only one of her old friends at the ceremony. Neither did she read it all to Martha. The old nurse was growing more feeble every year and she did not wish her blind faith in her bairn disturbed.

For many days she kept the letter locked in her desk, not having the courage to take it out again and read it. Then she sent for Captain Holt, the only one, beside Martha, with whom she could discuss the matter. She knew his strong, honest nature, and his blunt, outspoken way of giving vent to his mind, and she hoped that his knowledge of life might help to comfort her.

" Married to one o' them furriners, is she ? " the captain blurted out; " and goin' to keep right on livin' the lie she's lived ever since she left ye? You'll excuse me, Miss Jane,—you've been a mother, and a sister and everything to her, and you're nearer the angels than anybody I know. That's what I think when I look at you and Archie. I say it be-

206

hind your back and I say it now to your face, for it's true. As to Lucy, I may be mistaken, and I may not. I don't want to condemn nothin' 'less I'm on the survey and kin look the craft over; that's why I'm partic'lar. Maybe Bart was right in sayin' it warn't all his fault, whelp as he was to say it, and maybe he warn't. It ain't up before me and I ain't passin' on it,—but one thing is certain, when a ship's made as many voyages as Lucy has and ain't been home for repairs nigh on to seven years—ain't it?" and he looked at Jane for confirmation—" she gits foul and sometimes a little mite worm-eaten—especially her bilge timbers, unless they're copper-fastened or pretty good stuff. I've been thinkin' for some time that you ain't got Lucy straight, and this last kick-up of hers makes me sure of it. Some timber is growed right and some timber is growed crooked; and when it's growed crooked it gits leaky, and no 'mount o' tar and pitch kin stop it. Every twist the ship gives it opens the seams, and the pumps is goin' all the time. When your timber is growed right you kin all go to sleep and not a drop o' water'll git in. Your sister Lucy ain't growed right. Maybe she kin help it and maybe she can't, but she'll leak every time there comes a twist. See if she don't."

But Jane never lost faith nor wavered in her trust. With the old-time love strong upon her she continued to make excuses for this thoughtless, irresponsible woman, so easily influenced. " It is Maria Collins who has written the letter, and not Lucy," she kept saying to herself. " Maria has been her bad angel from her girlhood, and still dominates her. The poor child's sufferings have hardened her heart and destroyed for a time her sense of right and wrong— that is all."

With this thought uppermost in her mind she took the letter from her desk, and stirring the smouldering embers, laid it upon the coals. The sheet blazed and fell into ashes.

" No one will ever know," she said with a sigh.

CHAPTER XIII

Lying on Barnegat Beach, within sight of the House of Refuge and Fogarty's cabin, was the hull of a sloop which had been whirled in one night in a southeaster, with not a soul on board, riding the breakers like a duck, and landing high and dry out of the hungry clutch of the surf-dogs. She was light at the time and without ballast, and lay stranded upright on her keel. All attempts by the beach-combers to float her had proved futile; they had stripped her of her standing rigging and everything else of value, and had then abandoned her. Only the evenly balanced hull was left, its bottom timbers broken and its bent keelson buried in the sand. This hulk little Tod Fogarty, aged ten, had taken possession of; particularly the after-part of the hold, over which he had placed a trusty henchman armed with a cutlass made from the hoop of a fish barrel. The henchman—aged seven—wore knee-trousers and a cap and answered to the name of Archie. The refuge itself bore the title of " The Bandit's Home."

This new hulk had taken the place of the old

209

schooner which had served Captain Holt as a land-
mark on that eventful night when he strode Barnegat
Beach in search of Bart, and which by the action
of the ever-changing tides, had gradually settled until
now only a hillock marked its grave—a fate which
sooner or later would overtake this newly landed
sloop itself.

These Barnegat tides are the sponges that wipe
clean the slate of the beach. Each day a new record is made and each day it is wiped out: records
from passing ships, an empty crate, broken spar or
useless barrel grounded now and then by the tide
in its flow as it moves up and down the sand at the
will of the waters. Records, too, of many foot-
prints,—the lagging steps of happy lovers; the dimpled feet of joyous children; the tread of tramp,
coast-guard or fisherman—all scoured clean when the
merciful tide makes ebb.

Other records are strewn along the beach; these
the tide alone cannot efface—the bow of some hap-
less schooner it may be, wrenched from its hull, and
sent whirling shoreward; the shattered mast and
crosstrees of a stranded ship beaten to death in the
breakers; or some battered capstan carried in the
white teeth of the surf-dogs and dropped beyond the
froth-line. To these with the help of the south wind,
the tides extend their mercy, burying them deep with
successive blankets of sand, hiding their bruised

bodies, covering their nakedness and the marks of their sufferings. All through the restful summer and late autumn these battered derelicts lie buried, while above their graves the children play and watch the ships go by, or stretch themselves at length, their eyes on the circling gulls.

With the coming of the autumn all this is changed. The cruel north wind now wakes, and with a loud roar joins hands with the savage easter; the startled surf falls upon the beach like a scourge. Under their double lash the outer bar cowers and sinks; the frightened sand flees hither and thither. Soon the frenzied breakers throw themselves headlong, tearing with teeth and claws, burrowing deep into the hidden graves. Now the forgotten wrecks, like long-buried sins, rise and stand naked, showing every scar and stain. This is the work of the sea-puss—the revolving maniac born of close-wed wind and tide; a beast so terrible that in a single night, with its auger-like snout, it bites huge inlets out of farm lands—mouthfuls deep enough for ships to sail where but yesterday the corn grew.

In the hull of this newly stranded sloop, then—sitting high and dry, out of the reach of the summer surf,—Tod and Archie spent every hour of the day they could call their own; sallying forth on various piratical excursions, coming back laden with drift-wood for a bonfire, or hugging some bottle, which was always opened with trembling, eager fingers in the inmost recesses of the Home, in the hope that some tidings of a lost ship might be found inside; or with their pockets crammed with clam-shells and other sea spoils with which to decorate the inside timbers of what was left of the former captain's cabin.

Jane had protested at first, but the doctor had looked the hull over, and found that there was nothing wide enough, nor deep enough, nor sharp enough to do them harm, and so she was content. Then again, the boys were both strong for their age, and looked it, Tod easily passing for a lad of twelve or fourteen, and Archie for a boy of ten. The one danger discovered by the doctor lay in its height, the only way of boarding the stranded craft being by means of a hand-over-hand climb up the rusty chains of the bowsprit, a difficult and trousers-tearing operation. This was obviated by Tod's father, who made a ladder for the boys out of a pair of old oars, which the two pirates pulled up after them whenever an enemy hove in sight. When friends approached it was let down with more than elaborate ceremony, the guests being escorted by Archie and welcomed on board by Tod.

Once Captain Holt's short, sturdy body was descried in the offing tramping the sand-dunes on his way to Fogarty's, and a signal flag—part of Mother Fogarty's flannel petticoat, and blood-red, as befitted the desperate nature of the craft over which it floated, was at once set in his honor. The captain put his helm hard down and came up into the wind and alongside the hulk.

" Well! well! well! " he cried in his best quarter-deck voice—" what are you stowaways doin' here? " and he climbed the ladder and swung himself over the battered rail.

Archie took his hand and led him into the most sacred recesses of the den, explaining to him his plans for defence, his armament of barrel hoops, and his ammunition of shells and pebbles, Tod standing silently by and a little abashed, as was natural in one of his station; at which the captain laughed more loudly than before, catching Archie in his arms, rubbing his curly head with his big, hard hand, and telling him he was a chip of the old block, every inch of him—none of which did either Archie or Tod understand. Before he climbed down the ladder he announced with a solemn smile that he thought the craft was well protected so far as collisions on foggy nights were concerned, but he doubted if their arms were sufficient and that he had better leave them his big sea knife which had been twice around Cape Horn, and which might be useful in lopping off arms and legs whenever the cutthroats got too impudent and aggressive; whereupon Archie threw his arms around his grizzled neck and said he was a "bully commodore," and that if he would come and live with them aboard the hulk they would obey his orders to a man.

Archie leaned over the rotten rail and saw the old salt stop a little way from the hulk and stand looking at them for some minutes and then wave his hand, at which the boys waved back, but the lad did not see the tears that lingered for an instant on the captain's eyelids, and which the sea-breeze caught away; nor did he hear the words, as the captain resumed his walk: " He's all I've got left, and yet he don't know it and I can't tell him. Ain't it hell ? "

Neither did they notice that he never once raised his eyes toward the House of Refuge as he passed its side. A new door and a new roof had been added, but in other respects it was to him the same grewsome, lonely hut as on that last night when he had denounced his son outside its swinging door.

Often the boys made neighborly visits to friendly tribes and settlers. Fogarty was one of these, and Doctor Cavendish was another. The doctor's country was a place of buttered bread and preserves and a romp with Rex, who was almost as feeble as Meg had been in his last days. But Fogarty's cabin was a mine of never-ending delight. In addition to the quaint low house of clapboards and old ship-timber, with its sloping roof and little toy windows, so unlike his own at Yardley, and smoked ceilings, there was

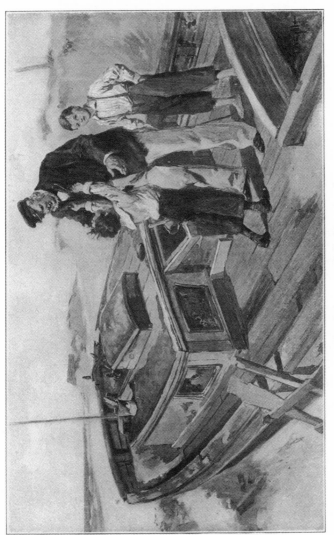

Archie said he was a "Bully Commodore."

a scrap heap piled up and scattered over the yard which in itself was a veritable treasure-house. Here were rusty chains and wooden figure-heads of broken-nosed, blind maidens and tailless dolphins. Here were twisted iron rods, fish-baskets, broken lobster-pots, rotting seines and tangled, useless nets—some used as coverings for coops of restless chickens—old worn-out rope, tangled rigging—everything that a fisherman who had spent his life on Barnegat beach could pull from the surf or find stranded on the sand.

Besides all these priceless treasures, there was an old boat lying afloat in a small lagoon back of the house, one of those seepage pools common to the coast—a boat which Fogarty had patched with a bit of sail-cloth, and for which he had made two pairs of oars, one for each of the " crew," as he called the lads, and which Archie learned to handle with such dexterity that the old fisherman declared he would make a first-class boatman when he grew up, and would " shame the whole bunch of 'em."

But these two valiant buccaneers were not to remain in undisturbed possession of the Bandit's Home with its bewildering fittings and enchanting possibilities—not for long. The secret of the uses to which the stranded craft had been put, and the attendant fun which Commodore Tod and his dauntless henchman, Archibald Cobden, Esquire, were

215

daily getting out of its battered timbers, had already
become public property. The youth of Barnegat—
the very young youth, ranging from nine to twelve,
and all boys—received the news at first with hilarious
joy. This feeling soon gave way to unsuppressed
indignation, followed by an active bitterness when
they realized in solemn conclave—the meeting was
held in an open lot on Saturday morning—that the
capture of the craft had been accomplished, not by
dwellers under Barnegat Light, to whom every piece
of sea-drift from a tomato-can to a full-rigged ship
rightfully belonged, but by a couple of aliens, one of
whom wore knee-pants and a white collar,—a distinction in dress highly obnoxious to these lords of the
soil.

All these denizens of Barnegat had at one time
or another climbed up the sloop's chains and peered
down the hatchway to the sand covering the keelson,
and most of them had used it as a shelter behind
which, in swimming-time, they had put on or peeled
off such mutilated rags as covered their nakedness,
but no one of them had yet conceived the idea of
turning it into a Bandit's Home. That touch of
the ideal, that gilding of the commonplace, had been
reserved for the brain of the curly-haired boy who,
with dancing eyes, his sturdy little legs resting on
Tod's shoulder, had peered over the battered rail,
and who, with a burst of enthusiasm, had shouted:

" Oh, cracky! isn't it nice, Tod! It's got a place we can fix up for a robbers' den; and we'll be bandits and have a flag. Oh, come up here! You never saw anything so fine," etc., etc.

When, therefore, Scootsy Mulligan, aged nine, son of a ship-caulker who worked in Martin Farguson's ship-yard, and Sandy Plummer, eldest of three, and their mother a widow—plain washing and ironing, two doors from the cake-shop—heard that that French " spad," Arch Cobden what lived up to Yardley, and that red-headed Irish cub, Tod Fogarty—Tod's hair had turned very red—had pre-empted the Black Tub, as the wreck was irreverently called, claiming it as their very own, " and-a-sayin' they wuz pirates and bloody Turks and sich," these two quarrelsome town rats organized a posse in lower Barnegat for its recapture.

Archie was sweeping the horizon from his perch on the " poop-deck " when his eagle eye detected a strange group of what appeared to be human beings advancing toward the wreck from the direction of Barnegat village. One, evidently a chief, was in the lead, the others following bunched together. All were gesticulating wildly. The trusty henchman immediately gave warning to Tod, who was at work in the lower hold arranging a bundle of bean-poles which had drifted inshore the night before—part of the deck-load, doubtless, of some passing vessel.

"Ay, ay, sir!" cried the henchman with a hoist of his knee-pants, as a prelude to his announcement.

"Ay, ay, yerself!" rumbled back the reply. "What's up?" The commodore had not read as deeply in pirate lore as had Archie, and was not, therefore, so ready with its lingo.

"Band of savages, sir, approaching down the beach."

"Where away?" thundered back the commodore, his authority now asserting itself in the tones of his voice.

"On the starboard bow, sir—six or seven of 'em."

"Armed or peaceable?"

"Armed, sir. Scootsy Mulligan is leadin' 'em."

"Scootsy Mulligan! Crickety! he's come to make trouble," shouted back Tod, climbing the ladder in a hurry—it was used as a means of descent into the shallow hold when not needed outside. "Where are they? Oh, yes! I see 'em—lot of 'em, ain't they? Saturday, and they ain't no school. Say, Arch, what are we goin' to do?" The terminal vowels softening his henchman's name were omitted in grave situations; so was the pirate lingo.

"Do!" retorted Archie, his eyes snapping. "Why, we'll fight 'em; that's what we are pirates for. Fight 'em to the death. Hurray! They're not coming aboard—no sir-ee! You go down, Toddy

218

[the same free use of terminals], and get two of the biggest bean-poles and I'll run up the death flag. We've got stones and shells enough. Hurry—big ones, mind you!"

The attacking party, their leader ahead, had now reached the low sand heap marking the grave of the former wreck, but a dozen yards away—the sand had entombed it the year before.

"You fellers think yer durned smart, don't ye?" yelled Mr. William Mulligan, surnamed "Scootsy" from his pronounced fleetness of foot. "We're goin' to run ye out o' that Tub. 'Tain't yourn, it's ourn—ain't it, fellers?"

A shout went up in answer from the group on the hillock.

"You can come as friends, but not as enemies," cried Archie grandiloquently. "The man who sets foot on this ship without permission dies like a dog. We sail under the blood-red flag!" and Archie struck an attitude and pointed to the fragment of mother Fogarty's own nailed to a lath and hanging limp over the rail.

"Hi! hi! hi!" yelled the gang in reply. "Oh, ain't he a beauty! Look at de cotton waddin' on his head!" (Archie's cropped curls.) "Say, sissy, does yer mother know ye're out? Throw that ladder down; we're comin' up there—don't make no dif-f'rence whether we got yer permish or not—and we'll knock the stuffin' out o' ye if ye put up any job on us. H'ist out that ladder!"

"Death and no quarter!" shouted back Archie, opening the big blade of Captain Holt's pocket knife and grasping it firmly in his wee hand. "We'll defend this ship with the last drop of our blood!"

"Ye will, will ye!" retorted Scootsy. "Come on, fellers—go for 'em! I'll show 'em," and he dodged under the sloop's bow and sprang for the overhanging chains.

Tod had now clambered up from the hold. Under his arm were two stout hickory saplings. One he gave to Archie, the other he kept himself.

"Give them the shells first," commanded Archie, dodging a beach pebble; "and when their hands come up over the rail let them have this," and he waved the sapling over his head. "Run, Tod,—they're trying to climb up behind. I'll take the bow. Avast there, ye lubbers!"

With this Archie dropped to his knees and crouched close to the heel of the rotting bowsprit, out of the way of the flying missiles—each boy's pockets were loaded—and looking cautiously over the side of the hulk, waited until Scootsy's dirty fingers—he was climbing the chain hand over hand, his feet resting on a boy below him—came into view.

"Off there, or I'll crack your fingers!"

" Crack and be———"

Bang! went Archie's hickory and down dropped the braggart, his oath lost in his cries.

" He smashed me fist! He smashed me fist! Oh! Oh!" whined Scootsy, hopping about with the pain, sucking the injured hand and shaking its mate at Archie, who was still brandishing the sapling and yelling himself hoarse in his excitement.

The attacking party now drew off to the hillock for a council of war. Only their heads could be seen —their bodies lay hidden in the long grass of the dune.

Archie and Tod were now dancing about the deck in a delirium of delight—calling out in true piratical terms, "We die, but we never surrender!" Tod now and then falling into his native vernacular to the effect that he'd " knock the liver and lights out o' the hull gang," an expression the meaning of which was wholly lost on Archie, he never having cleaned a fish in his life.

Here a boy in his shirt-sleeves straightened up in the yellow grass and looked seaward. Then Sandy Plummer gave a yell and ran to the beach, rolling up what was left of his trousers legs, stopping now and then to untie first one shoe and then the other. Two of the gang followed on a run. When the three reached the water's edge they danced about like Crusoe's savages, waving their arms and shouting.

Sandy by this time had stripped off his clothes and had dashed into the water. A long plank from some lumber schooner was drifting up the beach in the gentle swell of the tide. Sandy ran abreast of it for a time, sprang into the surf, threw himself upon it flat like a frog, and then began paddling shoreward. The other two now rushed into the water, grasping the near end of the derelict, the whole party pushing and paddling until it was hauled clean of the brine and landed high on the sand.

A triumphant yell here came from the water's edge, and the balance of the gang—there were seven in all—rushed to the help of the dauntless three.

Archie heaped a pile of pebbles within reach of his hand and waited the attack. What the savages were going to do with the plank neither he nor Tod could divine. The derelict was now dragged over the sand to the hulk, Tod and Archie pelting its rescuers with stones and shells as they came within short range.

" Up with her, fellers ! " shouted Sandy, who, since Scootsy's unmanly tears, had risen to first place. " Run it under the bowsprit—up with her—there she goes ! Altogether ! "

Archie took his stand, his long sapling in his hand, and waited. He thought first he would unseat the end of the plank, but it was too far below him and then again he would be exposed to their volleys of stones, and if he was hurt he might not get back on his craft. Tod, who had resigned command in favor of his henchman after Archie's masterly defence in the last fight, stood behind him. Thermopylæ was a narrow place, and so was the famous Bridge of Horatius. He and his faithful Tod would now make the fight of their lives. Both of these close shaves for immortality were closed books to Tod, but Archie knew every line of their records, Doctor John having spent many an hour reading to him, the boy curled up in his lap while Jane listened.

Sandy, emboldened by the discovery of the plank, made the first rush up and was immediately knocked from his perch by Tod, whose pole swung around his head like a flail. Then Scootsy tried it, crawling up, protecting his head by ducking it under his elbows, holding meanwhile by his hand. Tod's blows fell about his back, but the boy struggled on until Archie reached over the gunwale, and with a twist of his wrist, using all his strength, dropped the invader to the sand below.

The success of this mode of attack was made apparent, provided they could stick to the plank. Five boys now climbed up. Archie belabored the first one with the pole and Tod grappled with the second, trying to throw him from the rail to the sand, some ten feet below, but the rat close behind him, in spite of their efforts, reached forward, caught the rail, and scrambled up to his mate's assistance. In another instant both had leaped to the sloop's deck.

" Back! back! Run, Toddy! " screamed Archie, waving his arms. " Get on the poop-deck; we can lick them there. Run! "

Tod darted back, and the two defenders clearing the intervening rotten timbers with a bound, sprang upon the roof of the old cabin—Archie's " poop."

With a whoop the savages followed, jumping over the holes in the planking and avoiding the nails in the open beams.

In the melee Archie had lost his pole, and was now standing, hat off, his blue eyes flashing, all the blood of his overheated little body blazing in his face. The tears of defeat were trembling under his eyelids. He had been outnumbered, but he would die game. In his hand he carried, unconsciously to himself, the big-bladed pocket knife the captain had given him. He would as soon have used it on his mother as upon one of his enemies, but the Barnegat invaders were ignorant of that fact, knives being the last resort in their environment.

" Look out, Sandy! " yelled Scootsy to his leader, who was now sneaking up to Archie with the movement of an Indian in ambush;—" he's drawed a knife."

Sandy stopped and straightened himself within three feet of Archie. His hand still smarted from the blow Archie had given it. The "spad" had not stopped a second in that attack, and he might not in this; the next thing he knew the knife might be between his ribs.

"Drawed a knife, hev ye!" he snarled. "Drawed a knife, jes' like a spad that ye are! Ye oughter put yer hair in curl-papers!"

Archie looked at the harmless knife in his hand.

"I can fight you with my fists if you *are* bigger than me," he cried, tossing the knife down the open hatchway into the sand below. "Hold my coat, Tod," and he began stripping off his little jacket.

"I ain't fightin' no spads," sneered Sandy. He didn't want to fight this one. "Yer can't skeer nobody. You'll draw a pistol next. Yer better go home to yer mammy, if ye kin find her."

"He ain't got no mammy," snarled Scootsy. "He's a pick-up—me father says so."

Archie sprang forward to avenge the insult, but before he could reach Scootsy's side a yell arose from the bow of the hulk.

"Yi! yi! Run, fellers! Here comes old man Fogarty! he's right on top o' ye! Not that side— this way. Yi! yi!"

The invaders turned and ran the length of the deck, scrambled over the side and dropped one after the other to the sand below just as the Fogarty head appeared at the bow. It was but a step and a spring

225

for him, and with a lurch he gained the deck of the wreck.

"By jiminy, boys, mother thought ye was all killed! Has them rats been botherin' ye? Ye oughter broke the heads of 'em. Where did they get that plank? Come 'shore, did it? Here, Tod, catch hold of it; I jes' wanted a piece o' floorin' like that. Why, ye're all het up, Archie! Come, son, come to dinner; ye'll git cooled off, and mother's got a mess o' clams for ye. Never mind 'bout the ladder; I'll lift it down."

On the way over to the cabin, Fogarty and Tod carrying the plank and Archie walking beside them, the fisherman gleaned from the boys the details of the fight. Archie had recovered the captain's knife and it was now in his hand.

"Called ye a 'pick-up' did he, the rat, and said ye didn't have no mother. He's a liar! If ye ain't got a mother, and a good one, I don't know who has. That's the way with them town-crabs, allus cussin' somebody better'n themselves."

When Fogarty had tilted the big plank against the side of the cabin and the boys had entered the kitchen in search of the mess of clams, the fisherman winked to his wife, jerked his head meaningly over one shoulder, and Mrs. Fogarty, in answer, followed him out to the woodshed.

"Them sneaks from Barnegat, Mulligan's and

Farguson's boys, and the rest of 'em, been lettin' out on Archie: callin' him names, sayin' he ain't got no mother and he's one o' them pass-ins ye find on yer doorstep in a basket. I laughed it off and he 'peared to forgit it, but I thought he might ask ye, an' so I wanted to tip ye the wink."

"Well, ye needn't worry. I ain't goin' to tell him what I don't know," replied the wife, surprised that he should bring her all the way out to the wood-shed to tell her a thing like that.

"But ye *do* know, don't ye?"

"All I know is what Uncle Ephraim told me four or five years ago, and he's so flighty half the time and talks so much ye can't believe one-half he says— something about Miss Jane comin' across Archie's mother in a horsepital in Paris, or some'er's and promisin' her a-dyin' that she'd look after the boy, and she has. She'd do that here if there was women and babies up to Doctor John's horsepital 'stead o' men. It's jes' like her," and Mrs. Fogarty, not to lose her steps, stooped over a pile of wood and began gathering up an armful.

"Well, she ain't his mother, ye know," rejoined Fogarty, helping his wife with the sticks. "That's what they slammed in his face to-day, and he'll git it ag'in as he grows up. But he don't want to hear it from us."

"And he won't. Miss Jane ain't no fool. She

227

knows more about him than anybody else, and when she gits ready to tell him she'll tell him. Don't make no difference who his mother was—the one he's got now is good enough for anybody. Tod would have been dead half a dozen times if it hadn't been for her and Doctor John, and there ain't nobody knows it better'n me. It's just like her to let Archie come here so much with Tod; she knows I ain't goin' to let nothin' happen to him. And as for mothers, Sam Fogarty," here Mrs. Fogarty lifted her free hand and shook her finger in a positive way— " when Archie gits short of mothers he's got one right here, don't make no difference what you or anybody else says," and she tapped her broad bosom meaningly.

Contrary, however, to Fogarty's hopes and surmises, Archie had forgotten neither Sandy's insult nor Scootsy's epithet. " He's a pick-up " and " he ain't got no mammy " kept ringing in his ears as he walked back up the beach to his home. He remembered having heard the words once before when he was some years younger, but then it had come from a passing neighbor and was not intended for him. This time it was flung square in his face. Every now and then as he followed the trend of the beach on his way home he would stop and look out over the sea, watching the long threads of smoke being unwound from the spools of the steamers and the sails of the fishing-boats as they caught the light of the setting sun. The epithet worried him. It was something to be ashamed of, he knew, or they would not have used it.

Jane, standing outside the gate-post, shading her eyes with her hand, scanning the village road, caught sight of his sturdy little figure the moment he turned the corner and ran to meet him.

" I got so worried—aren't you late, my son ? " she asked, putting her arm about him and kissing him tenderly.

" Yes, it's awful late. I ran all the way from the church when I saw the clock. I didn't know it was past six. Oh, but we've had a bully day, mother! And we've had a fight. Tod and I were pirates, and Scootsy Mulligan tried to——"

Jane stopped the boy's joyous account with a cry of surprise. They were now walking back to Yardley's gate, hugging the stone wall.

" A fight! Oh, my son! "

" Yes, a bully fight; only there were seven of them and only two of us. That warn't fair, but Mr. Fogarty says they always fight like that. I could have licked 'em if they come on one at a time, but they got a plank and crawled up——"

" Crawled up where, my son? " asked Jane in astonishment. All this was an unknown world to her. She had seen the wreck and had known, of course, that the boys were making a playhouse of it, but this latter development was news to her.

"Why, on the pirate ship, where we've got our Bandit's Home. Tod is commodore and I'm first mate. Tod and I did all we could, but they didn't fight fair, and Scootsy called me a ' pick-up ' and said I hadn't any mother. I asked Mr. Fogarty what he meant, but he wouldn't tell me. What's a ' pick-up,' dearie ? " and he lifted his face to Jane's, his honest blue eyes searching her own.

Jane caught her hand to her side and leaned for a moment against the stone wall. This was the question which for years she had expected him to ask—one to which she had framed a hundred imaginary answers. When as a baby he first began to talk she had determined to tell him she was not his mother, and so get him gradually accustomed to the conditions of his birth. But every day she loved him the more, and every day she had put it off. To-day it was no easier. He was too young, she knew, to take in its full meaning, even if she could muster up the courage to tell him the half she was willing to tell him—that his mother was her friend and on her sick-bed had entrusted her child to her care. She had wanted to wait until he was old enough to understand, so that she should not lose his love when he came to know the truth. There had been, moreover, always this fear—would he love her for shielding his mother, or would he hate Lucy when he came to know? She had once talked it all over with Captain Holt, but she could never muster up the courage to take his advice.

"Tell him," he had urged. "It'll save you a lot o' trouble in the end. That'll let me out and I kin do for him as I want to. You've lived under this cloud long enough—there ain't nobody can live a lie a whole lifetime, Miss Jane. I'll take my share of the disgrace along of my dead boy, and you ain't done nothin', God knows, to be ashamed of. Tell him! It's grease to yer throat halyards and everything'll run smoother afterward. Take my advice, Miss Jane."

All these things rushed through her mind as she stood leaning against the stone wall, Archie's hand in hers, his big blue eyes still fixed on her own.

"Who said that to you, my son?" she asked in assumed indifference, in order to gain time in which to frame her answer and recover from the shock.

"Scootsy Mulligan."

"Is he a nice boy?"

"No, he's a coward, or he wouldn't fight as he does."

"Then I wouldn't mind him, my boy," and she smoothed back the hair from his forehead, her eyes avoiding the boy's steady gaze. It was only when someone opened the door of the closet concealing this

231

spectre that Jane felt her knees give way and her heart turn sick within her. In all else she was fearless and strong.

"Was he the boy who said you had no mother?"

"Yes. I gave him an awful whack when he came up the first time, and he went heels over head."

"Well, you have got a mother, haven't you, darling?" she continued, with a sigh of relief, now that Archie was not insistent.

"You bet I have!" cried the boy, throwing his arms around her.

"Then we won't either of us bother about those bad boys and what they say," she answered, stooping over and kissing him.

And so for a time the remembrance of Scootsy's epithet faded out of the boy's mind.

CHAPTER XIV

Ten years have passed away.

The sturdy little fellow in knee-trousers is a lad of seventeen, big and strong for his age; Tod is three years older, and the two are still inseparable. The brave commander of the pirate ship is now a full-fledged fisherman and his father's main dependence. Archie is again his chief henchman, and the two spend many a morning in Tod's boat when the blue-fish are running. Old Fogarty does not mind it; he rather likes it, and Mother Fogarty is always happier when the two are together.

" If one of 'em gits overboard," she said one day to her husband, " t'other kin save him."

" Save him! Well, I guess! " he replied. " Salt water skims off Archie same's if he was a white-bellied gull; can't drown him no more'n you kin a can buoy."

The boy has never forgotten Scootsy's epithet, although he has never spoken of it to his mother— no one knows her now by any other name. She

233

thought the episode had passed out of his mind, but she did not know everything that lay in the boy's heart. He and Tod had discussed it time and again, and had wondered over his own name and that of his nameless father, as boys wonder, but they had come to no conclusion. No one in the village could tell them, for no one ever knew. He had asked the doctor, but had only received a curious answer.

"What difference does it make, son, when you have such a mother? You have brought her only honor, and the world loves her the better because of you. Let it rest until she tells you; it will only hurt her heart if you ask her now."

The doctor had already planned out the boy's future; he was to be sent to Philadelphia to study medicine when his schooling was over, and was then to come into his office and later on succeed to his practice.

Captain Holt would have none of it.

"He don't want to saw off no legs," the bluff old man had blurted out when he heard of it. "He wants to git ready to take a ship 'round Cape Horn. If I had my way I'd send him some'er's where he could learn navigation, and that's in the fo'c's'le of a merchantman. Give him a year or two before the mast. I made that mistake with Bart—he loafed round here too long and when he did git a chance he was too old."

Report had it that the captain was going to leave the lad his money, and had therefore a right to speak; but no one knew. He was closer-mouthed than ever, though not so gruff and ugly as he used to be; Archie had softened him, they said, taking the place of that boy of his he " druv out to die a good many years ago."

Jane's mind wavered. Neither profession suited her. She would sacrifice anything she had for the boy provided they left him with her. Philadelphia was miles away, and she would see him but seldom. The sea she shrank from and dreaded. She had crossed it twice, and both times with an aching heart. She feared, too, its treachery and cruelty. The waves that curled and died on Barnegat beach —messengers from across the sea—brought only tidings fraught with suffering.

Archie had no preferences—none yet. His future was too far off to trouble him much. Nor did anything else worry him.

One warm September day Archie turned into Yardley gate, his so'wester still on his head framing his handsome, rosy face; his loose jacket open at the throat, the tarpaulins over his arm. He had been outside the inlet with Tod—since daybreak, in fact—fishing for bass and weakfish.

Jane had been waiting for him for hours. She

235

held an open letter in her hand, and her face was happier, Archie thought as he approached her, than he had seen it for months.

There are times in all lives when suddenly and without warning, those who have been growing quietly by our side impress their new development upon us. We look at them in full assurance that the timid glance of the child will be returned, and are astounded to find instead the calm gaze of the man; or we stretch out our hand to help the faltering step and touch a muscle that could lead a host. Such changes are like the breaking of the dawn; so gradual has been their coming that the full sun of maturity is up and away flooding the world with beauty and light before we can recall the degrees by which it rose.

Jane realized this—and for the first time—as she looked at Archie swinging through the gate, waving his hat as he strode toward her. She saw that the sailor had begun to assert itself. He walked with an easy swing, his broad shoulders—almost as broad as the captain's and twice as hard—thrown back, his head up, his blue eyes and white teeth laughing out of a face brown and ruddy with the sun and wind, his throat and neck bare except for the silk handkerchief—one of Tod's—wound loosely about it; a man really, strong and tough, with hard sinews and capable thighs, back, and wrists—the kind of sailorman that could wear tarpaulins or broadcloth at his pleasure and never lose place in either station.

In this rude awakening Jane's heart-strings tightened. She became suddenly conscious that the Cobden look had faded out of him; Lucy's eyes and hair were his, and so was her rounded chin, with its dimple, but there was nothing else about him that recalled either her own father or any other Cobden she remembered. As he came near enough for her to look into his eyes she began to wonder how he would impress Lucy, what side of his nature would she love best—his courage and strength or his tenderness?

The sound of his voice shouting her name recalled her to herself, and a thrill of pride illumined her happy face like a burst of sunlight as he tossed his tarpaulins on the grass and put his strong arms about her.

"Mother, dear! forty black bass, eleven weakfish, and half a barrel of small fry—what do you think of that?"

"Splendid, Archie. Tod must be proud as a peacock. But look at this!" and she held up the letter. "Who do you think it's from? Guess now," and she locked one arm through his, and the two strolled back to the house.

"Guess now!" she repeated, holding the letter behind her back. The two were often like lovers together.

" Let me see," he coaxed. " What kind of a stamp has it got ? "

" Never you mind about the stamp."

" Uncle John—and it's about my going to Philadelphia."

Jane laughed. " Uncle John never saw it."

"Then it's from— Oh, you tell me, mother!"

" No—guess. Think of everybody you ever heard of. Those you have seen and those you——"

" Oh, I know—Aunt Lucy."

" Yes, and she's coming home. Home, Archie, think of it, after all these years! "

" Well, that's bully! She won't know me, will she? I never saw her, did I? "

" Yes, when you were a little fellow." It was difficult to keep the tremor out of her voice.

" Will she bring any dukes and high daddies with her ? "

" No," laughed Jane, " only her little daughter Ellen, the sweetest little girl you ever saw, she writes."

" How old is she? "

He had slipped his arm around his mother's waist now and the two were " toeing it " up the path, he stopping every few feet to root a pebble from its bed. The coming of the aunt was not a great event in his life.

" Just seven her last birthday."

" All right, she's big enough. We'll take her out and teach her to fish. Hello, granny! " and the boy loosened his arm as he darted up the steps toward Martha. " Got the finest mess of fish coming up here in a little while you ever laid your eyes on," he shouted, catching the old nurse's cap from her head and clapping it upon his own, roaring with laughter, as he fled in the direction of the kitchen.

Jane joined in the merriment and, moving a chair from the hall, took her seat on the porch to await the boy's return. She was too happy to busy herself about the house or to think of any of her outside duties. Doctor John would not be in until the afternoon, and so she would occupy herself in thinking out plans to make her sister's home-coming a joyous one.

As she looked down over the garden as far as the two big gate-posts standing like grim sentinels beneath the wide branches of the hemlocks, and saw how few changes had taken place in the old home since her girl sister had left it, her heart thrilled with joy. Nothing really was different; the same mass of tangled rose-vines climbed over the porch—now quite to the top of the big roof, but still the same dear old vines that Lucy had loved in her childhood; the same honeysuckle hid the posts; the same box bordered the paths. The house was just as she left it; her bedroom had really never been touched. What few changes had taken place she would not miss. Meg would not run out to meet her, and Rex was under a stone that the doctor had placed over his grave; nor would Ann Gossaway peer out of her eyrie of a window and follow her with her eyes as she drove by; her tongue was quiet at last, and she and her old mother lay side by side in the graveyard. Doctor John had exhausted his skill upon them both, and Martha, who had forgiven her enemy, had sat by her bedside until the end, but nothing had availed. Mrs. Cavendish was dead, of course, but she did not think Lucy would care very much. She and Doctor John had nursed her for months until the end came, and had then laid her away near the apple-trees she was so fond of. But most of the faithful hearts who had loved her were still beating, and all were ready with a hearty welcome.

Archie was the one thing new—new to Lucy. And yet she had no fear either for him or for Lucy. When she saw him she would love him, and when she had known him a week she would never be separated from him again. The long absence could not have wiped out all remembrance of the boy, nor would the new child crowd him from her heart.

When Doctor John sprang from his gig (the custom of his daily visits had never been broken) she could hardly wait until he tied his horse—poor Bess had long since given out—to tell him the joyful news.

He listened gravely, his face lighting up at her happiness. He was glad for Jane and said so frankly, but the situation did not please him. He at heart really dreaded the effect of Lucy's companionship on the woman he loved. Although it had been years since he had seen her, he had followed her career, especially since her marriage, with the greatest interest and with the closest attention. He had never forgotten, nor had he forgiven her long silence of two years after her marriage, during which time she had never written Jane a line, nor had he ever ceased to remember Jane's unhappiness over it. Jane had explained it all to him on the ground that Lucy was offended because she had opposed the marriage, but the doctor knew differently. Nor had he ceased to remember the other letters which followed, and how true a story they told of Lucy's daily life and ambitions. He could almost recall the wording of one of them. "My husband is too ill," it had said, "to go south with me, and so I will run down to Rome for a month or so, for I really need the change." And a later one, written since his death, in which she wrote of her winter in Paris and at Monte Carlo, and "how good my mother-in-law is to take care of Ellen." This last letter to her sister, just received—the one he then held in his hand, and which gave Jane such joy, and which he was then reading as carefully as if it had been a prescription —was to his analytical mind like all the rest of its predecessors. One sentence sent a slight curl to his lips. " I cannot stay away any longer from my precious sister," it said, " and am coming back to the home I adore. I have no one to love me, now that my dear husband is dead, but you and my darling Ellen."

The news of Lucy's expected return spread rapidly. Old Martha in her joy was the mouthpiece. She gave the details out at church the Sunday morning following the arrival of Lucy's letter. She was almost too ill to venture out, but she made the effort, stopping the worshippers as they came down the board walk; telling each one of the good news, the tears streaming down her face. To the children and the younger generation the announcement made but little difference; some of them had never heard that Miss Jane had a sister, and others only that she lived abroad. Their mothers knew, of course, and so did the older men, and all were pleased over the news. Those of them who remembered the happy, joyous girl with her merry eyes and ringing laugh were ready to give her a hearty welcome; they felt complimented that the distinguished lady—fifteen years' residence abroad and a rich husband had gained her this position—should be willing to exchange the great Paris for the simple life of Warehold. It touched their civic pride.

Great preparations were accordingly made. Billy Tatham's successor (his son)—in his best open carriage—was drawn up at the station, and Lucy's drive through the village with some of her numerous boxes covered with foreign labels piled on the seat beside the young man—who insisted on driving Lucy and the child himself—was more like the arrival of a princess revisiting her estates than anything else. Martha and Archie and Jane filled the carriage, with little Ellen on Archie's lap, and more than one neighbor ran out of the house and waved to them as they drove through the long village street and turned into the gate.

Archie threw his arms around Lucy when he saw her, and in his open, impetuous way called her his " dear aunty," telling her how glad he was that she had come to keep his good mother from getting so sad at times, and adding that she and granny had not slept for days before she came, so eager were they to see her. And Lucy kissed him in return, but with a different throb at her heart. She felt a thrill when she saw how handsome and strong he was, and for an instant there flashed through her a feeling of pride that he was her own flesh and blood. Then there had come a sudden revulsion, strangling

243

every emotion but the one of aversion—an aversion so overpowering that she turned suddenly and catching Ellen in her arms kissed her with so lavish a display of affection that those at the station who witnessed the episode had only praise for the mother's devotion. Jane saw the kiss Lucy had given Archie, and a cry of joy welled up in her heart, but she lost the shadow that followed. My lady of Paris was too tactful for that.

Her old room was all ready. Jane, with Martha helping, had spent days in its preparation. White dimity curtains starched stiff as a petticoat had been hung at the windows; a new lace cover spread on the little mahogany, brass-mounted dressing-table— her great grandmother's, in fact—with its tiny swinging mirror and the two drawers (Martha remembered when her bairn was just high enough to look into the mirror), and pots of fresh flowers placed on the long table on which her books used to rest. Two easy-chairs had also been brought up from the sitting-room below, covered with new chintz and tied with blue ribbons, and, more wonderful still, a candle-box had been covered with cretonne and studded with brass tacks by the aid of Martha's stiff fingers that her bairn might have a place in which to put her dainty shoes and slippers.

When the trunks had been carried upstairs and Martha with her own hands had opened my lady's gorgeous blue morocco dressing-case with its bottles capped with gold and its brushes and fittings emblazoned with cupids swinging in garlands of roses, the poor woman's astonishment knew no bounds. The many scents and perfumes, the dainty boxes, big and little, holding various powders—one a red paste which the old nurse thought must be a salve, but about which, it is needless to say, she was greatly mistaken—as well as a rabbit's foot smirched with rouge (this she determined to wash at once), and a tiny box of court-plaster cut in half moons. So many things, in fact, did the dear old nurse pull from this wonderful bag that the modest little bureau could not hold half of them, and the big table had to be brought up and swept of its plants and belongings.

The various cosmetics and their uses were especial objects of comment.

"Did ye break one of the bottles, darlin'?" she asked, sniffing at a peculiar perfume which seemed to permeate everything. "Some of 'em must have smashed; it's awful strong everywhere—smell that" —and she held out a bit of lace which she had taken from the case, a dressing-sacque that Lucy had used on the steamer.

Lucy laughed. "And you don't like it? How funny, you dear old thing! That was made specially for me; no one else in Paris has a drop."

And then the dresses! Particularly the one she

was to wear the first night—a dress flounced and
furbelowed and of a creamy white (she still wore
mourning—delicate purples shading to white—the
exact tone for a husband six months dead). And
the filmy dressing-gowns, and, more wonderful than
all, the puff of smoke she was to sleep in, held together by a band of violet ribbon; to say nothing
of the dainty slippers bound about with swan's-
down, and the marvellous hats, endless silk stockings
of mauve, white, and black, and long and short
gloves. In all her life Martha had never seen or
heard of such things. The room was filled with them
and the two big closets crammed to overflowing, and
yet a dozen trunks were not yet unpacked, including
the two small boxes holding little Ellen's clothes.

The night was one long to be remembered. Everyone said the Manor House had not been so gay for
years. And they were all there—all her old friends
and many of Jane's new ones, who for years had
looked on Lucy as one too far above them in station
to be spoken of except with bated breath.

The intimates of the house came early. Doctor
John first, with his grave manner and low voice—
so perfectly dressed and quiet: Lucy thought she
had never seen his equal in bearing and demeanor,
nor one so distinguished-looking—not in any circle in
Europe; and Uncle Ephraim, grown fat and gouty,
leaning on a cane, but still hearty and wholesome,

and overjoyed to see her; and Pastor Dellenbaugh—
his hair was snow-white now—and his complacent
and unruffled wife; and the others, including Captain Holt, who came in late. It was almost a repeti-
tion of that other home-coming years before, when
they had gathered to greet her, then a happy, joyous
girl just out of school.

Lucy in their honor wore the dress that had so
astonished Martha, and a diamond-studded ornament
which she took from her jewel-case and fastened in
her hair. The dress followed the wonderful curves
of her beautiful body in all its dimpled plumpness
and the jewel set off to perfection the fresh, oval
face, laughing blue eyes—wet forget-me-nots were
the nearest their color—piquant, upturned nose and
saucy mouth. The color of the gown, too, harmon-
ized both with the delicate pink of her cheeks and
with the tones of her rather too full throat showing
above the string of pearls that clasped it.

Jane wore a simple gray silk gown which followed
closely the slender and almost attenuated lines of
her figure. This gown the doctor always loved because, as he told her, it expressed so perfectly the
simplicity of her mind and life. Her only jewels
were her deep, thoughtful eyes, and these, to-night,
were brilliant with joy over her sister's return.

As Jane moved about welcoming her guests the
doctor, whose eyes rarely left her face, became con-

scious that at no time in their lives had the contrast between the two sisters been greater.

One, a butterfly of thirty-eight, living only in the glow of the sunlight, radiant in plumage, alighting first on one flower and then on another, but always on flowers, never on weeds; gathering such honey as suited her taste; never resting where she might by any chance be compelled to use her feet, but always poised in air; a woman, rich, brilliant, and beautiful, and—here was the key-note of her life—always, year in and year out, warmed by somebody's admiration, whose she didn't much mind nor care, so that it gratified her pride and relieved her of *ennui*. The other—and this one he loved with his whole soul —a woman of forty-six, with a profound belief in her creeds; quixotic sometimes in her standards, but always sincere; devoted to her traditions, to her friends and to her duty; unselfish, tender-hearted, and self-sacrificing; whose feet, though often tired and bleeding, had always trodden the earth.

As Lucy greeted first one neighbor and then another, sometimes with one hand, sometimes with two, offering her cheek now and then to some old friend who had known her as a child, Jane's heart swelled with something of the pride she used to have when Lucy was a girl. Her beautiful sister, she saw, had lost none of the graciousness of her old manner, nor of her tact in making her guests feel perfectly at home. Jane noticed, too—and this was new to her —a certain well-bred condescension, so delicately managed as never to be offensive—more the air of a woman accustomed to many sorts and conditions of men and women, and who chose to be agreeable as much to please herself as to please her guests.

And yet with all this poise of manner and condescending graciousness, there would now and then dart from Lucy's eyes a quick, searching glance of inquiry, as she tried to read her guests' thoughts, followed by a relieved look on her own face as she satisfied herself that no whisper of her past had ever reached them. These glances Jane never caught.

Doctor John was most cordial in his greeting and talked to her a long time about some portions of Europe, particularly a certain café in Dresden where he used to dine, and another in Paris frequented by the *beau monde*. She answered him quite frankly, telling him of some of her own experiences in both places, quite forgetting that she was giving him glimpses of her own life while away—glimpses which she had kept carefully concealed from Jane or Martha. She was conscious, however, after he had left her of a certain uncomfortable feeling quivering through her as his clear, steadfast eyes looked into hers. He listened, and yet she thought she detected his brain working behind his steadfast gaze. It was as if he was searching for some hidden disease. " He knows something," she said to herself, when the doctor moved to let someone else take his place. "How much I can't tell. I'll get it all out of sister."

Blunt and bluff Captain Holt, white-whiskered and white-haired now, but strong and hearty, gave her another and a different shock. What his first words would be when they met and how she would avoid discussing the subject uppermost in their minds if, in his rough way, he insisted on talking about it, was one of the things that had worried her greatly when she decided to come home, for there was never any doubt in her mind as to his knowledge. But she misjudged the captain, as had a great many others who never looked beneath the rugged bark covering his heart of oak.

"I'm glad you've come at last," he said gravely, hardly touching her hand in welcome, "you ought to have been here before. Jane's got a fine lad of her own that she's bringin' up; when you know him ye'll like him."

She did not look at him when she answered, but a certain feeling of relief crept over her. She saw that the captain had buried the past and intended never to revive it.

The stern look on his face only gave way when little Ellen came to him of her own accord and climbing up into his lap said in her broken English that she heard he was a great captain and that she wanted him to tell her some stories like her good papa used to tell her. " He was gray like you," she said, " and big," and she measured the size with her plump little arms that showed out of her dainty French dress.

With Doctor John and Captain Holt out of the way Lucy's mind was at rest. " Nobody else round about Yardley except these two knows," she kept saying to herself with a bound of relief, " and for these I don't care. The doctor is Jane's slave, and the captain is evidently wise enough not to uncover skeletons locked up in his own closet."

These things settled in her mind, my lady gave herself up to whatever enjoyment, compatible with her rapidly fading mourning, the simple surroundings afforded, taking her cue from the conditions that confronted her and ordering her conduct accordingly and along these lines: Archie was her adopted nephew, the son of an old friend of Jane's, and one whom she would love dearly, as, in fact, she would anybody else whom Jane had brought up ; she herself was a gracious widow of large means recovering from a great sorrow; one who had given up the delights of foreign courts to spend some time among her dear people who had loved her as a child. Here for a time would she bring up and educate her daughter.

" To be once more at home, and in dear old Ware-hold, too!" she had said with upraised Madonna-like eyes and clasped hands to a group of women who were hanging on every word that dropped from her pretty lips. " Do you know what that is to me? There is hardly a day I have not longed for it. Pray, forgive me if I do not come to see you as often as I would, but I really hate to be an hour outside of the four walls of my precious home."

CHAPTER XV

Under the influence of the new arrival it was not at all strange that many changes were wrought in the domestic life at Cobden Manor.

My lady was a sensuous creature, loving color and flowers and the dainty appointments of life as much in the surroundings of her home as in the adornment of her person, and it was not many weeks before the old-fashioned sitting-room had been transformed into a French boudoir. In this metamorphosis she had used but few pieces of new furniture—one or two, perhaps, that she had picked up in the village, as well as some bits of mahogany and brass that she loved—but had depended almost entirely upon the rearrangement of the heirlooms of the family. With the boudoir idea in view, she had pulled the old tables out from the walls, drawn the big sofa up to the fire, spread a rug—one of her own—before the mantel, hung new curtains at the windows and ruffled their edges with lace, banked the sills with geraniums and begonias, tilted a print or two beside the clock, scattered a few books and magazines over the centre-table, on which she had placed a big, generous lamp, under whose umbrella shade she could see to read as she sat in her grandmother's rocking-chair—in fact, had, with that taste inherent in some women—touched with a knowing hand the dead things about her and made them live and mean something;—her talisman being an unerring sense of what contributed to personal comfort. Heretofore Doctor John had been compelled to drag a chair half-way across the room in order to sit and chat with Jane, or had been obliged to share her seat on the sofa, too far from the hearth on cold days to be comfortable. Now he could either stand on the hearth-rug and talk to her, seated in one corner of the pulled-up sofa, her work-basket on a small table beside her, or he could drop into a big chair within reach of her hand and still feel the glow of the fire. Jane smiled at the changes and gave Lucy free rein to do as she pleased. Her own nature had never required these nicer luxuries; she had been too busy, and in these last years of her life too anxious, to think of them, and so the room had been left as in the days of her father.

The effect of the rearrangement was not lost on the neighbors. They at once noticed the sense of cosiness everywhere apparent, and in consequence called twice as often, and it was not long before the old-fashioned sitting-room became a stopping-place for everybody who had half an hour to spare.

These attractions, with the aid of a generous hospitality, Lucy did her best to maintain, partly because she loved excitement and partly because she intended to win the good-will of her neighbors—those who might be useful to her. The women succumbed at once. Not only were her manners most gracious, but her jewels of various kinds, her gowns of lace and frou-frou, her marvellous hats, her assortment of parasols, her little personal belongings and niceties—gold scissors, thimbles, even the violet ribbons that rippled through her transparent underlaces—so different from those of any other woman they knew—were a constant source of wonder and delight. To them she was a beautiful Lady Bountiful who had fluttered down among them from heights above, and whose departure, should it ever take place, would leave a gloom behind that nothing could illumine.

To the men she was more reserved. Few of them ever got beyond a handshake and a smile, and none of them ever reached the borders of intimacy. Popularity in a country village could never, she knew, be gained by a pretty woman without great discretion. She explained her foresight to Jane by telling her that there was no man of her world in Warehold but the doctor, and that she wouldn't think of setting her cap for him as she would be gray-haired before he would have the courage to propose. Then she kissed Jane in apology, and breaking out into a rippling laugh that Martha heard upstairs, danced out of the room.

Little Ellen, too, had her innings; not only was she prettily dressed, presenting the most joyous of pictures, as with golden curls flying about her shoulders she flitted in and out of the rooms like a sprite, but she was withal so polite in her greetings, dropping to everyone a little French courtesy when she spoke, and all in her quaint, broken dialect, that everybody fell in love with her at sight. None of the other mothers had such a child, and few of them knew that such children existed.

Jane watched the workings of Lucy's mind with many misgivings. She loved her lightheartedness and the frank, open way with which she greeted everybody who crossed their threshold. She loved, too, to see her beautifully gowned and equipped and to hear the flattering comments of the neighbors on her appearance and many charms; but every now and then her ear caught an insincere note that sent a shiver through her. She saw that the welcome Lucy gave them was not from her heart, but from her lips; due to her training, no doubt, or perhaps to her unhappiness, for Jane still mourned over the unhappy years of Lucy's life—an unhappiness, had she known it, which had really ended with Archie's safe adoption and Bart's death. Another cause of anxiety was Lucy's restlessness. Every day she must have some new excitement—a picnic with the young girls and young men, private theatricals in the town hall, or excursions to Barnegat Beach, where they were building a new summer hotel. Now and then she would pack her bag and slip off to New York or Philadelphia for days at a time to stay with friends she had met abroad, leaving Ellen with Jane and Martha. To the older sister she seemed like some wild, untamable bird of brilliant plumage used to long, soaring flights, perching first on one dizzy height and then another, from which she could watch the world below.

The thing, however, which distressed Jane most was Lucy's attitude towards Archie. She made every allowance for her first meeting at the station, and knew that necessarily it must be more or less constrained, but she had not expected the almost cold indifference with which she had treated the boy ever since.

As the days went by and Lucy made no effort to attach Archie to her or to interest herself either in his happiness or welfare, Jane became more and more disturbed. She had prayed for this home-coming and had set her heart on the home-building which was sure to follow, and now it seemed farther off than ever. One thing troubled and puzzled her:

while Lucy was always kind to Archie indoors, kissing him with the others when she came down to breakfast, she never, if she could help it, allowed him to walk with her in the village, and she never on any occasion took him with her when visiting the neighbors.

"Why not take Archie with you, dear?" Jane had said one morning to Lucy, who had just announced her intention of spending a few days in Phildelphia with Max Feilding's sister Sue, whom she had met abroad when Max was studying in Dresden—Max was still a bachelor, and his sister kept house for him. He was abroad at the time, but was expected by every steamer.

"Archie isn't invited, you old goosie, and he would be as much out of place in Max's house as Uncle Ephraim Tipple would be in Parliament."

"But they would be glad to see him if you took him. He is just the age now when a boy gets impressions which last him through——"

"Yes, the gawky and stumble-over-things age! Piano-stools, rugs, anything that comes in his way. And the impressions wouldn't do him a bit of good. They might, in fact, do him harm," and she laughed merrily and spread her fingers to the blaze. A laugh was often her best shield. She had in her time dealt many a blow and then dodged behind a laugh to prevent her opponent from striking back.

A PACKAGE OF LETTERS

"But, Lucy, don't you want to do something to help him?" Jane asked in a pleading tone.

"Yes, whatever I can, but he seems to me to be doing very well as he is. Doctor John is devoted to him and the captain idolizes him. He's a dear, sweet boy, of course, and does you credit, but he's not of my world, Jane, dear, and I'd have to make him all over again before he could fit into my atmosphere. Besides, he told me this morning that he was going off for a week with some fisherman on the beach—some person by the name of Fogarty, I think."

"Yes, a fine fellow; they have been friends from their boyhood." She was not thinking of Fogarty, but of the tone of Lucy's voice when speaking of her son.

"Yes—most estimable gentleman, no doubt, this Mr. Fogarty, but then, dear, we don't invite that sort of people to dinner, do we?" and another laugh rippled out.

"Yes, sometimes," answered Jane in all sincerity. "Not Fogarty, because he would be uncomfortable if he came, but many of the others just as humble. We really have very few of any other kind. I like them all. Many of them love me dearly."

"Not at all strange; nobody can help loving you," and she patted Jane's shoulder with her jewelled fingers.

"But you like them, too, don't you? You treat them as if you did."

Lucy lifted her fluted petticoat, rested her slippered foot on the fender, glanced down at the embroidered silk stocking covering her ankle, and said in a graver tone:

"I like all kinds of people—in their proper place. This is my home, and it is wise to get along with one's neighbors. Besides, they all have tongues in their heads like the rest of the human race, and it is just as well to have them wag for you as against you."

Jane paused for a moment, her eyes watching the blazing logs, and asked with almost a sigh:

"You don't mean, dear, that you never intend to help Archie, do you?"

"Never is a long word, Jane. Wait till he grows up and I see what he makes of himself. He is now nothing but a great animal, well built as a young bull, and about as awkward."

Jane's eyes flashed and her shoulders straightened. The knife had a double edge to its blade.

"He is your own flesh and blood, Lucy," she said with a ring of indignation in her voice. "You don't treat Ellen so; why should you Archie?"

Lucy took her foot from the fender, dropped her skirts, and looked at Jane curiously. From underneath the half-closed lids of her eyes there flashed a quick glance of hate—a look that always came into Lucy's eyes whenever Jane connected her name with Archie's.

"Let us understand each other, sister," she said icily. "I don't dislike the boy. When he gets into trouble I'll help him in any way I can, but please remember he's not my boy—he's yours. You took him from me with that understanding and I have never asked him back. He can't love two mothers. You say he has been your comfort all these years. Why, then, do you want to unsettle his mind?"

Jane lifted her head and looked at Lucy with searching eyes—looked as a man looks when some-one he must not strike has flung a glove in his face.

"Do you really love anything, Lucy?" she asked in a lower voice, her eyes still fastened on her sister's.

"Yes, Ellen and you."

"Did you love her father?" she continued in the same direct tone.

"Y-e-s, a little—— He was the dearest old man in the world and did his best to please me; and then he was never very well. But why talk about him, dear?"

"And you never gave him anything in return for all his devotion?" Jane continued in the same cross-examining voice and with the same incisive tone.

"Yes, my companionship—whenever I could. About what you give Doctor John," and she looked at Jane with a sly inquiry as she laughed gently to herself.

Jane bit her lips and her face flushed scarlet. The cowardly thrust had not wounded her own heart. It had only uncovered the love of the man who lay enshrined in its depths. A sudden sense of the injustice done him arose in her mind and then her own helplessness in it all.

"I would give him everything I have, if I could," she answered simply, all her insistency gone, the tears starting to her eyes.

Lucy threw her arms about her sister and held her cheek to her own.

"Dear, I was only in fun; please forgive me. Everything is so solemn to you. Now kiss me and tell me you love me."

That night when Captain Holt came in to play with the little "Pond Lily," as he called Ellen, Jane told him of her conversation with Lucy, not as a reflection on her sister, but because she thought he ought to know how she felt toward Archie. The kiss had wiped out the tears, but the repudiation of Archie still rankled in her breast.

The captain listened patiently to the end. Then he said with a pause between each word:

"She's sailin' without her port and starboard lights, Miss Jane. One o' these nights with the tide settin' she'll run up ag'in somethin' solid in a fog, and then—God help her! If Bart had lived he might have come home and done the decent thing, and then we could git her into port some'er's for repairs, but that's over now. She better keep her lights trimmed. Tell her so for me."

What this " decent thing " was he never said—perhaps he had but a vague idea himself. Bart had injured Lucy and should have made reparation, but in what way except by marriage—he, perhaps, never formulated in his own mind.

Jane winced under the captain's outburst, but she held her peace. She knew how outspoken he was and how unsparing of those who differed from him and she laid part of his denunciation to this cause.

Some weeks after this conversation the captain started for Yardley to see Jane on a matter of business, and incidentally to have a romp with the Pond Lily. It was astonishing how devoted the old sea-dog was to the child, and how she loved him in return. " My big bear," she used to call him, tugging away at his gray whiskers. On his way he stopped at the post-office for his mail. It was mid-winter and the roads were partly blocked with snow, making walking difficult except for sturdy souls like Captain Nat.

" Here, Cap'n Holt, yer jest the man I been a-waitin' for," cried Miss Tucher, the postmistress, from behind the sliding window. " If you ain't goin' up to the Cobdens, ye kin, can't ye? Here's a lot o' letters jest come that I know they're expectin'. Miss Lucy's" (many of the village people still called her Miss Lucy, not being able to pronounce her dead husband's name) " come in yesterday and seems as if she couldn't wait. This storm made everything late and the mail got in after she left. There ain't nobody comin' out to-day and here's a pile of 'em— furrin' most of 'em. I'd take 'em myself if the snow warn't so deep. Don't mind, do ye? I'd hate to have her disapp'inted, for she's jes' 's sweet as they make 'em."

" Don't mind it a mite, Susan Tucher," cried the captain. " Goin' there, anyhow. Got some business with Miss Jane. Lord, what a wad o' them! "

" That ain't half what she gits sometimes," replied the postmistress, " and most of 'em has seals and crests stamped on 'em. Some o' them furrin lords, I guess, she met over there."

These letters the captain held in his hand when he pushed open the door of the sitting-room and stood before the inmates in his rough pea-jacket, his ruddy face crimson with the cold, his half-moon whiskers all the whiter by contrast.

" Good-mornin' to the hull o' ye! " he shouted. " Cold as blue blazes outside, I tell ye, but ye look snug enough in here. Hello, little Pond Lily! why ain't you out on your sled? Put two more roses in your cheeks if there was room for 'em. There, ma'am," and he nodded to Lucy and handed her the letters, " that's 'bout all the mail that come this mornin'. There warn't nothin' else much in the bag. Susan Tucher asked me to bring 'em up to you 'count of the weather and 'count o' your being in such an all-fired hurry to read 'em."

Little Ellen was in his arms before this speech was finished and everybody else on their feet shaking hands with the old salt, except poor, deaf old Martha, who called out, "Good-mornin', Captain Holt," in a strong, clear voice, and in rather a positive way, but who kept her seat by the fire and continued her knitting; and complacent Mrs. Dellenbaugh, the pastor's wife, who, by reason of her position, never got up for anybody.

The captain advanced to the fire, Ellen still in his arms, shook hands with Mrs. Dellenbaugh and extended three fingers, rough as lobster's claws and as red, to the old nurse. Of late years he never met Martha without feeling that he owed her an apology for the way he had treated her the day she begged him to send Bart away. So he always tried to make it up to her, although he had never told her why.

" Hope you're better, Martha? Heard ye was under the weather; was that so? Ye look spry 'nough now," he shouted in his best quarter-deck voice.

" Yes, but it warn't much. Doctor John fixed me up," Martha replied coldly. She had no positive animosity toward the captain—not since he had shown some interest in Archie—but she could never make a friend of him.

During this greeting Lucy, who had regained her chair, sat with the letters unopened in her lap. None of the eagerness Miss Tucher had indicated was apparent. She seemed more intent on arranging the folds of her morning-gown accentuating the graceful outlines of her well-rounded figure. She had glanced through the package hastily, and had found the one she wanted and knew that it was there warm under her touch—the others did not interest her.

" What a big mail, dear," remarked Jane, drawing up a chair. " Aren't you going to open it ? " The captain had found a seat by the window and the child was telling him everything she had done since she last saw him.

" Oh, yes, in a minute," replied Lucy. " There's plenty of time." With this she picked up the bunch of letters, ran her eye through the collection, and then, with the greatest deliberation, broke one seal after another, tossing the contents on the table. Some she merely glanced at, searching for the signatures and ignoring the contents; others she read through to the end. One was from Dresden, from a student she had known there the year before. This was sealed with a wafer and bore the address of the café where he took his meals. Another was stamped with a crest and emitted a slight perfume; a third was enlivened by a monogram in gold and began: " Ma chère amie," in a bold round hand. The one under her hand she did not open, but slipped into the pocket of her dress. The others she tore into bits and threw upon the blazing logs.

" I guess if them fellers knew how short a time it would take ye to heave their cargo overboard," blurted out the captain, " they'd thought a spell 'fore they mailed their manifests."

Lucy laughed good-naturedly and Jane watched the blaze roar up the wide chimney. The captain settled back in his chair and was about to continue his " sea yarn," as he called it, to little Ellen, when he suddenly loosened the child from his arms, and leaning forward in his seat toward where Jane sat, broke out with:

" God bless me! I believe I'm wool-gathering. I clean forgot what I come for. It is you, Miss Jane, I come to see, not this little curly head that'll git me ashore yet with her cunnin' ways. They're goin' to build a new life-saving station down Barnegat way. That Dutch brig that come ashore last fall in that so'easter and all them men drownded could have been saved if we'd had somethin' to help 'em with. We did all we could, but that House of Refuge ain't half rigged and most o' the time ye got to break the door open to git at what there is if ye're in a hurry, which you allus is. They ought to have a station with everything 'bout as it ought to be and a crew on hand all the time; then, when somethin' comes ashore you're right there on top of it. That one down to Squam is just what's wanted here."

"Will it be near the new summer hotel?" asked Lucy carelessly, just as a matter of information, and without raising her eyes from the rings on her beautiful hands.

"'Bout half a mile from the front porch, ma'am"—he preferred calling her so—"from what I hear. 'Tain't located exactly yet, but some'er's along there. I was down with the Gov'ment agent yesterday."

"Who will take charge of it, captain?" inquired Jane, reaching over her basket in search of her scissors.

"Well, that's what I come up for. They're talkin' about me," and the captain put his hands behind Ellen's head and cracked his big knuckles close to her ear, the child laughing with delight as she listened.

The announcement was received with some surprise. Jane, seeing Martha's inquiring face, as if she wanted to hear, repeated the captain's words to her in a loud voice. Martha laid down her knitting and looked at the captain over her spectacles.

" Why, would you take it, captain?" Jane asked in some astonishment, turning to him again.

" Don't know but I would. Ain't no better job for a man than savin' lives. I've helped kill a good many; 'bout time now I come 'bout on another tack. I'm doin' nothin'—haven't been for years. If I could get the right kind of a crew 'round me—men I could depend on—I think I could make it go."

" If you couldn't nobody could, captain," said Jane in a positive way. " Have you picked out your crew ? "

" Yes, three or four of 'em. Isaac Polhemus and Tom Morgan—Tom sailed with me on my last voyage—and maybe Tod."

" Archie's Tod?" asked Jane, replacing her scissors and searching for a spool of cotton.

" Archie's Tod," repeated the captain, nodding his head, his big hand stroking Ellen's flossy curls. " That's what brought me up. I want Tod, and he won't go without Archie. Will ye give him to me ? "

" My Archie!" cried Jane, dropping her work and staring straight at the captain.

" Your Archie, Miss Jane, if that's the way you put it," and he stole a look at Lucy. She was conscious of his glance, but she did not return it; she merely continued listening as she twirled one of the rings on her finger.

"Well, but, captain, isn't it very dangerous work? Aren't the men often drowned?" protested Jane.

"Anything's dangerous 'bout salt water that's worth the doin'. I've stuck to the pumps seventy-two hours at a time, but I'm here to tell the tale."

"Have you talked to Archie?"

"No, but Tod has. They've fixed it up betwixt 'em. The boy's dead set to go."

"Well, but isn't he too young?"

"Young or old, he's tough as a marline-spike— A1, and copper fastened throughout. There ain't a better boatman on the beach. Been that way ever since he was a boy. Won't do him a bit of harm to lead that kind of life for a year or two. If he was mine it wouldn't take me a minute to tell what I'd do."

Jane leaned back in her chair, her eyes on the crackling logs, and began patting the carpet with her foot. Lucy became engrossed in a book that lay on the table beside her. She didn't intend to take any part in the discussion. If Jane wanted Archie to serve as a common sailor that was Jane's business. Then again, it was, perhaps, just as well for a number of reasons to have him under the captain's care. He might become so fond of the sea as to want to follow it all his life.

"What do you think about it, Lucy?" asked Jane.

" Oh, I don't know anything about it. I don't really. I've lived so long away from here I don't know what the young men are doing for a living. He's always been fond of the sea, has he not, Captain Holt? "

" Allus," said the captain doggedly; " it's in his blood." Her answer nettled him. " You ain't got no objections, have you, ma'am? " he asked, looking straight at Lucy.

Lucy's color came and went. His tone offended her, especially before Mrs. Dellenbaugh, who, although she spoke but seldom in public had a tongue of her own when she chose to use it. She was not accustomed to being spoken to in so brusque a way. She understood perfectly well the captain's covert meaning, but she did not intend either to let him see it or to lose her temper.

" Oh, not the slightest," she answered with a light laugh. " I have no doubt that it will be the making of him to be with you. Poor boy, he certainly needs a father's care."

The captain winced in turn under the retort and his eyes flashed, but he made no reply.

Little Ellen had slipped out of the captain's lap during the colloquy. She had noticed the change in her friend's tone, and, with a child's intuition, had seen that the harmony was in danger of being broken. She stood by the captain's knee, not knowing whether to climb back again or to resume her seat by the window. Lucy, noticing the child's discomfort, called to her:

"Come here, Ellen, you will tire the captain."

The child crossed the room and stood by her mother while Lucy tried to rearrange the glossy curls, tangled by too close contact with the captain's broad shoulder. In the attempt Ellen lost her balance and fell into her mother's lap.

"Oh, Ellen!" said her mother coldly; "stand up, dear. You are so careless. See how you have mussed my gown. Now go over to the window and play with your dolls."

The captain noted the incident and heard Lucy's reproof, but he made no protest. Neither did he contradict the mother's statement that the little girl had tired him. His mind was occupied with other things—the tone of the mother's voice for one, and the shade of sadness that passed over the child's face for another. From that moment he took a positive dislike to her.

"Well, think it over, Miss Jane," he said, rising from his seat and reaching for his hat. "Plenty of time 'bout Archie. Life-savin' house won't be finished for the next two or three months; don't expect to git into it till June. Wonder, little Pond Lily, if the weather's goin' to be any warmer?" He slipped his hand under the child's chin and leaning over her

272

head peered out of the window. " Don't look like it, does it, little one? Looks as if the snow would hold on. Hello! here comes the doctor. I'll wait a bit—good for sore eyes to see him, and I don't git a chance every day. Ask him 'bout Archie, Miss Jane. He'll tell ye whether the lad's too young."

There came a stamping of feet on the porch outside as Doctor John shook the snow from his boots, and the next instant he stepped into the room bringing with him all the freshness and sunshine of the outside world.

" Good-morning, good people,". he cried, " every one of you! How very snug and cosey you look here! Ah, captain, where have you been keeping yourself? And Mrs. Dellenbaugh! This is indeed a pleasure. I have just passed the dear doctor, and he is looking as young as he did ten years ago. And my Lady Lucy! Down so early! Well, Mistress Martha, up again I see; I told you you'd be all right in a day or two."

This running fire of greetings was made with a pause before each inmate of the room—a hearty hand-shake for the bluff captain, the pressing of Mrs. Dellenbaugh's limp fingers, a low bow to Lucy, and a pat on Martha's plump shoulder.

Jane came last, as she always did. She had risen to greet him and was now unwinding the white silk handkerchief wrapped about his throat and helping him off with his fur tippet and gloves.

"Thank you, Jane. No, let me take it; it's rather wet," he added as he started to lay the heavy overcoat over a chair. "Wait a minute. I've some violets for you if they are not crushed in my pocket. They came last night," and he handed her a small parcel wrapped in tissue paper. This done, he took his customary place on the rug with his back to the blazing logs and began unbuttoning his trim frock-coat, bringing to view a double-breasted, cream-white waistcoat—he still dressed as a man of thirty, and always in the fashion—as well as a fluffy scarf which Jane had made for him with her own fingers.

"And what have I interrupted?" he asked, looking over the room. "One of your sea yarns, captain?"—here he reached over and patted the child's head, who had crept back to the captain's arms—"or some of my lady's news from Paris? You tell me, Jane," he added, with a smile, opening his thin, white, almost transparent fingers and holding them behind his back to the fire, a favorite attitude.

"Ask the captain, John." She had regained her seat and was reaching out for her work-basket, the violets now pinned in her bosom—her eyes had long since thanked him.

"No, do *you* tell me," he insisted, moving aside

the table with her sewing materials and placing it nearer her chair.

"Well, but it's the captain who should speak," Jane replied, laughing, as she looked up into his face, her eyes filled with his presence. "He has startled us all with the most wonderful proposition. The Government is going to build a life-saving station at Barnegat beach, and they have offered him the position of keeper, and he says he will take it if I will let Archie go with him as one of his crew."

Doctor John's face instantly assumed a graver look. These forked roads confronting the career of a young life were important and not to be lightly dismissed.

"Well, what did you tell him?" he asked, looking down at Jane in the effort to read her thoughts.

"We are waiting for you to decide, John." The tone was the same she would have used had the doctor been her own husband and the boy their child.

Doctor John communed with himself for an instant. "Well, let us take a vote," he replied with an air as if each and every one in the room was interested in the decision. "We'll begin with Mistress Martha, and then Mrs. Dellenbaugh, and then you, Jane, and last our lady from over the sea. The captain has already sold his vote to his affections, and so must be counted out."

"Yes, but don't count me *in,* please," exclaimed

275

Lucy with a merry laugh as she arose from her seat. " I don't know a thing about it. I've just told the dear captain so. I'm going upstairs this very moment to write some letters. Bonjour, Monsieur le Docteur; bonjour, Monsieur le Capitaine and Madame Dellenbaugh," and with a wave of her hand and a little dip of her head to each of the guests, she courtesied out of the room.

When the door was closed behind her she stopped in the hall, threw a glance at her face in the old-fashioned mirror, satisfied herself of her skill in preserving its beautiful rabbit's-foot bloom and freshness, gave her blonde hair one or two pats to keep it in place, rearranged the film of white lace about her shapely throat, and gathering up the mass of ruffled skirts that hid her pretty feet, slowly ascended the staircase.

Once inside her room and while the vote was being taken downstairs that decided Archie's fate she locked her door, dropped into a chair by the fire, took the unopened letter from her pocket, and broke the seal.

" Don't scold, little woman," it read. ". I would have written before, but I've been awfully busy getting my place in order. It's all arranged now, however, for the summer. The hotel will be opened in June, and I have the best rooms in the house, the three on the corner overlooking the sea. Sue says

"Yes, but don't count me *in*, please," exclaimed Lucy.

she will, perhaps, stay part of the summer with me. Try and come up next week for the night. If not I'll bring Sue with me and come to you for the day.

Your own   Max."

For some minutes she sat gazing into the fire, the letter in her hand.

" It's about time, Mr. Max Feilding," she said at last with a sigh of relief as she rose from her seat and tucked the letter into her desk. " You've had string enough, my fine fellow; now it's my turn. If I had known you would have stayed behind in Paris all these months and kept me waiting here I'd have seen you safe aboard the steamer. The hotel opens in June, does it? Well, I can just about stand it here until then; after that I'd go mad. This place bores me to death."

CHAPTER XVI

Spring has come and gone. The lilacs and cro-
cuses, the tulips and buttercups, have bloomed and
faded; the lawn has had its sprinkling of dandelions,
and the fluff of their blossoms has drifted past the
hemlocks and over the tree-tops. The grass has
had its first cutting; the roses have burst their buds
and hang in clusters over the arbors; warm winds
blow in from the sea laden with perfumes from beach
and salt-marsh; the skies are steely blue and the
cloud puffs drift lazily. It is summer-time—the season of joy and gladness, the season of out-of-doors.

All the windows at Yardley are open; the porch
has donned an awning—its first—colored white and
green, shading big rocking-chairs and straw tables
resting on Turkish rugs. Lucy had wondered why
in all the years that Jane had lived alone at Yardley
she had never once thought of the possibilities of this
porch. Jane had agreed with her, and so, under
Lucy's direction, the awnings had been put up and
the other comforts inaugurated. Beneath its shade

Lucy sits and reads or embroiders or answers her constantly increasing correspondence.

The porch serves too as a reception-room, the vines being thick and the occupants completely hidden from view. Here Lucy often spreads a small table, especially when Max Feilding drives over in his London drag from Beach Haven on Barnegat beach. On these occasions, if the weather is warm, she refreshes him with delicate sandwiches and some of her late father's rare Scotch whiskey (shelved in the cellar for thirty years) or with the more common brands of cognac served in the old family decanters.

Of late Max had become a constant visitor. His own ancestors had made honorable records in the preceding century, and were friends of the earlier Cobdens during the Revolution. This, together with the fact that he had visited Yardley when Lucy was a girl—on his first return from Paris, in fact—and that the acquaintance had been kept up while he was a student abroad, was reason enough for his coming with such frequency.

His drag, moreover, as it whirled into Yardley's gate, gave a certain air of *éclat* to the Manor House that it had not known since the days of the old colonel. Nothing was lacking that money and taste could furnish. The grays were high-steppers and smooth as satin, the polished chains rattled and clanked about the pole; the body was red and the wheels yellow, the lap-robe blue, with a monogram; and the diminutive boy studded with silver buttons bearing the crest of the Feilding family was as smart as the tailor could make him.

And the owner himself, in his whity-brown driving-coat with big pearl buttons, yellow gloves, and gray hat, looked every inch the person to hold the ribbons. Altogether it was a most fashionable equipage, owned and driven by a most fashionable man.

As for the older residents of Warehold, they had only words of praise for the turnout. Uncle Ephraim declared that it was a " Jim Dandy," which not only showed his taste, but which also proved how much broader that good-natured cynic had become in later years. Billy Tatham gazed at it with staring eyes as it trundled down the highway and turned into the gate, and at once determined to paint two of his hacks bright yellow and give each driver a lap-robe with the letter " T " worked in high relief.

The inmates of Yardley were not quite so enthusiastic. Martha was glad that her bairn was having such a good time, and she would often stand on the porch with little Ellen's hand in hers and wave to Max and Lucy as they dashed down the garden road and out through the gate, the tiger behind; but Jane, with that quick instinct which some women possess, recognized something in Feilding's manner which she could not put into words, and so held her peace. She had nothing against Max, but she did not like him. Although he was most considerate of her feelings and always deferred to her, she felt that any opposition on her part to their outings would have made no difference to either one of them. He asked her permission, of course, and she recognized the courtesy, but nothing that he ever did or said overcame her dislike of him.

Doctor John's personal attitude and bearing toward Feilding was an enigma not only to Jane, but to others who saw it. He invariably greeted him, whenever they met, with marked, almost impressive cordiality, but it never passed a certain limit of reserve; a certain dignity of manner which Max had recognized the first day he shook hands with him. It recalled to Feilding some of his earlier days, when he was a student in Paris. There had been a supper in Max's room that ended at daylight—no worse in its features than dozens of others in the Quartier— to which an intimate friend of the doctor's had been invited, and upon which, as Max heard afterward, the doctor had commented rather severely.

Max realized, therefore, but too well that the distinguished physician—known now over half the State —understood him, and his habits, and his kind as thoroughly as he did his own case of instruments. He realized, too, that there was nothing about his present appearance or surroundings or daily life that could lead so thoughtful a man of the world as Dr. John Cavendish, of Barnegat, to conclude that he had changed in any way for the better.

And yet this young gentleman could never have been accused of burning his candle at both ends. He had no flagrant vices really—none whose posters were pasted on the victim's face. Neither cards nor any other form of play interested him, nor did the wine tempt him when it was red—or of any other color, for that matter, nor did he haunt the dressing-rooms of chorus girls and favorites of the hour. His innate refinement and good taste prevented any such uses of his spare time. His weakness—for it could hardly be called a vice—was narrowed down to one infirmity, and one only: this was his inability to be happy without the exclusive society of some one woman.

Who the woman might be depended very largely on whom he might be thrown with. In the first ten years of his majority—his days of poverty when a student—it had been some girl in exile, like himself. During the last ten years—since his father's death and his inheritance—it had been a loose end picked out of the great floating drift—that social flotsam and jetsam which eddies in and out of the casinos of Nice and Monte Carlo, flows into Aix and Trouville in summer and back again to Rome and Cairo in winter—a discontented wife perhaps;

or an unmarried woman of thirty-five or forty, with means enough to live where she pleased; or it might be some self-exiled Russian countess or English-woman of quality who had a month off, and who meant to make the most of it. All most respectable people, of course, without a breath of scandal attaching to their names—Max was too careful for that—and yet each and every one on the lookout for precisely the type of man that Max represented: one never happy or even contented when outside the radius of a waving fan or away from the flutter of a silken skirt.

It was in one of these resorts of the idle, a couple of years before, while Lucy's husband and little Ellen were home in Geneva, that Max had met her, and where he had renewed the acquaintance of their childhood—an acquaintance which soon ripened into the closest friendship.

Hence his London drag and appointments; hence the yacht and a four-in-hand—then a great novelty—all of which he had promised her should she decide to join him at home. Hence, too, his luxuriously fitted-up bachelor quarters in Philadelphia, and his own comfortable apartments in his late father's house, where his sister Sue lived; and hence, too, his cosey rooms in the best corner of the Beach Haven hotel, with a view overlooking Barnegat Light and the sea.

None of these things indicated in the smallest degree that this noble gentleman contemplated finally settling down in a mansion commensurate with his large means, where he and the pretty widow could enjoy their married life together; nothing was further from his mind—nothing could be—he loved his freedom too much. What he wanted, and what he intended to have, was her undivided companionship—at least for the summer; a companionship without any of the uncomfortable complications which would have arisen had he selected an unmarried woman or the wife of some friend to share his leisure and wealth.

The woman he picked out for the coming season suited him exactly. She was blonde, with eyes, mouth, teeth, and figure to his liking (he had become critical in forty odd years—twenty passed as an expert) ; dressed in perfect taste, and wore her clothes to perfection; had a Continental training that made her mistress of every situation, receiving with equal ease and graciousness anybody, from a postman to a prince, sending them away charmed and delighted; possessed money enough of her own not to be too much of a drag upon him; and—best of all (and this was most important to the heir of Walnut Hill)— had the best blood of the State circling in her veins. Whether this intimacy might drift into something closer, compelling him to take a reef in his sails, never troubled him. It was not the first time that he had steered his craft between the Scylla of matrimony and the Charybdis of scandal, and he had not the slightest doubt of his being able to do it again.

As for Lucy, she had many plans in view. One was to get all the fun possible out of the situation; another was to provide for her future. How this was to be accomplished she had not yet determined. Her plans were laid, but some of them she knew from past experience might go astray. On one point she had made up her mind—not to be in a hurry. In furtherance of these schemes she had for some days—some months, in fact—been making preparations for an important move. . She knew that its bare announcement would come as a surprise to Jane and Martha and, perhaps, as a shock, but that did not shake her purpose. She furthermore expected more or less opposition when they fully grasped her meaning. This she intended to overcome. Neither Jane nor Martha, she said to herself, could be angry with her for long, and a few kisses and an additional flow of good-humor would soon set them to laughing again.

To guard against the possibility of a too prolonged interview with Jane, ending, perhaps, in a disagreeable scene—one beyond her control—she had selected a sunny summer morning for the stage setting of her little comedy and an hour when Feilding was expected to call for her in his drag. She and

Max were to make a joint inspection that day of his new apartment at Beach Haven, into which he had just moved, as well as the stable containing the three extra vehicles and equine impedimenta, which were to add to their combined comfort and enjoyment.

Lucy had been walking in the garden looking at the rose-beds, her arm about her sister's slender waist, her ears open to the sound of every passing vehicle— Max was expected at any moment—when she began her lines.

" You won't mind, Jane, dear, will you, if I get together a few things and move over to Beach Haven for a while ? " she remarked simply, just as she might have done had she asked permission to go upstairs to take a nap. " I think we should all encourage a new enterprise like the hotel, especially old families like ours. And then the sea air always does me so much good. Nothing like Trouville air, my dear husband used to tell me, when I came back in the autumn. You don't mind, do you ? "

" For how long, Lucy ? " asked Jane, with a tone of disappointment in her voice, as she placed her foot on the top step of the porch.

" Oh, I can't tell. Depends very much on how I like it." As she spoke she drew up an easy-chair for Jane and settled herself in another. Then she added carelessly : " Oh, perhaps a month—perhaps two."

" Two months ! " exclaimed Jane in astonishment, dropping into her seat. " Why, what do you want to leave Yardley for ? O Lucy, don't—please don't go ! "

" But you can come over, and I can come here," rejoined Lucy in a coaxing tone.

" Yes; but I don't want to come over. I want you at home. And it's so lovely here. I have never seen the garden look so beautiful; and you have your own room, and this little porch is so cosey. The hotel is a new building, and the doctor says a very damp one, with everything freshly plastered. He won't let any of his patients go there for some weeks, he tells me. Why should you want to go ? I really couldn't think of it, dear. I'd miss you dreadfully."

" You dear old sister," answered Lucy, laying her parasol on the small table beside her, " you are so old-fashioned. Habit, if nothing else, would make me go. I have hardly passed a summer in Paris or Geneva since I left you; and you know how delightful my visits to Biarritz used to be years ago. Since my marriage I have never stayed in any one place so long as this. I must have the sea air."

" But the salt water is right here, Lucy, within a short walk of our gate, and the air is the same." Jane's face wore a troubled look, and there was an anxious, almost frightened tone in her voice.

"No, it is not exactly the same," Lucy answered positively, as if she had made a life-long study of climate; "and if it were, the life is very different. I love Warehold, of course; but you must admit that it is half-asleep all the time. The hotel will be some change; there will be new people and something to see from the piazzas. And I need it, dear. I get tired of one thing all the time—I always have."

"But you will be just as lonely there." Jane in her astonishment was like a blind man feeling about for a protecting wall.

"No; Max and his sister will be at Beach Haven, and lots of others I know. No, I won't be lonely," and an amused expression twinkled in her eyes.

Jane sat quite still. Some of Captain Holt's blunt, outspoken criticisms floated through her brain.

"Have you any reason for wanting to leave here?" she asked, raising her eyes and looking straight at Lucy.

"No, certainly not. How foolish, dear, to ask me! I'm never so happy as when I am with you."

"Well, why then should you want to give up your home and all the comforts you need—your flowers, garden, and everything you love, and this porch, which you have just made so charming, to go to a damp, half-completed hotel, without a shrub about it—only a stretch of desolate sand with the tide going in and out?" There was a tone of suspicion in

Jane's voice that Lucy had never heard from her sister's lips—never, in all her life.

"Oh, because I love the tides, if nothing else," she answered with a sentimental note in her voice. "Every six hours they bring me a new message. I could spend whole mornings watching the tides come and go. During my long exile you don't know how I dreamed every night of the dear tides of Barnegat. If you had been away from all you love as many years as I have, you would understand how I could revel in the sound of the old breakers."

For some moments Jane did not answer. She knew from the tones of Lucy's voice and from the way she spoke that she did not mean it. She had heard her talk that way to some of the villagers when she wanted to impress them, but she had never spoken in the same way to her.

"You have some other reason, Lucy. Is it Max?" she asked in a strained tone.

Lucy colored. She had not given her sister credit for so keen an insight into the situation. Jane's mind was evidently working in a new direction. She determined to face the suspicion squarely; the truth under some conditions is better than a lie.

"Yes," she replied, with an assumed humility and with a tone as if she had been detected in a fault and wanted to make a clean breast of it. "Yes—now that you have guessed it—it *is* Max."

"Don't you think it would be better to see him here instead of at the hotel?" exclaimed Jane, her eyes still boring into Lucy's.

"Perhaps "—the answer came in a helpless way —" but that won't do much good. I want to keep my promise to him if I can."

"What was your promise?" Jane's eyes lost their searching look for an instant, but the tone of suspicion still vibrated.

Lucy hesitated and began playing with the trimming on her dress.

"Well, to tell you the truth, dear, a few days ago in a burst of generosity I got myself into something of a scrape. Max wants his sister Sue to spend the summer with him, and I very foolishly promised to chaperon her. She is delighted over the prospect, for she must have somebody, and I haven't the heart to disappoint her. Max has been so kind to me that I hate now to tell him I can't go. That's all, dear. I don't like to speak of obligations of this sort, and so at first I only told you half the truth."

"You should always keep your promise, dear," Jane answered thoughtfully and with a certain relieved tone. (Sue was nearly thirty, but that did not occur to Jane.) "But this time I wish you had not promised. I am sorry, too, for little Ellen. She will miss her little garden and everything she loves here; and then again, Archie will miss her, and so will Captain Holt and Martha. You know as well as I do that a hotel is no place for a child."

" I am glad to hear you say so. That's why I shall not take her with me." As she spoke she shot an inquiring glance from the corner of her eyes at the anxious face of her sister. These last lines just before the curtain fell were the ones she had dreaded most.

Jane half rose from her seat. Her deep eyes were wide open, gazing in astonishment at Lucy. For an instant she felt as if her heart had stopped beating.

" And you—you—are not going to take Ellen with you!" she gasped.

" No, of course not." She saw her sister's agitation, but she did not intend to notice it. Besides, her expectant ear had caught the sound of Max's drag as it whirled through the gate. " I always left her with her grandmother when she was much younger than she is now. She is very happy here and I wouldn't be so cruel as to take her away from all her pleasures. Then she loves old people. See how fond she is of the Captain and Martha! No, you are right. I wouldn't think of taking her away."

Jane was standing now, her eyes blazing, her lips quivering.

" You mean, Lucy, that you would leave your child here and spend two months away from her?"

The wheels were crunching the gravel within a rod of the porch. Max had already lifted his hat.

"But, sister, you don't understand——" The drag stopped and Max, with uncovered head, sprang out and extended his hand to Jane.

Before he could offer his salutations Lucy's joyous tones rang out.

"Just in the nick of time, Max," she cried. "I've just been telling my dear sister that I'm going to move over to Beach Haven to-morrow, bag and baggage, and she is delighted at the news. Isn't it just like her?"

CHAPTER XVII

BREAKERS AHEAD

The summer-home of Max Feilding, Esq., of Walnut Hill, and of the beautiful and accomplished widow of the dead Frenchman was located on a levelled sand-dune in full view of the sea. Indeed, from beneath its low-hooded porticos and piazzas nothing else could be seen except, perhaps, the wide sky—gray, mottled, or intensely blue, as the weather permitted—the stretch of white sand shaded from dry to wet and edged with tufts of yellow grass; the circling gulls and the tall finger of Barnegat Light pointing skyward. Nothing, really, but some scattering buildings in silhouette against the glare of the blinding light—one the old House of Refuge, a mile away to the north, and nearer by, the new Life Saving Station (now complete) in charge of Captain Nat Holt and his crew of trusty surfmen.

This view Lucy always enjoyed. She would sit for hours under her awnings and watch the lazy boats crawling in and out of the inlet, or the motionless steamers—motionless at that distance—slowly unwinding their threads of smoke. The Station particularly interested her. Somehow she felt a certain satisfaction in knowing that Archie was at work and that he had at last found his level among his own people—not that she wished him any harm; she only wanted him out of her way.

The hostelry itself was one of those low-roofed, shingle-sided and shingle-covered buildings common in the earlier days along the Jersey coast, and now supplanted by more modern and more costly structures. It had grown from a farm-house and out-buildings to its present state with the help of an architect and a jig-saw; the former utilizing what remained of the house and its barns, and the latter transforming plain pine into open work patterns with which to decorate its gable ends and façade. When the flags were raised, the hanging baskets suspended in each loop of the porches, and the merciless, omnipresent and ever-insistent sand was swept from its wide piazzas and sun-warped steps it gave out an air of gayety so plausible and enticing that many otherwise sane and intelligent people at once closed their comfortable homes and entered their names in its register.

The amusements of these habitués—if they could be called habitués, this being their first summer—were as varied as their tastes. There was a band which played mornings and afternoons in an unpainted pine pagoda planted on a plot of slowly dying grass and decorated with more hanging baskets and Chinese lanterns; there was bathing at eleven and four; and there was croquet on the square of cement fenced about by poles and clothes-lines at all hours. Besides all this there were driving parties to the villages nearby; dancing parties at night with the band in the large room playing away for dear life, with all the guests except the very young and very old tucked away in twos in the dark corners of the piazzas out of reach of the lights and the inquisitive—in short, all the diversions known to such retreats, so necessary for warding off *ennui* and thus inducing the inmates to stay the full length of their commitments.

In its selection Max was guided by two considerations: it was near Yardley—this would materially aid in Lucy's being able to join him—and it was not fashionable and, therefore, not likely to be overrun with either his own or Lucy's friends. The amusements did not interest him; nor did they interest Lucy. Both had seen too much and enjoyed too much on the other side of the water, at Nice, at Monte Carlo, and Biarritz, to give the amusements a thought. What they wanted was to be let alone; this would furnish all the excitement either of them needed. This exclusiveness was greatly helped by the red and yellow drag, with all its contiguous and connecting impedimenta, a turnout which never ceased to occupy everybody's attention whenever the small tiger stood by the heads of the satin-coated grays awaiting the good pleasure of his master and his lady. Its possession not only marked a social eminence too lofty for any ordinary habitué to climb to unless helped up by the proffered hand of the owner, but it prevented anyone of these would-be climbers from inviting either its owner or his companion to join in other outings no matter how enjoyable. Such amusements as they could offer were too simple and old-fashioned for two distinguished persons who held the world in their slings and who were whirling it around their heads with all their might. The result was that their time was their own.

They filled it at their pleasure.

When the tide was out and the sand hard, they drove on the beach, stopping at the new station, chatting with Captain Holt or Archie; or they strolled north, always avoiding the House of Refuge —that locality had too many unpleasant associations for Lucy, or they sat on the dunes, moving back out of the wet as the tide reached them, tossing pebbles in the hollows, or gathering tiny shells, which Lucy laid out in rows of letters as she had done when a child. In the afternoon they drove by way of Yardley to see how Ellen was getting on, or idled about Warehold, making little purchases at the shops and chatting with the village people, all of whom would come out to greet them. After dinner they would generally betake themselves to Max's portico, opening out of his rooms, or to Lucy's—they were at opposite ends of the long corridor—where the two had their coffee while Max smoked.

The opinions freely expressed regarding their social and moral status, and individual and combined relations, differed greatly in the several localities in which they were wont to appear. In Warehold village they were looked upon as two most charming and delightful people, rich, handsome, and of proper age and lineage, who were exactly adapted to each other and who would prove it before the year was out, with Pastor Dellenbaugh officiating, assisted by some dignitary from Philadelphia.

At the hostelry many of the habitués had come to a far different conclusion. Marriage was not in either of their heads, they maintained; their intimacy was a purely platonic one, born of a friendship dating back to childhood—they were cousins really—Max being the dearest and most unselfish creature in the world, he having given up all his pleasures elsewhere to devote himself to a most sweet and gracious lady whose grief was still severe and who would really be quite alone in the world were it not for her little daughter, now temporarily absent.

This summary of facts, none of which could be questioned, was supplemented and enriched by another conclusive instalment from Mrs. Walton Coates, of Chestnut Plains, who had met Lucy at Aix the year before, and who therefore possessed certain rights not vouchsafed to the other habitués of Beach Haven—an acquaintance which Lucy, for various reasons, took pains to encourage—Mrs. C.'s social position being beyond question, and her house and other appointments more than valuable whenever Lucy should visit Philadelphia: besides, Mrs. Coates's own and Lucy's apartments joined, and the connecting door of the two sitting-rooms was often left open, a fact which established a still closer intimacy. This instalment, given in a positive and rather lofty way, made plain the fact that in her enforced exile the distinguished lady not only deserved the thanks of every habitué of the hotel, but of the whole country around, for selecting the new establishment in which to pass the summer, instead of one of the more fashionable resorts elsewhere.

This outburst of the society leader, uttered in the hearing of a crowded piazza, had occurred after a conversation she had had with Lucy concerning little Ellen.

" Tell me about your little daughter," Mrs. Coates had said. " You did not leave her abroad, did you ? "

" Oh, no, my dear Mrs. Coates! I am really here on my darling's account," Lucy answered with a sigh. " My old home is only a short distance from here. But the air does not agree with me there, and so I came here to get a breath of the real sea. Ellen is with her aunt, my dear sister Jane. I wanted to bring her, but really I hadn't the heart to take her from them; they are so devoted to her. Max loves her dearly. He drives me over there almost every day. I really do not know how I could have borne all the sorrows I have had this year without dear Max. He is like a brother to me, and *so* thoughtful. You know we have known each other since we were children. They tell such dreadful stories, too, about him, but I have never seen that side of him. He's a perfect *saint* to me."

From that time on Mrs. Coates was her loyal mouthpiece and devoted friend. Being separated from one's child was one of the things she could not brook; Lucy was an angel to stand it as she did. As for Max—no other woman had ever so influenced him for good, nor did she believe any other woman could.

At the end of the second week a small fly no larger than a pin's head began to develop in the sunshine of their amber. It became visible to the naked eye when Max suddenly resolved to leave his drag, his tiger, his high-stepping grays, and his fair companion, and slip over to Philadelphia—for a day or two, he explained. His lawyer needed him, he said, and then again he wanted to see his sister Sue, who had run down to Walnut Hill for the day. (Sue, it might as well be stated, had not yet put in an appearance at Beach Haven, nor had she given any notice of her near arrival; a fact which had not disturbed Lucy in the least until she attempted to explain to Jane.)

"I've got to pull up, little woman, and get out for a few days," Max had begun. "Morton's all snarled up, he writes me, over a mortgage, and I must straighten it out. I'll leave Bones [the tiger] and everything just as it is. Don't mind, do you?"

"Mind! Of course I do!" retorted Lucy. "When did you get this marvellous idea into that wonderful brain of yours, Max? I intended to go to Warehold myself to-morrow." She spoke with her usual good-humor, but with a slight trace of surprise and disappointment in her tone.

"When I opened my mail this morning; but my going won't make any difference about Warehold. Bones and the groom will take care of you."

Lucy leaned back in her chair and looked over the rail of the porch. She had noticed lately a certain restraint in Max's manner which was new to her. Whether he was beginning to get bored, or whether it was only one of his moods, she could not decide—

even with her acute knowledge of similar symptoms. That some change, however, had come over him she had not the slightest doubt. She never had any trouble in lassoing her admirers. That came with a glance of her eye or a lift of her pretty shoulders: nor for that matter in keeping possession of them as long as her mood lasted.

"Whom do you want to see in Philadelphia, Max?" she asked, smiling roguishly at him. She held him always by presenting her happiest and most joyous side, whether she felt it or not.

"Sue and Morton—and you, you dear girl, if you'll come along."

"No; I'm not coming along. I'm too comfortable where I am. Is this woman somebody you haven't told me of, Max?" she persisted, looking at him from under half-closed lids.

"Your somebodies are always thin air, little girl; you know everything I have ever done in my whole life," Max answered gravely. She had for the last two weeks.

Lucy threw up her hands and laughed so loud and cheerily that an habitué taking his morning constitutional on the boardwalk below turned his head in their direction. The two were at breakfast under the awnings of Lucy's portico, Bones standing out of range.

"You don't believe it?"

301

"Not one word of it, you fraud; nor do you. You've forgotten one-half of all you've done and the other half you wouldn't dare tell any woman. Come, give me her name. Anybody Sue knows?"

"Nobody that anybody knows, Honest John." Then he added as an after-thought, "Are you sorry?" As he spoke he rose from his seat and stood behind her chair looking down over her figure. She had her back to him. He thought he had never seen her look so lovely. She was wearing a light-blue morning-gown, her arms bare to the elbows, and a wide Leghorn hat—the morning costume of all others he liked her best in.

"No—don't think I am," she answered lightly. "Fact is I was getting pretty tired of you. How long will you be gone?"

"Oh, I think till the end of the week—not longer." He reached over the chair and was about to play with the tiny curls that lay under the coil of her hair, when he checked himself and straightened up. One of those sudden restraints which had so puzzled Lucy had seized him. She could not see his face, but she knew from the tones of his voice that the enthusiasm of the moment had cooled.

Lucy shifted her chair, lifted her head, and looked up into his eyes. She was always entrancing from this point of view: the upturned eyelashes, round of the cheeks, and the line of the throat and swelling shoulders were like no other woman's he knew.

" I don't want you to go, Max," she said in the same coaxing tone of voice that Ellen might have used in begging for sugar-plums. " Just let the mortgage and old Morton and everybody else go. Stay here with me."

Max straightened up and threw out his chest and a determined look came into his eyes. If he had had any doubts as to his departure Lucy's pleading voice had now removed them.

" No, can't do it," he answered in mock positiveness. " Can't 'pon my soul. Business is business. Got to see Morton right away; ought to have seen him before." Then he added in a more serious tone, " Don't get worried if I stay a day or two longer."

" Well, then, go, you great bear, you," and she rose to her feet and shook out her skirts. " I wouldn't let you stay, no matter what you said." She was not angry—she was only feeling about trying to put her finger on the particular button that controlled Max's movements. " Worried ? Not a bit of it. Stay as long as you please."

There *was* a button, could she have found it. It was marked " Caution," and when pressed communicated to the heir of Walnut Hill the intelligence that he was getting too fond of the pretty widow and that his only safety lay in temporary flight. It was a favorite trick of his. In the charting of his course he had often found two other rocks beside Scylla and Charybdis in his way; one was boredom and the other was love. When a woman began to bore him, or he found himself liking her beyond the limit of his philosophy, he invariably found relief in change of scene. Sometimes it was a sick aunt or a persistent lawyer or an engagement nearly forgotten and which must be kept at all hazards. He never, however, left his inamorata in either tears or anger.

" Now, don't be cross, dear," he cried, patting her shoulder with his fingers. " You know I don't want to leave you. I shall be perfectly wretched while I'm gone, but there's no help for it. Morton's such a fussy old fellow—always wanting to do a lot of things that can, perhaps, wait just as well as not. Hauled me down from Walnut Hill half a dozen times once, and after all the fellow wouldn't sell. But this time it's important and I must go. Bones," and he lifted his finger to the boy, " tell John I want the light wagon. I'll take the 11.12 to Philadelphia."

The tiger advanced ten steps and stood at attention, his finger at his eyebrow. Lucy turned her face toward the boy. " No, Bones, you'll do nothing of the kind. You tell John to harness the grays to the drag. I'll go to the station with Mr. Feilding."

Max shrugged his shoulders. He liked Lucy for

304

"I don't want you to go, Max," she said.

a good many things—one was her independence, another was her determination to have her own way. Then, again, she was never so pretty as when she was a trifle angry; her color came and went so deliciously and her eyes snapped so charmingly. Lucy saw the shrug and caught the satisfied look in his face. She didn't want to offend him and yet she didn't intend that he should go without a parting word from her—tender or otherwise, as circumstances might require. She knew she had not found the button, and in her doubt determined for the present to abandon the search.

"No, Bones, I've changed my mind," she called to the boy, who was now half way down the piazza. "I don't think I will go. I'll stop here, Max, and do just what you want me to do," she added in a softened voice. "Come along," and she slipped her hand in his and the two walked toward the door of his apartments.

When the light wagon and satin-skinned sorrel, with John on the seat and Bones in full view, stopped at the sanded porch, Mrs. Coates and Lucy formed part of the admiring group gathered about the turn-out. All of Mr. Feilding's equipages brought a crowd of onlookers, no matter how often they appeared—he had five with him at Beach Haven, including the four-in-hand which he seldom used—but the grays and the light wagon, by common consent, were considered the most "stylish" of them all, not excepting the drag.

After Max had gathered the reins in his hands, had balanced the whip, had settled himself comfortably and with a wave of his hand to Lucy had driven off, Mrs. Coates slipped her arm through my lady's and the two slowly sauntered to their rooms.

"Charming man, is he not?" Mrs. Coates ventured. "Such a pity he is not married! You know I often wonder whom such men will marry. Some pretty school-girl, perhaps, or prim woman of forty."

Lucy laughed.

"No," she answered, "you are wrong. The bread-and-butter miss would never suit Max, and he's past the eye-glass and side-curl age. The next phase, if he ever reaches it, will be somebody who will make him do—not as he pleases, but as *she* pleases. A man like Max never cares for a woman any length of time who humors his whims."

"Well, he certainly was most attentive to that pretty Miss Billeton. You remember her father was lost overboard four years ago from his yacht. Mr. Coates told me he met her only a day or so ago; she had come down to look after the new ball-room they are adding to the old house. You know her, don't you?"

"No—never heard of her. How old is she?" rejoined Lucy in a careless tone.

"I should say twenty, maybe twenty-two—you can't always tell about these girls; very pretty and very rich. I am quite sure I saw Mr. Feilding driving with her just before he moved his horses down here, and she looked prettier than ever. But then he has a new flame every month, I hear."

"Where were they driving?" There was a slight tone of curiosity in Lucy's voice. None of Max's love-affairs ever affected her, of course, except as they made for his happiness; all undue interest, therefore, was out of place, especially before Mrs. Coates.

"I don't remember. Along the River Road, perhaps—he generally drives there when he has a pretty woman with him."

Lucy bit her lip. Some other friend, then, had been promised the drag with the red body and yellow wheels! This was why he couldn't come to Yardley when she wrote for him. She had found the button. It rang up another woman.

The door between the connecting sitting-rooms was not opened that day, nor that night, for that matter. Lucy pleaded a headache and wished to be alone. She really wanted to look the field over and see where her line of battle was weak. Not that she really cared—unless the girl should upset her plans; not as Jane would have cared had Doctor John been guilty of such infidelity. The eclipse was what hurt her. She had held the centre of the stage with the

307

lime-light full upon her all her life, and she intended to retain it against Miss Billeton or Miss Anybody else. She decided to let Max know at once, and in plain terms, giving him to understand that she didn't intend to be made a fool of, reminding him at the same time that there were plenty of others who cared for her, or who would care for her if she should but raise her little finger. She *would* raise it, too, even if she packed her trunks and started for Paris—and took him with her.

These thoughts rushed through her mind as she sat by the window and looked out over the sea. The tide was making flood, and the fishing-boats anchored in the inlet were pointing seaward. She could see, too, the bathers below and the children digging in the sand. Now and then a boat would head for the inlet, drop its sail, and swing round motionless with the others. Then a speck would break away from the anchored craft and with the movement of a water-spider land the fishermen ashore.

None of these things interested her. She could not have told whether the sun shone or whether the sky was fair or dull. Neither was she lonely, nor did she miss Max. She was simply angry—disgusted—disappointed at the situation; at herself, at the woman who had come between them, at the threatened failure of her plans. One moment she was building up a house of cards in which she held all the trumps, and the next instant she had tumbled it to the ground. One thing she was determined upon —not to take second place. She would have all of him or none of him.

At the end of the third day Max returned. He had not seen Morton, nor any of his clerks, nor anybody connected with his office. Neither had he sent him any message or written him any letter. Morton might have been dead and buried a century so far as Max or his affairs were concerned. Nor had he laid his eyes on the beautiful Miss Billeton; nor visited her house; nor written her any letters; nor inquired for her. What he did do was to run out to Walnut Hill, have a word with his manager, and slip back to town again and bury himself in his club. Most of the time he read the magazines, some pages two or three times over. Once he thought he would look up one or two of his women friends at their homes—those who might still be in town—and then gave it up as not being worth the trouble. At the end of the third day he started for Barnegat. The air was bad in the city, he said to himself, and everybody he met was uninteresting. He would go back, hitch up the grays, and he and Lucy have a spin down the beach. Sea air always did agree with him, and he was a fool to leave it.

Lucy met him at the station in answer to his telegram sent over from Warehold. She was dressed in her very best: a double-breasted jacket and straw turban, a gossamer veil wound about it. Her cheeks were like two red peonies and her eyes bright as diamonds. She was perched up in the driver's seat of the drag, and handled the reins and whip with the skill of a turfman. This time Bones, the tiger, did not spring into his perch as they whirled from the station in the direction of the beach. His company was not wanted.

They talked of Max's trip, of the mortgage, and of Morton; of how hot it was in town and how cool it was on her portico; of Mrs. Coates and of pater-familias Coates, who held a mortgage on Beach Haven; of the dance the night before—Max leading in the conversation and she answering either in mono-syllables or not at all, until Max hazarded the state-ment that he had been bored to death waiting for Morton, who never put in an appearance, and that the only human being, male or female, he had seen in town outside the members of the club, was Sue.

They had arrived off the Life-Saving Station now, and Archie had called the captain to the door, and both stood looking at them, the boy waving his hand and the captain following them with his eyes. Had either of them caught the captain's remark they, perhaps, would have drawn rein and asked for an explanation:

"Gay lookin' hose-carriage, ain't it? Looks as if they was runnin' to a fire!"

But they didn't hear it; would not, probably have heard it, had the captain shouted it in their ears. Lucy was intent on opening up a subject which had lain dormant in her mind since the morning of Max's departure, and the gentleman himself was trying to cipher out what new "kink," as he expressed it to himself, had "got it into her head."

When they had passed the old House of Refuge Lucy drew rein and stopped the drag where the widening circle of the incoming tide could bathe the horses' feet. She was still uncertain as to how she would lead up to the subject-matter without betraying her own jealousy or, more important still, without losing her temper. This she rarely displayed, no matter how goading the provocation. Nobody had any use for an ill-tempered woman, not in her atmosphere; and no fly that she had ever known had been caught by vinegar when seeking honey. There might be vinegar-pots to be found in her larder, but they were kept behind closed doors and sampled only when she was alone. As she sat looking out to sea, Max's brain still at work on the problem of her unusual mood, a schooner shifted her mainsail in the light breeze and set her course for the inlet.

"That's the regular weekly packet," Max ventured. "She's making for Farguson's ship-yard. She runs between Amboy and Barnegat—Captain Ambrose Farguson sails her." At times like these any topic was good enough to begin on.

"How do you know?" Lucy asked, looking at the incoming schooner from under her half-closed lids. The voice came like the thin piping of a flute preceding the orchestral crash, merely sounded so as to let everybody know it was present.

"One of my carriages was shipped by her. I paid Captain Farguson the freight just before I went away."

"What's her name?"—slight tremolo—only a note or two.

"The *Polly Walters*," droned Max, talking at random, mind neither on the sloop nor her captain.

"Named after his wife?" The flute-like notes came more crisply.

"Yes, so he told me." Max had now ceased to give any attention to his answers. He had about made up his mind that something serious was the matter and that he would ask her and find out.

"Ought to be called the *Max Feilding*, from the way she tacks about. She's changed her course three times since I've been watching her."

Max shot a glance athwart his shoulder and caught a glimpse of the pretty lips thinned and straightened and the half-closed eyes and wrinkled forehead.

312

He was evidently the disturbing cause, but in what way he could not for the life of him see. That she was angry to the tips of her fingers was beyond question; the first time he had seen her thus in all their acquaintance.

"Yes—that would fit her exactly," he answered with a smile and with a certain soothing tone in his voice. "Every tack her captain makes brings him the nearer to the woman he loves."

"Rather poetic, Max, but slightly farcical. Every tack you make lands you in a different port—with a woman waiting in every one of them." The first notes of the overture had now been struck.

"No one was waiting in Philadelphia for me except Sue, and I only met her by accident," he said good-naturedly, and in a tone that showed he would not quarrel, no matter what the provocation; "she came in to see her doctor. Didn't stay an hour."

"Did you take her driving?" This came in a thin, piccolo tone—barely enough room for it to escape through her lips. All the big drums and heavy brass were now being moved up.

"No; had nothing to take her out in. Why do you ask? What has happened, little——"

"Take anybody else?" she interrupted.

"No."

He spoke quite frankly and simply. At any other

time she would have believed him. She had always done so in matters of this kind, partly because she didn't much care and partly because she made it a point never to doubt the word of a man, either by suspicion or inference, who was attentive to her. This time she did care, and she intended to tell him so. All she dreaded was that the big horns and the tom-toms would get away from her leadership and the hoped-for, correctly played symphony end in an uproar.

" Max," she said, turning her head and lifting her finger at him with the movement of a conductor's baton, " how can you lie to me like that? You never went near your lawyer; you went to see Miss Bille-ton, and you've spent every minute with her since you left me. Don't tell me you didn't. I know everything you've done, and—" Bass drums, bass viols, bassoons—everything—was loose now.

She had given up her child to be with him! Everything, in fact—all her people at Yardley; her dear old nurse. She had lied to Jane about chaperon-ing Sue—all to come down and keep him from being lonely. What she wanted was a certain confidence in return. It made not the slightest difference to her how many women he loved, or how many women loved him; she didn't love him, and she never would; but unless she was treated differently from a child and like the woman that she was, she was going straight back to Yardley, and then back to Paris, etc., etc.

She knew, as she rushed on in a flood of abuse such as only a woman can let loose when she is thoroughly jealous and entirely angry, that she was destroying the work of months of plotting, and that he would be lost to her forever, but she was powerless to check the torrent of her invective. Only when her breath gave out did she stop.

Max had sat still through it all, his eyes express- ing first astonishment and then a certain snap of admiration, as he saw the color rising and falling in her cheeks. It was not the only time in his experi- ence that he had had to face similar outbursts. It was the first time, however, that he had not felt like striking back. Other women's outbreaks had bored him and generally had ended his interest in them— this one was more charming than ever. He liked, too, her American pluck and savage independence. Jealous she certainly was, but there was no whine about it; nor was there any flop at the close—floppy women he detested—had always done so. Lucy struck straight out from her shoulder and feared nothing.

As she raged on, the grays beating the water with their well-polished hoofs, he continued to sit per- fectly still, never moving a muscle of his face nor changing his patient, tolerant expression. The best

315

plan, he knew, was to let all the steam out of the
boiler and then gradually rake the fires.

" My dear little woman," he began, " to tell you
the truth, I never laid eyes on Morton; didn't want
to, in fact. All that was an excuse to get away. I
thought you wanted a rest, and I went away to let
you have it. Miss Billeton I haven't seen for three
months, and couldn't if I would, for she is engaged
to her cousin and is now in Paris buying her wedding clothes. I don't know who has been humbug-
ging you, but they've done it very badly. There is
not one word of truth in what you've said from beginning to end."

There is a certain ring in a truthful statement
that overcomes all doubts. Lucy felt this before
Max had finished. She felt, too, with a sudden thrill,
that she still held him. Then there came the instantaneous desire to wipe out all traces of the outburst and keep his good-will.

" And you swear it?" she asked, her belief already asserting itself in her tones, her voice falling
to its old seductive pitch.

" On my honor as a man," he answered simply.

For a time she remained silent, her mind working
behind her mask of eyes and lips, the setting sun
slanting across the beach and lighting up her face
and hair, the grays splashing the suds with their
impatient feet. Max kept his gaze upon her. He

saw that the outbreak was over and that she was a little ashamed of her tirade. He saw, too, man of the world as he was, that she was casting about in her mind for some way in which she could regain for herself her old position without too much humiliation.

"Don't say another word, little woman," he said in his kindest tone. "You didn't mean a word of it; you haven't been well lately, and I oughtn't to have left you. Tighten up your reins; we'll drive on if you don't mind."

That night after the moon had set and the lights had been turned out along the boardwalk and the upper and lower porticos and all Beach Haven had turned in for the night, and Lucy had gone to her apartments, and Mr. and Mrs. Coates and the rest of them, single and double, were asleep, Max, who had been pacing up and down his dressing-room, stopped suddenly before his mirror, and lifting the shade from the lamp, made a critical examination of his face.

"Forty, and I look it!" he said, pinching his chin with his thumb and forefinger, and turning his cheek so that the light would fall on the few gray hairs about his temples. "That beggar Miggs said so yesterday at the club. By gad, how pretty she was, and how her eyes snapped! I didn't think it was in her!"

CHAPTER XVIII

Captain Holt had selected his crew—picked surf-men, every one of them—and the chief of the bureau had endorsed the list without comment or inquiry. The captain's own appointment as keeper of the new Life-Saving Station was due as much to his knowledge of men as to his skill as a seaman, and so when his list was sent in—men he said he could " vouch for "—it took but a moment for the chief to write " Approved " across its face.

Isaac Polhemus came first: Sixty years of age, silent, gray, thick-set; face scarred and seamed by many weathers, but fresh as a baby's; two china-blue eyes—peep-holes through which you looked into his open heart; shoulders hard and tough as cordwood; hands a bunch of knots; legs like snubbing-posts; body quick-moving; brain quick-thinking; alert as a dog when on duty, calm as a sleepy cat beside a stove when his time was his own. Sixty only in years, this man; forty in strength and in skill, twenty in suppleness, and a one-year-old toddling infant in

318

all that made for guile. " Uncle Ike " some of the younger men once called him, wondering behind their hands whether he was not too old and believing all the time that he was. " Uncle Ike " they still called him, but it was a title of affection and pride; affection for the man underneath the blue woollen shirt, and pride because they were deemed worthy to pull an oar beside him.

The change took place the winter before when he was serving at Manasquan and when he pulled four men single-handed from out of a surf that would have staggered the bravest. There was no life-boat within reach and no hand to help. It was at night—a snowstorm raging and the sea a corral of hungry beasts fighting the length of the beach. The ship-wrecked crew had left their schooner pounding on the outer bar, and finding their cries drowned by the roar of the waters, had taken to their boat. She came bow on, the sea-drenched sailors clinging to her sides. Uncle Isaac Polhemus caught sight of her just as a savage pursuing roller dived under her stern, lifted the frail shell on its broad back, and whirled it bottom side up and stern foremost on to the beach. Dashing into the suds, he jerked two of the crew to their feet before they knew what had struck them; then sprang back for the others clinging to the seats and slowly drowning in the smother. Twice he plunged headlong after them, bracing himself against the backsuck, then with the help of his steel-like grip all four were dragged clear of the souse. Ever after it was " Uncle Isaac " or " that old hang-on," but always with a lifting of the chin in pride.

Samuel Green came next: Forty-five, long, Lincoln-bodied, and bony; coal-black hair, coal-black eyes, and charcoal-black mustache; neck like a loop in standing rigging; arms long as cant-hooks, with the steel grips for fingers; sluggish in movement and slow in action until the supreme moment of danger tautened his nerves to breaking point; then came an instantaneous spring, quick as the recoil of a parted hawser. All his life a fisherman except the five years he spent in the Arctic and the year he served at Squan; later he had helped in the volunteer crew alongshore. Loving the service, he had sent word over to Captain Holt that he'd like " to be put on," to which the captain had sent back word by the same messenger " Tell him he *is* put on." And he *was,* as soon as the papers were returned from Washington. Captain Nat had no record to look up or inquiries to make as to the character or fitness of Sam Green. He was the man who the winter before had slipped a rope about his body, plunged into the surf and swam out to the brig *Gorgus* and brought back three out of the five men lashed to the rigging, all too benumbed to make fast the shot-line fired across her deck.

Charles Morgan's name followed in regular order, and then Parks—men who had sailed with Captain Holt, and whose word and pluck he could depend upon; and Mulligan from Barnegat, who could pull a boat with the best of them; and last, and least in years, those two slim, tightly knit, lithe young tiger-cats, Tod and Archie.

Captain Nat had overhauled each man and had inspected him as closely as he would have done the timber for a new mast or the manila to make its rigging. Here was a service that required cool heads, honest hearts, and the highest technical skill, and the men under him must be sound to the core. He intended to do his duty, and so should every man subject to his orders. The Government had trusted him and he held himself responsible. This would probably be his last duty, and it would be well done. He was childless, sixty-five years old, and had been idle for years. Now he would show his neighbors something of his skill and his power to command. He did not need the pay; he needed the occupation and the being in touch with the things about him. For the last fifteen or more years he had nursed a sorrow and lived the life almost of a recluse. It was time he threw it off.

During the first week of service, with his crew about him, he explained to them in minute detail their several duties. Each day in the week would have its special work: Monday would be beach drill, practising with the firing gun and line and the safety car. Tuesday was boat drill; running the boat on its wagon to the edge of the sea, unloading it, and pushing it into the surf, each man in his place, oars poised, the others springing in and taking their seats beside their mates. On Wednesdays flag drills; practising with the international code of signals, so as to communicate with stranded vessels. Thursdays, beach apparatus again. Friday, resuscitation of drowning men. Saturday, scrub-day; every man except himself and the cook (each man was cook in turn for a week) on his knees with bucket and brush, and every floor, chair, table, and window scoured clean. Sunday, a day of rest, except for the beach patrol, which at night never ceased, and which by day only ceased when the sky was clear of snow and fog.

This night patrol would be divided into watches of four hours each at eight, twelve, and four. Two of the crew were to make the tramp of the beach, separating opposite the Station, one going south two and a half miles to meet the surfman from the next Station, and the other going north to the inlet; exchanging their brass checks each with the other, as a record of their faithfulness.

In addition to these brass checks each patrol would carry three Coston signal cartridges in a water-proof box, and a holder into which they were fitted, the handle having an igniter working on a spring to explode the cartridge, which burned a red light. These will-o'-the-wisps, flashed suddenly from out a desolate coast, have sent a thrill of hope through the heart of many a man clinging to frozen rigging or lashed to some piece of wreckage that the hungry surf, lying in wait, would pounce upon and chew to shreds.

The men listened gravely to the captain's words and took up their duties. Most of them knew them before, and no minute explanations were necessary. Skilled men understand the value of discipline and prefer it to any milder form of government. Archie was the only member who raised his eyes in astonishment when the captain, looking his way, mentioned the scrubbing and washing, each man to take his turn, but he made no reply except to nudge Tod and say under his breath:

" Wouldn't you like to see Aunt Lucy's face when she comes some Saturday morning ? She'll be pleased, won't she ? " As to the cooking, that did not bother him ; he and Tod had cooked many a meal on Fogarty's stove, and mother Fogarty had always said Archie could beat her any day making biscuit and doughnuts and frying ham.

Before the second week was out the Station had fallen into its regular routine. The casual visitor

during the sunny hours of the soft September days
when practice drill was over might see only a lonely
house built on the sand; and upon entering, a few
men leaning back in their chairs against the wall of
the living-room reading the papers or smoking their
pipes, and perhaps a few others leisurely overhauling
the apparatus, making minor repairs, or polishing
up some detail the weather had dulled. At night,
too, with the radiance of the moon making a pathway
of silver across the gentle swell of the sleepy surf,
he would doubtless wonder at their continued idle
life as he watched the two surfmen separate and begin
their walk up and down the beach radiant in the
moonlight. But he would change his mind should
he chance upon a north-easterly gale, the sea a froth
in which no boat could live, the slant of a sou'wester
the only protection against the cruel lash of the wind.
If this glimpse was not convincing, let him stand in
the door of their house in the stillness of a winter's
night, and catch the shout and rush of the crew tumbling from their bunks at the cry of "Wreck
ashore!" from the lips of some breathless patrol
who had stumbled over sand-dunes or plunged
through snowdrifts up to his waist to give warning.
It will take less than a minute to swing wide the
doors, grapple the life-boat and apparatus and whirl
them over the dunes to the beach; and but a moment
more to send a solid shot flying through the air on

its mission of mercy. And there is no time lost. Ten men have been landed in forty-five minutes through or over a surf that could be heard for miles; rescuers and rescued half dead. But no man let go his grip nor did any heart quail. Their duty was in front of them; that was what the Government paid for, and that was what they would earn—every penny of it.

The Station house in order, the captain was ready for visitors—those he wanted. Those he did not want—the riffraff of the ship-yard and the loungers about the taverns—he told politely to stay away; and as the land was Government property and his will supreme, he was obeyed.

Little Ellen had been the first guest, and by special invitation.

" All ready, Miss Jane, for you and the doctor and the Pond Lily; bring her down any time. That's what kind o' makes it lonely lyin' shut up with the men. We ain't got no flowers bloomin' 'round, and the sand gits purty white and blank-lookin' sometimes. Bring her down, you and the doctor; she's better'n a pot full o' daisies."

The doctor, thus commanded, brought her over in his gig, Jane, beside him, holding the child in her lap. And Archie helped them out, lifting his good mother in his arms clear of the wheel, skirts and all—the crew standing about looking on. Some of them knew Jane and came in for a hearty hand-shake, and all of them knew the doctor. There was hardly a man among them whose cabin he had not visited—not once, but dozens of times.

With her fair cheeks, golden curls, and spotless frock, the child, among those big men, some in their long hip boots and rough reefing jackets, looked like some fairy that had come in with the morning mist and who might be off on the next breeze.

Archie had her hugged close to his breast and had started in to show her the cot where he slept, the kitchen where he was to cook, and the peg in the hall where he hung his sou'wester and tarpaulins— every surfman had his peg, order being imperative with Captain Nat—when that old sea-dog caught the child out of the young fellow's arms and placed her feet on the sand.

" No, Cobden,"—that was another peculiarity of the captain's,—every man went by his last name, and he had begun with Archie to show the men he meant it. " No, that little posy is mine for to-day. Come along, you rosebud; I'm goin' to show you the biggest boat you ever saw, and a gun on wheels; and I've got a lot o' shells the men has been pickin' up for ye. Oh, but you're goin' to have a beautiful time, lassie ! "

The child looked up in the captain's face, and her wee hand tightened around his rough stubs of fingers.

Archie then turned to Jane and with Tod's help the three made a tour of the house, the doctor following, inspecting the captain's own room with its desk and papers, the kitchen with all its appointments, the outhouse for wood and coal, the staircase leading to the sleeping-rooms above, and at the very top the small ladder leading to the cupola on the roof, where the lookout kept watch on clear days for incoming steamers. On their return Mulligan spread a white oil-cloth on the pine table and put out a china plate filled with some cake that he had baked the night before, and which Green supplemented by a pitcher of water from the cistern.

Each one did something to please her. Archie handed her the biggest piece of cake on the dish, and Uncle Isaac left the room in a hurry and stumbling upstairs went through his locker and hauled out the head of a wooden doll which he had picked up on the beach in one of his day patrols and which he had been keeping for one of his grand-children—all blighted with the sun and scarred with salt water, but still showing a full set of features, much to Ellen's delight; and Sam Green told her of his own little girl, just her age, who lived up in the village and whom he saw every two weeks, and whose hair was just the color of hers. Meanwhile the doctor chatted with the men, and Jane, with her arm locked in Archie's, so proud and so tender over

him, inspected each appointment and comfort of the
house with ever-increasing wonder.

And so, with the visit over, the gig was loaded
up, and with Ellen waving her hand to the men
and kissing her finger-tips in true French style
to the captain and Archie, and the crew respond-
ing in a hearty cheer, the party drove past the
old House of Refuge, and so on back to Warehold
and Yardley.

One August afternoon, some days after this visit,
Tod stood in the door of the Station looking out to
sea. The glass had been falling all day and a dog-
day haze had settled down over the horizon. This,
as the afternoon advanced, had become so thick that
the captain had ordered out the patrols, and Archie
and Green were already tramping the beach—Green
to the inlet and Archie to meet the surfmen of the
station below. Park, who was cook this week, had
gone to the village for supplies, and so the captain
and Tod were alone in the house, the others, with the
exception of Morgan, who was at his home in the village with a sprained ankle, being at work some distance away on a crosshead over which the life-line
was always fired in gun practice.

Suddenly Tod, who was leaning against the jamb
of the door speculating over what kind of weather
the night would bring, and wondering whether the

worst of it would fall in his watch, jerked his neck out of his woollen shirt and strained his eyes in the direction of the beach until they rested upon the figure of a man slowly making his way over the dunes. As he passed the old House of Refuge, some hundreds of yards below, he stopped for a moment as if undecided on his course, looked ahead again at the larger house of the Station, and then, as if reassured, came stumbling on, his gait showing his want of experience in avoiding the holes and tufts of grass cresting the dunes. His movements were so awkward and his walk so unusual in that neighborhood that Tod stepped out on the low porch of the Station to get a better view of him.

From the man's dress, and from his manner of looking about him, as if feeling his way, Tod concluded that he was a stranger and had tramped the beach for the first time. At the sight of the surfman the man left the dune, struck the boat path, and walked straight toward the porch.

"Kind o' foggy, ain't it?"

"Yes," replied Tod, scrutinizing the man's face and figure, particularly his clothes, which were queerly cut and with a foreign air about them. He saw, too, that he was strong and well built, and not over thirty years of age.

"You work here?" continued the stranger, mounting the steps and coming closer, his eyes taking in

Tod, the porch, and the view of the sitting-room through the open window.

" I do," answered Tod in the same tone, his eyes still on the man's face.

" Good job, is it ? " he asked, unbuttoning his coat.

" I get enough to eat," answered Tod curtly, " and enough to do." He had resumed his position against the jamb of the door and stood perfectly impassive, without offering any courtesy of any kind. Strangers who asked questions were never very welcome. Then, again, the inquiry about his private life nettled him.

The man, without noticing the slight rebuff, looked about for a seat, settled down on the top step of the porch, pulled his cap from his head, and wiped the sweat from his forehead with the back of one hand. Then he said slowly, as if to himself:

" I took the wrong road and got consid'able het up."

Tod watched him while he mopped his head with a red cotton handkerchief, but made no reply. Curiosity is not the leading characteristic of men who follow the sea.

" Is the head man around ? His name's Holt, ain't it ? " continued the stranger, replacing his cap and stuffing his handkerchief into the side-pocket of his coat.

THE SWEDE'S STORY

As the words fell from his lips Tod's quick eye caught a sudden gleam like that of a search-light flashed from beneath the heavy eyebrows of the speaker.

"That's his name," answered Tod. "Want to see him? He's inside." The surfman had not yet changed his position nor moved a muscle of his body. Tiger cats are often like this.

Captain Holt's burly form stepped from the door. He had overheard the conversation, and not recognizing the voice had come to find out what the man wanted.

"You lookin' for me? I'm Captain Holt. What kin I do for ye?" asked the captain in his quick, imperious way.

"That's what he said, sir," rejoined Tod, bringing himself to an erect position in deference to his chief.

The stranger rose from his seat and took his cap from his head.

"I'm out o' work, sir, and want a job, and I thought you might take me on."

Tod was now convinced that the stranger was a foreigner. No man of Tod's class ever took his hat off to his superior officer. They had other ways of showing their respect for his authority—instant obedience, before and behind his back, for instance.

The captain's eyes absorbed the man from his thick shoes to his perspiring hair.

" Norwegian, ain't ye ? "

" No, sir ; Swede."

" Not much difference. When did ye leave Sweden ? You talk purty good."

" When I was a boy."

" What kin ye do ? "

" I'm a good derrick man and been four years with a coaler."

" You want steady work, I suppose."

The stranger nodded.

" Well, I ain't got it. Gov'ment app'ints our men. This is a Life-Saving Station."

The stranger stood twisting his cap. The first statement seemed to make but little impression on him ; the second aroused a keener interest.

" Yes, I know. Just new built, ain't it ? and you just put in charge ? Captain Nathaniel Holt's your name—am I right ? "

" Yes, you're just right." And the captain, dismissing the man and the incident from his mind, turned on his heel, walked the length of the narrow porch and stood scanning the sky and the blurred horizon line. The twilight was now deepening and a red glow shimmered through the settling fog.

" Fogarty ! " cried the captain, beckoning over his shoulder with his head.

Tod stepped up and stood at attention ; as quick

in reply as if two steel springs were fastened to his heels.

"Looks rather soapy, Fogarty. May come on thick. Better take a turn to the inlet and see if that yawl is in order. We might have to cross it to-night. We can't count on this weather. When you meet Green send him back here. That shot-line wants overhaulin'." Here the captain hesitated and looked intently at the stranger. "And here, you Swede," he called in a louder tone of command, "you go 'long and lend a hand, and when you come back I'll have some supper for ye."

One of Tod's springs must have slid under the Swede's shoes. Either the prospect of a meal or of having a companion to whom he could lend a hand—nothing so desolate as a man out of work—a stranger at that—had put new life into his hitherto lethargic body.

"This way," said Tod, striding out toward the surf.

The Swede hurried to his side and the two crossed the boat runway, ploughed through the soft drift of the dune, and striking the hard, wet sand of the beach, headed for the inlet. Tod having his high, waterproof boots on, tramped along the edge of the incoming surf, the half-circles of suds swashing past his feet and spreading themselves up the slope. The sand was wet here and harder on that account, and the walking better. The Swede took the inside course nearer the shore. Soon Tod began to realize that the interest the captain had shown in the unknown man and the brief order admitting him for a time to membership in the crew placed the stranger on a different footing. He was, so to speak, a comrade and, therefore, entitled to a little more courtesy. This clear in his mind, he allowed his tongue more freedom; not that he had any additional interest in the man—he only meant to be polite.

" What you been workin' at ? " he asked, kicking an empty tin can that the tide had rolled within his reach. Work is the universal topic; the weather is too serious a subject to chatter about lightly.

" Last year or two ? " asked the Swede, quickening his pace to keep up. Tod's steel springs always kept their original temper while the captain's orders were being executed and never lost their buoyancy until these orders were entirely carried out.

" Yes," replied Tod.

" Been a-minin'; runnin' the ore derricks and the shaft h'isters. What you been doin' ? " And the man glanced at Tod from under his cap.

" Fishin'. See them poles out there ? You kin just git sight o' them in the smoke. Them's my father's. He's out there now, I guess, if he ain't come in."

" You live 'round here ? " The man's legs were

shorter than Tod's, and he was taking two steps to Tod's one.

"Yes, you passed the House o' Refuge, didn't ye, comin' up? I was watchin' ye. Well, you saw that cabin with the fence 'round it?"

"Yes; the woman told me where I'd find the cap'n. You know her, I s'pose?" asked the Swede.

"Yes, she's my mother, and that's my home. I was born there." Tod's words were addressed to the perspective of the beach and to the way the hazè blurred the horizon; surfmen rarely see anything else when walking on the beach, whether on or off duty.

"You know everybody 'round here, don't you?" remarked the Swede in a casual tone. The same quick, inquiring glance shot out of the man's eyes.

"Yes, guess so," answered Tod with another kick. Here the remains of an old straw hat shared the fate of the can.

"You ever heard tell of a woman named Lucy Cobden, lives 'round here somewheres?"

Tod came to a halt as suddenly as if he had run into a derelict.

"I don't know no *woman*," he answered slowly, accentuating the last word. "I know a *lady* named Miss Jane Cobden. Why?" and he scrutinized the man's face.

"One I mean's got a child—big now—must be fifteen or twenty years old—girl, ain't it?"

"No, it's a boy. He's one of the crew here; his name's Archie Cobden. Me and him's been brothers since we was babies. What do you know about him?" Tod had resumed his walk, but at a slower pace.

"Nothin'; that's why I ask." The man had also become interested in the flotsam of the beach, and had stopped to pick up a clam-shell which he shied into the surf. Then he added slowly, and as if not to make a point of the inquiry, "Is she alive?"

"Yes. Here this week. Lives up in Warehold in that big house with the brick gate-posts."

The man walked on for some time in silence and then asked:

"You're sure the child is livin' and that the mother's name is Jane?"

"Sure? Don't I tell ye Cobden's in the crew and Miss Jane was here this week! He's up the beach on patrol or you'd 'a' seen him when you fust struck the Station."

The stranger quickened his steps. The information seemed to have put new life into him again.

"Did you ever hear of a man named Bart Holt," he asked, "who used to be 'round here?" Neither man was looking at the other as they talked. The conversation was merely to pass the time of day.

"Yes; he's the captain's son. Been dead for years.

Died some'er's out in Brazil, so I've heard my father say. Had fever or something."

The Swede walked on in silence for some minutes. Then he stopped, faced Tod, took hold of the lapel of his coat, and said slowly, as he peered into his eyes:

" He ain't dead, no more'n you and I be. I worked for him for two years. He run the mines on a percentage. I got here last week, and he sent me down to find out how the land lay. If the woman was dead I was to say nothing and come back. If she was alive I was to tell the captain, his father, where a letter could reach him. They had some bad blood 'twixt 'em, but he didn't tell me what it was about. He may come home here to live, or he may go back to the mines; it's just how the old man takes it. That's what I've got to say to him. How do you think he'll take it?"

For a moment Tod made no reply. He was trying to make up his mind what part of the story was true and what part was skilfully put together to provide, perhaps, additional suppers. The improbability of the whole affair struck him with unusual force. Raising hopes of a long-lost son in the breast of a father was an old dodge and often meant the raising of money.

" Well, I can't say," Tod answered carelessly; he had his own opinion now of the stranger. " You'll have to see the captain about that. If the man's alive it's rather funny he ain't showed up all these years."

" Well, keep mum 'bout it, will ye, till I talk to him? Here comes one o' your men."

Green's figure now loomed up out of the mist.

" Where away, Tod?" the approaching surfman cried when he joined the two.

" Captain wants me to look after the yawl," answered Tod.

" It's all right," cried Green; " I just left it. Went down a-purpose. Who's yer friend?"

" A man the cap'n sent along to lend a hand. This is Sam Green," and he turned to the Swede and nodded to his brother surfman.

The two shook hands. The stranger had not volunteered his name and Tod had not asked for it. Names go for little among men who obey orders; they serve merely as labels and are useful in a payroll, but they do not add to the value of the owner or help his standing in any way. " Shorty " or " Fatty " or " Big Mike " is all sufficient. What the man can *do* and how he does it, is more important.

" No use goin' to the inlet," continued Green. " I'll report to the captain. Come along back. I tell ye it's gettin' thick," and he looked out across the breakers, only the froth line showing in the dim twilight.

The three turned and retraced their steps.

Tod quickened his pace and stepped into the house ahead of the others. Not only did he intend to tell the captain of what he had heard, but he intended to tell him at once.

Captain Holt was in his private room, sitting at his desk, busy over his monthly report. A swinging kerosene lamp hanging from the ceiling threw a light full on his ruddy face framed in a fringe of gray whiskers. Tod stepped in and closed the door behind him.

" I didn't go to the inlet, sir. Green had thought of the yawl and had looked after it; he'll report to you about it. I just heard a strange yarn from that fellow you sent with me and I want to tell ye what it is."

The captain laid down his pen, pushed his glasses from his eyes, and looked squarely into Tod's face.

" He's been askin' 'bout Miss Jane Cobden and Archie, and says your son Bart is alive and sent him down here to find out how the land lay. It's a cock-and-bull story, but I give it to you just as I got it."

Once in the South Seas the captain awoke to look into the muzzle of a double-barrelled shot-gun held in the hand of the leader of a mutiny. The next instant the man was on the floor, the captain's fingers twisted in his throat.

Tod's eyes were now the barrels of that gun. No

cat-like spring followed; only a cold, stony stare, as if he were awaking from a concussion that had knocked the breath out of him.

"He says Bart's *alive!*" he gasped. "Who? That feller I sent with ye?"

"Yes."

The captain's face grew livid and then flamed up, every vein standing clear, his eyes blazing.

"He's a liar! A dirty liar! Bring him in!" Each word hissed from his lips like an explosive.

Tod opened the door of the sitting-room and the Swede stepped in. The captain whirled his chair suddenly and faced him. Anger, doubt, and the flicker of a faint hope were crossing his face with the movement of heat lightning.

"You know my son, you say?"

"I do." The answer was direct and the tone positive.

"What's his name?"

"Barton Holt. He signs it different, but that's his name."

"How old is he?" The pitch of the captain's voice had altered. He intended to riddle the man's statement with a cross-fire of examination.

"'Bout forty, maybe forty-five. He never told me."

"What kind of eyes?"

"Brown, like yours."

340

"You know my son, you say?"

"What kind of hair?"

"Curly. It's gray now; he had fever, and it turned."

"Where—when?" Hope and fear were now struggling for the mastery.

"Two years ago—when I first knew him; we were in hospital together."

"What's he been doin'?" The tone was softer. Hope seemed to be stronger now.

"Mining out in Brazil."

The captain took his eyes from the face of the man and asked in something of his natural tone of voice:

"Where is he now?"

The Swede put his hand in his inside pocket and took out a small time-book tied around with a piece of faded tape. This he slowly unwound, Tod's and the captain's eyes following every turn of his fingers. Opening the book, he glanced over the leaves, found the one he was looking for, tore it carefully from the book, and handed it to the captain.

"That's his writing. If you want to see him send him a line to that address. It'll reach him all right. If you don't want to see him he'll go back with me to Rio. I don't want yer supper and I don't want yer job. I done what I promised and that's all there is to it. Good-night," and he opened the door and disappeared in the darkness.

Captain Holt sat with his head on his chest looking at the floor in front of him. The light of the hanging lamp made dark shadows under his eyebrows and under his chin whiskers. There was a firm set to his clean-shaven lips, but the eyes burned with a gentle light; a certain hope, positive now, seemed to be looming up in them.

Tod watched him for an instant, and said:

" What do ye think of it, cap'n? "

" I ain't made up my mind."

" Is he lyin'? "

" I don't know. Seems too good to be true. He's got some things right; some things he ain't. Keep your mouth shut till I tell ye to open it—to Cobden, mind ye, and everybody else. Better help Green overhaul that line. That'll do, Fogarty."

Tod dipped his head—his sign of courteous assent—and backed out of the room. The captain continued motionless, his eyes fixed on space. Once he turned, picked up the paper, scrutinized the handwriting word for word, and tossed it back on the desk. Then he rose from his seat and began pacing the floor, stopping to gaze at a chart on the wall, at the top of the stove, at the pendulum of the clock, surveying them leisurely. Once he looked out of the window at the flare of light from his swinging lamp, stencilled on the white sand and the gray line of the dunes beyond. At each of these resting-places his face assumed a different expression; hope, fear, and anger again swept across it as his judgment struggled with his heart. In one of his turns up and down the small room he laid his hand on a brick lying on the window-sill—one that had been sent by the builders of the Station as a sample. This he turned over carefully, examining the edges and color as if he had seen it for the first time and had to pass judgment upon its defects or merits. Laying it back in its place, he threw himself into his chair again, exclaiming aloud, as if talking to someone:

"It ain't true. He'd wrote before if he were alive. He was wild and keerless, but he never was dirt-mean, and he wouldn't a-treated me so all these years. The Swede's a liar, I tell ye!"

Wheeling the chair around to face the desk, he picked up a pen, dipped it into the ink, laid it back on the desk, picked it up again, opened a drawer on his right, took from it a sheet of official paper, and wrote a letter of five lines. This he enclosed in the envelope, directed to the name on the slip of paper. Then he opened the door.

"Fogarty."

"Yes, cap'n."

"Take this to the village and drop it in the post yourself. The weather's clearin', and you won't be wanted for a while," and he strode out and joined his men.

CHAPTER XIX

THE BREAKING OF THE DAWN

September weather on Barnegat beach! Fine
gowns and fine hats on the wide piazzas of Beach
Haven! Too cool for bathing, but not too cool to
sit on the sand and throw pebbles and loll under
kindly umbrellas; air fresh and bracing, with a touch
of June in it; skies full of mares'-tails—slips of a
painter's brush dragged flat across the film of blue;
sea gone to rest; not a ripple, no long break of the
surf, only a gentle lift and fall like the breathing
of a sleeping child.

Uncle Isaac shook his head when he swept his
eye round at all this loveliness; then he turned on
his heel and took a look at the aneroid fastened to
the wall of the sitting-room of the Life-Saving Station. The arrow showed a steady shrinkage. The
barometer had fallen six points.

"What do ye think, Captain Holt?" asked the
old surfman.

"I ain't thinkin', Polhemus; can't tell nothin'
'bout the weather this month till the moon changes;
may go on this way for a week or two, or it may let

344

loose and come out to the sou'-east. I've seen these dog-days last till October."

Again Uncle Isaac shook his head, and this time kept his peace; now that his superior officer had spoken he had no further opinion to express.

Sam Green dropped his feet to the floor, swung himself over to the barometer, gazed at it for a moment, passed out of the door, swept his eye around, and resumed his seat—tilted back against the wall. What his opinion might be was not for publication— not in the captain's hearing.

Captain Holt now consulted the glass, picked up his cap bearing the insignia of his rank, and went out through the kitchen to the land side of the house. The sky and sea—feathery clouds and still, oily flatness—did not interest him this September morning. It was the rolling dune that caught his eye, and the straggly path that threaded its way along the marshes and around and beyond the clump of scrub pines and bushes until it was lost in the haze that hid the village. This land inspection had been going on for a month, and always when Tod was returning from the post-office with the morning mail. The men had noticed it, but no one had given vent to his thoughts.

Tod, of course, knew the cause of the captain's impatience, but no one of the others did, not even Archie; time enough for that when the Swede's story was proved true. If the fellow had lied that was an end to it; if he had told the truth Bart would answer, and the mystery be cleared up. This same silence had been maintained toward Jane and the doctor; better not raise hopes he could not verify—certainly not in Jane's breast.

Not that he had much hope himself; he dared not hope. Hope meant a prop to his old age; hope meant joy to Jane, who would welcome the prodigal; hope meant relief to the doctor, who could then claim his own; hope meant redemption for Lucy, a clean name for Archie, and honor to himself and his only son.

No wonder, then, that he watched for an answer to his letter with feverish impatience. His own missive had been blunt and to the point, asking the direct question: "Are you alive or dead, and if alive, why did you fool me with that lie about your dying of fever in a hospital and keep me waiting all these years?" Anything more would have been superfluous in the captain's judgment—certainly until he received some more definite information as to whether the man was his son.

Half a dozen times this lovely September morning the captain had strolled leisurely out of the back door and had mounted the low hillock for a better view. Suddenly a light flashed in his face, followed by a look in his eyes that they had not known for weeks—not since the Swede left. The light came when his

346

glance fell upon Tod's lithe figure swinging along the road; the look kindled when he saw Tod stop and wave his hand triumphantly over his head.

The letter had arrived!

With a movement as quick as that of a horse touched by a whip, he started across the sand to meet the surfman.

"Guess we got it all right this time, captain," cried Tod. "It's got the Nassau postmark, anyhow. There warn't nothin' else in the box but the newspapers," and he handed the package to his chief.

The two walked to the house and entered the captain's office. Tod hung back, but the captain laid his hand on his shoulder.

"Come in with me, Fogarty. Shut the door. I'll send these papers in to the men soon's I open this."

Tod obeyed mechanically. There was a tone in the captain's voice that was new to him. It sounded as if he were reluctant to be left alone with the letter.

"Now hand me them spectacles."

Tod reached over and laid the glasses in his chief's hand. The captain settled himself deliberately in his revolving chair, adjusted his spectacles, and slit the envelope with his thumb-nail. Out came a sheet of foolscap closely written on both sides. This he read to the end, turning the page as carefully as if it had been a set of official instructions, his face growing paler and paler, his mouth tight shut. Tod

347

stood beside him watching the lights and shadows playing across his face. The letter was as follows:

" NASSAU, No. 4 Calle Valenzuela,
" Aug. 29, 18——.

" FATHER: Your letter was not what I expected, although it is, perhaps, all I deserve. I am not going into that part of it, now I know that Lucy and my child are alive. What has been done in the past I can't undo, and maybe I wouldn't if I could, for if I am worth anything to-day it comes from what I have suffered; that's over now, and I won't rake it up, but I think you would have written me some word of kindness if you had known what I have gone through since I left you. I don't blame you for what you did—I don't blame anybody; all I want now is to get back home among the people who knew me when I was a boy, and try and make up for the misery I have caused you and the Cobdens. I would have done this before, but it has only been for the last two years that I have had any money. I have got an interest in the mine now and am considerably ahead, and I can do what I have always determined to do if I ever had the chance and means—come home to Lucy and the child; it must be big now—and take them back with me to Bolivia, where I have a good home and where, in a few years, I shall be able to give them everything they need. That's due to her and to the child, and it's due to you; and if she'll come I'll do my best to make her happy while she lives. I heard about five years ago from a man who worked for a short time in Farguson's ship-yard how she was suffering, and what names the people called the child, and my one thought ever since has been to do the decent thing by both. I couldn't then, for I was living in a hut back in the mountains a thousand miles from the coast, or tramping from place to place; so I kept still. He told me, too, how you felt toward me, and I didn't want to come and have bad blood between us, and so I stayed on. When Olssen Strom, my foreman, sailed for Perth Amboy, where they are making some machinery for the company, I thought I'd try again, so I sent him to find out. One thing in your letter is wrong. I never went to the hospital with yellow fever; some of the men had it aboard ship, and I took one of them to the ward the night I ran away. The doctor at the hospital wanted my name, and I gave it, and this may have been how they thought it was me, but I did not intend to deceive you or anybody else, nor cover up any tracks. Yes, father, I'm coming home. If you'll hold out your hand to me I'll take it gladly. I've had a hard time since I left you; you'd forgive me if you knew how hard it has been. I haven't had anybody out here to care whether I lived or died, and I would like to see how it feels. But if you don't I can't help it. My hope is that Lucy and the boy will feel differently. There is a steamer sailing from here next Wednesday; she goes direct to Amboy, and you may expect me on her.　　　Your son,

"　Barton."

"It's him, Tod," cried the captain, shaking the letter over his head; "it's him!" The tears stood

in his eyes now, his voice trembled; his iron nerve
was giving way. "Alive, and comin' home! Be
here next week! Keep the door shut, boy, till I pull
myself together. Oh, my God, Tod, think of it! I
haven't had a day's peace since I druv him out nigh
on to twenty year ago. He hurt me here"—and
he pointed to his breast—" where I couldn't forgive
him. But it's all over now. He's come to himself
like a man, and he's square and honest, and he's goin'
to stay home till everything is straightened out. O
God! it can't be true! it *can't* be true!"

He was sobbing now, his face hidden by his wrist
and the cuff of his coat, the big tears striking his pea-
jacket and bounding off. It had been many years
since these springs had yielded a drop—not when
anybody could see. They must have scalded his
rugged cheeks as molten metal scalds a sand-pit.

Tod stood amazed. The outburst was a revelation.
He had known the captain ever since he could remember, but always as an austere, exacting man.

"I'm glad, captain," Tod said simply; "the
men'll be glad, too. Shall I tell 'em?"

The captain raised his head.

"Wait a minute, son." His heart was very tender, all discipline was forgotten now; and then he
had known Tod from his boyhood. "I'll go myself
and tell 'em," and he drew his hand across his eyes
as if to dry them. "Yes, tell 'em. Come, I'll go

'long with ye and tell 'em myself. I ain't 'shamed of the way I feel, and the men won't be 'shamed neither."

The sitting-room was full when he entered. Dinner had been announced by Morgan, who was cook that week, by shouting the glad tidings from his place beside the stove, and the men were sitting about in their chairs. Two fishermen who had come for their papers occupied seats against the wall.

The captain walked to the corner of the table, stood behind his own chair and rested the knuckles of one hand on the white oilcloth. The look on his face attracted every eye. Pausing for a moment, he turned to Polhemus and spoke to him for the others:

"Isaac, I got a letter just now. Fogarty brought it over. You knew my boy Bart, didn't ye, the one that's been dead nigh on to twenty years?"

The old surfman nodded, his eyes still fastened on the captain. This calling him "Isaac" was evidence that something personal and unusual was coming. The men, too, leaned forward in attention; the story of Bart's disappearance and death had been discussed up and down the coast for years.

"Well, he's alive," rejoined the captain with a triumphant tone in his voice, "and he'll be here in a week—comin' to Amboy on a steamer. There ain't no mistake about it; here's his letter."

The announcement was received in dead silence.

To be surprised was not characteristic of these men, especially over a matter of this kind. Death was a part of their daily experience, and a resurrection neither extraordinary nor uncommon. They were glad for the captain, if the captain was glad—and he evidently was. But what did Bart's turning up at this late day mean? Had his money given out, or was he figuring to get something out of his father—something he couldn't get as long as he remained dead?

The captain continued, his voice stronger and with a more positive ring in it:

" He's part owner in a mine now, and he's comin' home to see me and to straighten out some things he's interested in." It was the first time in nearly twenty years that he had ever been able to speak of his son with pride.

A ripple of pleasure went through the room. If the prodigal was bringing some money with him and was not to be a drag on the captain, that put a new aspect on the situation. In that case the father was to be congratulated.

" Well, that's a comfort to you, captain," cried Uncle Isaac in a cheery tone. " A good son is a good thing. I never had one, dead or alive, but I'd 'a' loved him if I had had. I'm glad for you, Captain Nat, and I know the men are." (Polhemus's age and long friendship gave him this privilege. Then, of course, the occasion was not an official one.)

"Been at the mines, did ye say, captain?" remarked Green. Not that it was of any interest to him; merely to show his appreciation of the captain's confidence. This could best be done by prolonging the conversation.

"Yes, up in the mountains of Brazil some'er's, I guess, though he don't say," answered the captain in a tone that showed that the subject was still open for discussion.

Mulligan now caught the friendly ball and tossed it back with:

"I knowed a feller once who was in Brazil—so he said. Purty hot down there, ain't it, captain?"

"Yes; on the coast. I ain't never been back in the interior."

Tod kept silent. It was not his time to speak, nor would it be proper for him, nor necessary. His chief knew his opinion and sympathies and no word of his could add to their sincerity.

Archie was the only man in the room, except Uncle Isaac, who regarded the announcement as personal to the captain. Boys without fathers and fathers without boys had been topics which had occupied his mind ever since he could remember. That this old man had found one of his own whom he loved and whom he wanted to get his arms around, was an inspiring thought to Archie.

"There's no one happier than I am, captain,"

he burst out enthusiastically. "I've often heard of your son, and of his going away and of your giving him up for dead. I'm mighty glad for you," and he grasped his chief's hand and shook it heartily.

As the lad's fingers closed around the rough hand of the captain a furtive look flashed from out Morgan's eyes. It was directed to Parks—they were both Barnegat men—and was answered by that surfman with a slow-falling wink. Tod saw it, and his face flushed. Certain stories connected with Archie rose in his mind; some out of his childhood, others since he had joined the crew.

The captain's eyes filled as he shook the boy's hand, but he made no reply to Archie's outburst. Pausing for a moment, as if willing to listen to any further comments, and finding that no one else had any word for him, he turned on his heel and re-entered his office.

Once inside, he strode to the window and looked out on the dunes, his big hands hooked behind his back, his eyes fixed on vacancy.

"It won't be long, now, Archie, not long, my lad," he said in a low voice, speaking aloud to himself. "I kin say you're my grandson out loud when Bart comes, and nothin' kin or will stop me! And now I kin tell Miss Jane."

Thrusting the letter into his inside pocket, he

picked up his cap, and strode across the dune in the direction of the new hospital.

Jane was in one of the wards when the captain sent word to her to come to the visiting-room. She had been helping the doctor in an important operation. The building was but half way between the Station and Warehold, which made it easier for the captain to keep his eye on the sea should there be any change in the weather.

Jane listened to the captain's outburst covering the announcement that Bart was alive without a comment. Her face paled and her breathing came short, but she showed no signs of either joy or sorrow. She had faced too many surprises in her life to be startled at anything. Then again, Bart alive or dead could make no difference now in either her own or Lucy's future.

The captain continued, his face brightening, his voice full of hope:

" And your troubles are all over now, Miss Jane; your name will be cleared up, and so will Archie's, and the doctor'll git his own, and Lucy kin look everybody in the face. See what Bart says," and he handed her the open letter.

Jane read it word by word to the end and handed it back to the captain. Once in the reading she had tightened her grasp on her chair as if to steady herself, but she did not flinch; she even read some sentences twice, so that she might be sure of their meaning.

In his eagerness the captain had not caught the expression of agony that crossed her face as her mind, grasping the purport of the letter, began to measure the misery that would follow if Bart's plan was carried out.

" I knew how ye'd feel," he went on, " and I've been huggin' myself ever since it come when I thought how happy ye'd be when I told ye; but I ain't so sure 'bout Lucy. What do you think? Will she do what Bart wants?"

" No," said Jane in a quiet, restrained voice; " she will not do it."

" Why?" said the captain in a surprised tone. He was not accustomed to be thwarted in anything he had fixed his mind upon, and he saw from Jane's expression that her own was in opposition.

" Because I won't permit it."

The captain leaned forward and looked at Jane in astonishment.

" You won't permit it!"

" No, I won't permit it."

" Why?" The word came from the captain as if it had been shot from a gun.

" Because it would not be right." Her eyes were still fixed on the captain's.

" Well, ain't it right that he should make some

amends for what he's done?" he retorted with in-creasing anger. "When he said he wouldn't marry her I druv him out; now he says he's sorry and wants to do squarely by her and my hand's out to him. She ain't got nothin' in her life that's doin' her any good. And that boy's got to be baptized right and take his father's name, Archie Holt, out loud, so every-body kin hear."

Jane made no answer except to shake her head. Her eyes were still on the captain's, but her mind was neither on him nor on what fell from his lips. She was again confronting that spectre which for years had lain buried and which the man before her was exorcising back to life.

The captain sprang from his seat and stood before her; the words now poured from his lips in a torrent.

"And you'll git out from this death blanket you been sleepin' under, bearin' her sin; breakin' the doctor's heart and your own; and Archie kin hold his head up then and say he's got a father. You ain't heard how the boys talk 'bout him behind his back. Tod Fogarty's stuck to him, but who else is there 'round here? We all make mistakes; that's what half the folks that's livin' do. Everything's been a lie—nothin' but lies—for near twenty years. You've lived a lie motherin' this boy and breakin' your heart over the whitest man that ever stepped in

shoe leather. Doctor John's lived a lie, tellin' folks
he wanted to devote himself to his hospital when he'd
rather live in the sound o' your voice and die a
pauper than run a college anywhere else. Lucy has
lived a lie, and is livin' it yet—and *likes it, too,* that's
the worst of it. And I been muzzled all these years;
mad one minute and wantin' to twist his neck, and
the next with my eyes runnin' tears that the only
boy I got was lyin' out among strangers. The only
one that's honest is the little Pond Lily. She ain't
got nothin' to hide and you see it in her face. Her
father was square and her mother's with her and
nothin' can't touch her and don't. Let's have this
out. I'm tired of it——"

The captain was out of breath now, his emotions
still controlling him, his astonishment at the unex-
pected opposition from the woman of all others on
whose assistance he most relied unabated.

Jane rose from her chair and stood facing him,
a great light in her eyes:

"*No!* no! NO! A thousand times, no! You
don't know Lucy; I do. What you want done now
should have been done when Archie was born. It
was my fault. I couldn't see her suffer. I loved her
too much. I thought to save her, I didn't care how.
It would have been better for her if she had faced
her sin then and taken the consequences; better for
all of us. I didn't think so then, and it has taken

me years to find it out. I began to be conscious of it first in her marriage, then when she kept on living her lie with her husband, and last when she deserted Ellen and went off to Beach Haven alone—that broke my heart, and my mistake rose up before me, and I *knew!*"

The captain stared at her in astonishment. He could hardly credit his ears.

"Yes, better, if she'd faced it. She would have lived here then under my care, and she might have loved her child as I have done. Now she has no tie, no care, no responsibility, no thought of anything but the pleasures of the moment. I have tried to save her, and I have only helped to ruin her."

"Make her settle down, then, and face the music!" blurted out the captain, resuming his seat. "Bart warn't all bad; he was only young and foolish. He'll take care of her. It ain't never too late to begin to turn honest. Bart wants to begin; make her begin, too. He's got money now to do it; and she kin live in South America same's she kin here. She's got no home anywhere. She don't like it here, and never did; you kin see that from the way she swings 'round from place to place. *Make* her face it, I tell ye. You been too easy with her all your life; pull her down now and keep her nose p'inted close to the compass."

"You do not know of what you talk," Jane

359

answered, her eyes blazing. "She hates the past; hates everything connected with it; hates the very name of Barton Holt. Never once has she mentioned it since her return. She never loved Archie; she cared no more for him than a bird that has dropped its young out of its nest. Besides, your plan is impossible. Marriage does not condone a sin. The power to rise and rectify the wrong lies in the woman. Lucy has not got it in her, and she never will have it. Part of it is her fault; a large part of it is mine. She has lived this lie all these years, and I have only myself to blame. I have taught her to live it. I began it when I carried her away from here; I should have kept her at home and had her face the consequences of her sin then. I ought to have laid Archie in her arms and kept him there. I was a coward and could not, and in my fear I destroyed the only thing that could have saved her—the mother-love. Now she will run her course. She's her own mistress; no one can compel her to do anything."

The captain raised his clenched hand:

"Bart will, when he comes."

"How?"

"By claimin' the boy and shamin' her before the world, if she don't. She liked him well enough when he was a disgrace to himself and to me, without a dollar to his name. What ails him now, when he comes back and owns up like a man and wants to do the square thing, and has got money enough to see it through ? She's nothin' but a *thing,* if she knew it, till this disgrace's wiped off'n her. By God, Miss Jane, I tell you this has got to be put through just as Bart wants it, and quick! "

Jane stepped closer and laid her hand on the captain's arm. The look in her eyes, the low, incisive, fearless ring in her voice, overawed him. Her courage astounded him. This side of her character was a revelation. Under their influence he became silent and humbled—as a boisterous advocate is humbled by the measured tones of a just judge.

" It is not my friend, Captain Nat, who is talking now. It is the father who is speaking. Think for a moment. Who has borne the weight of this, you or I ? You had a wayward son whom the people here think you drove out of your home for gambling on Sunday. No other taint attaches to him or to you. Dozens of other sons and fathers have done the same. He returns a reformed man and lives out his life in the home he left.

" I had a wayward sister who forgot her mother, me, her womanhood, and herself, and yet at whose door no suspicion of fault has been laid. I stepped in and took the brunt and still do. I did this for my father's name and for my promise to him and for my love of her. To her child I have given my

361

life. To him I am his mother and will always be—always, because I will stand by my fault. That is a redemption in itself, and that is the only thing that saves me from remorse. You and I, outside of his father and mother, are the only ones living that know of his parentage. The world has long since forgotten the little they suspected. Let it rest; no good could come—only suffering and misery. To stir it now would only open old wounds and, worst of all, it would make a new one."

" In you ? "

" No, worse than that. My heart is already scarred all over; no fresh wound would hurt."

" In the doctor ? "

" Yes and no. He has never asked the truth and I have never told him."

" Who, then ? "

" In little Ellen. Let us keep that one flower untouched."

The captain rested his head in his hand, and for some minutes made no answer. Ellen was the apple of his eye.

" But if Bart insists ? "

" He won't insist when he sees Lucy. She is no more the woman that he loved and wronged than I am. He would not know her if he met her outside this house."

" What shall I do ? "

" Nothing. Let matters take their course. If he is the man you think he is he will never break the silence."

" And you will suffer on—and the doctor ? "

Jane bowed her head and the tears sprang to her eyes.

" Yes, always; there is nothing else to do."

CHAPTER XX

THE UNDERTOW

Within the month a second letter was handed to the captain by Tod, now regularly installed as post-man. It was in answer to one of Captain Holt's which he had directed to the expected steamer and which had met the exile on his arrival. It was dated " Amboy," began " My dear father," and was signed " Your affectionate son, Barton."

This conveyed the welcome intelligence—welcome to the father—that the writer would be detained a few days in Amboy inspecting the new machinery, after which he would take passage for Barnegat by the *Polly Walters,* Farguson's weekly packet. Then these lines followed: " It will be the happiest day of my life when I can come into the inlet at high tide and see my home in the distance."

Again the captain sought Jane.

She was still at the hospital, nursing some ship-wrecked men—three with internal injuries—who had been brought in from Forked River Station, the crew having rescued them the week before. Two of the regular attendants were worn out with the constant nursing, and so Jane continued her vigils.

She had kept at her work—turning neither to the right nor to the left, doing her duty with the bravery and patience of a soldier on the firing-line, knowing that any moment some stray bullet might end her usefulness. She would not dodge, nor would she cower; the danger was no greater than others she had faced, and no precaution, she knew, could save her. Her lips were still sealed, and would be to the end; some tongue other than her own must betray her sister and her trust. In the meantime she would wait and bear bravely whatever was sent to her.

Jane was alone when the captain entered, the doctor having left the room to begin his morning inspection. She was in her gray-cotton nursing-dress, her head bound about with a white kerchief. The pathos of her face and the limp, tired movement of her figure would have been instantly apparent to a man less absorbed in his own affairs than the captain.

" He'll be here to-morrow or next day! " he cried, as he advanced to where she sat at her desk in the doctor's office, the same light in his eyes and the same buoyant tone in his voice, his ruddy face aglow with his walk from the station.

" You have another letter then? " she said in a resigned tone, as if she had expected it and was prepared to meet its consequences. In her suffering she had even forgotten her customary welcome of him—for whatever his attitude and however gruff he might be, she never forgot the warm heart beneath.

"Yes, from Amboy," panted the captain, out of breath with his quick walk, dragging a chair beside Jane's desk as he spoke. "He got mine when the steamer come in. He's goin' to take the packet so he kin bring his things—got a lot o' them, he says. And he loves the old home, too—he says so—you kin read it for yourself." As he spoke he unbuttoned his jacket, and taking Bart's letter from its inside pocket, laid his finger on the paragraph and held it before her face.

"Have you talked about it to anybody?" Jane asked calmly; she hardly glanced at the letter.

"Only to the men; but it's all over Barnegat. A thing like that's nothin' but a cask o' oil overboard and the bung out—runs everywhere—no use tryin' to stop it." He was in the chair now, his arms on the edge of the desk.

"But you've said nothing to anybody about Archie and Lucy, and what Bart intends to do when he comes, have you?" Jane inquired in some alarm.

"Not a word, and won't till ye see him. She's more your sister than she is his wife, and you got most to say 'bout Archie, and should. You been everything to him. When you've got through I'll take a hand, but not before." The captain always spoke the truth, and meant it; his word settled at once any anxieties she might have had on that score.

"What have you decided to do?" She was not looking at him as she spoke; she was toying with a penholder that lay before her on the desk, apparently intent on its construction.

"I'm goin' to meet him at Farguson's ship-yard when the *Polly* comes in," rejoined the captain in a positive tone, as if his mind had long since been made up regarding details, and he was reciting them for her guidance—"and take him straight to my house, and then come for you. You kin have it out together. Only one thing, Miss Jane "—here his voice changed and something of his old quarter-deck manner showed itself in his face and gestures—" if he's laid his course and wants to keep hold of the tiller I ain't goin' to block his way and he shall make his harbor, don't make no difference who or what gits in the channel. Ain't neither of us earned any extry pay for the way we've run this thing. You've got Lucy ashore flounderin' 'round in the fog, and I had no business to send him off without grub or compass. If he wants to steer now he'll *steer*. I don't want you to make no mistake 'bout this, and you'll excuse me if I put it plain."

Jane put her hand to her head and looked out of the window toward the sea. All her life seemed to be narrowing to one small converging path which grew smaller and smaller as she looked down its perspective.

"I understand, captain," she sighed. All the fight was out of her; she was like one limping across a battle-field, shield and spear gone, the roads unknown.

The door opened and the doctor entered. His quick, sensitive eye instantly caught the look of despair on Jane's face and the air of determination on the captain's. What had happened he did not know, but something to hurt Jane; of that he was positive. He stepped quickly past the captain without accosting him, rested his hand on Jane's shoulder, and said in a tender, pleading tone:

"You are tired and worn out; get your cloak and hat and I'll drive you home." Then he turned to the captain: "Miss Jane's been up for three nights. I hope you haven't been worrying her with anything you could have spared her from—at least until she got rested," and he frowned at the captain.

"No, I ain't and wouldn't. I been a-tellin' her of Bart's comin' home. That ain't nothin' to worry over—that's something to be glad of. You heard about it, of course?"

"Yes, Morgan told me. Twenty years will make a great difference in Bart. It must have been a great surprise to you, captain."

Both Jane and the captain tried to read the doctor's face, and both failed. Doctor John might have been commenting on the weather or some equally unimportant topic, so light and casual was his tone.

He turned to Jane again.

" Come, dear—please," he begged. It was only when he was anxious about her physical condition or over some mental trouble that engrossed her that he spoke thus. The words lay always on the tip of his tongue, but he never let them fall unless someone was present to overhear.

" You are wrong, John," she answered, bridling her shoulders as if to reassure him. " I am not tired —I have a little headache, that's all." With the words she pressed both hands to her temples and smoothed back her hair—a favorite gesture when her brain fluttered against her skull like a caged pigeon. " I will go home, but not now—this afternoon, perhaps. Come for me then, please," she added, looking up into his face with a grateful expression.

The captain picked up his cap and rose from his seat. One of his dreams was the marriage of these two. Episodes like this only showed him the clearer what lay in their hearts. The doctor's anxiety and Jane's struggle to bear her burdens outside of his touch and help only confirmed the old sea-dog in his determination. When Bart had his way, he said to himself, all this would cease.

"I'll be goin' along," he said, looking from one to the other and putting on his cap. "See you later, Miss Jane. Morgan's back ag'in to work, thanks to you, doctor. That was a pretty bad sprain he had—he's all right now, though; went on practice yesterday. I'm glad of it—equinox is comin' on and we can't spare a man, or half a one, these days. May be blowin' a livin' gale 'fore the week's out. Good-by, Miss Jane; good-by, doctor." And he shut the door behind him.

With the closing of the door the sound of wheels was heard—a crisp, crunching sound—and then the stamping of horses' feet. Max Feilding's drag, drawn by the two grays and attended by the diminutive Bones, had driven up and now stood beside the stone steps of the front door of the hospital. The coats of the horses shone like satin and every hub and plate glistened in the sunshine. On the seat, the reins in one pretty gloved hand, a gold-mounted whip in the other, sat Lucy. She was dressed in her smartest driving toilette—a short yellow-gray jacket fastened with big pearl buttons and a hat bound about with the breast of a tropical bird. Her eyes were dancing, her cheeks like ripe peaches with all the bloom belonging to them in evidence, and something more, and her mouth all curves and dimples.

When the doctor reached her side—he had heard the sound of the wheels, and looking through the window had caught sight of the drag—she had risen from her perch and was about to spring clear of the equipage without waiting for the helping hand of either Bones or himself. She was still a girl in her suppleness.

"No, wait until I can give you my hand," he said, hurrying toward her.

"No—I don't want your hand, Sir Esculapius. Get out of the way, please—I'm going to jump! There—wasn't that lovely?" And she landed beside him. "Where's sister? I've been all the way to Yardley, and Martha tells me she has been here almost all the week. Oh, what a dreadful, gloomy-looking place! How many people have you got here anyhow, cooped up in this awful— Why, it's like an almshouse," she added, looking about her. "Where did you say sister was?"

"I'll go and call her," interpolated the doctor when he could get a chance to speak.

"No, you won't do anything of the kind; I'll go myself. You've had her all the week, and now it's my turn."

Jane had by this time closed the lid of her desk, had moved out into the hall, and now stood on the top step of the entrance awaiting Lucy's ascent. In her gray gown, simple head-dress, and resigned face, the whole framed in the doorway with its connecting background of dull stone, she looked like one of

Correggio's Madonnas illumining some old cloister wall.

" Oh, you dear, *dear* sister! " Lucy cried, running up the short steps to meet her. " I'm so glad I've found you; I was afraid you were tying up somebody's broken head or rocking a red-flannelled baby." With this she put her arms around Jane's neck and kissed her rapturously.

" Where can we talk ? Oh, I've got such a lot of things to tell you! You needn't come, you dear, good doctor. Please take yourself off, sir—this way, and out the gate, and don't you dare come back until I'm gone."

My Lady of Paris was very happy this morning; bubbling over with merriment—a condition that set the doctor to thinking. Indeed, he had been thinking most intently about my lady ever since he had heard of Bart's resurrection. He had also been thinking of Jane and Archie. These last thoughts tightened his throat; they had also kept him awake the past few nights.

The doctor bowed with one of his Sir Roger bows, lifted his hat first to Jane in all dignity and reverence, and then to Lucy with a flourish—keeping up outwardly the gayety of the occasion and seconding her play of humor—walked to the shed where his horse was tied and drove off. He knew these moods of Lucy's; knew they were generally assumed and that they always concealed some purpose—one which neither a frown nor a cutting word nor an outbreak of temper would accomplish; but that fact rarely disturbed him. Then, again, he was never anything but courteous to her—always remembering Jane's sacrifice and her pride in her.

"And now, you dear, let us go somewhere where we can be quiet," Lucy cried, slipping her arm around Jane's slender waist and moving toward the hall.

With the entering of the bare room lined with bottles and cases of instruments her enthusiasm began to cool. Up to this time she had done all the talking. Was Jane tired out nursing? she asked herself; or did she still feel hurt over her refusal to take Ellen with her for the summer? She had remembered for days afterward the expression on her face when she told of her plans for the summer and of her leaving Ellen at Yardley; but she knew this had all passed out of her sister's mind. This was confirmed by Jane's continued devotion to Ellen and her many kindnesses to the child. It was true that whenever she referred to her separation from Ellen, which she never failed to do as a sort of probe to be assured of the condition of Jane's mind, there was no direct reply—merely a changing of the topic, but this had only proved Jane's devotion in avoiding a subject which might give her beautiful sister pain. What, then, was disturbing her to-day? she asked herself with a slight chill at her heart. Then she raised her head and assumed a certain defiant air. Better not notice anything Jane said or did; if she was tired she would get rested and if she was provoked with her she would get pleased again. It was through her affections and her conscience that she could hold and mould her sister Jane—never through opposition or fault-finding. Besides, the sun was too bright and the air too delicious, and she herself too bliss-fully happy to worry over anything. In time all these adverse moods would pass out of Jane's heart as they had done a thousand times before.

"Oh, you dear, precious thing!" Lucy began again, all these matters having been reviewed, set-tled, and dismissed from her mind in the time it took her to cross the room. "I'm so sorry for you when I think of you shut up here with these dreadful peo-ple; but I know you wouldn't be happy anywhere else," she laughed in a meaning way. (The bring-ing in of the doctor even by implication was always a good move.) "And Martha looks so desolate. Dear, you really ought to be more with her; but for my darling Ellen I don't know what Martha would do. I miss the child so, and yet I couldn't bear to take her from the dear old woman."

Jane made no answer. Lucy had found a chair now and had laid her gloves, parasol, and handkerchief on another beside her. Jane had resumed her seat; her slender neck and sloping shoulders and sparely modelled head with its simply dressed hair— she had removed the kerchief—in silhouette against the white light of the window.

" What is it all about, Lucy ? " she asked in a grave tone after a slight pause in Lucy's talk.

" I have a great secret to tell you—one you mustn't breathe until I give you leave."

She was leaning back in her chair now, her eyes trying to read Jane's thoughts. Her bare hands were resting in her lap, the jewels flashing from her fingers; about her dainty mouth there hovered, like a butterfly, a triumphant smile; whether this would alight and spread its wings into radiant laughter, or disappear, frightened by a gathering frown, depended on what would drop from her sister's lips.

Jane looked up. The strong light from the window threw her head into shadow; only the slight fluff of her hair glistened in the light. This made an aureole which framed the Madonna's face.

" Well, Lucy, what is it ? " she asked again simply.

" Max is going to be married."

" When ? " rejoined Jane in the same quiet tone. Her mind was not on Max or on anything connected with him. It was on the shadow slowly settling upon all she loved.

" In December," replied Lucy, a note of triumph in her voice, her smile broadening.

" Who to ? "

" Me."

With the single word a light ripple escaped from her lips.

Jane straightened herself in her chair. A sudden faintness passed over her—as if she had received a blow in the chest, stopping her breath.

" You mean—you mean—that you have promised to marry Max Feilding ! " she gasped.

" That's exactly what I do mean."

The butterfly smile about Lucy's mouth had vanished. That straightening of the lips and slow contraction of the brow which Jane knew so well was taking its place. Then she added nervously, unclasping her hands and picking up her gloves :

" Aren't you pleased ? "

" I don't know," answered Jane, gazing about the room with a dazed look, as if seeking for a succor she could not find. " I must think. And so you have promised to marry Max ! " she repeated, as if to herself. " And in December." For a brief moment she paused, her eyes again downcast ; then she raised her voice quickly and in a more positive tone asked, " And what do you mean to do with Ellen ? "

" That's what I want to talk to you about, you dear thing." Lucy had come prepared to ignore any unfavorable criticisms Jane might make and to give her only sisterly affection in return. "I want to give her to you for a few months more," she added blandly, "and then we will take her abroad with us and send her to school either in Paris or Geneva, where her grandmother can be near her. In a year or two she will come to us in Paris."

Jane made no answer.

Lucy moved uncomfortably in her chair. She had never, in all her life, seen her sister in any such mood. She was not so much astonished over her lack of enthusiasm regarding the engagement; that she had expected—at least for the first few days, until she could win her over to her own view. It was the deadly poise—the icy reserve that disturbed her. This was new.

"Lucy!" Again Jane stopped and looked out of the window. "You remember the letter I wrote you some years ago, in which I begged you to tell Ellen's father about Archie and Barton Holt?"

Lucy's eyes flashed.

"Yes, and you remember my answer, don't you?" she answered sharply. "What a fool I would have been, dear, to have followed your advice!"

Jane went straight on without heeding the interruption or noticing Lucy's changed tone.

"Do you intend to tell Max?"

"I tell Max! My dear, good sister, are you

crazy! What should I tell Max for? All that is dead and buried long ago! Why do you want to dig up all these graves? Tell Max—that aristocrat! He's a dear, sweet fellow, but you don't know him. He'd sooner cut his hand off than marry me if he knew!"

" I'm afraid you will have to—and this very day," rejoined Jane in a calm, measured tone.

Lucy moved uneasily in her chair; her anxiety had given way to a certain ill-defined terror. Jane's voice frightened her.

" Why?" she asked in a trembling voice.

" Because Captain Holt or someone else will, if you don't."

" What right has he or anybody else to meddle with my affairs?" Lucy retorted in an indignant tone.

" Because he cannot help it. I intended to keep the news from you for a time, but from what you have just told me you had best hear it now. Barton Holt is alive. He has been in Brazil all these years, in the mines. He has written to his father that he is coming home."

All the color faded from Lucy's cheeks.

" Bart! Alive! Coming home! When?"

" He will be here day after to-morrow; he is at Amboy, and will come by the weekly packet. What I can do I will. I have worked all my life to save you, and I may yet, but it seems now as if I had reached the end of my rope."

"Who said so? Where did you hear it? It *can't* be true!"

Jane shook her head. "I wish it was not true—but it is—every word of it. I have read his letter."

Lucy sank back in her chair, her cheeks livid, a cold perspiration moistening her forehead. Little lines that Jane had never noticed began to gather about the corners of her mouth; her eyes were wide open, with a strained, staring expression. What she saw was Max's eyes looking into her own, that same cold, cynical expression on his face she had sometimes seen when speaking of other women he had known.

"What's he coming for?" Her voice was thick and barely audible.

"To claim his son."

"He—says—he'll—claim—Archie—as—his—son!" she gasped. "I'd like to see any man living dare to——"

"But he can *try,* Lucy—no one can prevent that, and in the trying the world will know."

Lucy sprang from her seat and stood over her sister:

"I'll deny it!" she cried in a shrill voice; "and face him down. He can't prove it! No one about here can!"

"He may have proofs that you couldn't deny, and that I would not if I could. Captain Holt knows everything, remember," Jane replied in her same calm voice.

"But nobody else does but you and Martha!" The thought gave her renewed hope—the only ray she saw.

"True; but the captain is enough. His heart is set on Archie's name being cleared, and nothing that I can do or say will turn him from his purpose. Do you know what he means to do?"

"No," she replied faintly, more terror than curiosity in her voice.

"He means that you shall marry Barton, and that Archie shall be baptized as Archibald Holt. Barton will then take you both back to South America. A totally impossible plan, but——"

"I marry Barton Holt! Why, I wouldn't marry him if he got down on his knees. Why, I don't even remember what he looks like! Did you ever hear of such impudence! What is he to me?" The outburst carried with it a certain relief.

"What he is to you is not the question. It is what *you* are to Archie! Your sin has been your refusal to acknowledge him. Now you are brought face to face with the consequences. The world will forgive a woman all the rest, but never for deserting her child, and that, my dear sister, *is precisely what you did to Archie.*"

Jane's gaze was riveted on Lucy. She had never dared to put this fact clearly before—not even to herself. Now that she was confronted with the calamity she had dreaded all these years, truth was the only thing that would win. Everything now must be laid bare.

Lucy lifted her terrified face, burst into tears, and reached out her hands to Jane.

"Oh, sister,—sister!" she moaned. "What shall I do? Oh, if I had never come home! Can't you think of some way? You have always been so good— Oh, please! please!"

Jane drew Lucy toward her.

"I will do all I can, dear. If I fail there is only one resource left. That is the truth, and all of it. Max can save you, and he will if he loves you. Tell him everything!"

CHAPTER XXI

THE MAN IN THE SLOUCH HAT

The wooden arrow on the top of the cupola of the Life-Saving Station had had a busy night of it. With the going down of the sun the wind had continued to blow east-southeast—its old course for weeks—and the little sentinel, lulled into inaction, had fallen into a doze, its feather end fixed on the glow of the twilight.

At midnight a rollicking breeze that piped from out the north caught the sensitive vane napping, and before the dawn broke had quite tired it out, shifting from point to point, now west, now east, now nor'east-by-east, and now back to north again. By the time Morgan had boiled his coffee and had cut his bacon into slivers ready for the frying-pan the restless wind, as if ashamed of its caprices, had again veered to the north-east, and then, as if determined ever after to lead a better life, had pulled itself together and had at last settled down to a steady blow from that quarter.

The needle of the aneroid fastened to the wall of the sitting-room, and in reach of everybody's eye, had also made a night of it. In fact, it had not had a moment's peace since Captain Holt reset its register the day before. All its efforts for continued good weather had failed. Slowly but surely the baffled and disheartened needle had sagged from " Fair " to " Change," dropped back to " Storm," and before noon the next day had about given up the fight and was in full flight for " Cyclones and Tempests."

Uncle Isaac Polhemus, sitting at the table with one eye on his game of dominoes (Green was his partner) and the other on the patch of sky framed by the window, read the look of despair on the honest face of the aneroid, and rising from his chair, a " double three " in his hand, stepped to where the weather prophet hung.

" Sompin's comin', Sam," he said solemnly. " The old gal's got a bad setback. Ain't none of us goin' to git a wink o' sleep to-night, or I miss my guess. Wonder how the wind is." Here he moved to the door and peered out. " Nor'-east and puffy, just as I thought. We're goin' to hev some weather, Sam— ye hear?—some *weather!* " With this he regained his chair and joined the double three to the long tail of his successes. Good weather or bad weather— peace or war—was all the same to Uncle Isaac. What he wanted was the earliest news from the front.

Captain Holt took a look at the sky, the aneroid and the wind—not the arrow; old sea-dogs know which way the wind blows without depending on any such contrivance—the way the clouds drift, the trend of the white-caps, the set of a distant sail, and on black, almost breathless nights, by the feel of a wet finger held quickly in the air, the coolest side determining the wind point.

On this morning the clouds attracted the captain's attention. They hung low and drifted in long, straggling lines. Close to the horizon they were ashy pale; being nearest the edge of the brimming sea, they had, no doubt, seen something the higher and rosier-tinted clouds had missed; something of the ruin that was going on farther down the round of the sphere. These clouds the captain studied closely, especially a prismatic sun-dog that glowed like a bit of rainbow snipped off by wind-scissors, and one or two dirt spots sailing along by themselves.

During the captain's inspection Archie hove in sight, wiping his hands with a wad of cotton waste. He and Parks had been swabbing out the firing gun and putting the polished work of the cart apparatus in order.

"It's going to blow, captain, isn't it?" he called out. Blows were what Archie was waiting for. So far the sea had been like a mill-pond, except on one or two occasions, when, to the boy's great regret, nothing came ashore.

"Looks like it. Glass's been goin' down and the

wind has settled to the nor'east. Some nasty dough-balls out there I don't like. See 'em goin' over that three-master?"

Archie looked, nodded his head, and a certain thrill went through him. The harder it blew the better it would suit Archie.

"Will the *Polly* be here to-night?" he added. "Your son's coming, isn't he?"

"Yes; but you won't see him to-night, nor to-morrow, not till this is over. You won't catch old Ambrose out in this weather" (Captain Ambrose Farguson sailed the *Polly*). "He'll stick his nose in the basin some'er's and hang on for a spell. I thought he'd try to make the inlet, and I 'spected Bart here to-night till I saw the glass when I got up. Ye can't fool Ambrose—he knows. Be two or three days now 'fore Bart comes," he added, a look of disappointment shadowing his face.

Archie kept on to the house, and the captain, after another sweep around, turned on his heel and re-entered the sitting-room.

"Green!"

"Yes, captain." The surfman was on his feet in an instant, his ears wide open.

"I wish you and Fogarty would look over those new Costons and see if they're all right. And, Polhemus, perhaps you'd better overhaul them cork jackets; some o' them straps seemed kind o' awkward on practice yesterday—they ought to slip on easier; guess they're considerable dried out and a little mite stiff."

Green nodded his head in respectful assent and left the room. Polhemus, at the mention of his name, had dropped his chair legs to the floor; he had finished his game of dominoes and had been tilted back against the wall, awaiting the dinner-hour.

" It's goin' to blow a livin' gale o' wind, Polhemus," the captain continued; " that's what it's goin' to do. Ye kin see it yerself. There she comes now! "

As he spoke the windows on the sea side of the house rattled as if shaken by the hand of a man and as quickly stopped.

" Them puffs are jest the tootin' of her horn "— this with a jerk of his head toward the windows. " I tell ye, it looks ugly! "

Polhemus gained his feet and the two men stepped to the sash and peered out. To them the sky was always an open book—each cloud a letter, each mass a paragraph, the whole a warning.

" But I'm kind o' glad, Isaac." Again the captain forgot the surfman in the friend. " As long as it's got to blow it might as well blow now and be over. I'd kind o' set my heart on Bart's comin', but I guess I've waited so long I kin wait a day or two more. I wrote him to come by train, but he wrote back he had a lot o' plunder and he'd better put it 'board the *Polly;* and, besides, he said he kind o' wanted to sail into the inlet like he used to when he was a boy. Then ag'in, I couldn't meet him; not with this weather comin' on. No—take it all in all, I'm glad he ain't comin'."

" Well, I guess yer right, captain," answered Uncle Isaac in an even tone, as he left the room to overhaul the cork jackets. The occasion was not one of absorbing interest to Isaac.

By the time the table was cleared and the kitchen once more in order not only were the windows on the sea side of the house roughly shaken by the rising gale, but the sand caught from the dunes was being whirled against their panes. The tide, too, egged on by the storm, had crept up the slope of the dunes, the spray drenching the grass-tufts.

At five o'clock the wind blew forty miles an hour; at sundown it had increased to fifty; at eight o'clock it bowled along at sixty. Morgan, who had been to the village for supplies, reported that the tide was over the dock at Barnegat and that the roof of the big bathing-house at Beach Haven had been ripped off and landed on the piazza. He had had all he could do to keep his feet and his basket while crossing the marsh on his way back to the station. Then he added:

" There's a lot o' people there yit. That feller

from Philadelphy who's mashed on Cobden's aunt was swellin' around in a potato-bug suit o' clothes as big as life." This last was given from behind his hand after he had glanced around the room and found that Archie was absent.

At eight o'clock, when Parks and Archie left the Station to begin their patrol, Parks was obliged to hold on to the rail of the porch to steady himself, and Archie, being less sure of his feet, was blown against the water-barrel before he could get his legs well under him. At the edge of the surf the two separated for their four hours' patrol, Archie breasting the gale on his way north, and Parks hurrying on, helped by the wind, to the south.

At ten o'clock Parks returned. He had made his first round, and had exchanged his brass check with the patrol at the next station. As he mounted the sand-dune he quickened his steps, hurried to the Station, opened the sitting-room door, found it empty, the men being in bed upstairs awaiting their turns, and then strode on to the captain's room, his sou'wester and tarpaulin drenched with spray and sand, his hip-boots leaving watery tracks along the clean floor.

" Wreck ashore at No. 14, sir ! " Parks called out in a voice hoarse with fighting the wind.

The captain sprang from his cot—he was awake, his light still burning.

" Anybody drownded ? "

" No, sir; got 'em all. Seven of 'em, so the patrol said. Come ashore 'bout supper-time."

" What is she ? "

" A two-master from Virginia loaded with cord-wood. Surf's in bad shape, sir; couldn't nothin' live in it afore; it's wuss now. Everything's a bob-ble; turrible to see them sticks thrashin' 'round and slammin' things."

" Didn't want no assistance, did they ? "

" No, sir; they got the fust line 'round the fore-mast and come off in less'n a hour; warn't none of 'em hurted."

" Is it any better outside ? "

" No, sir; wuss. I ain't seen nothin' like it 'long the coast for years. Good-night," and Parks took another hole in the belt holding his tarpaulins to-gether, opened the back door, walked to the edge of the house, steadied himself against the clapboards, and boldly facing the storm, continued his patrol.

The captain stretched himself again on his bed; he had tried to sleep, but his brain was too active. As he lay listening to the roar of the surf and the shrill wail of the wind, his thoughts would revert to Bart and what his return meant; particularly to its effect on the fortunes of the doctor, of Jane and of Lucy.

Jane's attitude continued to astound him. He

389

had expected that Lucy might not realize the advantages of his plan at first—not until she had seen Bart and listened to what he had to say; but that Jane, after the confession of her own weakness, should still oppose him, was what he could not understand. He would keep his promise, however, to the very letter. She should have free range to dissuade Bart from his purpose. After that Bart should have his way. No other course was possible, and no other course either honest or just.

Then he went over in his mind all that had happened to him since the day he had driven Bart out into the night, and from that same House of Refuge, too, which, strange to say, lay within sight of the Station. He recalled his own and Bart's sufferings; his loneliness; the bitterness of the terrible secret which had kept his mouth closed all these years, depriving him of even the intimate companionship of his own grandson. With this came an increased love for the boy; he again felt the warm pressure of his hand and caught the look in his eyes the morning Archie congratulated him so heartily on Bart's expected return. He had always loved him; he would love him now a thousand times more when he could put his hand on the boy's shoulder and tell him everything.

With the changing of the patrol, Tod and Polhemus taking the places of Archie and Parks, he fell into a doze, waking with a sudden start some hours later, springing from his bed, and as quickly turning up the lamp.

Still in his stocking feet and trousers—on nights like this the men lie down in half their clothes—he walked to the window and peered out. It was nearing daylight; the sky still black. The storm was at its height; the roar of the surf incessant and the howl of the wind deafening. Stepping into the sitting-room he glanced at the aneroid—the needle had not advanced a point; then turning into the hall, he mounted the steps to the lookout in the cupola, walked softly past the door of the men's room so as not to waken the sleepers, particularly Parks and Archie, whose cots were nearest the door—both had had four hours of the gale and would have hours more if it continued—and reaching the landing, pressed his face against the cool pane and peered out.

Below him stretched a dull waste of sand hardly distinguishable in the gloom until his eyes became accustomed to it, and beyond this the white line of the surf, whiter than either sky or sand. This writhed and twisted like a cobra in pain. To the north burned Barnegat Light, only the star of its lamp visible. To the south stretched alternate bands of sand, sky, and surf, their dividing lines lost in the night. Along this beach, now stopping to get their breath, now slanting the brim of their sou'-

westers to escape the slash of the sand and spray, strode Tod and Polhemus, their eyes on and beyond the tumbling surf, their ears open to every unusual sound, their Costons buttoned tight under their coats to keep them from the wet.

Suddenly, while his eyes were searching the horizon line, now hardly discernible in the gloom, a black mass rose from behind a cresting of foam, seesawed for an instant, clutched wildly at the sky, and dropped out of sight behind a black wall of water. The next instant there flashed on the beach below him, and to the left of the station, the red flare of a Coston signal.

With the quickness of a cat Captain Holt sprang to the stairs shouting:

" A wreck, men, a wreck! " The next instant he had thrown aside the door of the men's room. " Out every one of ye! Who's on the beach? " And he looked over the cots to find the empty ones.

The men were on their feet before he had ceased speaking, Archie before the captain's hand had left the knob of the door.

" Who's on the beach, I say? " he shouted again.

" Fogarty and Uncle Ike," someone answered.

" Polhemus! Good! All hands on the cart, men; boat can't live in that surf. She lies to the north of us! " And he swung himself out of the door and down the stairs.

"God help 'em, if they've got to come through that surf!" Parks said, slinging on his coat. "The tide's just beginnin' to make flood, and all that cord-wood 'll come a-waltzin' back. Never see nothin' like it!"

The front door now burst in and another shout went ringing through the house:

"Schooner in the breakers!"

It was Tod. He had rejoined Polhemus the moment before he flared his light and had made a dash to rouse the men.

"I seen her, Fogarty, from the lookout," cried the captain, in answer, grabbing his sou'wester; he was already in his hip-boots and tarpaulin. "What is she?"

"Schooner, I guess, sir."

"Two or three masts?" asked the captain hurriedly, tightening the strap of his sou'wester and slipping the leather thong under his gray whiskers.

"Can't make out, sir; she come bow on. Uncle Ike see her fust." And he sprang out after the men.

A double door thrown wide; a tangle of wild cats springing straight at a broad-tired cart; a grappling of track-lines and handle-bars; a whirl down the wooden incline, Tod following with the quickly lighted lanterns; a dash along the runway, the sand cutting their cheeks like grit from a whirling stone; over the dune, the men bracing the cart on either

393

side, and down the beach the crew swept in a rush to where Polhemus stood waving his last Coston.

Here the cart stopped.

"Don't unload nothin'," shouted Polhemus. "She ain't fast; looks to me as if she was draggin' her anchors."

Captain Holt canted the brim of his sou'wester, held his bent elbow against his face to protect it from the cut of the wind, and looked in the direction of the surfman's fingers. The vessel lay about a quarter of a mile from the shore and nearer the House of Refuge than when the captain had first seen her from the lookout. She was afloat and drifting broadside on to the coast. Her masts were still standing and she seemed able to take care of herself. Polhemus was right. Nothing could be done till she grounded. In the meantime the crew must keep abreast of her. Her fate, however, was but a question of time, for not only had the wind veered to the southward—a-dead-on-shore wind—but the set of the flood must eventually strand her.

At the track-lines again, every man in his place, Uncle Isaac with his shoulder under the spokes of the wheels, the struggling crew keeping the cart close to the edge of the dune, springing out of the way of the boiling surf or sinking up to their waists into crevices of sluiceways gullied out by the hungry sea. Once Archie lost his footing and would have been sucked under by a comber had not Captain Holt grapped him by the collar and landed him on his feet again. Now and then a roller more vicious than the others would hurl a log of wood straight at the cart with the velocity of a torpedo, and swoop back again, the log missing its mark by a length.

When the dawn broke the schooner could be made out more clearly. Both masts were still standing, their larger sails blown away. The bowsprit was broken short off close to her chains. About this dragged the remnants of a jib sail over which the sea soused and whitened. She was drifting slowly and was now but a few hundred yards from the beach, holding, doubtless, by her anchors. Over her deck the sea made a clean breach.

Suddenly, and while the men still tugged at the track-ropes, keeping abreast of her so as to be ready with the mortar and shot-line, the ill-fated vessel swung bow on toward the beach, rose on a huge mountain of water, and threw herself headlong. When the smother cleared her foremast was overboard and her deck-house smashed. Around her hull the waves gnashed and fought like white wolves, leaping high, flinging themselves upon her. In the recoil Captain Holt's quick eye got a glimpse of the crew; two were lashed to the rigging and one held the tiller—a short, thickset man, wearing what appeared to be a slouch hat tied over his ears by a white handkerchief.

With the grounding of the vessel a cheer went up from around the cart.

" Now for the mortar ! "

" Up with it on the dune, men ! " shouted the captain, his voice ringing above the roar of the tempest.

The cart was forced up the slope—two men at the wheels, the others straining ahead—the gun lifted out and set, Polhemus ramming the charge home, Captain Holt sighting the piece; there came a belching sound, a flash of dull light, and a solid shot carrying a line rose in the air, made a curve like a flying rocket, and fell athwart the wreck between her forestay and jib. A cheer went up from the men about the gun. When this line was hauled in and the hawser attached to it made fast high up on the mainmast and above the raging sea, and the car run off to the wreck, the crew could be landed clear of the surf and the slam of the cord-wood.

At the fall of the line the man in the slouch hat was seen to edge himself forward in an attempt to catch it. The two men in the rigging kept their hold. The men around the cart sprang for the hawser and tally-blocks to rig the buoy, when a dull cry rose from the wreck. To their horror they saw the mainmast waver, flutter for a moment, and sag over the schooner's side. The last hope of using the life-car was gone! Without the elevation of the mast and with nothing but the smashed hull to make fast to, the shipwrecked men would be pounded into pulp in the attempt to drag them through the boil of wreckage.

" Haul in, men! " cried the captain. " No use of another shot; we can't drag 'em through that surf! "

" I'll take my chances," said Green, stepping forward. " Let me, cap'n. I can handle 'em if they haul in the slack and make fast."

" No, you can't," said the captain calmly. " You couldn't get twenty feet from shore. We got to wait till the tide cleans this wood out. It's workin' right now. They kin stand it for a while. Certain death to bring 'em through that smother—that stuff'd knock the brains out of 'em fast as they dropped into it. Signal to 'em to hang on, Parks."

An hour went by—an hour of agony to the men clinging to the grounded schooner, and of impatience to the shore crew, who were powerless. The only danger was of exhaustion to the shipwrecked men and the breaking up of the schooner. If this occurred there was nothing left but a plunge of rescuing men through the surf, the life of every man in his hand.

The beach began filling up. The news of a shipwreck had spread with the rapidity of a thundershower. One crowd, denser in spots where the stronger men were breasting the wind, which was now happily on the wane, were moving from the village along the beach, others were stumbling on through the marshes. From the back country, along the road leading from the hospital, rattled a gig, the horse doing his utmost. In this were Doctor John and Jane. She had, contrary to his advice, remained at the hospital. The doctor had been awakened by the shouts of a fisherman, and had driven with all speed to the hospital to get his remedies and instruments. Jane had insisted upon accompanying him, although she had been up half the night with one of the sailors rescued the week before by the crew of No. 14. The early morning air—it was now seven o'clock—would do her good, she pleaded, and she might be of use if any one of the poor fellows needed a woman's care.

Farther down toward Beach Haven the sand was dotted with wagons and buggies; some filled with summer boarders anxious to see the crew at work. One used as the depot omnibus contained Max Feilding, Lucy, and half a dozen others. She had passed a sleepless night, and hearing the cries of those hurrying by had thrown a heavy cloak around her and opening wide the piazza door had caught sight of the doomed vessel fighting for its life. Welcoming the incident as a relief from her own maddening thoughts, she had joined Max, hoping that the excitement might divert her mind from the horror that overshadowed her. Then, too, she did not want to be separated a single moment from him. Since the fatal hour when Jane had told her of Bart's expected return Max's face had haunted her. As long as he continued to look into her eyes, believing and trusting in her there was hope. He had noticed her haggard look, but she had pleaded one of her headaches, and had kept up her smiles, returning his caresses. Some way would be opened; some way *must* be opened!

While waiting for the change of wind and tide predicted by Captain Holt to clear away the deadly drift of the cord-wood so dangerous to the imperilled men, the wreckage from the grounded schooner began to come ashore—crates of vegetables, barrels of groceries, and boxes filled with canned goods. Some of these were smashed into splinters by end-on collisions with cord-wood; others had dodged the floatage and were landed high on the beach.

During the enforced idleness Tod occupied himself in rolling away from the back-suck of the surf the drift that came ashore. Being nearest a stranded crate he dragged it clear and stood bending over it, reading the inscription. With a start he beckoned to Parks, the nearest man to him, tore the card from the wooden slat, and held it before the surfman's face.

" What's this? Read! That's the *Polly Walters*

out there, I tell ye, and the captain's son's aboard!
I've been suspicionin' it all the mornin'. That's him
with the slouch hat. I knowed he warn't no sailor
from the way he acted. Don't say nothin' till we're
sure."

Parks lunged forward, dodged a stick of cord-wood
that drove straight at him like a battering-ram and,
watching his chance, dragged a floating keg from the
smother, rolled it clear of the surf, canted it on end,
and took a similar card from its head. Then he
shouted with all his might:

"It's the *Polly,* men! It's the *Polly*—the *Polly
Walters!* O God, ain't that too bad! Captain Ambrose's drowned, or we'd a-seen him! That feller
in the slouch hat is Bart Holt! Gimme that line!"
He was stripping off his waterproofs now ready for
a plunge into the sea.

With the awful words ringing in his ears Captain
Holt made a spring from the dune and came running
toward Parks, who was now knotting the shot-line
about his waist.

"What do you say she is?" he shouted, as he
flung himself to the edge of the roaring surf and
strained his eyes toward the wreck.

"The *Polly*—the *Polly Walters!*"

"My God! How do ye know? She ain't left
Amboy, I tell ye!"

"She has! That's her—see them kerds! They

come off that stuff behind ye. Archie got one and
I got t'other!" He held the bits of cardboard under
the rim of the captain's sou'wester.

Captain Holt snatched the cards from Parks's
hand, read them at a glance, and a dazed, horror-
stricken expression crossed his face. Then his eye
fell upon Parks knotting the shot-line about his
waist.

"Take that off! Parks, stay where ye are; don't
ye move, I tell ye."

As the words dropped from the captain's lips a
horrified shout went up from the bystanders. The
wreck, with a crunching sound, was being lifted from
the sand. She rose steadily, staggered for an instant
and dropped out of sight. She had broken amidships.
With the recoil two ragged bunches showed above the
white wash of the water. On one fragment—a splin-
tered mast—crouched the man with the slouch hat;
to the other clung the two sailors. The next instant
a great roller, gathering strength as it came, threw
itself full length on both fragments and swept on.
Only wreckage was left and one head.

With a cry to the men to stand by and catch the
slack, the captain ripped a line from the drum of
the cart, dragged off his high boots, knotted the
bight around his waist, and started on a run for the
surf.

Before his stockinged feet could reach the edge of

the foam, Archie seized him around the waist and held him with a grip of steel.

"You sha'n't do it, captain!" he cried, his eyes blazing. "Hold him, men—I'll get him!" With the bound of a cat he landed in the middle of the floatage, dived under the logs, rose on the boiling surf, worked himself clear of the inshore wreckage, and struck out in the direction of the man clinging to the shattered mast, and who was now nearing the beach, whirled on by the inrushing seas.

Strong men held their breath, tears brimming their eyes. Captain Holt stood irresolute, dazed for the moment by Archie's danger. The beach women— Mrs. Fogarty among them—were wringing their hands. They knew the risk better than the others.

Jane, at Archie's plunge, had run down to the edge of the surf and stood with tight-clenched fingers, her gaze fixed on the lad's head as he breasted the breakers—her face white as death, the tears streaming down her cheeks. Fear for the boy she loved, pride in his pluck and courage, agony over the result of the rescue, all swept through her as she strained her eyes seaward.

Lucy, Max, and Mrs. Coates were huddled together under the lee of the dune. Lucy's eyes were staring straight ahead of her; her teeth chattering with fear and cold. She had heard the shouts of Parks and the captain, and knew now whose life was at stake. There was no hope left; Archie would win and pull him out alive, and her end would come.

The crowd watched the lad until his hand touched the mast, saw him pull himself hand over hand along its slippery surface and reach out his arms. Then a cheer went up from a hundred throats, and as instantly died away in a moan of terror. Behind, towering over them like a huge wall, came a wave of black water, solemn, merciless, uncrested, as if bent on deadly revenge. Under its impact the shattered end of the mast rose clear of the water, tossed about as if in agony, veered suddenly with the movement of a derrick-boom, and with its living freight dashed headlong into the swirl of cord-wood.

As it ploughed through the outer drift and reached the inner line of wreckage, Tod, whose eyes had never left Archie since his leap into the surf, made a running jump from the sand, landed on a tangle of drift, and sprang straight at the section of the mast to which Archie clung. The next instant the surf rolled clear, submerging the three men.

Another ringing order now rose above the roar of the waters, and a chain of rescuing surfmen—the last resort—with Captain Nat at the head dashed into the turmoil.

It was a hand-to-hand fight now with death. At the first onslaught of the battery of wreckage Polhemus was knocked breathless by a blow in the stomach and rescued by the bystanders just as a log was curling over him. Green was hit by a surging crate, and Mulligan only saved from the crush of the cordwood by the quickness of a fisherman. Morgan, watching his chance, sprang clear of a tangle of barrels and cord-wood, dashed into the narrow gap of open water, and grappling Tod as he whirled past, twisted his fingers in Archie's waistband. The three were then pounced upon by a relay of fishermen led by Tod's father and dragged from under the crunch and surge of the smother. Both Tod and Morgan were unhurt and scrambled to their feet as soon as they gained the hard sand, but Archie lay insensible where the men had dropped him, his body limp, his feet crumpled under him.

All this time the man in the slouch hat was being swirled in the hell of wreckage, the captain meanwhile holding to the human chain with one hand and fighting with the other until he reached the half-drowned man whose grip had now slipped from the crate to which he clung. As the two were shot in toward the beach, Green, who had recovered his breath, dodged the recoil, sprang straight for them, threw the captain a line, which he caught, dashed back and dragged the two high up on the beach, the captain's arm still tightly locked about the rescued man.

A dozen hands were held out to relieve the captain of his burden, but he only waved them away.

"I'll take care of him!" he gasped in a voice almost gone from buffeting the waves, as the body slipped from his arms to the wet sand. "Git out of the way, all of you!"

Once on his feet, he stood for an instant to catch his breath, wrung the grime from his ears with his stiff fingers, and then shaking the water from his shoulders as a dog would after a plunge, he passed his great arms once more under the bedraggled body of the unconscious man and started up the dune toward the House of Refuge, the water dripping from both their wet bodies. Only once did he pause, and then to shout:

"Green,—Mulligan! Go back, some o' ye, and git Archie. He's hurt bad. Quick, now! And one o' ye bust in them doors. And— Polhemus, pull some coats off that crowd and a shawl or two from them women if they can spare 'em, and find Doctor John, some o' ye! D'ye hear! *Doctor John!*"

A dozen coats were stripped from as many backs, a shawl of Mrs. Fogarty's handed to Polhemus, the doors burst in and Uncle Isaac lunging in tumbled the garments on the floor. On these the captain laid the body of the rescued man, the slouch hat still clinging to his head.

While this was being done another procession was

approaching the house. Tod and Parks were carrying Archie's unconscious form, the water dripping from his clothing. Tod had his hands under the boy's armpits and Parks carried his feet. Behind the three walked Jane, half supported by the doctor.

" Dead! " she moaned. " Oh, no—no—no, John; it cannot be! Not my Archie! my brave Archie! "

The captain heard the tramp of the men's feet on the board floor of the runway outside and rose to his feet. He had been kneeling beside the form of the rescued man. His face was knotted with the agony he had passed through, his voice still thick and hoarse from battling with the sea.

" What's that she says? " he cried, straining his ears to catch Jane's words. " What's that! Archie dead! No! 'Tain't so, is it, doctor? "

Doctor John, his arm still supporting Jane, shook his head gravely and pointed to his own forehead.

" It's all over, captain," he said in a broken voice. " Skull fractured."

" Hit with them logs! Archie! Oh, my God! And this man ain't much better off—he ain't hardly breathin'. See for yerself, doctor. Here, Tod, lay Archie on these coats. Move back that boat, men, to give 'em room, and push them stools out of the way. Oh, Miss Jane, maybe it ain't true, maybe he'll come round! I've seen 'em this way more'n a dozen times. Here, doctor let's get these wet

The Captain started up the dune with the bedraggled body of the unconscious man.

clo'es off 'em." He dropped between the two limp, soggy bodies and began tearing open the shirt from the man's chest. Jane, who had thrown herself in a passion of grief on the water-soaked floor beside Archie, commenced wiping the dead boy's face with her handkerchief, smoothing the short wet curls from his forehead as she wept.

The man's shirt and collar loosened, Captain Holt pulled the slouch hat from his head, wrenched the wet shoes loose, wrapped the cold feet in the dry shawl, and began tucking the pile of coats closer about the man's shoulders that he might rest the easier. For a moment he looked intently at the pallid face smeared with ooze and grime, and limp body that the doctor was working over, and then stepped to where Tod now crouched beside his friend, the one he had loved all his life. The young surf-man's strong body was shaking with the sobs he could no longer restrain.

" It's rough, Tod," said the captain, in a choking voice, which grew clearer as he talked on. " Almighty rough on ye and on all of us. You did what you could—ye risked yer life for him, and there ain't nobody kin do more. I wouldn't send ye out again, but there's work to do. Them two men of Cap'n Ambrose's is drowned, and they'll come ashore some'er's near the inlet, and you and Parks better hunt 'em up. They live up to Barnegat, ye know, and their folks'll be wantin' 'em." It was strange how calm he was. His sense of duty was now controlling him.

Tod had raised himself to his feet when the captain had begun to speak and stood with his wet sou'-wester in his hand.

" Been like a brother to me," was all he said, as he brushed the tears from his eyes and went to join Parks.

The captain watched Tod's retreating figure for a moment, and bending again over Archie's corpse, stood gazing at the dead face, his hands folded across his girth—as one does when watching a body being slowly lowered into a grave.

" I loved ye, boy," Jane heard him say between her sobs. " I loved ye! You knowed it, boy. I hoped to tell ye so out loud so everybody could hear. Now they'll never know."

Straightening himself up, he walked firmly to the open door about which the people pressed, held back by the line of surfmen headed by Polhemus, and calmly surveyed the crowd. Close to the opening, trying to press her way in to Jane, his eyes fell on Lucy. Behind her stood Max Feilding.

" Friends," said the captain, in a low, restrained voice, every trace of his grief and excitement gone, " I've got to ask ye to git considerable way back and keep still. We got Doctor John here and Miss

Jane, and there ain't nothin' ye kin do. When there is I'll call ye. Polhemus, you and Green see this order is obeyed."

Again he hesitated, then raising his eyes over the group nearest the door, he beckoned to Lucy, pushed her in ahead of him, caught the swinging doors in his hands, and shut them tight. This done, he again dropped on his knees beside the doctor and the now breathing man.

CHAPTER XXII

THE CLAW OF THE SEA-PUSS

With the closing of the doors the murmur of the crowd, the dull glare of the gray sky, and the thrash of the wind were shut out. The only light in the House of Refuge now came from the two small windows, one above the form of the suffering man and the other behind the dead body of Archie. Jane's head was close to the boy's chest, her sobs coming from between her hands, held before her face. The shock of Archie's death had robbed her of all her strength. Lucy knelt beside her, her shoulder resting against a pile of cordage. Every now and then she would steal a furtive glance around the room—at the boat, at the rafters overhead, at the stove with its pile of kindling—and a slight shudder would pass through her. She had forgotten nothing of the past, nor of the room in which she crouched. Every scar and stain stood out as clear and naked as those on some long-buried wreck dug from shifting sands by a change of tide.

A few feet away the doctor was stripping the wet clothes from the rescued man and piling the dry coats over him to warm him back to life. His emer-

410

gency bag, handed in by Polhemus through the crack of the closed doors, had been opened, a bottle selected, and some spoonfuls of brandy forced down the sufferer's throat. He saw that the sea-water had not harmed him; it was the cordwood and wreckage that had crushed the breath out of him. In confirmation he pointed to a thin streak of blood oozing from one ear. The captain nodded, and continued chafing the man's hands—working with the skill of a surfman over the water-soaked body. Once he remarked in a half-whisper—so low that Jane could not hear him:

"I ain't sure yet, doctor. I thought it was Bart when I grabbed him fust; but he looks kind o' different from what I expected to see him. If it's him he'll know me when he comes to. I ain't changed so much maybe. I'll rub his feet now," and he kept on with his work of resuscitation.

Lucy's straining ears had caught the captain's words of doubt, but they gave her no hope. She had recognized at the first glance the man of all others in the world she feared most. His small ears, the way the hair grew on the temples, the bend of the neck and slope from the chin to the throat. No—she had no misgivings. These features had been part of her life—had been constantly before her since the hour Jane had told her of Bart's expected return. Her time had come; nothing could save her. He would regain consciousness, just as the captain had said, and would open those awful hollow eyes and would look at her, and then that dreadful mouth, with its thin, ashen lips, would speak to her, and she could deny nothing. Trusting to her luck—something which had never failed her—she had continued in her determination to keep everything from Max. Now it would all come as a shock to him, and when he asked her if it was true she could only bow her head.

She dared not look at Archie—she could not. All her injustice to him and to Jane; her abandonment of him when a baby; her neglect of him since, her selfish life of pleasure; her triumph over Max— all came into review, one picture after another, like the unrolling of a chart. Even while her hand was on Jane's shoulder, and while comforting words fell from her lips, her mind and eyes were fixed on the face of the man whom the doctor was slowly bringing back to life.

Not that her sympathy was withheld from Archie and Jane. It was her terror that dominated her— a terror that froze her blood and clogged her veins and dulled every sensibility and emotion. She was like one lowered into a grave beside a corpse upon which every moment the earth would fall, entombing the living with the dead.

The man groaned and turned his head, as if in

pain. A convulsive movement of the lips and face followed, and then the eyes partly opened.

Lucy clutched at the coil of rope, staggered to her feet, and braced herself for the shock. He would rise now, and begin staring about, and then he would recognize her. The captain knew what was coming; he was even now planning in his mind the details of the horrible plot of which Jane had told her!

Captain Holt stooped closer and peered under the half-closed lids.

"Brown eyes," she heard him mutter to himself, "just 's the Swede told me." She knew their color; they had looked into her own too often.

Doctor John felt about with his hand and drew a small package of letters from inside the man's shirt. They were tied with a string and soaked with salt water. This he handed to the captain.

The captain pulled them apart and examined them carefully.

"It's him," he said with a start, "it's Bart! It's all plain now. Here's my letter," and he held it up. "See the printing at the top—'Life-Saving Service'? And here's some more—they're all stuck together. Wait! here's one—fine writing." Then his voice dropped so that only the doctor could hear: "Ain't that signed 'Lucy'? Yes—'Lucy'—and it's an old one."

The doctor waved the letters away and again laid

413

his hand on the sufferer's chest, keeping it close to his heart. The captain bent nearer. Jane, who, crazed with grief, had been caressing Archie's cold cheeks, lifted her head as if aware of the approach of some crisis, and turned to where the doctor knelt beside the rescued man. Lucy leaned forward with straining eyes and ears.

The stillness of death fell upon the small room. Outside could be heard the pound and thrash of the surf and the moan of the gale; no human voice— men and women were talking in whispers. One soul had gone to God and another life hung by a thread.

The doctor raised his finger.

The man's face twitched convulsively, the lids opened wider, there came a short, inward gasp, and the jaw dropped.

" He's dead," said the doctor, and rose to his feet. Then he took his handkerchief from his pocket and laid it over the dead man's face.

As the words fell from his lips Lucy caught at the wall, and with an almost hysterical cry of joy threw herself into Jane's arms.

The captain leaned back against the life-boat and for some moments his eyes were fixed on the body of his dead son.

" I ain't never loved nothin' all my life, doctor," he said, his voice choking, " that it didn't go that way."

Doctor John made no·reply except with his eyes. Silence is ofttimes more sympathetic than the spoken word. He was putting his remedies back into his bag so that he might rejoin Jane. The captain continued:

"All I've got is gone now—the wife, Archie, and now Bart. I counted on these two. Bad day's work, doctor—bad day's work." Then in a firm tone, " I'll open the doors now and call in the men; we got to git these two bodies up to the Station, and then we'll get 'em home somehow."

Instantly all Lucy's terror returned. An unaccountable, unreasoning panic took possession of her. All her past again rose before her. She feared the captain now more than she had Bart. Crazed over the loss of his son he would blurt out everything. Max would hear and know—know about Archie and Bart and all her life!

Springing to her feet, maddened with an undefinable terror, she caught the captain's hand as he reached out for the fastenings of the door.

"Don't—don't tell them who he is! Promise me you won't tell them anything! Say it's a stranger! You are not sure it's he—I heard you say so! "

" Not say it's my own son! Why? " He was entirely unconscious of what was in her mind.

Jane had risen to her feet at the note of agony

in Lucy's voice and had stepped to her side as if to protect her. The doctor stood listening in amazement to Lucy's outbreak. He knew her reasons, and was appalled at her rashness.

"No! Don't—*don't!*" Lucy was looking up into the captain's face now, all her terror in her eyes.

"Why, I can't see what good that'll do!" For the moment he thought that the excitement had turned her head. "Isaac Polhemus 'll know him," he continued, "soon's he sets his eyes on him. And even if I was mean enough to do it, which I ain't, these letters would tell. They've got to go to the Superintendent 'long with everything else found on bodies. Your name's on some o' 'em and mine's on some others. We'll git 'em ag'in, but not till Gov'-ment see 'em."

These were the letters which had haunted her!

"Give them to me! They're mine!" she cried, seizing the captain's fingers and trying to twist the letters from his grasp.

A frown gathered on the captain's brow and his voice had an ugly ring in it:

"But I tell ye the Superintendent's got to have 'em for a while. That's regulations, and that's what we carry out. They ain't goin' to be lost—you'll git 'em ag'in."

"He sha'n't have them, I tell you!" Her voice rang now with something of her old imperious tone.

416

"Nobody shall have them. They're mine—not yours—nor his. Give them——"

"And break my oath!" interrupted the captain. For the first time he realized what her outburst meant and what inspired it.

"What difference does that make in a matter like this? Give them to me. You dare not keep them," she cried, tightening her fingers in the effort to wrench the letters from his hand. "Sister—doctor —speak to him! Make him give them to me—I will have them!"

The captain brushed aside her hand as easily as a child would brush aside a flower. His lips were tight shut, his eyes flashing.

"You want me to lie to the department?"

"*Yes!*" She was beside herself now with fear and rage. "I don't care who you lie to! You brute—you coward— I want them! I will have them!" Again she made a spring for the letters.

"See here, you she-devil. Look at me!"—the words came in cold, cutting tones. "You're the only thing livin', or dead, that ever dared ask Nathaniel Holt to do a thing like that. And you think I'd do it to oblige ye? You're rotten as punk—that's what ye are! Rotten from yer keel to yer top-gallant! and allus have been since I knowed ye!"

Jane started forward and faced the now enraged man.

"You must not, captain—you *shall* not speak to my sister that way!" she commanded.

The doctor stepped between them: "You forget that she is a woman. I forbid you to——"

"I will, I tell ye, doctor! It's true, and you know it." The captain's voice now dominated the room.

"That's no reason why you should abuse her. You're too much of a man to act as you do."

"It's because I'm a man that I do act this way. She's done nothin' but bring trouble to this town ever since she landed in it from school nigh twenty year ago. Druv out that dead boy of mine lyin' there, and made a tramp of him; throwed Archie off on Miss Jane; lied to the man who married her, and been livin' a lie ever since. And now she wants me to break my oath! Damn her——"

The doctor laid his hand over the captain's mouth. "Stop! And I mean it!" His own calm eyes were flashing now. "This is not the place for talk of this kind. We are in the presence of death, and——"

The captain caught the doctor's wrist and held it like a vice.

"I won't stop. I'll have it out—I've lived all the lies I'm goin' to live! I told you all this fifteen year ago when I thought Bart was dead, and you wanted me to keep shut, and I did, and you did, too, and you ain't never opened your mouth since. That's

418

because you're a man—all four square sides of ye. You didn't want to hurt Miss Jane, and no more did I. That's why I passed Archie there in the street; that's why I turned round and looked after him when I couldn't see sometimes for the tears in my eyes; and all to save that *thing* there that ain't worth savin'! By God, when I think of it I want to tear my tongue out for keepin' still as long as I have!"

Lucy, who had shrunk back against the wall, now raised her head:

" Coward! Coward!" she muttered.

The captain turned and faced her, his eyes blazing, his rage uncontrollable:

" Yes, you're a *thing,* I tell ye!—and I'll say it ag'in. I used to think it was Bart's fault. Now I know it warn't. It was yours. You tricked him, damn ye! Do ye hear? Ye tricked him with yer lies and yer ways. Now they're over—there'll be no more lies—not while I live! I'm goin' to strip ye to bare poles so's folks 'round here kin see. Git out of my way—all of ye! Out, I tell ye!"

The doctor had stepped in front of the infuriated man, his back to the closed door, his open palm upraised.

" I will not, and you shall not!" he cried. " What you are about do to is ruin—for Lucy, for Jane, and for little Ellen. You cannot—you shall not put such a stain upon that child. You love her, you——"

" Yes—too well to let that woman touch her ag'in if I kin help it!" The fury of the merciless sea was in him now—the roar and pound of the surf in his voice. " She'll be a curse to the child all her days; she'll go back on her when she's a mind to just as she did on Archie. There ain't a dog that runs the streets that would 'a' done that. She didn't keer then, and she don't keer now, with him a-lyin' dead there. She ain't looked at him once nor shed a tear. It's too late. All hell can't stop me! Out of my way, I tell ye, doctor, or I'll hurt ye!"

With a wrench he swung back the doors and flung himself into the light.

" Come in, men! Isaac, Green—all of ye—and you over there! I got something to say, and I don't want ye to miss a word of it! You, too, Mr. Feilding, and that lady next ye—and everybody else that kin hear!

" That's my son, Barton Holt, lyin' there dead! The one I druv out o' here nigh twenty year ago. It warn't for playin' cards, but on account of a woman; and there she stands—Lucy Cobden! That dead boy beside him is their child—my own grandson, Archie! Out of respect to the best woman that ever lived, Miss Jane Cobden, I've kep' still. If anybody ain't satisfied all they got to do is to look over these letters. That's all!"

Lucy, with a wild, despairing look at Max, had

"Come in, men!" he shouted.

sunk to the floor and lay cowering beneath the life-boat, her face hidden in the folds of her cloak.

Jane had shrunk back behind one of the big folding doors and stood concealed from the gaze of the astonished crowd, many of whom were pressing into the entrance. Her head was on the doctor's shoulder, her fingers had tight hold of his sleeve. Doctor John's arms were about her frail figure, his lips close to her cheek.

"Don't, dear—don't," he said softly. "You have nothing to reproach yourself with. Your life has been one long sacrifice."

"Oh, but Archie, John! Think of my boy being gone! Oh, I loved him so, John!"

"You made a man of him, Jane. All he was he owed to you." He was holding her to him—comforting her as a father would a child.

"And my poor Lucy," Jane moaned on, "and the awful, awful disgrace!" Her face was still hidden in his shoulder, her frame shaking with the agony of her grief, the words coming slowly, as if wrung one by one out of her breaking heart.

"You did your duty, dear—all of it." His lips were close to her ear. No one else heard.

"And you knew it all these years, John—and you did not tell me?"

"It was your secret, dear; not mine."

"Yes, I know—but I have been so blind—so fool-

421

ish. I have hurt you so often, and you have been so true through it all. O John, please—please forgive me! My heart has been so sore at times—I have suffered so!"

Then, with a quick lifting of her head, as if the thought alarmed her, she asked in sudden haste:

"And you love me, John, just the same? Say you love me, John!"

He gathered her closer, and his lips touched her cheek:

"I never remember, my darling, when I did not love you. Have you ever doubted me?"

"No, John, no! Never, never! Kiss me again, my beloved. You are all I have in the world!"

THE END